STAR TREK GIANT:
FINAL FRONTIER

D1143574

STAR TREK NOVELS

STAR TREK: THE NEXT GENERATION NOVELS

STAR TREK GIANT NOVELS

STAR TREK LARGE FORMAT

A *STAR TREK*®
GIANT NOVEL

FINAL FRONTIER
DIANE CAREY

TITAN BOOKS
LONDON

STAR TREK GIANT: FINAL FRONTIER
ISBN 1 85286 059 6

Published by
Titan Books Ltd
58 St Giles High St
London WC2H 8LH

First Titan Edition March 1988
10 9 8 7 6 5 4 3 2 1

British edition by arrangement with Pocket Books, a division of
Simon & Schuster, Inc., Under Exclusive License from
Paramount Pictures Corporation, The Trademark Owner.

Printed and bound in Great Britain by Cox and Wyman Ltd,
Reading, Berkshire.

To the spirit of exploration
and the dignity it brings home

Foreword

It was a dark and stormy sector. Suddenly, a starship appeared on the horizon. The Vulcan screamed! . . .

Well . . . maybe not.

When Diane first suggested that I write the foreword for *Final Frontier,* I accepted the task with the comforting thought that she had 127,000 words to write before I had to make good on this promise. Surely I could come up with a few paragraphs of insightful prose in the same amount of time.

Surely . . .

Now that we are a few days from sending the novel to Pocket Books, I feel much the same as I did in college on those Sunday nights when I had a term paper due on Monday morning. In those days, my best bet was to start with a list of possible topics in the hope that one would inspire me.

One topic here could be revenge. I could repay Diane for putting me on the spot like this by describing what it's like to be her husband and collaborator. Unfortunately, we've all heard so many eccentric-writer stories at conventions that anything I could say would be redundant. I think I'll let this topic slide with merely a sidebar. Psychologists generally agree that a major childhood trauma will often result in people's becoming thieves, murderers, drug addicts, prostitutes, or writers. Generally, I'm pleased that Diane chose the last. However, when the light clicks on at 3:00 A.M. because Captain Kirk is whispering something into Diane's ear, I must admit that those thieves and murderers don't look so bad.

Another, always popular possibility would be to take a humorous look at our favorite shared-universe. I could, for instance, fantasize about being able to remove one scene from the series or the movies and rewrite it to my specifications. Which scene would it be? No, that might get me into trouble. And while *Star Trek* parodies are a lot of fun for true Trek fans, they are often misinterpreted by non-Trek people (the unclean) as ridicule of *Star Trek*.

How about commenting on some of the technical and scientific . . . uh . . . liberties that were occasionally taken during the series to move the plot along. No, that would be longer than the book.

Let's try another tack.

How, it is so often asked, could a twenty-year-old television show develop such a vast and loyal following? Even the fans can't reach an agreement on this. Some people feel that the *Star Trek* characters, the "Four from the *Enterprise*" especially, are a classic combination of compassion, humor, and conflict that the years cannot diminish. Others argue that the series itself always aspired to be "a cut above," its episodes not directed, like so much of television, at an audience with the collective IQ of a swarm of lobotomized houseflies. While I agree with these observations, I think that there is an even more important aspect of *Star Trek* that has made it so enduring—one that is often overlooked.

For several thousand years, philosophical and religious leaders have been preaching that man is basically evil. When *Star Trek* was conceived in the 1960's, this fact seemed to be demonstrated by the events all around us. We were plagued with war, racial unrest, pollution, overpopulation, and the threat of nuclear annihilation. These combined to support the belief that the human race was going to have a very short and miserable future on this planet. Those who looked into this future envisioned a massively over-populated, polluted world of such poverty and violence that we would all be locked into a daily life-and-death struggle for our basic needs. A very depressing outlook, to say the least. *Star Trek* thumbed its nose at our culture's Chicken Littles by giving us a much more reassuring look at humanity.

The overall theme of *Star Trek* must surely be that we have a grand future. Yes, we will have troubles. Some of them may seem insurmountable. But mankind is not just an upstart species, an aberration of nature destined to cause its own inevitable slide back into the muck. The creators of *Star Trek* wanted us to know that we *are* special, we *are* in charge of our destinies. That destiny can be a fine one as long as we never allow the problems of today to overwhelm our aspirations for the future. Diane and I consider it an honor to be part of the *Star Trek* universe and we will always try to maintain the respect for mankind that has made *Star Trek* an ever-increasing force in the social consciousness of today.

Final Frontier is a *Star Trek* historical, taking place twenty-five years before James Kirk's time aboard the *Enterprise* (the framework involving James Kirk takes place immediately after the television episode "The City on the Edge of Forever," and the reader may wish to refer to it). Diane and I have worked conscientiously to project backward on both technology and philosophy, to a point where we can see the emergence of the Trek familiar to us all. This is before everything—before starship technology was polished, before Federation policy was tested, before captains really knew how to handle what they encountered. It involves the inevitable conflicts between our philosophies, our aspirations, and the brutal reality that often exists when intelligence clashes with intelligence. We hope that as *Star Trek* continues, more and more people who see life as merely a living and dying process without meaning or direction will stand with us and demand that "There must be more!"

Gregory Brodeur

Part I

Space . . .

Prologue

A TIME BEFORE stardates. And a captain's privilege to go there.

Even with the unchanged cornfields lying beneath sprawling blue skies and the barn smell all around him, Jim Kirk discovered he couldn't quite get away from reality when the communicator in his pocket suddenly chirped. His hand automatically went for the utility belt that usually held his phaser and communicator when he wasn't on board the ship, and only then did he remember he wasn't wearing a uniform.

"Mind your own business, Bones," he muttered as he found the device inside the lightweight indigo fabric of his sailing jacket. He snapped the grip open with too much ease—not something he ordinarily perceived in his movements—and spoke firmly into it. "Mind your own business, McCoy. I'm on leave."

"On leave and suddenly psychic, too, I see," the familiar voice plunged back.

"Who else has the gall to disobey direct orders?" Kirk shifted the communicator to his left hand and used his right to wrench open a sliding panel in the barn's loft wall. Not easy; it hadn't been open in—no, he didn't want to count years right now. The eddies of time weren't his best friends at the moment. The backwashes . . .

"What do you want?" he asked as he reached into the metal cubbyhole behind the panel of century-old barnwood. He was quite aware of the guilty hesitation on the other end of the frequency when McCoy didn't answer right away.

"I thought you might want company for dinner."

"That's the best excuse you've got?"

"Well, it's hard to come up with a shipboard emergency hanging here in spacedock, you know. Dangling a juicy stuffed Cornish hen dinner in front of you was all I could come up with. I'm a surgeon, not a . . . not a . . . damn, I can't think of anything."

"Then you have something to keep you busy," Kirk said sharply. "There are some days when a man doesn't want to be cheered up. Kirk out."

He flipped the grid closed and stuffed the communicator and everything it represented back into his pocket. In his mind he saw McCoy's squarish face skewered with helpless empathy and knew he'd been unfair, but everything was unfair. Where was it written that a starship captain always had to be the exception? This wasn't his day to be exceptional. Today he wanted to be what he remembered himself as—a tough, curly-haired blond kid with big aspirations and a painfully pragmatic edge to his imagination. He knew that if he looked out the loft door he'd see his mother peeking out the farmhouse window like she had during his entire boyhood, wondering what her son was thinking and not having the nerve to come out and ask. Either that or she just had more respect for his privacy than McCoy did.

No surprise. Bacteria had more respect for privacy than McCoy did.

Kirk shook away an urge to glance over his shoulder and reached into the hidden metal box inside the loft wall. Carefully he pulled out an uneven bundle of letters, ragged and yellowed, a bundle of Starfleet notepaper preserved only with a child's obsessive care for something particularly precious. His lips curled up on one side as he ran his thumb across the discolored ink of a handwritten line.

"Stone knives and bearskins," he murmured. His throat closed around any further comment. Suddenly he was glad he was alone. He straightened up —certainly one thing that had been easier twenty-five years ago—strode through old hay to the loft door, and sat down in a wedge of sunlight with the bundle of notepaper.

The sunlight on his face, real sunlight, made the natural ruddiness rise in his cheeks again. He could feel the color seep back into his skin, aware of how pale starship duty sometimes made him in spite of special whole-spectrum artificial lighting with all its pretense of sunlight. Like pills instead of solid food. The same, but not. Maybe that was because starship lighting had no warmth.

Starship . . . how could a word so beautiful seem so sinister to him now? It hadn't been the ship's fault, this tragedy that crushed him to the Earth's surface like sudden gravity. It hadn't been McCoy's fault, though McCoy felt otherwise. It hadn't been Spock's fault, though Spock hadn't been able to help no matter how much he wanted to. *So, it must be my own fault. My fault, because I earned command. And for my reward, I pay.*

Squinting in the bright daylight, he divided the pile in two, just for the sake of mystery, then picked up a letter and started reading.

May 10, 2183

Dear George and Jim —
This letter is going to be late reaching you — sorry. Your letter

had to find me after being
delivered to the wrong starbase.
That's Star Fleet for you — we
can patrol a galaxy, but we
can't get a letter through.

I feel bad about last
month, troopers. I know
I promised to be there, but
there's a problem with promises
and you might as well learn
it. Even fathers have to break
them sometimes.

George, I want you to know
I'm proud of that green ribbon
you won at the science fair.
You already know more about
biology than I ever could. I
hung the ribbon right on the
door of the base recreation
deck, so everybody who goes
in has to look at it. I'm
getting congrats for you from
all over the starbase.

About the other idea, Jimmy—
probably not. Space isn't really
very pretty when it's all you
have to look at. Someday
you'll appreciate having

*a planet under your feet
when you look at the stars.
Okay, so it's not much of
an answer.*

"No," Kirk sighed, "it's not. But I probably wasn't listening anyway." He leaned back on the gray barnwood and crossed his ankles, then indulged in a sip of the coffee he'd brought out here with him. Doused with honey and milk like his aunt used to make for him when she thought he was too young to take coffee black, it was more of a liquid candy bar than coffee. The taste of nostalgia.

He tipped the crusty letter away from the sun and spoke to the handwriting.

"Keep talking. I'm listening now."

Chapter One

THE SECURITY COMMANDER set his pen down and spun the sensor camera roller, then gazed up at the row of monitors. Each monitor was carefully positioned so that he got a clear view of his own reflection, and it was a damned annoyance to always have to be looking past that fellow with the rusty red hair and the stern expression that reminded him of bleached-out dreams. He blinked to clear the reflection from his mind and looked toward the monitors, each of which showed a different compartment or lab or lounge on the starbase. At two o'clock in the simulated night, things were quiet. At least temporarily.

The officer set the computer sentry on automatic survey, picked up his pen, and went back to his writing while he had the chance.

Of course there's no reason you can't visit here when school's over, boys. But living on Starbase Two is out of the question. After all, your mother has her own career to consider, and even as Chief of Security here, I wouldn't have

*enough free time to make it
worth your while to give up
the life you have on Earth.
There aren't any meadows here,
or any lakes, or frogs, or race
tracks, or anything. Just labs,
classrooms and simulators,
and a couple of gyms not
even big enough to throw a
baseball in.*

He stopped writing, dissatisfied with the shielded truth he was sending home. Not even shielded truth. Shielded lies, really; better servants than a truth that would hurt the tender trust he was writing home to. At this point, trust meant more to him than truth. And he could never get far enough into space to ease the ache of his own integrity.

Distraction was welcome when it came—the startling buzz of one of the monitors. He pressed a switch that stopped the buzz, and leaned forward. Like a lie detector working on physiological cues, the monitor farthest to the left had focused in on the pool hall, its sensors triggered by the infinitesimal rise in body heat and other stress factors interpreted as hostile by the computer. Four men were clustered around one of the pool tables—well, more precisely, three of the men were clustered around the fourth. The biggest of the three had the prey by the collar and was pressing him against the pool table.

The security chief leaned still closer, his hazel eyes narrowing. He recognized the three as intersystem traders. "Scratch" Jones and his seamy crew. Local system troublemakers who stayed just close enough to a loose interpretation of the law that they were still allowed on the starbase to stock up, fuel up, and hawk their questionable services to anyone who would pay. But the tawny-faced, umber-haired man they were harassing was no trader. He was starbase personnel, and he had no business being there at this hour.

"But fellows," the tawny-faced one said in the accented but perfect English of the West Indies, "twice you've beaten me already. I'm better than you, I'm simply having a terrible day. The terrible-est. If I put my mind on it, I could smoke you."

"Sure, Reed," one of the men responded. "I've heard that talk all night and I'm sick of the insults. I'm still waiting for a real game."

Scratch Jones tightened his grip on the starbase man's neck. "Why don't you put your mind 'on it' and put your month's pay up against all of ours."

"I would, but lordy, I've got to go. I'm on duty, you see. It means my commission if I'm found here with you prehistorics."

"He's got to go," muttered the third trader. "What a coincidence."

"On the rail," Scratch Jones growled.

With some difficulty, since there was a two-hundred-pound man leaning against him, Drake Reed tugged his pay voucher from his pocket and placed it on the table's rail beside him. He'd lost two games already, and his pay voucher looked like easy pickings to Jones' crew as they too dumped handfuls of Federation credit slips and assorted interplanetary tokens, promissory notes, and other tender on top of the helpless Fleet ticket.

Jones smiled and released Reed. He nodded to the bearded one of his herd. "Rack 'em up, Chainsaw."

Reed shrugged. "You're going to need a warp power cue just to keep up with my juju, man."

10

"And chickens quack. You break."

Reed shook his head, catching the cue stick rudely tossed to him by Jones.

In the security office, the chief tightened his weapons harness and kept an eye on the monitor while Reed flexed his shoulders beneath a standard red Starfleet uniform and leaned over the pool table. "Amateur night at Starfleet," the chief muttered just as Reed's cue made a sudden snap at the cue ball and the triangle of colored balls exploded across the table.

Scratch Jones and his men dropped their jaws as at least half of the balls toppled neatly into convenient pockets. They'd seen nothing like that from Reed before this, the chief knew, and that's where the trouble lay.

When the balls stopped clacking into the pockets, Chainsaw shook his head and leered at Reed. "You can open your eyes now," he mocked.

With his brown eyes gleaming and quite open, Reed offered that innocent shrug again and responded, "Must have been a sudden gust of gravity . . ."

"Better have been," Jones growled. On the wake of his words, he drew a Rigellian dagger and held it with casual but naked threat. "Take your next shot, rum-runner."

The security chief quickly set the monitor on automatic and hurried out into the corridor to the security lift across the hall. Behind him the door panel to starbase security whispered shut.

By the time Reed made his next two shots, Jones and his crew clearly smelled the scam. But the bet was already made, lying there on the table's rail, just waiting to see if Reed was incomparably lucky or a king's own liar.

Reed's shots grew more complicated. He avoided

11

the easiest shots now and openly displayed a penchant for banked shots and double sinkers, until finally the acreage of green felt was cleared of all its colors. It was the last shot that destroyed Reed's chances of ever being accepted as an easy touch again—the three and the seven dunked at opposite ends of the table by a shot that banked the poor cue ball three times.

"He fleeced us, Scratch," the third man said.

"I did warn you," was Reed's weak defense.

"You reekin' fraud," Jones accused as Reed put down the cue stick and stuffed the assorted currency into his boot cuffs. "Put it back. You're gonna play us again. And this time you're gonna play *me.*"

Reed straightened and waved his hands in calculated decline. "No, no, no, two-dimensionals, I can't do it. I've got to go. On duty, you see. I'm going to be in deep disgusting trouble."

He had been backing toward the door, none too gracefully, when Chainsaw lunged at him and got him by the throat again.

Reed squirmed. "Look, I'm not done healing from the last time—"

"You're not gonna be done healing for a long time, swindler."

"See here, gas weed—take your flippers off my flesh!"

Jones raised his Rigellian dagger to Reed's eye level. Crusted blood flaked across the blade like some ignoble sash of conquest from the last time someone felt its bite. What planet, what situation, what defense, none of that mattered; all that remained was the dried blood. Blood that looked quite human.

With the hiss of the door panel, a flurry of hits broke up the attack. The security commander rammed his knee into Reed's ribs to bring him down, then grasped Reed's arm and twisted it behind his back, and held Jones and his men off with the hand-cannon extended in a no-fooling stance. "Neutral corners!"

"He cheated us!" Chainsaw protested instantly.

"All I see is armed assault," the chief snapped back. "If you want me to forget I saw it, you'd better be off this starbase in ten minutes!"

Reed twisted to look up at the officer. "I can explain, your officerness—"

"Name, mister."

"Francis Drake Reed, sir. I can explain—"

"Explain in the brig. You're up to your privates in infractions. Out the door."

Jones took a step forward. "But he's got our—"

The hand-cannon stiffened at the end of the chief's arm, a none-too-subtle reminder of the chief's fighting prowess that even Jones hesitated to challenge. "Ten minutes! Flat!"

The door panel breathed open as the chief dragged a wincing Reed through it, then closed again. Left behind, in Scratch Jones' oily hands, a pool cue snapped in two.

Reed gasped in relief as the security chief led him into the turbo-lift, then leaned against the lift wall and rubbed his side.

"You okay?" the commander asked him.

"Jesus on a hill, George," Reed responded, his expression wounded, "you hit me."

George brushed a lock of rust hair from his forehead and leaned forward, glaring. "Are . . . you . . . okay?"

"Well, considering that you might have made your appearance a thought earlier—"

"Then shut up. And hand it over."

Reed punished George with another wince as he pulled the currency from his boot. George took it and gave it a rough count.

"Looks like Jones had a good month," he said, brows raised in appreciation.

"All muscle," Drake scoffed. "No talent. You really came in like Moco Jumbie dancing the bamboola. *Antic terrible.*"

"Here's your half. And you can keep whatever's in the other boot."

Looking insulted, Drake straightened. "What makes you think there's anything in the other boot?"

George tried to resist the grin tugging at his lips. "Drake, you are not an honest man."

"Oh, tut. Honesty is a matter of interpretation, George. I told Jones the truth from the very beginning."

"Sure, but you engineered it so they wouldn't believe you."

"I'm a simple man of little ornament."

"You're an opportunist with an innocent face, is what you are," George pointed out, giving Reed's tawny cheek a tap. "You lie like a rug."

"I protest."

"You're a rogue with a cute accent. Admit it. You sound like a Trinidad priest and you know how to use it."

"This from the man for whose pocket I risk my life."

George gazed down at the handful of Federation-acceptable notes and bonds and chips, feeling guilty about taking ill-gotten booty. But only a little. After all, the gains he held really belonged to whoever Jones had bilked it out of to begin with. At least it would be spent for a kindness and not on cheap alien rotgut. "Thanks, Drake. This means a lot to me. I could never put together this much by next month."

"Great minds, George, great minds. We work together like a steel band on Dimanche Gras."

The lift door opened and the two men crossed the corridor to the security office. The first thing George did was check the pool-hall monitor—sure enough, Jones and his men had taken him seriously enough to vacate the area. People like Jones didn't cross Starfleet security if they could avoid it; there were considerably more problems for them in losing starbase privileges than in losing a bet, even if the sacrifice was three men's pay for a whole month. All quiet.

"You'd better get back in uniform before somebody walks in here," George suggested.

"How can it matter? My best friend is security commander."

"Don't press your luck, pirate."

Drake Reed immediately went to a closet and began systematically donning his security harness, jacket, and weapon. Even fully armed, he still looked like the priest George had accused him of imitating. "You've not yet told me what it is you need the money for, Geordie."

George settled into his seat at the monitor station and picked up the magnetic writing board again. The faint light glowed through several layers of paper, making his own handwriting leap up at him. "I'm going to buy Jimmy a birthday present. I told you that."

"Certainly you did, and very vaguely indeed. What present?"

"Well . . ."

"A woman of his own, yes?"

"He's not a midshipman yet, you know," George complained with a grin.

"Then what does he want for his grand number ten?"

15

"He wants . . . well, he wants a sailboat. That's what I get for taking him to museums, I guess."

"In Iowa, he'll need a horse to pull it. Did you think of that?" Drake reminded as he joined George at the console.

George's hazel gaze came up without a blink. "It's not going to Iowa. It's going to Ontario. The boys visit their aunt every summer on Georgian Bay. And this year, Drake, you whitewashed racketeer, there's going to be a pretty little sailboat waiting for them with Jimmy's name on the captain's hat."

"And sailing lessons, I hope to God."

George's eyes lost their focus. The writing board in his hand blurred before him. "What I wouldn't give to be there holding its leash when they arrive . . ."

"Leash?"

"Rein, rope, whatever grows off a sailboat. Don't confuse me."

Drake held up a scolding finger. "These details are critical to island men, George. What will Geordie Junior think of all this, hmm?"

George raised his brows. "What should he think? After all, the whole bay's got his name on it. My boys aren't competitive, you know that. Georgie's the practical type, like me. No imagination at all. He just wants to know how things work. It's Jimmy who's the idealist. He wants the universe in order." The memories flooded back and drove George reaching for his pen once more, lapsing into silence as he reread the last few lines of his letter.

Drake's voice shook his reverie. "Why do you do that?"

"Do what?"

"Write letters. Would the boys not rather look at your face on a screen and see their papa talking to them? And it costs you a ransom every time you send

16

one of those all the way back to Earth. Why not just make a recording?"

George sighed. "You know I can't think and talk at the same time."

I know it's a little weird that I send letters instead of comp tapes, but there's a reason. Remember when I took you to the Seafarer's Museum and we read the log from that 1910 merchant ship? Remember how close we felt to the captain when we looked at his handwriting and the words on the page? We could almost feel what he felt. That's because it's lonely at sea, and the feelings come to the surface whether you like it or not. There's something private and personal about a pen and paper. I remember the looks on your faces. I hope you boys can look at my letters that way some day, even if I never cross an ocean on a toothpick like they did. You'll touch the paper and

*know I touched it too. And
I'll know you're touching it —*

"Don't make it a sad letter, George."

George looked up into Drake's eyes, shaded by that awning of umber hair that reflected his West Indies heritage. Drake was doing his priest thing again, but this time it was no sham.

"How do you know it's a sad letter?" George asked. A sudden shiver ran down his arms.

Drake sat on the console and gazed down at him. "I see your face."

George's complexion, normally peach-pale, flushed russet. "Hang you."

"End the letter before it gets sad, George," Drake pressed.

For a moment George's eyes grew cold, his brows flattened over them, and the threatening look he'd used on Jones returned. *Don't tamper with my privacy,* the look warned. *It's all I have.*

"Love . . . Dad," Drake prodded. He pointed at the paper.

Indignant and embarrassed at being so transparent, George felt the sting of regret. He tore his gaze away from Drake and dragged his attention back to the paper. If only he could allow his family to know him so well. If only.

His fingers were stiff as he wrote the final words.

*George, look after the family.
You're my second-in-command.
I'll write to you both when
you get to Georgian Bay.
And Jim, don't get mad*

when Aunt Ilsa calls you
"Yeemee."
                        Signing Off,
                           Dad

He folded the paper immediately, then again, as
though the act would seal out any invasion. Knowing
Drake was watching, he slipped the letter into a
Starfleet envelope, slid his fingers along the pressure
seal, addressed it sloppily, then opened the communications chute and dropped the letter in. The sound of
automatic suction told him it was gone. Two weeks
from now his boys would be reading it. And it was too
late for him to catch it back and change anything. The
commitment made him nervous. He closed his eyes
for a moment and covered his mouth with a cool
hand. Strange how just writing a letter . . .

"You always get surly when you write to your
puppies, Geordie," Drake said as he folded his arms
and shifted against the console. "You have the temper
of a resting alligator, you know, and I'd like to hear
you admit it freely."

George glanced at him briefly and let his indignation flow away. He fiddled with the monitor equipment. "I'd rather sleep with a Romulan."

"You might. You don't even know what a Romulan
looks like."

"I don't have to."

"George, you are a bigot."

"I know."

Without the slightest warning, the office door slid
open. That in itself was a surprise; the security office
doors weren't supposed to open except for cleared
personnel, and the people who entered, two men and
a woman, didn't seem to be wearing any of the coded
clearance badges for the computer sentry to read.

How had they gotten the door open? George swiveled around slightly in his chair, just enough to get a good look at the woman, who was in the lead. All he had time to register were her grape-green eyes and the color of her shoulder-length hair—like a wheat field just after dawn. Biscuit-blond.

She took two measured steps into the office, followed by the two nondescript men, and without a pause asked, "George Kirk?"

The answer was automatic. "Yes?"

The two men lunged around her, one heading for George, the other for Drake.

Drake was taken by surprise, training or not, and his attacker managed to pinion his arms before he could draw his hand-cannon. The woman moved in instantly and pressed a moist cloth over Drake's nose and mouth. Drake's eyes widened in terror and disgust at the stifling medicinal odor in the cloth, and his arms and legs turned to putty in the grip of his attackers.

George had had that extra second necessary to raise his feet and kick off the other man's first lunge, and by the time he rolled to the floor and came up, he had managed to draw his weapon. Lacking time to aim and fire it, though, he simply brought it upward in a sweep and butt-stroked the stranger's jaw. Had he not been startled by Drake's sudden collapse at the hands of the woman, he might not have been overtaken. But when Drake went down, the second man moved in on George and kicked him hard across the pelvis. Stunned, George fought the numbness and tried to keep his balance, but the only way to do that was to lean on the hand that held his cannon. The two men grabbed his arms and held him as he writhed and tried to kick back, and the woman moved in.

George bellowed an animal protest as the cloth closed in on his mouth, and the woman had a fight just getting near his face. Something about her told him she was a professional. She seemed to know the moves he would make as he twisted and tugged against the two strong men, and she anticipated him enough to force the odorous narcotic into his nostrils. His muscles turned to jelly, and the room to sizzling colors. A tunnel began to close around his vision, snuffing out the colors. He felt himself sinking. The cloth pressed tighter over his mouth, and the heavy drug drowned his universe. A black, black universe.

Chapter Two

THE ONLY TANGIBLE sensation was that of unreality. Not tangible . . . but identifiable, at least. The uncomfortable dream gradually gathered itself into the feeling of a hard floor beneath his shoulder blades. There was a faint vibration along his spine. The air itself was an oppressive weight.

George came around slowly. He tried to lift his arms, but they wouldn't come up. His eyes wouldn't open. And the arms definitely wouldn't come up. Somehow the drug had left him stone blind and paralyzed.

Don't panic, he warned himself. *Panic kills. Do something else.* He thought about his right shoulder, his right arm, his right hand. With hard concentration he willed the arm to trace an arc along the floor. It tingled and ached, but it moved, and it struck something solid. His hand slowly closed around the object —a leg, or arm. Warm.

"Drake," he whispered. He concentrated now on opening his eyes. Nothing. He closed them again, opened them a second time, and yes, this time there was a sensation of light. Instantly his muggy brain registered the yellowish glow of shipboard running lights at the edge of the ceiling. That explained the steady vibration—engines.

Urgency shot through him. He was being taken

somewhere against his will. That meant he had to move, and soon.

The next project was lifting his head.

"If I turn over," he murmured, clinging to the sound of his own voice, "I could use my arms and maybe . . . sit up."

He gave up trying to focus on the yellow lights and instead thought about rolling over onto his side. As if thinking about it wasn't enough of a strain, he re-arranged his legs and pressed the floor until the whole ship moved. Was he . . . yes, he was on his side now. When he blinked his eyes again, a streak of dark-ness clouded one of them. Redness. Blood on his eye?

Pushing the panic down like a rung on a rubber ladder, George brought a hand up to his eye and fingered it. Hair. Was his hair that red? He turned his head toward the running lights and got a clearer view of a cinnamon strand. Yes, it was his hair. He wasn't bleeding after all.

That left him free to move without worrying about his head falling off unexpectedly. He got his shoulder under him, arranged his legs again, and heaved him-self over.

And his head fell off.

He grabbed it with both hands. "Oh . . . God . . . *damn!* Ow!"

"George?"

"Dammmmmn—"

"George? I say, George?"

"Yeah," he gasped. "Yeah . . . don't sit up fast, whatever you do."

"George," the voice replied, "did you hit me again?"

"No, I didn't hit you. Of course I didn't hit you. Somebody drugged us. Don't move. It's all right. I'm coming over there."

23

He planted his hands on the floor and wobbled into a crawl.

The journey to Drake was exhausting. George hoped he was moving in the right direction under the distorting effects of yellow lights and double vision. His arms and thighs trembled with effort, but every movement brought him closer to regaining control. He moved toward the red and black blur of Drake's Security Division uniform, found Drake's rib cage, and palmed along it until he found Drake's shoulder. Judging from the Indies complexion made sallow by the running lights, this was indeed Drake and not just another corpse that happened to be lying around. "Corpse" was a good word for this feeling.

"Come on." George wrapped his hands around Drake's arm. "Try to sit up. Slowly."

Pulling Drake up against the bulkhead made George dizzy, but it also got his blood running. He flopped down beside the other man and breathed deeply, and gradually his sodden brain cleared.

"What've you done now?" he grumbled.

"I? I?"

"This must be your fault."

Beside him, Drake shifted. "My fault? *My* fault? And when they asked for George Kirk, was I supposed to answer?"

"They could've killed us, but they didn't," George thought aloud. "Why didn't they?"

"Small favors. Let's not remind them, eh? Oooh . . . I feel like a gutted calabash."

George gazed around their cramped prison, taking in the configuration of the bulkhead structure and colors. "Starfleet vessel . . . but old. And small. Maybe a personal transport of some kind."

"It's a Hubble VXT interstellar runabout, actually."

George blinked and turned to Drake accusatively. "What?"

"Interstellar runabout."

"How do you know that?"

"It says so right on the wall here. Construction contract number 116-B . . . commissioned January of twenty-one-sixty—"

"All right, all right."

"Second-generation warp drive—"

"Enough, Drake. On your feet."

"I have no feet left, George. They're gone. I tried to find them, but they're gone."

Since George had feet, he got up first and moved along the wall to the door panel. "Not very good security," he said, examining the door. "If it's meant to lock at all, this kind of hold is meant to keep people out, not keep them in. We should be able to get out . . . if we can find the hydraulics inside the wall, we can sever the lines and just push the doors open."

"Assuming," Drake began, "they're not also magnetically locked. You always assume."

"And you're still sitting on your ass. Get up and help."

"Patience. I'm still several toes short of a set, fellow."

George tapped the wall. Hollow. Typical low-security interior bulkhead, no heavy mechanics; no reason they shouldn't be able to get out. "This ship might be too old to have magnetics. I'll bet on that. Got any tools on you?"

"Brains. Only brains."

"Are you up yet?"

"Any minute now, I swear."

"Something to use as a pry bar . . ." George blinked his eyes to clear them one more time and scanned the small hold area. "Here. Here's the access." He

25

wedged his fingers into the rim of the small panel and wrenched it off, exposing a hollow area with some circuit boards and interior diagrams stretching down into the wall. "Good. No molecular circuitry. They didn't need anything fancy. We should be able to do this." He reached into the wall as far as he could. "Drake, come here. Your hand is smaller than mine. Reach in there and feel around for the lock release."

Drake took a deep breath and struggled to his feet.

"It's got to be down to the left," George told him. "I felt the tip of it. You were always better at circuitry than I was. Come on, hurry up." He grasped Drake's arm and pulled him up to the access hole.

"I hear and I do. Stand abreast." Drake squared his shoulders and kissed the tips of his fingers before they vanished into the hole. "Yes . . . I feel it . . . I think I have it."

"Be careful," George warned.

"Oh, yes. Oh, I love success." Drake drew back his lips and concentrated. Then—

plink

And the artificial gravity turned off.

"Drake!" George howled as they suddenly found themselves floating in place.

"Hmmm," Drake observed. "That isn't right."

"Get away from there before you shut down the life support too!"

"So serious all the time, Geordie," Drake scolded.

"You could stand a dose of serious—" An involuntary flex of his muscles sent him floating upward. George bumped his head on the light fixture running along the ceiling edge and turned to push away from it, then changed his mind. "Well, as long as I'm up here . . ." He braced his feet on the ceiling, worked his fingers between the lighting plate and the bulkhead, and heaved. The metal groaned and cut into his fingers, but he refused to ease up. His legs shook with

26

the strain. His cheeks flushed with color and his fingers throbbed, but the creaking of the metal plate urged him on.

The creak became a horrid shriek. Bolts popped and flew across the hold. Finally, the plate gave on one side, then the other, and with a great *clack* it came off in George's tortured hands. He let out a breath of victory that instantly became a gulp of surprise as he shot across the hold and smashed the back of his head and shoulders into the opposite bulkhead, bounced toward the floor, then floated back toward the ceiling.

"George!" Drake reached out for a passing ankle and pulled until he could get a better grip on George's arm and belt. "George, are you all right?"

George winced and rubbed his pounding head, becoming disoriented as his legs started to float sideways. "I'll get you for this. I *know* it's your fault."

"You know, George, you look just like Peter Pan! I never noticed it before. Has your wife ever seen you in zero-G?"

With a testing stretch of his ravaged shoulder muscles, George pulled himself back to the access hole and wedged the corner of the lighting plate into it. "All right. It's coming off now, whether it likes it or not. Stand aside." He leaned back, braced his feet against the bulkhead, and put his weight into his work. "One . . . two . . ."

"Hello, children."

The bridge crew shared a mutual smile at their captain's unique greeting. At first his manner had seemed awkward, but now they accepted it for what it was and simply appreciated his infectious charm. This wasn't their usual assignment ship; that was plain from their unfamiliarity with the design. This was nothing more than a getting-from-here-to-there ship, and this time the "there" was top secret. No one but the captain himself seemed to have any idea of where they were going or why.

The young man on helm turned immediately and said, "We have warp, Captain. Our ETA is thirty-nine minutes."

"Ah! Good," the captain responded in his reassuring Coventry chant. "Thank you, Carlos. You always do such a magnificent job." Clad in a sloppy Irish wool cardigan that hid much of his mustard-gold Starfleet uniform, the captain was a one-man destruction zone for the hackneyed image of the stuffy, passionless Englishman. That was evidenced as he dropped his hand on the helmsman's shoulder. "Have you had your lunch? This is a good time."

The helmsman looked up for confirmation and found it in the captain's offhand nod. "Thanks, sir . . . thank you."

"Not at all. Off you go." He waved a hand at the thick-set communications officer and said, "You too, Claw. Off you go. Dr. Poole and I can handle things up here for a short while, I 'magine."

The two junior officers gratefully left the bridge. On the port side, a woman with dark blond hair folded her arms and said nothing, but merely watched the captain.

He was a gentle-faced man in his early forties, with brown hair sloppily palmed to one side, a slightly hooked nose, and powder-blue eyes pouched with experience. Given to hanging his hands in the pockets of that nonregulation cardigan, he looked out of place on the tight little bridge. She remembered the time she'd pecked at him about the sweater, only to be informed by another officer that the captain suffered a rare blood deficiency that made him slightly chilly most of the time. While any other officer in Starfleet would feel obliged to wear a thermal layer *under* the uniform, this man simply slipped the sweater on and

28

called it solved. Over several years of service, the sweater, like its master, had acquired a slight sag and a lot of respect, not to mention a professorial image that smothered any hint of his Starfleet accolades —considerable ones.

When the juniors were gone, the captain lounged back in the helm chair instead of his command seat and shifted his gaze to the woman. She was still looking at him as though he needed looking at.

With a deep breath and an easy grin, he said, "Rolf tells me you knocked them out straightaway."

The woman shrugged. "I didn't want to have to explain anything to them. I don't have the answers."

The captain stuffed his hands into his old knitted friend. "I could give you the details of the mission—"

She held up a defensive hand. "No, thanks."

"You'll have to find out sooner or later, doctor, my dear."

"No, I don't. The less I know, the less involved I have to get, and the sooner I can get back to the colony I've been assigned to. The one I *requested* and was *granted* by the Federation."

The captain's thin lips curled in amusement. He tipped his head. "It's a compliment."

The woman leaned forward. "It's an intrusion. I have other work to do in another place."

"Can't you see that you must be the most qualified person? You'll be the first, you know."

"I'm sure there've been doctors on big boats before," she responded dryly. "I don't know how you arranged to get my orders changed, but I intend to log a formal protest as soon as we get back."

He chuckled. "Orders do change, Sarah. And this is an emergency mission, after all."

"You're not going to admit it, are you?" she accused.

The captain tossed his head and laughed. "In my

experience, it's wisest never to admit anything to a pretty woman who's also smart."

She grimaced, her ivory face made pasty by the poor lighting and given a green cast by the Medical Services smock. Only her eyes, as she narrowed them at him, seemed to have any substance in the unflattering light. She gave her head a shake as though to call attention to what she had once described to him as uneventful hair. "Don't smooth me, Captain. I'm over thirty. I've heard it before."

"Obviously not sincerely enough." He lolled back still farther in the wobbly helm chair and watched space stretch by at warp two. "At least I managed to convince the authorities to let me select my own command crew. And there was barely time for that. You've known me for a long time. You know I like to have familiar people around me. Perhaps it's a weakness . . . we'll see. Well," he said, giving the ship's navigation console an affectionate slap, "I'll explain it in full to you as soon as Kirk gets up here."

Dr. Poole settled into the science station seat and told him, "He's not going to get up here. I locked them in the hold."

"Oh, *that* won't make any difference."

She blinked. "Houdini?"

"Stubborn."

His rueful nod ushered in a silence that lasted several long, quiet minutes. Through the wide main portal, he watched space peel by at the kind of speed it takes time to get used to. It never ceased to be startling, or beautiful, or even a touch frightening, and none of it was natural. This speed was the accomplishment of inventive minds. Of all the wonders of the natural universe, this wonder belonged to intelligence alone. It was nice for something to be marvelous because it didn't know any better, but to be marvelous by *design* . . .

The captain sighed and contemplated the miracles he would see in the next few days. Inside the pockets, his hands clenched with anticipation. His eyes reflected the passage of hope's foothills.

Then the bridge entry panel shot open and the floor vibrated—and he knew the time for contemplation was over.

"On your feet!"

The captain and the doctor turned and stood up to face the two security men, the russet-haired one armed with a particle cutter from a ship's emergency kit. Though Dr. Poole froze, the captain swung his arms out wide and greeted, "George! How good to see you! You look strapping. How're the boys?" He strode to them and gave George a pat on the arm, then turned to Dr. Poole. "I told you they'd be right along." He gave George a little shake and drawled, "Ingenious fellow."

George Kirk let his breath out in a gasp and sucked in a new one, staring fiercely at the captain, then the doctor, then the bridge, then the captain again. "R—" He took another breath and tried again. "Robert!"

Behind him, Drake brandished the bent lighting panel they'd used to break out of the hold, still not quite convinced by the captain's joviality.

The captain rocked on his heels, devilishly pleased with the reunion he'd arranged. "Didn't think I could be so clandestine, did you?"

"You . . ." George began. *"You* kidnapped us?"

"Well, there simply wasn't time—"

"There'd better be time now!"

"Oh yes, plenty. A good eight or ten minutes yet, I'm sure," the captain said, glancing at the chronometer.

George took a few uncertain steps around the bridge, his head still swimming, and demanded,

"Where is everybody? This ship's practically empty. Where's the crew?"

"In the mess hall, I suppose, having a good lunch. There are only a few on board. Security reasons, you see."

George narrowed his eyes. "Security . . . what are you up to?"

"I want you to volunteer for a mission."

"What mission?"

"I can't specify."

"To where?"

"I can't tell you."

"For how long?"

The lopsided grin appeared. "Sorry."

"After I volunteer, then you can tell me?"

"Right."

"And I'm supposed to just trust you?"

"I'd be so grateful."

"All right. I volunteer."

"What about you, Drake?" the captain asked, starting to turn.

George stepped closer and waved a hand. "He volunteers too. Now, what's all this about?"

The captain's grin widened and he looked at Sarah. "Didn't I tell you?"

Sarah shrugged her innocence. "It wasn't my idea to drug them."

"Yes, would you care to explain that?" George demanded, glaring at the captain.

"Well, you see, this mission is the top-secret response to an emergency situation, and decisions had to be made quickly. They finally allowed me to choose my own officers, so—"

"Who did?"

"Starfleet Command."

"You got Starfleet Command to authorize you to

knock us out and kidnap us?" George shook his head. "I'd like to see that memo."

The captain held his hands out wide. "It was the *only* way they'd agree to it." Amused by Kirk's dubious expression, the captain suddenly touched his lips with one finger and said, "Oh, forgive me. I'm being inhospitable." He gestured gallantly between them and the woman. "May I present Commander George Kirk, and over there is Lieutenant Francis Drake Reed. Gentlemen . . . Dr. Sarah Poole."

George stared rudely at her, quite aware of the rude part, and once his memory made adjustments for the bridge lighting and the green smock, he recognized her. "We've met," he snapped.

Sarah bobbed her eyebrows. "Don't look at me like that. He did the same thing to get me here."

George snapped back at the captain, "You did that to her? And why pull Drake into this?"

The captain shrugged and strode a few steps to the upper bridge for a long look at Drake. "While it would be easier·if you'd just drag around a teddy bear or a blanket, I knew you'd want him along." His hands went back into the pockets, and the captain suddenly looked as though he was hovering in front of a blackboard, waiting to see if his students comprehended a new concept, so innocuous and self-assured that he was almost impossible to dislike. With that tolerant grin, he nodded. "Well, then. This is a good time for explanations. Gather round, children." He moved to the computer bank and tapped the access. "Computer on," he said.

"Working."

"This is Captain Robert April. Request security access, Starfleet Command authorization, graphic tape one."

The console buzzed to life, and its raspy voice responded, *"Authorization accepted. File on screen."*

Above them appeared a series of diagrams and photographs of a familiar colonial transport ship, one of the Seidman-class long-distance movers. Old, but time-proven. It meant nothing at all to anyone except, of course, Captain April. He nodded at the diagrams. "This is the United Federation Colonizer S.S. *Rosenberg*. She was off to colonize a newly discovered planet in the space just recently charted by the Federation. Five days ago we received a distress call from the *Rosenberg*. They don't, of course, have an advanced sensor system and weren't able to realize the severity of an ionic storm cluster they encountered until after they were already too deep inside it to stop the damage and reverse course. They're adrift. No engine power, and heavy radiation leakage in their storage compartments and engineering areas. Most of their foodstuffs have been contaminated. Actually, even if they did have the food, there's radiation leakage into the inhabited parts of the ship. It's only a matter of time, and not much time at that. To make a long story tolerable," April said with a sad sigh, "they're going to die out there."

George was the first to break the heavy silence. "How many?"

April half turned. "Fourteen families. Fifty-one people. Twenty-seven are under fifteen years old. Young families with babies, and without experience. And without food."

"God . . ." Sarah breathed, then caught the breath with the knuckle of her thumb.

"Of course, a shuttleplane was dispatched straight off," April went on, "but no conventional ship can risk going through the ionic storms until they've dissipated, and that could take years. The rescue ship is going around the storms, but even at warp three

34

that'll take four months. The *Rosenberg* only has about three weeks' worth of supplies on hand, and, of course, I mentioned the radiation leaks." He gazed at the graphic screen. It cast its pattern of lights on his face. "Fifty-one people who think they're going to die in space, hopelessly out of range. And the really tragic part is that we can communicate with them quite nicely, with communications at warp twenty. All of the Federation is listening to them die out there. Journalists are having a field day, you can well imagine."

He stepped off the upper deck, past the three pained faces of his chosen crew, only to find himself yanked around. He stared up into George Kirk's eyes, and the unmistakable image of two little boys in a cornfield, on a planet suddenly too far away for peaceful memory.

"You've got something planned," George snapped. "What is it? We'll try it."

April's light blue eyes filled with affection as he grinned up at the fierceness he knew he would need at his side. He opened his mouth to answer, only to be interrupted by the beeping of the ship's auto-nav. He turned as though responding to a dog barking outside his door. "Ah! We've arrived. Drake, do you know how to take the ship out of warp?"

Drake blinked out of his trance and recovered his usual false humility. "I shall die trying, sir." With that, he moved to the helm and pecked at the controls.

April moved toward the bridge viewing portal and watched in wonder as the ship smoothly fell out of warp drive and approached what appeared to be a spacedock behind a little cluster of asteroids.

George left the upper deck, his eyes fixed on his former commander, all the details of their mutual past flashing through his mind. He saw unshielded resolve in the captain's expression. It was infectious.

And confusing. "What is it, Robert?" he prodded. "What are you planning?"

"Think of it, George," April murmured. "An impossible rescue. A way to turn a four-month journey into a three-week epic triumph in the name of life. Think of it."

Now George moved around to face him, and to force April to look at him. In the upper edge of the view screen, unnoticed, the spacedock moved closer.

"Why all the cloak and dagger?" George pressed. "Why didn't you just ask me?"

"Couldn't take the chance, old boy."

"Why?"

April stepped closer to the helm, placed his hands on the console, and looked out, upward, at the looming spacedock. He nodded out, up. "That's why."

Soft lights from the spacedock played in his eyes.

George stepped closer, leaned over the console, and looked out. The lights bathed his ruddy cheeks and drew him onward, into astonishment.

"My God . . ." he whispered. "What is *that?*"

"That," April breathed, "is a starship."

Chapter Three

SPACE WAS BLACK. Innerspace every bit as black as the Outmarches or the Wide. Nothing would color it, ever.

"This is Field-Primus Kilyle. The Swarm accepts patrol."

"Acknowledged. Regards of the Grand-Primus go with you. We wish you adventure."

Space hummed now. Through it soared a gigantic winged craft, painted black as the space around it, but glossy and decorated with metallic painted feathers. From one wing, one at a time, bunches of feathers began to detach, like shingles falling from a rooftop in strong wind. Each bunch of feathers, once free of the bunch layered above it, became a ship. Where only one side of feathers, one wing, had been showing as it rested layered under the ship on top of it, each vessel now showed itself to be a small version of the mothership.

Like an organized molt, the Swarm of six patrol vessels detached from the mothership which had delivered it to its patrol space at hyperlight speed. Now, capable of only sublight propulsion, the six would be alone in this interior space. Not even interior—practically *an*terior. Such was the irony of the "regards of the Grand-Primus."

On the bridge of the Swarm's flagship, a ship they

called *Raze*—yet another irony—the commander stifled a sigh and ignored the irritated glances of the bridge crew. It was an effort for her to ignore them, but she was determined to do it without the slightest hint of self-awareness. In fact, they weren't glancing at her; they were glancing at each other. Their communication was subtle, but it carried enough resentment that she could nearly see their thoughts right through the backs of their bird-head helmets as they deliberately *didn't* look at her.

"Deploy patrol, Kai," she said, while watching in the main viewer as the mothership was suddenly and unceremoniously sucked into hyperlight to deliver the other Swarms to their own patrol space. A sense of relief followed.

From her own bridge, a familiar voice: "Deploying *War Thorn*. Acknowledge, *War Thorn*," her subcommander said, picking at his instruments.

"War Thorn *accepts patrol*," the communications panel rasped. In the viewer, one patrol vessel broke away from the Swarm and veered off at half sublight. Soon it was gone.

Subcommander Kai went on without a pause. "Deploying *Raffish*. Acknowledge, *Raffish*."

"Raffish *accepts patrol*."

And so on down the line of five cluster ships under command of *Raze. Soar, Experience,* and *Future Fire* soon followed, until *Raze* was alone, only her metallic feathers rupturing the smooth blackness of space.

The commander got out of her seat with measured casualness, habitually favoring her left leg. "I'm going to report status to Primus Kilyle."

She almost made it to the corridor entrance before a voice from behind halted her.

"Commander Idrys," said a young officer who was standing against the bridge strut, making it obvious that he had nothing to do. His colorless hair and ears

38

whose points were slightly turned forward had become symbols of annoyance for her. "My compliments to the Primus."

The commander paused only long enough to give him an unbending glare. "I'm sure the Primus will be thrilled to hear from you, Antecenturion." *And I'm sure he also craves eating roast butterflies with the Klingons.*

As she stepped toward the corridor, she involuntarily added a little more sway to her old limp than necessary, reminding him of her own long history of service to the Empire.

The ship seemed very small today. She chose to walk through it as long as possible, avoiding the lifts. Climbing the access ladders made her feel more potent and, she admitted, stalled her confrontation with Primus Kilyle, a man so intense that he burned her with his presence.

The command corridor was heavily guarded by sentries, and she stalked past them without even seeing them. Only when she stopped at the Primus' door did she acknowledge the existence of the two stuffed uniforms standing like cast stone on either side of the entrance. For a moment she said nothing, but only looked at the calligraphied letters on the door: T'CAEL ZANIIDOR KILYLE, FIELD-PRIMUS.

The letters looked foolish to her now, where for years they had not. They were being phased out, these announcements of who dwelled within. It was part of a growing paranoia on the part of the Senate, a symptom of the praetor's own insecurities.

"Advise the Field-Primus that I'm here," she said directly, not looking at either of the subcenturions.

One of the helmeted guards twisted a toggle on the door panel. "Field-Primus," he said, "Commander Idrys wishes audience with you."

"Admit her."

The subcenturion immediately produced a permission chip from his belt pack and attached it to the cowl of Idrys' uniform while the other guard tapped out the code that would open the door.

Entering the Primus' quarters was like entering another world. The air was moist here and very fresh, fed by the breath of hanging plants that crowded the ceiling. Unlike the austere military tone of the rest of the ship, this chamber was deep with color—plants by the dozens, exotic and shocking, so thick they seemed to be growing from the walls, ceiling, and deck. Mostly green, the foliage was complicated here and there with the bright yellows, purples, and blues of plants that fared less well in these atmospheric conditions, and some whose natural colors had nothing to do with greenness. Others had bizarre growths typical of alien environments visited by the Primus over the years. There were even a few that qualified as trees, with woody stems and drooping fronds.

"Come in, Commander," the Primus' deceptively soft voice invited from somewhere among the vegetation.

Idrys stepped inside. The door closed behind her with a mechanical breath. She moved carefully so as not to damage any of the plants, and took care to step widely around an intelligent-looking vine whose runners always seemed to be moving toward her. She stifled a cough brought on by the humidity and mossy smell, and parted a veil of bright amber hanging blossoms. "Primus?"

"To your right. Around the demontree."

Anything with a name like that got a wide berth. When she cleared it, Primus Kilyle stood in front of her, half smiling at her hesitation. "Welcome," he said simply.

Among the plants, he was a striking anomaly. His hair was raven black, without a trace of shine, his complexion darksome and disturbing. His eyes were large and extremely black and round, wreathed all around in shadows, and always seemed to be opened a little wider than was comfortable. They held a stubbornness, and certainly an intelligence of dangerous proportion. Over them, brows arched like sickles, in artistic contrast to the peaked ears, which were almost perfect by Rihannsu standards of beauty. Idrys knew the wedges of her own ears were too backturned to meet that standard, and at times regretted having won a rank higher than those who wore helmets. A vain regret, but one she always felt upon first glimpsing the Primus.

Primus Kilyle seemed determined to draw attention to himself, even in private. He preferred wearing the old-style officer's jacket, indigo blue and decorated only with a single river of gold fur up the right arm and hanging freely down the back, instead of the scarlet and black uniforms now favored by the Senate for military use. Though the padded shoulders and narrow waist of the jacket lent a wedged effect to his thread-thin frame, the glamour of his rank seemed to be lost on him. His old regalia was almost provincial now, as things turned more harsh in the Empire, including fashion, and only a simple silver rope around the high yellow collar marked him to other Rihannsu as Field-Primus of the Swarm.

"I always expect to come in here and find you've been consumed by a gang of seedbearers," she told him.

He gave her his cryptic grin again and continued pruning a stubborn shrub. "I will have died content," he said.

"You will have died off duty," she corrected. She stopped near a strange thin protrusion from one of the squatter plants, pointed at a grotesque black ball at the tip, and asked, "What's this?"

41

"Hmm? Oh, that's its idea of a flower."

"I see." She looked around at the other growths, which were more obviously flowers, a collection of beauty ranging from the exotic to the modest, and avoided making more useless chatter, no matter how uncomfortable she felt. "Primus . . . may I ask again that you come to the bridge when dispersing the Swarm."

"You may, of course. But am I needed to disperse the Swarm?"

"The crew needs to see you there. For your own safety, sir. Your absence from the bridge gives leverage to the other commanders."

T'Cael stopped his trimming and slid his thigh up onto a big pot from which a tree was crowding the ceiling, and looked at her with particular trenchance. Idrys' long toast-brown hair, pin-straight and heavily plaited to keep it from swinging, framed her face with very little style. Her cheekbones were hidden in fleshy bronze cheeks and a coloring closer to some Klingon races than to Rihannsu, a trait which he knew had made her climb to command all the more rigorous and all the more valuable. And during that rigorous climb she had learned a directness he deeply appreciated, no matter how risky it might be for her to speak candidly. He felt it coming. Old data.

"You're commander of the *Raze*," he said. "She is the Swarm flagship. For the sake of your future, you might as well be seen dispersing the Swarm yourself."

Twisted between her own goals and guilts, Idrys nodded and murmured, "I thank you for your trust."

"Go on," he invited.

"Antecenturion Ry'iak will be coming to see you soon with the Supreme Praetor's greeting," she said. "He's already spreading disaffection among the crew."

"This is dry duty, Idrys," t'Cael pointed out. "Hinterspace."

"Dry duty, yes, but even hinterspace has pirates to defend against."

"We're in far more danger from these plants than from pirates."

Idrys pressed her lips tight in frustration. "The other commanders of the Swarm will enjoy having the Praetor's whip hand on board your flagship. You know the Senate won't question the slightest excuse to remove you."

"Is this a warning?"

Idrys realized she had been staring past him, afraid of those black eyes. Now she looked at him squarely. "Never. A hope that you will come to the bridge."

Slipping off the edge of the pot, t'Cael grasped a handful of vines and started examining them again. "Hold this, please," he requested, handing her the end of one particularly swollen vine.

Reluctantly, Idrys accepted the duty and grasped the end of the vine. It was stiff, but she felt a spongy interior—and some resistance from the vine. It didn't want her to be holding it. Trying not to be obvious, she backed away and avoided committing her whole palm to holding the vine. The Primus grasped the center of the vine and raised a blade that looked like a medical implement, selected a spot with great care, then swiftly sliced into the plant's flesh and drew the blade all the way down to Idrys' fingers. The plant started fighting.

"Sir . . ." Idrys began, having to hold on tighter than she wanted, to keep the vine from twisting out of her grip.

"All things fight when they are cut," t'Cael said, with a tone one uses to quiet a child. Was he soothing her or the plant?

43

She determined not to let go, no matter what happened. Was this some strange little test? How long would she have to know him before she actually knew him?

Some of the plant waste went on the floor, and some of it was stuffed into t'Cael's pocket without a thought, suggesting the importance the regalia held for him. "Hold tight on to it."

Idrys tried to respond, but could manage only a nod through her suddenly morbid fascination with his mutilating of this plant. She watched unblinking as he dug his fingers into the seam he had cut and forced it to part. At first the plant resisted violation. Then, suddenly, the incision burst open. Idrys jumped slightly as a dozen long tiny vines exploded outward and filled the air in front of t'Cael, wet new leaves uncrinkling with what actually appeared to be joy.

"Birth," t'Cael murmured. With special familiarity he helped the little leaves unfold and escorted the supple new vines into shape.

Idrys' nose caught a blast of planty aroma from the baby vines. She grimaced and looked down at her hands. Her fingers were clenched around a long withered shell. The mother vine had shriveled.

With a shiver, she dropped it.

T'Cael was peering at her in a sidelong way. She couldn't tell whether he approved or not.

And he deliberately didn't tell her.

"I'm aware of the tensions you feel on the bridge," he said, still combing his fingers through the vines. "I have guarded my words for a quarter generation."

"You may have to do more than that now. Especially in front of the Praetor's eye."

"Ry'iak doesn't frighten me."

"He should," she said quickly. She had to say it quickly, before her tongue remembered she was talking to Primus Kilyle, hero of the Wide War. "As

44

senate proctor he holds great power, even with a rank of only antecenturion. He is a dagger over your head."

T'Cael allowed himself a rueful snicker and said, "In its way, even that is an honor to me."

"A dubious one. It says the Praetor is afraid of you."

"Ry'iak is too young to have gained his post by earning it. He is the Senate Proctor only because of some attachment to the right family, or as a payment for some favor he had little to do with. He hasn't the experience to know what his power really is. I can turn that to my favor."

"Sir, the Senate will listen to him, especially if he knows how to lie artistically. The Supreme Praetor will welcome such lies."

"Even the Supreme Praetor's power isn't sufficient to remove me from a position I earned. I am Field-Primus, don't forget, even if in this ignoble area of hindspace."

"Our area of patrol is your punishment, sir," she reminded, though she knew he had never misinterpreted the meaning of an assignment so far inside Rihannsu territory, where absolutely nothing could possibly happen and absolutely no further honor could be earned. It was a punitive assignment for a man of t'Cael's status, and utterly ruinous for those among his Swarm who had plans for their own advancement. Especially now.

"Ry'iak is the Praetor's eye. He is here," Idrys went on slowly, "because his presence pressures you. Each time the crew sees him, they are reminded of your reputation as a dove among preybirds. They see their chances for advancement moving further away."

"And you're here to tell me . . ."

"That a commander's dishonor is his crew's."

He plucked a predatory insect from his hand and crushed it. "Thank you."

With a sheepish grin, Idrys added, "It *is* my duty to say it."

"It is," he agreed. Now he left the baby vines and moved to another plant, a thick thing with spiky arms and fat seed sacks. He began palpating the seed sacks and selectively began pruning them. "Don't fear, Idrys. The Supreme Praetor doesn't yet have the power to remove me unless I dishonor myself. If I had refused backspace duty, then I would be a target. But I accepted it, and we're here."

"It's disgraceful duty to be shunted into such cushioned space," she said, daring to repeat herself. "Word of Federation military buildup is giving the Supreme Praetor leverage to gain power. There are twenty supervessels being built by the Federation, to be launched simultaneously as a statement of galactic might. Super battleships. The humans will instigate a war just as an excuse to take Rihannsu space under their control."

T'Cael tipped his head downward and scolded, "Idrys, you don't really believe such things."

"Don't you?"

"Exaggeration. I know something of the humans, don't forget."

"You're the closest thing to an expert that we have," she acknowledged. "No one denies that. But there is a time for flexing muscles, after all. Even now, our ships are gathering in the Outmarches, probing the Neutral Zone for reasons to attack the Federation before they attack us. That's why this hinterspace duty is so painful to us and dangerous to you, sir. The crews of our Swarm are hungry to be part of the vanguard. They're looking for an excuse to mutiny without dishonoring themselves. They'll find one just as our fleet will find an excuse to attack the Federation. There *will* be war."

As his hands fell away from the plant, t'Cael realized he had grown poor at hiding his feelings. There had been a time when no one could tell what he was thinking. Even his *least* radical ideas had earned him the Senate's distrust since the Wide War. With a gesture of unshielded disgust, he put down the blade as though afraid to have a sharp instrument in his hand at this moment. Absently he dropped a palmful of loosened seed pods into his pocket.

"Personal honor was once worth more than personal glory," he said with great regret. "Loyalty was once a greater trait than acclaim in battle. I do not care for what I see happening around me. It makes me ashamed."

Idrys took a step closer to him through the cloying leaves of his personal jungle. "You need not be ashamed! The only cure is for you to cast your lot with the Praetor so we can leave this laughable patrol and participate in the glorious confrontation. Your praises could still be sung in the Praetor's alcazar, Primus, and your deeds told with awe from here to ch'Havran!"

T'Cael moved slowly away from her, sitting once again on the edge of the big stone pot, dissipating her intensity with a smile. Idrys realized that he really did smile often for so mysterious a man, even though his smiles retained a touch of the cryptic.

He shook his head in amusement. "It isn't that far from here to ch'Havran," he said wryly.

He looked down now at his hands, which were dirtied with yellow-brown soil, and thought of how to put reality into words for her. "When we were attacked in the Wide, I was quite willing to fight. I rose to command my own fighter. My crew was loyal. Then our people reverted to what we had been when we transgressed into the humans' space all those years ago. We became the aggressors again. We used our victories to gain huge tracts of space from our enemies. Soon our enemies became our victims. Now I think we hunger for more reasons to get more victims. So we cross our space from the Wide back to the Outmarches, and we start watching the Federation, looking for reasons to bite into their space again. And we call it honor. Commander, believe me," he finished, his gaze sincere and penetrating, "if I truly thought the Federation was a threat to us, I would *disobey* orders to get there and fight them. That I promise you."

Idrys licked her lips thoughtfully. "Then what are these things we hear?"

"Rumors, partially, I imagine. Swelled by the wishful thoughts of our own leaders."

"Partially?"

"Oh, I have no doubt the Federation has made advancements. So have we. That's to be expected. And in a generation, we'll be more advanced, and another generation after that, and so on forever. If we attack each other every time we fear advancements, we'll be at war until we're all dead. Not much glory there," he added with a little chuckle. "Advancement is natural to civilization. Attacking a society because it advances is akin to killing a person because he breathes."

Idrys felt her face grow warm with confusion. He sounded right, but . . . "What if you're mistaken? It took us a half generation to rebuild after the Federation War. This time they will give us no second chance."

T'Cael stood straight once more, raising the crescent end of one black eyebrow. "That," he said, "is why I still do my duty."

The commander inhaled deeply. Once again, she was telling him nothing new. The Primus had long ago decided to stand by his principles. There was nowhere for him to go and no way for him to escape when enemies loomed on all sides. Things would probably be all right for him if it weren't for this noise about tension hatching once again between the Supreme Praetor's burgeoning control and the Federation, tensions the Federation didn't even know about yet. The Praetor liked it that way; it gave him advantage.

Idrys tried to move backward, only to find herself held fast by the plaits in her hair. She tried to look around, but couldn't turn her head. Something was crawling around her ear. She clamped her mouth shut to avoid yelping, and saw in her periphery that something with little suckers was moving up her cheek toward her eye.

A moment later t'Cael sensed it, looked up, and came to her rescue with his blade. He took hold of a great handful of her hair and held her head steady, then one by one pried the suckers from her face. "This one," he explained as he sliced a tentacle from her hair, where it had quietly entwined itself, "has to be watched constantly. If I don't keep it trimmed back, it encroaches upon the nearest living thing and crushes the life from it. Other plants . . . sleeping animals . . . I even have to cut it before I rest. There you are. Free again." He made a small ritual of smoothing down the plaits in her hair that had been tugged out of place, then brushed off the soil left there by his fingers. Unable to keep traces of himself from staining her, he turned away and was silent.

Idrys watched his back for a long moment, then tried to shield herself in formality—to shield both of them, really.

"I only came to inform you about the attitude of the Swarm crews. If this is no help to you, then forgive me. I can only suggest that you express your feelings with more subtlety as long as the Praetor's eye remains among us."

49

T'Cael smiled his impenetrable smile again. "Idrys, these expressions that are bringing me trouble," he said, *"are* my most subtle ones."

She sighed. "Ry'iak will come. I only thought you should know."

Feeling as though she was leaving a funeral pyre after having been the only mourner, Idrys began to pick her way through the hanging foliage only to be stopped by his voice again.

"Among the crew," he began, "where do you stand?"

Her bronze face puckered with hurt, which she controlled before turning.

He wasn't looking at her. He was back to his trimming, handling the clusters of leaves with the same boldness and familiarity he had used to handle her braids.

"I stand with you," she said. "It is not as though I was just assigned, Primus."

From her tone, t'Cael could tell instantly that he had wounded her. He gave her what he hoped was a comforting glance. "Forgive the question."

Idrys faced him again. "You know I covet your position," she admitted, "but I wish to get it through your advancement, not through your deposement. Be careful of yourself, sir. You may be your own greatest danger."

He nodded, for that was completely true. "I'm nowhere near the border, yet I feel surrounded by enemies."

The announcer bleeped then, saving Idrys from replying. The words that followed, however, made her long for silence.

"Primus Kilyle, Antecenturion Ry'iak desires an audience."

T'Cael looked at Idrys, and his smile returned, devilish this time. "Let's make him wait, shall we?"

Idrys bit her lip, but her own cheeks tightened with amusement. "You make a child of me, sir," she complained.

As he stepped past her he noted, "You're welcome." He tapped the nearest communications panel and spoke into it. "Request that the antecenturion stand by."

"Yes, Primus."

When t'Cael turned back to Idrys, his expression teemed with mischief. "How long do you suppose he'll stand out there letting the guards stare past him?"

"He dares not leave, having announced himself," she said, but he knew that already.

"Protocol can be a wonderful thing." T'Cael reached high over their heads and pulled several plants along a metal rod, then moved others on other rods, taking his time to arrange them until the path to the doorway had vanished entirely. "Do you suppose Ry'iak is an explorer as well as a hunter?"

Idrys folded her arms and put her fingers to her lips to keep herself from answering. All she could think of was Ry'iak standing in the corridor, unable to leave, unable to buzz a second time, with the two guards stoically ignoring him. Seldom was danger so entertaining.

When the plants had been arranged to his satisfaction, t'Cael gave one long look at the carnivorous plant with the suckered tentacles, but evidently dismissed a tempting idea. He tapped the wall panel once again. "Admit the antecenturion."

From their places in the chamber, neither Idrys nor t'Cael could see the door opening. They heard it, though, through the layers of plants, and exchanged a glance before burying their amusement in proper military expressions.

They heard the door shutting, then a few measured

footsteps, followed by the rustle of tangled leaves. Idrys pressed her fingers tighter against her lips. Evidently Ry'iak wasn't about to call out for rescue. Even when they heard him bump into a wall strut, neither said a thing.

The plants nearer by began to shiver, and they knew he was getting closer. T'Cael had arranged the plants to be sure Ry'iak couldn't take a step without getting a faceful of pots and leaves, and it was working. Only after several false starts did the senate proctor finally emerge into their company.

Idrys bit her finger hard. Ry'iak's plaster-pale hair was spiked up after being disordered by the plants, and there were tiny ferns stuck in it. He looked disoriented, and was blinking frantically, trying to recover.

"Ah, Antecenturion," t'Cael acknowledged, careful of his tone of voice.

"The . . . the Supreme Praetor's greetings, Field-Primus," Ry'iak managed, "and those of the Tricameron."

"Accepted."

"The air is thick here."

"Thick air is strong air, Antecenturion."

"Yes . . . of course." Ry'iak freed himself from the nearest cluster of leaves, which still had a grip on his shoulder, and positioned himself in a place where t'Cael and Idrys couldn't possibly communicate silently without his seeing them do it. "With my respects, Field-Primus, I have a list of suggestions to present."

"Yes."

"There seems to be some dissent among your crews," Ry'iak said, forcing himself to overcome the mockery of what he had thought would be a grand entrance. His face worked stiffly to assume a look of control. "This duty space is inglorious, and they seem . . . to blame you."

T'Cael acknowledged only with a nod this time.

"My suggestions include that you put me in charge of personnel assignments within the Swarm. I shall thereby do my best to ward off any disaffection."

This time t'Cael reacted only by sitting once again on the big pot. He dropped his eyes and folded his arms complacently.

"Second," Ry'iak continued. "I don't trust standard ship's security. Allow me to put my own chosen guards around you. These guards of mine will have no loyalty to anyone but me, and therefore will not be swayed by any ripples among your crews."

On the outskirts of this, Idrys stiffened, knowing she had no authority to speak. T'Cael seemed oblivious to the veiled threats, which Ry'iak was delivering with thievish care. Each threat was poised on the brink of suggestion. She suddenly regretted advising the Primus to avoid irritating the situation. She quaked with desire to shriek at the Praetor's eye and order him to never again dirty Primus Kilyle's quarters with his presence. She found herself glaring at t'Cael, wishing he would speak out against these shrouded insults.

"Last of all," Ry'iak continued, "I will rotate among the crews of your Swarm and remind them that any service to the Praetor is glorious. I'll be arranging removal of any slackers or dissidents. I'm sure that will please you. Crews must be kept pure, of course."

T'Cael continued gazing at nothing. "Of course."

Idrys clenched her hands, galled at Ry'iak's smugness. The self-important senate proctor believed t'Cael dared not deny him these "suggestions."

"Any dissidents," Ry'iak said, "will be temporarily

assigned to *Raze,* so they may be watched until the mothership returns to pick up the patrol string."

T'Cael nodded, once again in silence.

Idrys felt her fury boil. Translation: bring the most radical dissenting elements under one roof, better to effect a swift mutiny. Even if a mutiny flared and could be put down, it would be interpreted as the failure of the chief commander of that unit. Either way, the Field-Primus would be removed, the Praetor's wishes served. Message received.

"Is there anything else?" t'Cael asked emotionlessly.

Ry'iak took the opportunity to puff himself up again. "You will grant me the privilege of private communication to the nearest Praetor's coach, that I might more efficiently keep him apprised of our progress. I'm sure you'll want His Excellency to know you're encouraging proper behavior."

T'Cael nodded again. Not a ripple of change came into his expression. He seemed thoroughly shamed, and Idrys felt a keen responsibility for that. Better he should die than submit, she realized. She wished she had never come to his quarters.

Ry'iak waited several seconds, glaring at the Field-Primus with youth's own invulnerability. The ferns in his disarrayed hair made him look like a fighting cock strutting over a victim.

After another moment, Ry'iak couldn't contain himself. "When will you implement these changes?"

T'Cael licked his lips and stood up slowly, his arms folded in a contrite manner. He took a long, deep breath, and raised his head. "When you eat leeches."

Ry'iak's smugness dropped away. His eyes widened.

The explosion was instantaneous. T'Cael didn't even take another breath before backhanding Ry'iak across the chamber and into a wall. Leaves rippled. A splatter of blood left a dark jade trail on part of the wall. T'Cael stepped through the ravaged plants and grasped Ry'iak's collar until the Senate's puppet was nearly choked. When t'Cael spoke, even Idrys shivered.

"Remember who you vex," whispered the Field-Primus. "If you imagine I'm going to allow you to shuttle between the ships and cram praetorial vigilance down the throats of honorable men, you've been mistaught. You're a parasite. I don't like parasites. You won't think again of carrying your blight through my crews before I charge you with gross disloyalty and have you disemboweled." On the echo of the word, he pulled Ry'iak even closer, making himself clearly understood. "You may report my disposition to the Senate," he said, then slowly added, "if you survive."

Another horrid moment passed before t'Cael hauled Ry'iak to his feet, tore the permission chip from his sleeve, and gently invited him to exit the chamber by slamming him into the opposite wall of the corridor.

The guards made no effort to help him up.

When the door had once again closed, t'Cael straightened the strip of fur over his shoulder and turned to Idrys.

"Was that subtle?" he asked.

Chapter Four

PERHAPS IT WAS the way he said it. With all the awe and respect a human being could utter. *Staaarship.*

Her hull, every inch of it, was opaque ivory. There were no signs of call letters or decorative painting, and she stood out like a pearl against black velvet as she hovered in spacedock. The absence of decals, numbers, and letters made her all the more startling.

George had no idea how long it was before he took a breath. Robert April's quiet enunciation of that word made him quiver with empathy. Together they stared out the portal.

Shaped to awe and to threaten, a careful amalgam of size and line, the ship implied speed even though speed in space had nothing to do with shape. From the primary saucer to the sleek cigar-shaped power cells in back, her beauty had a harshness about it—almost a hauteur. The design, though not altogether unfamiliar, had been severely streamlined and made new. Her gleaming cream-white hull said she wasn't meant to melt in with the curtain of space; rather, she was meant to stand out against it. Her most impressive single feature, though, was her size. For a streamlined ship, she was thundrous. Yet there was no sense of bulk at all. She was like a gigantic swan, a bird grown a thousand times normal, yet somehow retaining its grace. George had seen big ships before—transports, space stations, freighters, starliners, carriers, frigates—but this . . . this ship sang a song of her own potential.

"Starship," he whispered, his eyes narrowing until the ship was hardly more than a blur. They were approaching from underneath; the starship loomed over them.

From his side, a voice came.

"She hasn't been named, hasn't been catalogued, announced, commissioned, or kissed goodbye. In fact, she doesn't even exist yet. And neither will we while we're aboard her."

George cleared his throat, but when he spoke, his voice still sounded raspy. "That's reassuring . . ."

April leaned farther toward his dream. "Superb, isn't she?" And he wasn't looking for an answer.

The bridge access panel hissed, and George instinctively pulled his eyes away from the starship to look. Two crewmen strode to their positions, the smaller of the two taking the helm from Drake, which was lucky; Drake could no more maneuver an approach to that starship than get out and walk there. The second man, a massive Indian type whose shoulders almost broke through his uniform shirt, went immediately to the upper deck and tapped out an approach request.

"Hello, boys," April chimed. "Let me introduce all of you. Face me, everybody. Fellows, this is Commander George Kirk and Lieutenant Reed. At the helm is Carlos Florida." He gave the starship a little nod and added, "He's going to drive that—and updeck is our astrotelemetrist, Spirit Claw Sanawey. Watch out for him. Mescalero Apache. A wholly dangerous man."

Holding a communications link to his ear, Sanawey nodded and lifted dark eyebrows. "Right," he said in a voice very deep but shockingly mild, "I may trip over you." He listened for a moment, then nodded to

April. "Permission to approach the dock is granted, sir. Spacedock commander acknowledges responsibility for the runabout, and we're cleared to board the starship."

"That's delightful," April said. "Respond accordingly."

"Where do we dock?" George asked, peering up once again at the starship, now hardly more than a stunning field of alabaster taking up most of their viewport.

"We're not going to dock."

George looked up. "What?"

April eyed him. "We're going to beam in."

George felt his mouth go dry. "Transporters?"

"Yes, and greatly improved from those aboard the Baton Rouge class of ships. There's much less power consumption, and they're much faster than before. A matter of seconds instead of minutes."

"I don't understand," George protested. "How can that be? I heard transporting takes too long to be practical. What changed?"

"Do you know anything about duotronics?"

"No."

"Oh. Well, about ten years ago, a young fellow named Daystrom developed a new computer concept. It was akin to the breakthrough when early man learned to write. It's taken a few years to wiggle the bugs out, but it seems to be working beautifully now, and this starship is fully mounted with it. With the transporter tied in to the computer bank, the process is advanced to mere seconds. The computer can assimilate the molecular pattern of the bodies it scrambles, and reassemble them virtually instantly. You're going to love it, George."

"I'm going to be sick, Robert."

April laughed and clapped him on the back. "Rogue."

George straightened, feeling a sudden need to head off a pile of complications by understanding them one by one. "What has all this got to do with the *Rosenberg?*"

"Oh, yes. This is the ship that's going to save those people's lives," April explained as Sarah Poole appeared opposite him and stared out at the looming starship. "She's a stockpile of new technological stuff. Fourth-generation warp drive, a vast increase in power, dilithium focusing that allows for a maximum cruise speed of warp six with bursts to warp eight, extremely tough new shielding—I could go on forever."

"You already have," Sarah murmured.

"We should be able to reach those people in record time."

"But you said it was a four-month journey at warp three. Even with fourth-generation drive, it'll take a month to go around the storms, and you said they don't have a month."

"It's not going to take a month."

George narrowed his eyes in doubt. No matter the size or power or beauty, even that ship out there couldn't bend space and make the trip any shorter than it absolutely had to be. He watched with great caution as April pressed his lips together and slipped his hands into his pockets again.

"With advanced shielding," April began, "and this ship's duotronic-enhanced navigation, we should be able to batter our way straight through the core of those ionic storms."

From behind him, George felt the ripple of astonishment from Drake and the lady doctor, but it was not that to which he responded. He stepped closer to April, leaning over the console that separated them. *"Through?* Through the heart of ion disruption? Robert, you're out of your mind!"

April raised his brows and looked straight at George. "We should be able to reach those people in a week. A *week.*"

"*Should* be able? Not *will* be?"

"Well . . . I'm an optimist, but not a cockeyed one. But the starship is a breakthrough. She's the culmination of several technological breakthroughs of the last decade that are only now coming into practical use."

George closed his eyes for a moment, dazzled and confused, then paced around April while staring at the deck. He put a hand to his head, trying to hold in all these new things. April waited in silence and watched him, a gaze George felt acutely, but stiffly ignored.

After a moment George spoke again, sharply and intuitively. "And it's Starfleet's gambit."

"It had to be." April responded with a shrug. "There was no other way to finance her. But she's a Federation vessel, George, not Starfleet alone. What do you think of her?"

"What am I supposed to think? Don't you know already?"

"I'd like to hear it."

George waved a hand. "We've been guarding that Neutral Zone for seventy-five years because we're afraid of another Romulan attack. And why? Because they haven't had any reason to be afraid of us, that's why. They haven't had to respect us." He jabbed a finger toward the viewport. "That's no rescue ship out there. That's a fighting machine!"

April quickly paced around the navigation console, which had somehow come between them. "This is not a spaceship, George," he insisted dramatically. "George . . . this is a *star*ship!"

"Starship, spaceship," George canted, knowing he was casting bait.

"George! *Star*. Listen to the word." April's voice

softened, but intensified. "Star. A luminary, far away in the cosmos, so far away that it seems only a sparkle in the night. A little titter of life so easily misinterpreted as mere mythology by those who just don't see it for what it is."

"Star, I got it." George sighed.

"Ship," April segued, easing the word in on a sweep of his arms that led from the stars outside to a pair of cupped hands. "Since those first squabby reed vessels waddled across the ocean from here to there, holding little nameless people who had nothing in common but their dreams of discovery, the word 'ship' has become profound!"

George shook his head, amazed at April's blind idealism. "Rob, this is first-rate. Have you copyrighted this?"

"Just take the tour. See the ship. *Feel* her around you." The captain's arms dropped to his sides. "Then we'll talk."

The process of beaming was nothing to look forward to, and George didn't. He'd never been beamed before, but he'd heard about it. Nothing good. So when they left the runabout hooked up to the spacedock and Claw Eagle, or whatever his name was, signaled the starship to "energize," George couldn't help holding his breath and waiting to die. The first sensation was of sound—a buzzing noise like insects, soon accompanied by the sensation of being crawled on by all those insects. Somehow he had climbed into a beehive, and now he couldn't find the door.

Vision went next, into a vortex of irritating color. Then came immobility. He tried to move his arms, just to reassure himself, but they didn't seem to be there anymore. He became acutely aware of his internal organs quivering. The bridge of the runabout rearranged itself around him—he sensed it more than

61

saw it—and then he saw something take form. A room with pale gray walls trimmed in red . . . a free-standing console with two men behind it . . . and he himself was standing in a wide cubbyhole framed with some kind of bracings. The room solidified, and a slight vertigo flushed over him. After a moment, he took a little breath, then a deeper one, then one more just to make sure.

"Everyone all right?"

April's voice was a shock in the suddenly quiet chamber.

"Not exactly a perfected process, is it?" came Sarah Poole's dry response from somewhere in the back.

"George?"

George dared to look down, and discovered he was standing on a frosted lens disk. "That's the most nauseating experience I've ever had in my life," he said. He looked around for Drake and found him in back. The other man's chocolate eyes were ringed with white, but he was in one piece.

"We'll get better at it," April assured him as he stepped off his own disk. "Breathtaking, though, isn't it? Not just one person at a time, but all six of us. We can conceivably beam a whole landing party up and down just that easily."

"If your hopes are so high for it," George asked immediately as he stepped down to April's level, trying not to wobble, "why does the ship still have a flight deck?"

April hesitated. "Eventually, just for backup, we hope."

"Won't there be alternative transporter rooms for backup?"

"Well, yes, but—"

"Seems like a whole lot of wasted space if you really expect the transporter to take over the duties of shuttles, doesn't it?"

April swung his hands and said, "George! I'm just a simple romantic. You know design engineers. They love new ideas but they refuse to give up old ones."

"Just asking."

"My friends," April offered, holding his hand toward the door. "To the bridge."

"There are only fifty-seven people on board," Captain April explained as they walked a long unadorned corridor on some unnamed deck, and in some places there were only structural beams for support, but no walls yet. "All are specialists in the building of this ship. There's no one on board who hasn't been rated and cleared of at least a level-eight security clearance. These are the best of Federation engineers, electrical and computer scientists, propulsion experts, and so on. All her parts were designed in secret, and built in separate places. No one who worked on the parts had any idea what it was he was contributing to. Other than the bridge, which you'll see in a moment, there are only two completed decks on the entire primary hull, and the engineering hull is still partially unfinished. There's no rec deck yet, but that area has been converted into an emergency medical area for the people we're going after." He turned to look back at the doctor. "Sarah, you'll want to inspect that right away, because there'll be no time to get provisions once we're under way."

"It sounds like there's already no time," Sarah commented, stepping aside to allow two technicians with antigravs to pass by with some kind of heavy electrical panel.

"What's finished?" George interrupted.

"The computer facilities . . . the sensors . . . the warp engines, though untested . . . all the bulkheads and conduits . . . life support throughout most of the ship . . . heavy weapons systems . . . exterior shields

63

. . . not auxiliary control yet, though I hoped it would be—"

"Sounds like preliminary testing conditions to me."

April nodded and gave George a look of approval. "Yes, you're precisely right."

"What are her weapons capabilities?"

"She's armed with laser streams and particle cannons for heavy short bolts, all adjustable from grade one through grade ten impact/burn. Not quite impotent, you might say," he added with a reluctant nod. "We were almost ready to test the primary equipment, just the things that make her go and let her defend herself against space elements. Shields, sensors, propulsion, and so on. When this emergency with *Rosenberg* came up, we decided it was time. The starship's time. She'll never have a better chance to prove herself before prejudices settle in around her."

"Prejudices?" George pulled his gaze from the sparkling new corridor and the doorless rooms he'd been peeking into and looked at April. "What kind of prejudices?"

"Well, time enough for that later. You need a tour of the ship if you're going to be first officer."

George stopped in his tracks. Drake and the astrotelemetrist bumped into each other trying to avoid bumping into him. "If I'm going to be *what*? Robert, I'm not qualified!"

April swung around easily and squashed George's objections with a tilt of his head. "Oh, qualified, George! Look around. All you see are qualified people. I don't need another one of those. I need you, George. I need an exec who's a counterbalance to myself. It's the only way I'll be able to trust my decisions."

"That's a foolish choice," George told him with raw honesty.

With a grin April gestured toward George, and to the others he said, "You see? Just what I need!"

George dropped his head in frustration.

The captain smiled tolerantly. "Come on, George. You've served in space before. And you don't get to be head of security at a starbase without having some mastery of current technology. Don't you think I know that? And whatever else there is, you'll figure out. You're a bright fellow, George."

April stepped into an elevator and waited for everyone to join him. His two bridge officers stepped in without hesitation, then Dr. Poole, not quite as boldly.

George hung back and glared at Drake. "You've been conspicuously silent through all this," he accused.

Drake rolled his eyes. "The dead say very little."

"What killed you?"

"Shock."

"Good. At least I'm not alone."

The turbo-lift was fast and also a little nauseating, but it gave George a perception of the size of the ship. *Darned big,* he thought. *That's the size of it.* As soon as the door opened and the bridge stretched out before them, Florida and Sanawey moved quickly to what George presumed were their respective posts.

The bridge was a circular place, still drab because much of its trim painting hadn't been finished yet. George glanced around and could see the code markings scribbled where the red and blue trim would eventually be. The floor was lightly carpeted in drab dove blue, and probably made to cut down on acoustics. All around the upper level near the ceiling were visual readout screens, each dwarfed by a huge main viewing screen directly at front and center. All those screens, including the big one, were dead gray. Several technicians were closing portals to electrical nightmares along the floor, and on a recessed deck in the center of the bridge, Florida was bringing life to the helm controls. A whisper of energy hummed through the console.

"This way," April invited, and moved to their right. He stood before a shiny black control console with colorful but unmarked switches, dials, toggles, and computer cartridge input notches. "This is our pride and joy," he said with supreme confidence. "It's called a 'library' computer. We can virtually store the knowledge of the galaxy in a computer bank and recall it instantly. This is the culmination of the duotronics discovery. Speed of analysis and recall has been increased ten thousand times. Ten thousand times! The Vulcans helped with its design and programming, but they wouldn't give us a specialist to run it. Apparently they couldn't find anyone among them who wanted to cast his lot with a pack of humans. But this"—he placed his hand affectionately on the console—"is the reason we can navigate at warp. Even at warp six. And even through completely unmapped territory. Astonishing. Because of this, the correlation between advanced sensors and the ship's navigation is extremely fine and fast. This is what's going to allow us to smash through those storms." He gave them a little glance then, just to reaffirm his connection with them, and said, "It's not going to be easy, you understand, not something even a starship will do every day, but it is possible in an emergency."

"Interesting disclaimer, Captain," George commented.

"Well, I felt obliged. But you can see the advantage. We don't have to do warp hops anymore—warp a little, stop, do a sensor scan to make sure you're not going to pile into somebody's planet, warp a little farther, stop again . . . no more of that. Thanks to the library computer, we can extend the explorable range of our galaxy a thousandfold."

"Why the secrecy?"

"Pardon?" April turned, forced back to the moment. "Oh . . . yes." He turned completely around and leaned on the console, thoughtfully staring down at the lower deck, evidently lacking the words to describe this ship and his hopes for her. Somehow she was the core of something easily perverted, and April wanted all the conceptualizations about her to be right. It was several seconds before he spoke.

"She's not meant to be a pageant wagon," April said, beginning slowly. "She has to be introduced gradually, carefully. She's easy to misunderstand, and many Federation member governments are suspicious of a centralized power. That's what this ship looks like—like one facility is trying to build a device so powerful that no one will be able to challenge its decisions. You see, if the Federation doesn't centralize soon, it'll ossify. It won't mean anything or do anything. This ship and a fleet like her will mean ideological unity if we play our cards right."

George paced across the upper deck to a place where he could scan the firing mechanisms on the helm console. Carlos Florida looked up at him self-consciously, but said nothing as the newly appointed first officer glared fiercely at the instruments as though the control panels themselves were capable of manipulating the people around them.

After a long time, George said, "This is the scariest thing I've ever seen."

April came forward and leaned on the bridge hand rail. Cagily he prodded, "Why?"

"Why? A ship like this . . . even just one of her . . . and you're talking about a whole fleet?"

"Yes, as many as ten starships. But I don't—"

"Don't you?" George attacked. "Don't you really? You're avoiding reality, Robert. That computer, those sensors, those weapons, all that compounded energy stored in this ship—it adds up to a power machine that could cut through enemy vessels a lot more easily than through those ion storms. For the first time, we can protect the frontier and our colony planets, and be taken seriously. We can intimidate the Romulans, the Klingons, and everyone else into leaving us alone."

April waved a hand desperately. "But do we want to do that?"

"Are you saying we don't?"

"How can we justify reaching out into the galaxy if we shut off anyone from looking in?" April's voice was softly insistent. "This ship is for exploration, George. That's what I want her to be seen as."

George stepped toward him. "A civilization flourishes best when it can protect itself."

"Yes, but you can't tell defensive weapons from offensive just by looking. Her philosophy *must* be established first! Any bravado will cheapen her and put our credibility at risk."

"You're too much of a poet, Robert."

"That's why I brought you along, George." April strode past Drake and Sarah, who were remaining safely silent, to what was obviously the captain's command chair. He leaned on it like an old soldier on a warhorse and searched for better words. He seemed to think he wasn't getting his point across, and that it was his own fault.

"George, try to understand. If the starship is misinterpreted as a military machine, exploration will be the sacrificial lamb to all that fear. We mustn't let that happen. Eventually we hope to encourage other races than humans to join the crews of these ships—those who can physically live together. Once the starship's benevolent capabilities are proven, the UFP Congress will accept her as a truly interstellar ship, not belonging to any one government or planet. It's the first step toward truly unifying the known galaxy. We have to overcome the paranoia that goes with a ship of this kind, that taste of the military you're talking about, and show the galaxy that this ship is a harbinger of growth and expansion that will give us all more quality of life in the long run. We can bring civilization to uncharted tracts, bring back alien technologies and ideas we never dreamed of—season ourselves with wisdoms we've never thought of before." He held out his hand as though to offer George the truth. "That's why an impossible rescue is her perfect first mission. This is not a military machine, George."

"It's not? Grade-ten laser and particle cannon intensities? How do you figure it's not? Do you realize how many systems could be protected just by the presence of one of these? People could sleep easier by the billions!" George moved around the deck, feeling it out, as if to see if the starship agreed with what he was saying. Several sets of eyes watched him, most of them afraid he might look at them and demand comment. Ultimately he turned on April again. "You keep talking about principles and philosophies, Captain, but men of principles have to be willing to stand their ground. There's nothing wrong with might as long as it's used to defend right. One of our principles has to be that you can't take something away from someone else just because you're able to."

"Exactly!" April insisted. "That's what we have to make clear! That this vessel *isn't* meant to take from others. She's an empress of ideals, George. She's our right, not our might."

"She's both!" George snapped back, heading for the turbo-lift. "She has to be."

On the heels of his own words he whipped a gesture toward Drake. "Come on. Let's look at this thing."

He stalked into the turbo-lift, followed quickly by Drake, who wasn't about to argue with either of these men.

When the lift doors breathed closed and silence fell on the bridge, Robert April folded his arms, shook his head, and sighed.

"God, I'm glad I brought him."

Chapter Five

"Go AHEAD, CLAW. Relay the message down here. On discreet, please."

"Relaying. Last message from S.S. Rosenberg, received at Starbase Two, one solar hour ago, sir."

Captain April tried to remain on his feet to hear the message, but found himself lowering into the desk chair in his quarters, unable to hide the effect that communicating with the disabled ship was having on him.

Sitting in the other chair, George watched him as the click of communications circuits focused their attention on the words that would come any moment. It was a grinding feeling, like bones in teeth, this waiting to hear from dying people. George leaned forward, but said nothing.

The message, when it finally came, was faint and crackling.

"This is the resea— . . . *—S.* Rosenberg." The voice was a woman's, chilling, distant, under great strain, and under great control. She went on without any dramatic pauses. *"The ion cluster is extending itself . . . severity now at eight on the scale. Repeat: eight on the scale. It's all around us now. Radiation leaks have contaminated . . . bulk of supplies. We're cannibalizing the . . . —oolant system from the impulse drive . . . engines aren't . . . —king anyway.*

71

Critical information: we're trying to build . . .
—nough suspended animation units for the children
under eight years old. We're just telling the kids they'll
be going to sleep. We hope there'll be enough power to
last . . . rescue gets here. Do you understand, Starbase?
You'll . . . be ready to help them understand why their
parents aren't alive when they wake up. We can only
hope the radiation doesn't affect the suspension cham-
bers before you get here. We know . . . can't save most
of us, but come anyway. Do you copy, Starbase? Don't
give up on our babies. No matter . . . long it takes, just
don't give up on our kids."

There was a hesitation, even more cryptic than the
silence that had overtaken the captain's cabin. George
felt his hands go cold.

"This will . . . final message unless you contact us.
We are attempting to conserve power. Captain Anita
Zagaroli, S.S. Rosenberg *. . . signing off."*

April's hand was pressed across his mouth. His eyes
had grown vacant as he listened. The pain of courage
had come across all too well in the woman's voice.
The courage of last hope.

George suddenly felt as if the artificial gravity had
been turned up too high. He was crushed to his chair.
Unbidden thoughts of Iowa, of his two boys, assaulted
him.

He forced his voice out.

"Tell them," he rasped. "We've got to tell them
we're coming."

Several noticeable seconds went by before April
moved, or even blinked.

Finally, from behind his hand, the captain murmured, "I've been aching to tell them." Now he
gathered himself and slumped back in the chair. "I
can't. You heard . . . what they're doing is almost
impossible with the supplies and engineering aboard a
ship of that type. They have nothing that can be

72

realistically converted into suspended animation shells, George. And those people aren't really engineers. They might succeed in building deep freezes of sorts, but the chances of our arriving and finding children alive in hypersleep . . ." He shook his head slowly. "They're just grasping at straws, trying to keep from going insane. Real engineers would know it's nearly impossible. I suspect the engineer aboard the ship is deluding them on purpose."

"But . . ."

"George, I can't tell them we're going to be there in a week when I don't know if it's possible. I can't even tell them we *hope* to be there at all. We're just not that sure we can even make it through those ion storms, and I can't—" Words suddenly failed him as he tried to express the torment he would cause by spreading his own faith in the starship. "I just can't."

George sat back, unable to argue. If it were he, what would he tell George Jr. and Jimmy? The prospect frightened him.

Jimmy . . . he never could lie to Jimmy and get away with it.

Through his reverie he heard the click of the desk intercom and looked up to see April touching the unit.

"Claw," April addressed.

"Bridge here. Sanawey."

"Contact Starbase Two. Ask them to acknowledge transmission from that ship on my personal behalf and assure them we're not giving up and we're not going to. Then repeat it. Make absolutely sure they understand. Make them feel they're not alone."

When the communications officer replied, it was with a dubious tone, as though he wasn't sure he could make that message ring true. *"I'll do my best, Captain. Sanawey out."*

"I'll have to ask you to wait until we're under way before I can introduce you to the rest of the crew complement," April said, still somewhat thoughtfully, trying to juggle too many responsibilities. Only then did he notice that George wasn't listening, but instead had gotten up and was pacing the cabin, his arms and shoulders tensed. "George?"

Turning from staring at a wall, George blinked. "Sorry. I'm just impatient to get under way."

"I know what you mean."

"Let's go, then." He leaned toward the door without actually taking a step.

April countered the tension by gesturing George back to his chair. "No, no. Sit down for a few more minutes. The matter/antimatter intermix has just begun, and I've found the engineers feel obligated to explain things whenever I'm around at moments like that. It only slows the process. Sit down, George. Sit down and tell me what else is on your mind."

Brows lowered over George's dark hazels. "What do you mean?"

"Come now, George. Is something wrong?"

"Is something wrong?" George repeated with a harshness he didn't really intend. "After that message, you can ask if something's wrong? Yes . . . I guess something's wrong."

"I'm listening."

George knew April was deliberately distracting him from tension about the *Rosenberg,* tension that could do no good at this moment. Unable to hide his feelings, he clenched and unclenched his hands, then sat down again. A moment or two later, he found his voice.

"I was . . . just hoping to get leave in time for Jimmy's birthday." He waved his hand at the silent communications panel. "That just made me think of it."

"Things haven't improved between you and your wife?"

74

George leaned to one side and tried not to feel invaded. Did he want to get into this at all?

"Pretty much the same. Stuck in idle."

"I'm sure that's hard on the boys," April said, with every bit as much empathy as he had displayed for the disabled ship.

George ignored it. "They're tough enough. I try to stay in their lives, in spite of the distance."

"Well, with a little luck and a miracle or two, you just might make it home for that birthday, eh?"

A sheepish smile crept over George's lips now. "Maybe. I hope. Well, I think I hope it. When he was seven, I made a promise I shouldn't have made."

April perked up. "Really? What was it?"

"I promised him that when he turned ten, I'd tell him why his middle name is Tiberius."

April tossed his head and chuckled. "Tiberius? You never told me that."

"I thought he'd forget."

"Jimmy? You were dreaming."

"I know that now, don't I?"

"So . . . why is it?"

"Why is what?"

"Why is his middle name Tiberius? Wasn't that a bit cumbersome for an infant?"

With an embarrassed shrug, George said, "He'll grow into it. When he was seven, he figured out that the *T* stood for something. I was on duty at Starbase Four, and Winn was afraid to tell him. After all, the kid slept with a handmade bow and arrow. You know Jimmy—that didn't stop him. He looked around and decided it stood for Tank. Until I got home on leave, his name was Jimmy Tank Kirk. I couldn't let that go on, could I?"

"Hardly." The hand was back in front of April's mouth now, but for a different reason.

"I taught him to say 'James T. Kirk' when people

asked his name and solemnly swore I'd tell him what it stood for when he turned ten. And here I am. The kid's got a self-propelled memory."

April's hand fell away. He laced his fingers on his chest and leaned back sagely. "Now you make me a promise."

George looked up. "What?"

"If we reach the *Rosenberg* without killing ourselves first," April said, "you tell me why his middle name is Tiberius."

For a long moment the two men gazed at each other.

Conviction stood firm in George's voice. "Deal." He couldn't quite keep the challenge out of his tone. Which brought forward another thought. "Robert," he began, "what do you call this ship? It has a name, doesn't it?"

"No name yet, George. No identity at all. Very spooky and clandestine, isn't it?"

"So what do we call her? How do we identify ourselves when we meet other ships? We shouldn't roll up to the *Rosenberg* and say, 'This is the Spaceship *Anonymous* calling.'"

April held up a corrective hand. "Starship. United Starship. The USS *Anonymous.*"

"One straight answer, Robert."

April nodded his understanding. Obviously there wasn't yet a straight answer for that question. "You must realize we've been drawing up plans for a while, and we had to call it something."

"Which is?"

"Well, I had suggested calling her *Constitution*. It says everything I hope to communicate about her. A whole heritage of justice, unity, plurality, or at least opportunity."

"Is that definite?"

76

With a shrug, April said, "No, I don't suppose 'definite' is the word for it. There *have* been several notable alterations in design and power during the actual building of the ship that make her quite different from the original *Constitution* designs, I admit. She's not quite the same ship as the one on the drawing boards, and her Naval Construction Contract number will be different, that's true—"

"Then it's not really the same ship."

With a sigh, April opted to tell the whole story before George badgered it out of the crew. "The *Constitution* was actually put on the boards before all the technological breakthroughs of recent years. Before they even laid the keel, things had vastly changed, from duotronics to the warp navigational tie-in we've got on board this one. Faced with virtually reengineering the whole heart of the ship, Starfleet just took out a new construction contract. On the drawing board, the ship is Number 1700. The actual vessel is 1701."

George nodded slowly. "Who makes the final decision?"

April paused, his mouth hanging open. "I'm . . . almost afraid to tell you," he said with a little laugh.

"You?"

"Yes, guilty. They've given me the option. The Federation, I mean. They like me."

"Fools that they are."

"Why, George? Have you got another idea?"

Put on the spot, George felt himself close up. He didn't belong here at all, much less involved in the nomenclature of the vessel. But this ship . . . he knew what April was feeling.

"Let me think about it," he said evasively.

"All right. Take your time. Naming the ship is probably the only thing we've got to do that *isn't* in a rush." April got to his feet, taking a moment to tap the intercom. "Engineering, this is the captain. Status report, please?"

"We're ready to begin impulse drive ignition sequence, Captain, on your order."

"Wonderful! This is what we've all been waiting for. Begin power-up."

"Engineering, aye."

"Come help me usher in a new age, George." Robert April gestured dramatically toward the door. "We're going to start her engines. For the very first time."

The bridge was buzzing with activity when they arrived. Several engineering specialists were patching together unfinished control panels, and almost as soon as Kirk and April appeared, the specialists scurried off the bridge, heading back to posts not meant to be handled by so few people. Soon the only people besides the captain and first officer were Sanawey on communications and telemetry, Florida on helm, Drake helping Florida try to fit the helm plate into place, and a small birdlike woman at the subsystems monitor whom April introduced quickly as Bernice Hart; she evidently was one of the design engineers for the bridge tie-in consoles.

"Ordinarily, we'll have several more people on the bridge, you understand," April said as he settled into his command chair.

"I would hope so," George commented. He glanced around, feeling like an albatross among the specialists and geniuses, perceiving that the bridge seemed very empty for its size and for all those buttons and buzzers and panels that seemed to need watching. He flinched when the lights on those panels suddenly hummed to life as newborn power was fed through to the bridge, then blushed at his reaction and turned away so April wouldn't see it. The whir of electronic life brought sudden color to the bridge—indicator lights flickered, then settled into bright reds, blues, and yellows, while monitors and dynoscanners burst alive with diagrams and crosspatterns of color, very few of which George could interpret. *Why am I here? I barely recognize half of this equipment. I'm a dinosaur around here. What if somebody asks me for something?*

His thoughts were jarred when the main viewscreen wavered from a board of flat gray and suddenly focused on the beautiful panorama of space outside the ship. The edge of spacedock poked into view at both sides, and beyond that—stars.

Then . . . April's voice. A pleasant, gentle, English voice above the hum of bridge noise.

"Engineering, this is the captain. We're about to implement impulse power. Go ahead with implementation of the warp propulsion intermix formula. Remember to clear personnel out of the Jeffries tubes before we start up. I don't want anyone in there, even when we're only on impulse."

"Aye aye, sir. Standing by for impulse generation."

George stepped down to the captain's chair. "What's all that mean?"

"Hmm? Oh—the engineers are up inside the support pylons, mother-henning the warp units. I don't want anyone caught in there. If the warp engines aren't working by now, we're hopeless anyway. But we're not hopeless. They'll be all right."

"The warp engines won't be used right away, will they?"

"No, not immediately, but as soon as we clear the asteroids. We're not out here to take our time, of course. I just want to be cautious. Those warp engines are warming up even now, and there are successive baffles that keep the matter/antimatter from flushing

79

back into the ship as the power level heats up. A half hour or so from now, they'll be fully ignited."

"Where's the power been coming from up until now?"

April smiled impishly. "You ask good questions, George."

"Captain . . ."

"Yes, well, batteries. The batteries are chemical, and they've been drawing power from the spacedock. They're energized quite fully by now. Of course, the ship itself will have vastly more power than the spacedock, once it's humming. Don't push yourself, George. It'll all start to make sense as you go along."

George pressed his finger into April's shoulder. "My ignorance about this job is your fault, not mine."

With another grin, April nodded. "All right. Whatever makes you comfortable." He turned to Sanawey then. "Claw, patch me through to the spacedock."

"Aye aye, sir. Tied in."

"Spacedock, this is April. Disconnect all external power sources, please."

"Acknowledged, starship. No more mother's milk. Good luck."

"Thank you. April out." Now he looked at the woman at the engineering station and cleared his throat before going on. "Bernice, divert battery power to impulse ignition."

"Diverting, sir," she acknowledged. "We have impulse ignition. We're alive, sir."

A shudder of anticipation moved across April's shoulders. He glanced at George, but kept his command-level cool.

"Seal all magnetic hatches."

"Hatches sealing, sir."

"Verify integrity of all safety and containment systems."

"Safety systems read green, sir."

"Carlos, establish helm control."

Carlos Florida gestured to Drake to sit down in the navigation chair—where Drake was completely useless but could probably not do much harm—and settled into his own post. He ran his hands over the control board, taking his time in spite of the obvious rush to get under way. "Helm answers, sir," he said with a subdued pride.

"Majestic," April whispered. He gripped the arms of his command chair and beamed at George. "Well, First Officer . . . go ahead. Move us out."

George snapped around. His eyes asked the silent question.

"Please," April said with a nod. A nod toward open space.

George stared at him for several seconds. Only when April nodded once more toward the viewscreen did George become sure that the captain really did want to shift this honor away from himself and onto his exec. That was it, of course. Neither one of them actually had to steer the ship; Florida would be doing that. But the honor of giving the first order, of being logged as the first person to issue the go-forward—it was Starfleet's version of being the one to break the champagne bottle against the keel. And on top of it all, George knew April truly wanted it this way. There was no martyrdom here.

With a long, deep, steadying breath, George moved stiffly forward. "All right," he said. "Let's see if the empress will fly."

Everyone felt the electricity. The first movement of the first starship.

George wasn't officially a Starfleet pilot, and he certainly didn't know how to drive a ship like this. He knew he was guessing. If he was wrong, he hoped

Florida would quietly compensate without pointing out the missteps.

Resisting one more glance at April for reassurance, he riveted his eyes on the forward viewer and said, "Ahead twenty percent sublight, Mr. Florida."

"Twenty percent sublight, aye."

The helm console hummed under Florida's hands.

Perhaps the sense of surging power behind the primary hull was imaginary, but they all sensed it. Though he knew he was surrounded by brilliant minds, George sensed a distinct childish excitement in the air about him that made him feel a little better about his place in this puzzle. They were just like him when it came to this ship and the promise it evoked. He hadn't even seen the starship before today and these people had been working on it for a long time, but sheer astonishment had jolted him into involvement. Body and soul, he was part of it now. And a little bundle of pioneers was waiting for him. If he had failed his own family, this would be his moment to make up for it.

His hands tightened with impatience. In the viewscreen, the spacedock was pulling slowly back. The ship was moving.

Then, quite abruptly, the ship made a nauseous groan—a sound so mournful it was nearly human. *Brrrrrrooooooooo . . .*

The lights flickered; the lights died. The bridge went pitch black. All motion stopped.

Standing in the dark, George didn't dare move.

Out of the darkness, out of the silence, came a voice from the navigator's seat. Drake's.

"I didn't touch a thing, George. I swear I didn't touch a thing."

Then, from behind, came the click of an intercom at the captain's chair, and the sound of April's voice in the blackness.

"Bridge to engineering . . . Dr. Brownell? Are you there?"

Seconds passed before an answer came, a blunt statement delivered by a squeaky voice.

"The power source completely uncoupled itself."

"Batteries too?"

"'Course the batteries too. What do you think 'completely' means?"

Surprised by the disrespectful tone, George automatically turned toward April's chair, even though they still couldn't see each other in the dark. "Who's that?" he demanded.

The emergency backup lights popped on then, a runner of tiny lights along the bridge deck, and two small lights in the ceiling, running on their own internal battery system. The bridge was still very dim, but at least they could see.

April's features were blurred by shadows as he hunched over the intercom. "What does that mean, doctor?"

"You want me to spend time explaining it to you, or you want me to start fixing it?"

Even April blinked at that one. He parted his lips to respond, but never got the chance. The horrid shriek of emergency alarms interrupted him, whooping throughout the ship like the sound of impending disaster.

George involuntarily grabbed the bridge rail and swiveled around, shocked.

"What is it?" April shouted into the intercom, his voice nearly drowned out by the klaxons. "Engineering!"

"—goddamned screwed-up hunka—"

"Dr. Brownell! What's happening?"

There was a shuffle of activity inside the intercom that added to the nerve-racking blast of alarms all around them, and when a response came, a different person was talking. *"Bridge! There's been an accident! We've got to reestablish power to the containment devices within fifteen minutes or we'll have to jettison the warp units!"*

"Good God," April murmured. He vaulted to his feet and headed for the turbo-lift. "George! Come with me!"

Chapter Six

ENGINEERING WAS JUST as dim as the bridge. Specialists scurried about, bumping into each other in spite of the broadness of the deck, which was still missing walls in a few places. Everyone was running, including the captain and first officer.

George followed April through an obstacle course of transport crates and disconnected machinery, which evidently was supposed to have been installed when the ship was under way.

They skidded to a stop at a group of technicians who were crowded around an access junction to a vast computer board that stretched the length of engineering, interrupted only by a ladder that led up to more panels.

"Dr. Brownell?" the captain began.

From within the bundle of engineers, up popped an animated face that was at least seventy years old, topped with a thick wave of white hair and wearing glasses—though nobody wore glasses anymore. It swiveled around until it found April. "What?" it snapped.

"What's the matter with the ship?"

"It's broken."

"Might you be more specific?"

"Could if I had time," the old man said, bobbing

wintry eyebrows as he twisted a dial on some kind of hand-held conductive unit and shoved it deep into an outlet. "Can't trust anything under fifty years old anymore."

"Is there a danger?" April pressed, leaning over the cluster of technicians.

"Woody!" the old man called, ignoring the captain.

From across the deck, a very young man appeared behind one of the separator grids. In blatant contrast to the relic who summoned him, this fellow could hardly be twenty years old. Blond and smooth-faced, he looked very out of place among the seasoned engineers around him. "Yes, sir?"

"Get over here and explain it to August."

"Yes, sir, be right there."

George pulled on April's arm. "Robert, who is that antique?"

April stepped away from the engineers and lowered his voice. "That's Dr. Leo Brownell from Starfleet Academy. He's a Starfleet institution, George. He's the one who formulated the combination of dilithium thrust with the new duotronics system that allows for continuous warp," he quickly explained.

"I thought Zefram Cochrane did that."

"No, Cochrane discovered the warp formula itself. But warp couldn't be used continually in uncharted space because sensors and computers simply weren't fast enough. Brownell managed to marry duotronics to the sensors. It eases our ability to move through uncharted space because we don't have to keep stopping to see if we're about to pile into somebody's planet. Please don't antagonize him, eh? He's absolutely brilliant."

"He's obnoxious!"

"And this is Anthony Wood, his assistant," April said, gesturing to the infant who was crossing the deck even now. "Equally brilliant. He graduated from college when he was all of seventeen. He's twenty-one now."

"Where do you find these people, Robert?" George complained under his breath as he watched Anthony Wood approach.

"Captain," Wood greeted.

"Woody, this is our first officer, George Kirk."

Wood made a little bow with his blond head. "Sir."

"What's happening, Woody? What's wrong?" April pressed.

Wood took a deep breath. "There's been an accidental misrouting of circuit coolant and for some reason the computer backup wasn't on line to that junction, so it all fused and everything shorted out. The batteries and the impulse drive are both fine, but there's no way to deliver the power to the warp containment hatches." As Wood talked, George recognized his voice as the one they'd heard from the bridge. The one who said something about jettisoning the warp units . . .

"You said something about a deadline," George urged.

"Yes, thirteen minutes now," Wood said, stepping out of the way as two engineers ran by at full tilt. He moved along the deck quickly, forcing George and April to follow him as he checked readouts and adjusted dials and did incomprehensible things with surface controls, only glancing back at them once or twice as he moved. "The safety hatches weren't meant to hold without magnetic seals, and we've already started the warp drive intermix. They're hot, and there's no cooling them down. If we don't reestablish connectivity, those units are going to have to be blown!"

April gasped.

George headed him off. "The engines themselves?"

"Yes, the nacelles themselves," Wood confirmed. "There'll be a complete meltdown without those seals, and there's nothing we can do to stop it. I'm sorry, sir, but could you excuse me, please?" The young man scooted past George and climbed halfway up a ladder to where he could reach a section of toggles. "It couldn't have happened at a worse time. Fifteen minutes ago the engines wouldn't have been hot enough to do any damage without a power source to the seals. Fifteen minutes *from* now, we could've gotten the power directly from the warp engines. A year's construction is going down the drain, and all because we don't have any way to reestablish power." Frustration added a slight whine to Wood's voice. His smooth face shriveled as he interpreted the readouts in front of him.

"Why don't we just hook back up to the spacedock?" George asked.

"They don't have enough external power to feed the system," Wood said. "There's just not enough for what the seals need. There's not enough anywhere that we can route fast enough."

"Woody, get down from there, you punk!"

George and April turned in time to be met by Dr. Brownell, who was wiping dirtied hands on his worksuit, which was just as dirty. He was at least a head shorter than April, but that didn't seem to have any effect on his attitude. He and Wood reached them at almost the same time.

"One constipated starship," the old man said. The antiquated glasses made his eyes look twice their normal size, and exaggerated his expression to cartoon proportions.

"There's nothing you can do?" April breathed. "Nothing at all?"

"Oh, sure. We can sit here and blow up." Despite his manner, Dr. Brownell couldn't hide his own deep disappointment. "You better get ready to blast those units free. At least we can salvage the hulls."

April paled. "Damn it all," he whispered, "damn it all."

George pushed through to April's side. "But those people on *Rosenberg!*"

"We can't add to the death toll by letting all these engineers be killed," April said cryptically.

"So you're giving up?"

"We haven't much of an option."

"No!" George said. "You're not."

All eyes struck him.

April grasped his shoulder. "You have an idea?"

"I have an idea that you're not giving up," George said, and even he was a bit surprised by his own ferocity. "Find an alternative."

Leo Brownell raised his wrinkled face and leveled a finger at George but looked at April. "Who is this?"

"Lives are on the line," George said, horrified by the idea of giving up so easily when lives were at stake. He wouldn't let them. He couldn't. "Find an alternative!"

The finger waggled, so close to George's head that it ruffled an auburn strand of hair. *"Who* is this? I want to know who this is before I die."

George turned to Wood. "Find a way to feed power to those hatches."

The young engineer blinked. "There's no way to do it, not in ten minutes. We could rebuild the circuit, but not in ten minutes."

Bristling, George closed the space between himself and Wood. "I don't accept that! Listen to what I'm saying. Forget about the circuit. Forget about the whole ship if you have to. Just the hatches! How can we feed power to *just* the containment field long enough to keep from blowing the warp units? Just long enough until the warp engines have enough power to keep the seals up themselves." He stepped to Wood and grasped the young man's arm. "What's the alternative?"

"I—I told you. There isn't one," Wood insisted. "The circuit is a mass of melted—"

George pressed closer. "There is. Pretend there's no way to blow the warp units. You're going to *die.* What do you do about it?"

Wood shrunk back against the engineering panel. His helpless stare was pathetic, but behind it there was a hint of hard thought. He never blinked, not once. He simply stared back into George's raving glare, trying to come up with a wild card. And no one looked more surprised than he did himself when he muttered a single word.

"Shuttlecraft."

Brownell pushed April aside and nosed up to Wood. "What? Shuttlecraft!"

April smacked his hands together. "Of course! Doctor!"

George was forced to back away a half step as Brownell whirled around faster than seemed possible for his degree of ripeness. "Outa my way, August. Thompson! Disconnect all power to the external feed except relays to the hatches. Chang! Run a power transfer device down to the hangar bay and hook it into the shuttlecraft engines! Hook it right up to the external power outlets for the magnetic hatches in the pylons. Woody, set up those connections. And find Marvick and tell him to nursemaid those engines till they're stabilized. Hop to, boy!"

As Wood slipped away and ran into an anteroom, George realized he was panting. He forcibly calmed himself while the engineering deck burst into organized insanity. Beside him, April's voice was so quiet it seemed out of place.

"Still think you don't belong here, George?"

A touch of color rose in George's cheeks. Fury or humility—he couldn't tell which. He shrugged. "They think like engineers. It can be a handicap." He glanced off in the direction Wood had disappeared. "I didn't mean to scare him."

"You scared him into saving the ship," April said gently. "I'm grateful."

"Think it'll work?"

"Well, it won't hold forever, but certainly long enough to repair the system," the captain assured. Only a film of sweat across his upper lip remained to show the panic of a few moments ago. He wiped it away with a forefinger and indulged in a deep sigh. "Let's get back to the bridge."

He stepped away, hands back in those pockets again as though to show everything was all right, but stopped when he realized George wasn't following. He turned back. "George?"

George said nothing, but frowned at the engineering controls.

"George? What's the matter?"

"Too much coincidence, that's what."

"I beg your pardon?"

George turned abruptly. "Something happens to go wrong in the one cooling tube that happens to be connected to a circuit with no backup system operating, at just the right moment when nothing can be done but abort the mission. Not fifteen minutes before, not fifteen minutes after. I don't like it."

"Oh, George, come now," April protested. "Who would want to sabotage a rescue mission?"

"Not the mission," George said. "The ship."

"Now, George, you don't understand. There are hundreds of cooling units aboard, and probably a score of them aren't working yet, on top of the thousands of computer connections, any number of which will have bugs to be worked out—"

"I don't care. I don't like it. It sounds wrong."

"But the collapse of the power grid wouldn't even have been a problem if we hadn't been in such a hurry to energize the warp engines."

"That's what I mean. The right circuit, the right moment."

"George, you've got to lax up on this military way of thinking."

"I thought that's why you wanted me on board."

"Only in part. You're being paranoid."

"Am I? A malfunction like that could scuttle your whole starship program and sink it under a sea of bureaucracy, and you know it."

"Well . . . that's true. But you don't understand the incredible tangle of engineering behind these consoles—"

"And it's a good thing I don't, too. Brownell and Wood didn't know how to think of something radical. Somebody knew how to use that against them."

April scratched his head, trying to come up with the right words. "You're overreacting, my friend."

April spoke so rationally George couldn't avoid being embarrassed. He licked his lips and forced himself to bury his suspicions for the moment, even though he knew April could still read them in his eyes.

"What would make you happy, George?" April asked with a placating tilt of his head.

"Who's in charge of security?"

"Security? We don't have any security forces on board."

"Put me in charge of it."

"There's nothing to be in charge of. We don't have a security division at all."

"All the more reason."

"George, have you forgotten? You're the first officer."

George paused. Yes, he had forgotten. It wasn't real yet. "Then make Drake chief of security."

With a little nod, April pulled a hand from a pocket and poked the nearest intercom link. "April to bridge. Drake, are you there?"

"Ever vigilant, sir. How can I serve you?"

Pretty convincing for a man who had nothing to do, George noticed, smirking at Drake's response.

"You're now chief of security," April said, "answerable to the first officer."

"Sir?"

"George'll explain it to you. Congratulations. April out." He waved a hand over the console as though he'd just worked a card trick, and said, "There you are."

George folded his arms and frowned. "You know, you could be a little more formal about things like that."

"Formal? I don't know what you mean."

"Formal. Protocol. The captain of a ship shouldn't be on a first-name basis with humanity," George said. "Discipline, Robert."

April tossed it off. "Oh, discipline! Everyone here wants the same thing, George." A hail from the bridge interrupted them, and April eyed George as he answered it. "April here."

"Sanawey, sir. Dr. Brownell's looking for you."

"Pipe me through to him."

"Aye, sir."

Brownell's voice came almost immediately. *"August? Where are you?"*

"I'm still in engineering, doctor," April answered, a grin curling his lips.

"Get out of there. You make my techs nervous."

"Do I detect a lilt of success, doctor?"

"Tell that redheaded intruder he got lucky."

"It's working, then? The hatches will hold?"

"Bet it's the first time a ship this size ever got jump-started."

April closed his eyes for a moment of relief and breathed, "Wonderful. Wonderful, doctor! How long before we're under way?"

"I'm an old man. I move slow. Two hours, including safety checks."

"I think we can all manage to give you that time. Is there anything I can do for you?"

"Yeah. Don't bother me."

"Oh, I'm very good at that, doctor. Best of luck."

"You're bothering me."

With a little laugh, the captain nodded as though the intercom could see him. "All right, April out."

George pointed at the intercom. "He's really in Starfleet?"

"He's really in Starfleet," April confirmed, folding his arms and leaning against the engineering console. "In fact, he's an admiral. Would you believe it?"

"I *don't* believe it."

"Admiral of Engineering and Computer Sciences. One of the very few to have such a rank in two separate areas of expertise."

"He's a fart."

"But isn't he a delightful one?"

"He's not senior commanding staff around here. He shouldn't treat you like that."

"I don't care how he treats me as long as the ship goes. Well, George, you have two hours. What are you going to do with it—besides sit back and be proud of yourself?"

His quarters were spartan and austere, like most of the half-finished interior of the ship. Eventually parts of the walls or structural beams would be painted blue or red or gold or some color to denote specific decks, and to make the crew feel less like they were living inside a giant beaker. But for now, "drab" was the operative word. There weren't even any cabin numbers painted on the doors yet; he'd had to count rooms down from the turbo-lift to find his quarters, and he hoped he wasn't sitting in somebody else's bedroom, using somebody else's computer terminal and somebody else's notepaper.

"With my luck, it's probably Brownell's cabin," he muttered as he tapped up another section of information on the screen and scanned it. When the door buzzer sounded, he grumbled and said, "Yeah, come."

The door slid open and Drake strode in, immediately snapping to attention. "Security Chief Me reporting for duty, *sah.*"

George didn't look up. "At least I know I'm in the right cabin."

"I hear congratulations are in order," Drake said, moving closer.

"Congratulations," George muttered, lost in the screen before him.

"Not to me, silly man. To you."

Now he did look up. "What for? Oh—that wasn't anything."

Drake sprawled out on Starfleet's idea of a bed and propped himself up on an elbow. "Not on board half a day before you save the ship. Pretty good score, I would call it."

"I didn't do anything so great. They made me mad, that's all. Their little bubble was about to burst and they were ready to cry about it instead of snow-plowing their way out. Engineers are used to taking their time. They can't think under pressure. I just made them think harder." He clicked off the computer and leaned back as though the effort had exhausted him.

"Snowplowing, do you say? What's that?"

"What are you? An apprentice alien? Even in Trinidad, they must've heard of snow."

"Heard of it, of course. But I don't understand—"

"When it snows, you have to get out and plow it back before it gets too packed and heavy. Snowplowing. Plow through a problem before it becomes a bigger problem."

Drake laughed and said, "Heavy! George, I have seen pictures of this stuff. It's all light and feathery and all you have to do is floof it out of your way with a little brush of your hand. Plowing, indeed. Such stories you tell."

With a threatening stare, George told him, "I know where you're spending your next winter leave, you can bet. I've got a nice long walkway at home that I'm going to introduce you to. You'll have a different use for that shovel you sling."

"What's that I see?" Drake pushed himself up and pointed at the notepad on George's lap. "Another letter? You just sent one this morning, and already something else is on your mind?"

George looked self-consciously down at the notepad with the scribbled letter and drew a blank on a reasonable response that wouldn't give him away. He knew if he looked up, if he let Drake get a good fix on his eyes and the pain within them, that his shields would drop. There would be no drawing them back up in time.

"Why are you unhappy, George?"

George hid a wince. Too late. He stared at his reflection in the blank computer screen.

From behind him, Drake sat up on the bed. "Don't say a word. I'll tell you why." His accent, that strange mixture of West Indies French, Creole, and educated English, seemed to give his analysis a cutting stability. "Captain made you feel your career is something less than noble. He made you think that perhaps the military aspects of the Federation are holding us back, and here you are contributing to them. You are suddenly a military man among philosophers. Actually, we both are, but the difference is that I don't take it personally, and you do. But that's all right, because I never take anything personally and you always take everything personally, thus all is well there."

George watched his reflection in the computer screen grow sallow. It stopped blinking; perhaps it even stopped breathing for a moment as the truth behind Drake's words drew the life from it. George felt his jaw grow stiff as he watched his face inside the screen and listened.

"You feel wounded," Drake went on, his tone suddenly less frivolous. "Captain made you think the niche you have dug for yourself may be a grave. When he talked about the stars and the ship and exploring, he made you feel dirty." Drake pointed at the letter in George's lap. "You wonder if you've wasted yourself, and you think your family has paid the price. You've given up the best things in a more normal life-style in order to help protect our space, and now Captain shows you there's something more to go for. The Federation moves forward, and Geordie Kirk doesn't. You've gotten neither 'best.' If you can't be a Robert April, you wonder if you might not at least be a better daddy."

George felt the weight of things that had no substance. Words. Thick as steel blocks, they dropped one by one on the deck, each with a ringing jar.

George parted his lips and whispered, "You're a son of a bitch."

The notepad slid off his leg and flopped facedown

97

on the carpet. Even the letter wanted nothing to do with him. Even it knew he was being less than honest with himself—about space duty, and about the home front as well. Neither "best."

"George," Drake began slowly, "Captain never meant harm, eh?"

He swiveled around in his chair, at least enough to glance at Drake before lowering his eyes again, still touched with shame. "Oh, I know that. April would cut his tongue out before he'd deliberately hurt anybody's self-esteem. He just . . . accidentally made me quit fooling myself about where my life is going."

"Even accidentally, the stinger goes in."

"Maybe he thinks he's doing me a favor. Maybe that's why he really brought me along. Maybe the only thing I'm really here for is so Robert can help me shake a life out of my existence."

"George," Drake scolded, "saving the ship and the lives of all those people out in space isn't enough to suggest something else to you?"

"I told you, I didn't save the ship. And those people are still out there."

"You are a professional underestimater, Geordie."

"All right, that's enough." George scooped up the notepad, pulled off the letter, folded it, and stuffed it into an envelope. Immediately he sealed it and got to his feet. "Come with me. I've got some things I want you to start on."

"Where are we going?"

"Sickbay."

"Are we sick?"

Sickbay was hard to find. The whole deck was only pretending to be habitable, and between the empty rooms and endless unmarked doors, the two men made several wrong turns before they found Sarah Poole and a handful of techs moving diagnostic beds

98

into place and hooking them up to the readout screens. Dr. Poole looked more attractive under these lights than she had under the lights in the runabout, though she still had a countryish plainness and the pale cheeks of someone who hadn't been under good sunlight for a while. And the disposition of someone who missed it.

"You gentlemen need something?" she demanded on first glimpse of them.

Drake stopped short, turned around, and started to leave, but George hooked his elbow and dragged him back in. "Can you teach Lieutenant Reed to use a mediscanner?"

"I suppose it's critical."

"It might be," George retaliated.

"Depends," she said. "Does Lieutenant Reed have the brains for it?"

"Depends. Does the teacher have the brains to make it clear without resorting to Latin?"

Dr. Poole glared at him, then accepted the inevitable and pawed through a transport crate. "All right," she sighed, pulling out a case of hand-sized mediscanners. "What is it you want him to scan for?"

"General metabolic rate," George said. "Heart, perspiration, things like that."

"Oh," she said with a caustic nod. "You want him to look for lies."

George stepped to her. "Is it going to be that obvious?"

Her unadorned green eyes suddenly sparkled with satisfaction at his concern, and she looked straight at him while she adjusted one of the units. "That's his problem, not mine." She turned away from him before he could respond. "All right, Reed. Come here."

With a subservient bow, Drake stepped to her.

Dr. Poole ran her finger down the side of the small

instrument, pointing out gradients of readings. "This is the norm range. It's not going to read the same for everybody, but humans have certain physiological common denominators. If the lights flow to the right, it's high. Low is to the left. Here's heart, here's blood pressure, here's respiratory function, here's brain wave activity, here's nerve activity in the extremities, and the slash on the bottom is muscle control."

"What are the numbers on this side?" Drake asked.

"Those are too complicated for a ten-second medical degree. Ignore them and just watch the lights." She wagged the instrument in his face. "This is set for humans. If Captain April has pulled any surprises on me and hired aliens that he didn't bother to tell me about, which wouldn't be the slightest surprise, it's not going to work on them properly and you'll get a red signal in this space right here. You'll have to come back for an instrument with a different setting."

"Madame, I shall nominate you for sainthood."

"No, thanks. I've already got all the odd jobs I need."

"On your way, Drake," George ordered. "And don't forget what I told you."

"My orders are burned indelibly on the skin of my brain," Drake said, bowing. He skittered out into the corridor and disappeared.

George found himself alone with Sarah Poole. Suddenly he felt relieved to be around someone who didn't know him at all, who couldn't find the subtle hiding places inside himself like Robert, and especially like Drake, were able to.

He turned to her and bluntly said, "I get the feeling you don't want to be here."

"I get the same readings from you," she said without a blink. "You really expect your friend to be able to feel out the crew without giving himself away?"

"Drake's intuitive. More than you think."

She nodded toward him. "What's that?"

"What's what?"

She pointed at his hand. "That."

He looked down. He'd forgotten he was still holding the envelope. "Just a letter home," he said, careful of his tone.

Evidently not careful enough.

"Is that the place you want to be instead of here?" she asked bluntly.

"Why do you ask that?" he snapped.

"I don't know many people who bother to actually write letters, do you?"

Had he put on transparent skin this morning or what? Somehow George managed to stifle a giveaway shake of his head.

"To your wife?" Dr. Poole added.

"No, to my sons," he snapped back quickly, and the frustration of having his privacy so easily ruptured bubbled to the surface.

"You don't have a wife?"

"Yes, I have a wife, doctor."

"All right, I'm sorry. Forget I asked."

"I will."

"How old are your sons?"

Stiff-jawed, George took a settling breath and absorbed what seemed to be genuine interest on her part. Whether the interest was professional or personal, he couldn't tell yet. "They're fourteen and ten."

"Ah . . ."

"What do you mean, 'ah'?"

She shrugged. "Oh, only that those are the ages when fathers and sons have the most in common. Just after childhood and just before adolescence. It's not surprising that you're feeling the distance. I assume your kids are on Earth."

Deflecting any further analysis, George went for

aggression. "Well, that's my life in a box. What about yours? Where did Robert kidnap you from?"

"Me?" With a sigh she sat on the edge of the transport case and picked at the equipment. "I'm a veterinarian."

"That's one way to look at it," George commented.

Her brows went up and she leaned forward a little to punctuate her point. "I'm not being facetious, Mr. Kirk. I'm supposed to be on assignment to a new farm colony."

George stared at her to see when the joke would break, but it didn't. He held out a hand to stay the flow of disbelief. "Wait a minute. You're a doctor. Robert's doctor, right?"

"I'm his *dog's* doctor, Commander."

George stared a few more moments, then paced across the floor before turning back. "Pardon my asking," he began hesitantly, "but why are you here?"

"Ask the captain," she said, ready with her answer. "I've already done all my arguing. I told him it was crazy and that I didn't want the assignment. But the River April only flows in one direction, as you probably know perfectly well."

"And we're caught in the rapids. Robert knows human nature. Nobody in his right mind would turn down a mission to save fifty-one people from deep space."

"Speak for yourself. I'd turn it down in a minute if he'd given me a choice. I'm the wrong person for this mission. I don't have enough training in radiation sickness, and I haven't spent enough time in space to be accustomed to its eccentricities, and we don't have any real idea of what condition we're going to find those people in. He'd have done much better to choose a doctor with deep-space experience."

Not to mention one who usually treats humans instead of spaniels, George thought, and only barely managed to keep from saying. *We haven't left spacedock and already we're in trouble.*

"We'll all have to do our best," he said. "There isn't time for less."

"Or more," she added.

He pressed his lips tight and vowed not to give her more ammunition. He might be annoyed with Robert April, but he was also loyal to him, and if you worked for somebody, you should damned well work *for* him. He wasn't about to spend the mission collecting grievances against April. If anything, it was his job to dilute them.

April himself defused the issue when he strolled in the main door, saw the two of them, and held out his arms in greeting. "So, getting to know each other? How very reassuring. George, I'm so surprised to see you here, but isn't it nice? I thought you were resting up. Sarah, my dear, we've had a little accident with an acid burn in impulse engineering. I told them I was just passing through and would send you down. Nothing serious, but would you see to it?"

Sarah pursed her lips in disapproval, reached into the packing crate, and came up with treatment cloths and a spray bottle. "Barn calls already." Without further comment, she glanced accusatively at Robert and strode out.

April watched her go with a pleased grin and stuffed his hands into his pockets. "Marvelous, isn't she?" he said after she was gone.

"Robert, would you like to explain to me why our ship's physician is an animal doctor?"

"Oh, she told you about that, did she?"

"In no uncertain terms."

"Well, you see, George, she's perfectly qualified as an M.D. A human doctor, I mean. She went back for a second degree in veterinary medicine well after she had already completed a medical degree. So she wasn't being altogether truthful with you. It's just that she *wants* to be a veterinarian and she doesn't want to be a human doctor anymore."

"She's managing that all right," George said caustically.

The captain smiled. "Now, George."

"Rob, she's a veterinarian!"

April shook his head. "George, she's the perfect choice for this mission. She's a stable, steady ally when the situation gets stressful, and she already knows me well enough that I don't have to explain myself in order to get the right action, and that's just what we'll need. It's the same reason I chose you for my exec. I don't want to work with strangers. Not on this mission, not with this ship."

Whether or not his doubt showed, George couldn't tell. With no way to argue a point he preferred not to discuss at all, he fell silent under April's gaze.

"What's this you've got?" April asked, changing the subject. "Oh, a letter home. How charming." He reached out without the slightest regard for privacy, which was becoming less and less available, and plucked the envelope from George's hand. "I think this is one of the things I like best about you, George."

George gazed at April's shoes. "It's one of the things I like least about myself," he admitted.

"Really? What brings this on?" April asked sympathetically.

"Nothing," George muttered.

"Needing to go home for a while? I can arrange it after we get back. No problem."

Those words didn't hold the promise of solution that George expected they might. Instead, there was little more than another sinking feeling, a drained hope.

"Won't that help?" April finally asked.

George shrugged. "When I'm home, the tension

104

gets focused," he said slowly. "At least when I'm in space, the boys have a fantasy to cling to."

With a fatherly nod, April said, "I understand." He tapped the letter against his palm. "I'll see that this gets out for you, if you like."

George looked up abruptly. "Now? What about security? Starfleet's managed to keep a black hole around this project. You don't expect they're going to let something like that get through, do you?"

"Oh, if command status doesn't offer a few advantages, what good is it? I'll pipe it through to the spacedock before we leave, and they'll funnel it back to Earth. I doubt even starbase security will find anything subversive about a letter to two little boys in Iowa."

In spite of the callous front George had put up, he felt a warmth rise in his chest. "That's damned generous of you, Rob."

April fanned the letter between them and clapped George's arm. "Not at all, George. Not at all."

Chapter Seven

Dear troopers —

How's the weather down there? Getting sunny? Not much sun out here, you know, even when you're in a star system. At least, not the nice kind of sunlight like what shines through an atmosphere and runs across the water of some little lake. The starbase is pretty dull and we're all feeling closed in. Next time I get leave, you'll both have to teach me how to ride a horse again. They say you never forget, but I think I did.

You wouldn't like it here after the first couple of days.

all the people are involved in
their jobs and themselves. Why
waste all the best summer
weather sitting around some
cold starbase, right? Besides,
Jimmy, there aren't any
little girls to tease.

I'm going to be leaving
Starbase Two for a while on
assignment. They've got a
security problem in another
sector, so I volunteered, just
to move around a little.
I don't know long this will
take and I'm not even sure
they'll let me send this
letter through. If you don't
hear from me for a while,
you won't give up on me,
okay, guys? It feels great
to have somebody I can
depend on.

Hand-me-down regrets. They fell off the page like
petals from a dying flower. He'd never seen them
before, in those days so far past, when the letters had
meant other things t him. Things that seemed magnified now, from this different perspective. Somehow
time had failed to gild the memories brought back by

these handwritten words. There was something different here, something ten-year-old eyes hadn't been able to see.

The letters were a kind of unconsummated love —the deepest kind of all, because all its hopes remain forever intact, unspent.

He knew that sensation too well today. His father's face had faded in his memory, and even these letters failed to call it back entirely. Instead of the masculine face he expected to see as his eyes scanned these curled pages, he saw a drably dressed Englishwoman rather out of place herself, or out of time, and he saw himself plunging in emotionally where he didn't belong.

"Anybody aboard?"

The familiar roughness of that voice rustled through his memories. He let the letters drop to his thigh and leaned his head back on the loft door. "I might've known."

"Anybody up there alive?"

Kirk turned his head slightly toward the sound and furrowed his brows. "What do I get if I don't answer?"

"Mouth-to-mouth resuscitation," came the response, along with the creak of the loft ladder.

"From you? No thanks." He turned just in time to see the frost-blue eyes and animated face of interference itself pop up over the edge of the loft.

"Your mother said you were up here," McCoy said as he maneuvered his thin frame around the top of the ladder and strolled through the hay, wiping dusty hands on his trousers.

Kirk frowned. "Last I heard from you, you were in orbit. What are you doing down here?"

McCoy's brows arched. "Just passing through."

"Nobody's ever just passing through Iowa, McCoy."

The brows went up even higher. "Well, *I* am." He rearranged his long legs and sat down on the opposite side of the doorway as though he couldn't help it that his loft door was on the same farm as Kirk's loft door.

Kirk leered at him, not surprised at his audacity. "I knew I could count on you to come up here and cheer me up, especially if I ordered you not to."

Dependably, McCoy changed the subject. "What're those?"

Kirk looked down at the yellowed piles of old-style Starfleet stationery and notepaper and wondered if there wasn't some way he could pretend they were something other than what they were. "They're letters."

"To whom?"

"To me. Sam and me."

"From?"

"From," he answered slowly, still stalling, "from our father."

McCoy leaned back, hanging one leg over the edge. "And I thought you were up here alone."

McCoy was nervous; Kirk could tell. Nervous and hiding it. Something had dragged him here, albeit unwillingly, as surely as a magnet drags a paperclip. A caution hovered over them, as though McCoy had expected to be verbally whipped for the intrusion, as though he still thought that might happen.

Kirk looked down at the letters again and knew McCoy was watching him. It was like having his own private Geiger counter; someone whose attention almost always came in direct proportion to some other emotion—concern, curiosity, guilt.

Guilt . . .

"How old were you then?" McCoy asked.

"This batch came the summer I was ten."

"That would've been twenty-one eighty . . . eighty-two."

"Eighty-three."

"And your father was about the age you are now? About thirty-four? Thirty-five?"

Kirk eyed him, knowing perfectly well what he was doing. "Give or take a year," he said evasively.

A light breeze came across the cornfield and ruffled the papers in his hand, as though to draw him back. He looked at the words for a second time. Back then, all those years and experiences ago, he'd thought his father was trying to let him down easy about spending the summer at Starbase 2. Now, perhaps the interpretation had to be different. Perhaps his father had been experiencing something entirely other than the message his sons got from the letters. Perhaps he had been realizing what it was he left behind—wife, sons, the human side of modern existence. At the time, it had only seem disappointing to little Jim. Back then, the feelings had been those of a ten-year-old kid.

Now, the feelings were his father's. He'd grown into them.

"When I was a boy," he began, his own voice a shock in the silence that had fallen, "I was so proud of him . . . he was head of security for a whole starbase. It sounded like a kingdom to me then."

There was a faint shuffle in the hay. "And now?"

"Now I see an undercurrent of boredom. I never saw it before. These letters are more apologetic than I remembered. It's shaded, but I can see it now. I don't think he shared the pride in himself that I had in him."

"Sounds familiar," McCoy muttered.

"And some of it was my fault."

"Oh, this I'd like to hear," McCoy shot back. "Let me get comfortable. How do you figure it was your fault?"

"I was always bothering him to let us come to the starbase, maybe even live there. It must have made him feel neglectful of us. I didn't realize what I was doing to him." He squinted as the sun broke from around a small cloud and struck the bright paper, making it appear suddenly new. Even through the clouds of time. "In a way, I'm jealous."

"Of your father?"

"At least when he did come home, he had somebody to come home to. The glory and excitement wears a little thin when you realize what you're paying for it, Bones. My father had a family. I don't even have that. I should've realized that a long time ago."

McCoy played with a bit of hay, to avoid looking up at the sandy hair and hazel eyes filled with regret. "Jim, we've all got enough to be sorry for without counting should'ves," he said quietly. "History abused us," he went on. "It's the price we pay for being able to travel through time in two directions instead of one. It would be wrong to let the past shrivel the future too."

The sun moved in the sky, slowly, ignorantly. Clouds made sleepy turns. Neither man looked at the other.

"It's the ship, Bones," Kirk said, in a tone softly accusatory, like a witness to a murder who'd suddenly realized what it was he saw happening in the dark of night. "It's her fault. It's a sacrifice of any personal happiness, this drug called a starship." He paused. "And I've made a decision."

This time McCoy did look up, but any prompting clogged in his throat. His lips parted, but nothing came out.

Kirk gazed out over the sunstruck corn. "I've lived the starship's life for her. It's time to live my own. It's time to take what I've got left, and get out."

111

Part II

These Are the Voyages

Chapter Eight

THE *RAZE* WAS in simulated night. In the "morning," they were scheduled to search a fleet of merchant cargo runners. Dry duty, yes.

Idrys divorced herself from plaguing thoughts of the Field-Primus, or tried to. He was a self-assured man. He seemed to know his future, seemed to have some time-earned understanding of how governments and people change like unstoppable tides. Yet she had seen in t'Cael's eyes a frustration that kept him forever trying to stall the changes, and forever suffering the agonies of never quite succeeding. Finally he was the victim of the changes.

She would welcome the sight of her own quarters tonight. The military austerity would be comforting. The unadorned walls and muted colors would remind her of nothing, and that would bring fleeting peace.

The peace might have stayed with her had she not been stricken by the unwelcome appearance of Antecenturion Ry'iak coming out of the turbo-lift just as she was going in. Idrys pressed her lips tight against a bitter grin; his forehead was colored by a verdant bruise with t'Cael's signature on it. She liked that very much. Certainly it was prideful to wear one's own medals of victory, but it was that much more pleasing when the enemy was forced to wear the medals of his defeat.

"Commander," he greeted.

"Antecenturion," she returned. "I'm surprised to see you up so late, after so full a day."

He bristled at her reminder of the day's humiliations. When he actually smiled and cocked his head with pleasure at his own words, Idrys felt her own pleasure drop away.

"Surprises are part of our duty, Commander," he said. "You should be ready for them."

With an infuriating nod, he strode away.

She watched him leave, but couldn't tell where he was headed. Why was he so pleased with himself? T'Cael had thoroughly cowed him. Where did this sudden return of smugness come from?

Perhaps it was his youth, she suggested to herself. Still, she knew better. He was up to something and he was too inexperienced and unprofessional to keep from giving himself away. He hadn't been able to resist gloating. Yet, if she had him tracked and he ended up doing nothing, she could be accused of dissolution and removed of her command.

She stood in the corridor, weighing her options, feeling the spider's web was thickening.

Ry'iak almost giggled as the panel to the cramped auxiliary bridge slid closed against his shoulder blades. He inhaled the recirculated air as though it gave him power.

The officer on duty turned and grew as cold as his helmet when he saw the Praetor's eye, for he knew what the visit meant.

"The Senate's regards, Subcenturion," Ry'iak said, twisting out a smile.

The subcenturion only managed a nod, knowing perfectly well that the greeting was a reminder of Ry'iak's power; the Senate would never pass its regards to a lower officer.

"It is my time," Ry'iak reminded.

Another nod.

Ry'iak moved to the control panel. "I will need a screened communication dispatch, direct to ch'Rihan system, in the cypher I gave you for the Supreme Praetor's alcazar, speed boosted and under code."

The subcenturion rose stiffly. "It's ready, sir. Time will be limited. You have until the blue mark. If you go beyond the mark, the bridge will be notified of the dispatch, and we will both be fodder."

Ry'iak smiled his smugness. "Don't feel you're being disloyal, Moyu. Loyalty to the Praetor takes precedence over loyalty to a Field-Primus who has shamed us all with his pacifism."

The subcenturion tried to absorb the complex ethic. "Primus Kilyle is hardly a soft kind, sir. He's a sovereign provincial Praetor in his own right and I do fear him."

"Oh, wisely so," Ry'iak placated. "But even he has crutches that can be kicked away."

Dubious, the subcenturion lowered his eyes and escaped from the auxiliary bridge, leaving Ry'iak alone for the precious minutes he would need to effect his subterfuge.

His eyes narrowing with a sinister joy, Ry'iak lowered into the seat and began tapping out his message.

Simulated morning slipped in almost unnoticed. A few more crewmen were on duty; the small ship's interior lights were slightly brighter. Already a hulking cargo vessel dwarfed the fighter-flagship, and a boarding party had been dispatched to search for contraband. Nothing would be found.

The *Raze*, though tiny against the large brown bulk of the carrier, was still intimidating. Despite the size difference, the bird-painted flagship could easily destroy the entire cargo vessel.

That fact meant little to the bridge crew as they went through the motions of monitoring the routine search. Only when the Praetor's eye joined them on the bridge did mundane duty gain a touch of spice.

For a very carefully measured amount of time, Ry'iak looked out the main viewer at the carrier's hull, which stretched out into space close enough to touch. Most of the carrier was still out of view simply because of the docking position. Monitors across the bridge displayed different views of the big ship, a placid cow awaiting permission to enter the feeding yard.

Ry'iak waited until Subcommander Kai couldn't stand it anymore and glanced at him. Then he issued a calculated sigh.

"Isn't it a pity," Ry'iak began, "that officers of your caliber must be reduced to such . . . busybody duty. Soldiers diminished to maidservants."

"Duty is duty," Kai said self-consciously, refusing to look at the antecenturion. "All is glorious in the name of the Empire."

"If it comforts you," Ry'iak agreed. He moved closer. "But to be the minions of disgrace . . . I sympathize."

"These inspections are necessary," Kai said, forcing himself to sound strong.

"A Praetorial Swarm reduced to territory snooping? Such waste." Ry'iak shook his head. "To be an animal sniffing at the hindquarters of another animal . . ."

From the master engineer to the bridge centurion to the navigational technicians, the bridge crew glanced uncomfortably at each other. Ry'iak made sure they all heard, his voice just loud enough to stitch disaffection together like a garment's threads, and tug it tight.

Kai drew his shoulders in and gripped the controls of the subcommand console. "We're protecting our space from smugglers and pirates."

"Protecting? Against ships that aren't allowed to carry armaments? Perhaps you think of it as a challenge . . . but then, perhaps you've spent enough time here to know more about innerspace dangers than I." He leaned on the console, maneuvering into a position that forced Kai to see his face. "Or perhaps you've attained your goal already. To be subcommander of a ship in an imperial Swarm is a worthy thing. I can see why you might be comfortable with it."

Kai dug his fingers into the console controls' spongy grips. His nose wrinkled at the stench of Ry'iak's words. He felt the eyes of the bridge officers from beneath the pointed browplates of their helmets. Empathy, anger, pity, bitterness—all ran like snakes at their feet.

His legs began to ache; he was stuck in this position, bent over the controls; if he turned, the crew would see his face.

"It's a good thing this ship has the authority of the Tricameron behind it," Ry'iak said, flexing his shoulders and gazing out the main viewer. He raised his voice now that he had the crew's attention. "Smugglers and pirates have to be intimidated."

Kai's eyes screwed shut.

The bridge crew exchanged another collective glance, each officer feeling the weight of his rank insignia—or perhaps, the lack of weight. On the cramped, low-roofed bridge, a faint heat rose. Each crewman felt the closeness of the next.

The bridge entrance panel sighed open and Idrys strode to the command seat. Conversation fell away. Not until she reached the command module did she notice Ry'iak standing half hidden behind a structural rib. She stopped short and stared at him. Only by a cultivated self-discipline was she able to break the glare and pretend to turn her attention to the cargo ship. What was he doing here so early?

"When will the inspection be complete?" she asked, lowering herself into the hard command seat.

Kai cleared his throat. "The inspection team is on its way back to airlock now, Commander."

"Good. Prepare to detach. Authorize passage for the carrier into home space. When the team returns, I want to see a list of cargo."

"Yes, Commander."

"Be sure the commander of the carrier—" she began, then stopped.

Kai was bent over the communications board, no longer hearing her. His brow was furrowed as he read an incoming message. His adjutant was also bent over the message, and a moment later, the master engineer. A subtle bleeping from the decoder said the message came from outside the Swarm.

"What is it, Kai?" Idrys demanded.

"A . . ." The subcommander leaned down even further to reread the message. "It comes . . . from the Supreme Praetor's citadel. I am . . ." He stood straight then, and she could see only his back, the tension in his neck, the balling of his fists. Stiffly, he nodded to his adjutant, then to the master engineer.

In a single movement, the three officers turned to Idrys.

Idrys put her weight on her good leg and turned in her seat. Some innate wisdom warned her to remain seated. Two reasons—to avoid the challenge implied by standing up, and to show them plainly that she alone deserved to sit there.

"Commander . . ." Kai began.

"Speak, if you can," she said sharply.

Kai cleared his throat. "Commander, you have

120

been named accessory to the assassination of your kinsman, Senior Senator Illiat d'Yn. I must place you under arrest."

She bolted to her feet, gripping the armrests of the chair. "My uncle!" she gasped. "Murdered?"

The bridge officers stared, horrified at the prospect, as Kai went on. "The order to hold you for questioning comes from the Senate Council. The charge is complicity in the murder of a member of your own house."

"Kai!" She stumbled toward him.

He backed away, frozen by revulsion and by a necessary coldness.

Another voice chilled the bridge even further. Ry'iak. "This must be some mistake."

Idrys whirled to look at him. As she expected, his expression proved he wasn't surprised at all by this turn of events.

"Centurion," Kai addressed, "Escort the commander to detention. No privileges."

The bridge centurion summoned two guards from the doorway. The three of them came to stand beside Idrys.

Idrys gathered herself and willed her legs to operate. At the last moment before leaving the bridge, she turned to the subcommander. "Kai—"

"Commander?"

"You must notify Primus Kilyle of this."

"That is out of order, Commander."

"But it must be done. I ask you to make it a priority." With her eyes she pleaded that he break the standard order, that he do one more thing to remain an individual before allowing irrevocable process to swallow them all.

He dipped his head in acknowledgment, but made no promises. As he watched her being escorted from the bridge, a keen awareness of his own vulnerabilities came home to him. He was in command now. A greater target.

When the bridge panel closed, the Praetor's eye moved to the center of the cubicle and gazed at the closed door. "The commander is sentimental. How pitiful that she could plot to murder a kinsman. Ah, but I've been fooled before . . ."

Kai ignored the younger man and turned to his adjutant. "Have the Supreme Praetor's message sent down to Primus Kilyle's quarters and notify him of the commander's arrest."

Ry'iak turned. "Subcommander," he said carefully, "it's dangerous to break the order of advisement. Your first duty as commander of the flagship is to notify the other commanders of the Swarm, then to—"

"My first duty as commander," Kai interrupted, "is to fulfill my last duty to the former commander." He waited until his words were firmly absorbed and the Senate Proctor had been stared into silence. Only then did he turn again to his adjutant. "Continue as I directed."

The adjutant nodded, and punched up the onboard code for Primus Kilyle's quarters.

She sat unmoving, controlling her emotions, though they were a deep and running river. But there were guards on the other side of the energy field, and her grief, if she allowed them to see it, would be interpreted as a weakness. So she simply sat on the cold metal bench, staring sightless at the wall. The only sound other than her own heartbeat was the unnerving sizzle of the energy field.

"Idrys."

She looked up, feeling drugged. With a blink, she pushed herself up. "Primus!"

The force field cast a strange ghostly glow around

t'Cael's lean form and made his blue coat seem almost green, but the sight couldn't have been more welcome. Idrys had to control herself from trying to go right through the energy wall.

"Are you well in there?" he asked.

"I'm here," she said. "It's all I can say."

He nodded slowly, then turned to the senior guard. "I want the commander released. Remand her to my personal custody."

The guard came to attention and tensely said, "My Lord Primus, I cannot."

"Why not?"

"Such a release would require authorization from each commander in the Swarm, plus a marked dictate from the Senate Council, plus an injunction from the Grand Primus stating—"

"Enough," t'Cael snapped. A constant amazement, how the praetorial system was learning to tie its own hands, and how quickly the ropes could be tightened. He folded his arms, pressed one finger against his lips, and strolled back to the center of the energy wall. "It seems you stay," he said to Idrys.

"And with my imprisonment, they bind you," she reminded. Her hands shook. "Collusion in the murder of my own kin . . . the suggestion alone will never lift from my reputation."

"It was a carefully chosen charge," t'Cael said. "A heinous sin as well as a political crime. Little else could so effectively and so swiftly cast revulsion over you in the eyes of the Swarm."

She moved closer to the energy field. "My uncle," she murmured. "Do you think they really did . . ."

Sympathy cut through him. He drew his arms in tighter against his chest. "Without doubt."

Misery and fury twisted Idrys' small mouth. "All to remove you from power?" she choked, her eyes clouding.

123

"From one perspective, yes," he answered. "Those who wish to excise me had only to find those who wished to remove your uncle from the Senate. In times past, the Council of Clans carried more weight than the Praetorate. Now, the Supreme Praetor cannot be removed by the Council. But the Praetor isn't yet powerful enough to defy the Council as he desires, at least not openly. All must be done with a mesh of scapegoats and accusations. A tidy patting of backs was involved in this one, I'm certain."

"And effective," she said bitterly. "Ry'iak."

T'Cael nodded. "He is a canker."

"How can it be? How can he have timed it so perfectly?"

"By planning ahead. Somehow he has set wheels in motion which were awaiting his signal." T'Cael paced slowly to the edge of the force field and made a leisurely turn. "I should have anticipated this."

"How could you?" she asked from behind the annoying buzz. "I don't understand."

"Ry'iak is a well-connected youngster who speaks of the glories of battle yet has never been in one. He could never be Senate Proctor on his own. He has help in the Supreme Praetor's alcazar. He's being advised. I should have known he would have an alternate plan."

"A plan to assassinate my uncle?" Her voice cracked.

"By assassinating your uncle, these elements win three victories, Idrys. Your uncle . . . you . . . and me."

"But how? How?"

Calmly he explained. "Ry'iak failed to intimidate me. I frightened him momentarily, but I underestimated his cockiness. His plan is now to undermine you."

"Because he knows I am loyal to you," she finished, weakened.

"Of course. He knows I depend on you. Cripple the legs, and the head will fall. The crew is loyal to you, but suspicious of me. He can use that. He knows I can't use the crew as efficiently as you can, so he had to eliminate you. And Ry'iak is in a position to use them *very* well. Now all he has to do is shift their loyalty from you to the Praetor."

Furious at her impotence, Idrys spun around and paced the cell. "I did beg you to attend the bridge," she said with a shuddering breath. "Time after time I begged it. Now you pay the price of your seclusion."

"Quite true." T'Cael's round, dark eyes widened in agreement. "Bide here as well as you can. I'll try to engineer a release, if only a temporary one."

Once again Idrys crowded the force field. She felt the energy sizzle against the fine hairs around her face. "An even bigger problem for you," she said. "The edges of order will fray very fast now, if Ry'iak is allowed to sink his fangs into the hearts of the crew. You'll have to hold tight if a mutiny is to be avoided. Mistakes at this point will be fatal for both of us."

T'Cael nodded serenely. "The two of us will be lost in a flood of fatalities, Commander, with the Empire continuing in this pathetic direction. Meanwhile, we row through the danger and hope fear hasn't taken over entirely. Even Ry'iak is being used, though he doesn't have the brains to realize it yet. Very sad."

He turned without ceremony and started away.

"Where are you going?" she called, looking at him at an image-warping angle through the force field.

He cast her one more glance.

"To the bridge. You'll be joining me very soon."

Chapter Nine

"ALL RIGHT, CHILDREN. This is it."

Captain April swirled onto the bridge and down to his command chair with such exuberance that his cardigan flapped at his sides like a cape. Everyone on the bridge fell into a sudden and quite childlike flu of excitement which put butterflies in even the most professional stomach. Sanawey manned the astro-telemetry station, Florida the helm, Hart and two staff engineers on loan from the impulse power deck the engineering console: George stood at the hand rail behind his captain, just being George. April looked around, making eye contact with every person around him, acknowledging both their presence and their contribution to the moment.

At last, he turned to George. His half-smile reappeared.

"Still your prerogative, George."

George touched the bridge hand rail as a sheepish grin pulled up one corner of his mouth, and said, "Don't forget what happened last time."

A collective chuckle rippled around the bridge crew. It told George that they didn't think of him as a Jonah.

"I brought you for good luck," April said. He gestured to the command console and Carlos Florida, who was waiting for orders. "Off with you, First Officer. Make the empress fly."

George went to stand beside Florida and clasped his hands behind his back to control the faint chill in his fingers. "Ahead, twenty percent sublight."

"Twenty percent sublight, aye."

Almost imperceptibly, the starship began to hum. On the big viewscreen, the spacedock slowly fell away to port and starboard, and all was space.

Before them was the shimmering beauty of a lifeless star system, a sun and its three uninhabitable planets, and a little cluster of asteroids.

"Test the sensors, George," April said, almost whispering.

George blinked and looked around, then understood. Tests. Of course. Muscle-stretching.

"Mr. Sanawey, specify composition of the asteroids we're coming up to," he requested, a little more stiffly than he intended.

"Aye, sir," Sanawey's tunnel-deep voice responded. The big man bent over a viewscope and did something with the controls near him at the library computer station. "Asteroids consist primarily of iron, titanium, nickel, and small amounts of gold, as well as traces of various inert ores. Largest reads out at roughly two thousand metric tons, and they break down to stones of about a pound or so in the dust field. Nice and boring."

April twisted around in his chair. "How do those instruments feel, Claw?"

"They feel like they know what they're doing, sir. There's even a percentage breakdown of ore content and density. We can get as detailed as we need to."

"Magnificent." He turned once again to face the view. "Go on, George."

"Mr. Florida, plot a course," George continued.

"Make it an obstacle course through those asteroids to the end of the belt and back again. Zigzag to port and starboard, plus full overturn. Just make use of the space you have and shake down the controls."

Florida looked up. "Really?"

"Sure, really. Arrange something that tests maneuverability at sublight."

"Quite right," April said from behind them. "And monitor gravitational compensation systems as well."

Florida raised his eyebrows but said nothing more. It took him a few moments to plot that kind of course, during which time George was careful not to look at anybody.

"Plotted," Florida said. "I think."

"What do you mean, you think?" George asked.

"The asteroids aren't stationary to one another, sir. They're constantly moving apart and together. It's not really a plottable course, in the true sense of plotting a course."

"That's perfect," George said. "Random gyrations."

"It is?"

"How else can we know how the ship responds to direct control by hand? Can't rely on computers for everything, can we?"

Florida couldn't quite manage to agree.

April punched his intercom, and his voice echoed throughout the ship. "All hands, alert for maneuverability and gravitational testing of the starship's systems. Brace yourselves." He nodded to Florida. "Execute."

Florida caressed his board. The ship veered into the asteroid belt.

George clung to the bridge rail as the pitch of the deck suddenly came high on the starboard side. He felt his body weight change as the artificial gravity fought to adjust, but the centrifugal force as they careened between space rocks nauseated him. There was a downturn that made the asteroids in the viewer seem to jump over them, and half the crew was scattered across the bridge as they lost grip.

Like a giant pendulum, the starship became an elegant courser involved in inelegant moves. She upended at Florida's touch, and pitched violently to sub-port. Brand-new, untested bulkheads, structural beams, braces, framework sections, and every bolt and sash and joint was stressed.

George gritted his teeth and held on. "Go to forty percent sublight," he shouted over the ship's whine of protest.

"Forty percent," Florida called back. He touched his controls with his free hand, since the other hand was holding on tight, and the ship's merry-go-round doubled its speed.

"Keep your eyes on the gyrostats!" Engineer Hart called from her position at the subsystems monitor.

George had no idea who she was talking to, but he just hoped it wasn't him because he also had no idea where to find gyrostats and he wasn't about to let go in order to look for them. His arms and legs turned to iron as the starship brushed by a huge asteroid, then between two others in stiffer and stiffer maneuvers. To anyone who didn't know better, it seemed that the ship's gravitational compensators weren't worth spitting on. In fact, if they *hadn't* been working, and working perfectly for that matter, everyone on the bridge would have been smacked through the bulkheads already and had his molecules sizzling in space by now.

"Go to seventy-five percent," George ordered. "Break out of the belt and head for the gas giant. Take her between the rings!"

Florida's hand crawled over his controls. "Point five . . . point six . . ."

The viewscreen compensated for the new sight—a vast gas planet suddenly at point-blank range, her brightly colored rings slapping down on them with unsettling speed.

"Point seven . . . five."

The crushing sensation intensified. Every breath was a concentrated effort now as the starship tested her capabilities in more and more sinewy maneuvers between the gaseous rings of the planet at such full-tilt speed that George gritted his teeth and hoped the nacelles didn't rip off. With the whines and groans she made, the empress told them she was enjoying the action.

Suddenly April's voice cut through the bridge noise. "Emergency stop!"

Florida leaned on his board, smashing toggles.

Shocked, George chose the wrong instant to look back toward April, trying to see in the captain's face what the emergency was. Instead, he was torn from his place and flung headlong onto the forward deck as the ship slammed to a halt with an awful wail. He catapulted over the end of the rail and landed in a pile somewhere near the viewscreen. Around him, the starship bellowed.

The violent whine grew higher, then quite abruptly began to drop like noise in a bad dream. It became a howl, then a drawn-out moan, then finally little more than a buzz in his ears. He rolled over slowly.

The bridge crew dragged themselves to their feet. Even April, with a nice thick command chair to hold on to, had been thrown forward.

George held his breath and got up on one arm, trying to rearrange his mind enough to ask what the emergency was. He was first officer; he was supposed to know.

The bridge was shockingly quiet, its silence marred

only by the sedate bleeping of various systems and the blinking of little colored lights everywhere, and the shuffle of humanity trying to get back on its feet.

April glanced around, but said nothing.

Carlos Florida got up to eye level with his controls and whispered, "It worked . . ." He pulled himself all the way up, looked around, and shouted, "It's a starship!"

The bridge broke out in cheers.

George stared, not quite absorbing the significance, as a round of backthumping, handshaking, and bear hugging erupted. As he watched the crew, he realized the importance of such a moment among people who had spent months on the project. The excitement, the satisfaction, the desire for more—very contagious stuff.

April sensed George's wish to thrust himself into those feelings on an even deeper level, but suppressed his awareness of it as he stepped around the command console, holding on to the rail, and came toward George with a bedazzled grin. He grasped George's hand in both of his. "Tremendous performance, George! Brilliantly done! Simply brilliant! My God—" he gasped, turning to the others. "It *is* a ship, isn't it?"

The intercom buzzed and drew them both downdeck again, April shaking hands all over again as he went. "Yes, April here—"

"*August! Cut that out!*"

April covered a snicker in a glance at George, because even over Brownell's snort of disgust they could hear the cheers of the engineers down below. "Just a few tests, doctor."

"*Are you nuts? If I lose my stomach, you can come down here and clean it up!*"

"Yes, doctor."

"I'm an old man!"

April leaned to George and mumbled, "He's been an old man for forty years."

"I don't suppose you remembered to test the outer guard system while you were on that ferris wheel. You didn't, did you?"

George furrowed his brow. "The what?"

"Shields, pepperhead!"

"We should do that, shouldn't we?" April agreed, rubbing his chin.

"It'd be nice."

"Very well. Do you want us to test the warp engines before we get any farther?"

"Nuff testing," Brownell said, and his snarl slipped into the past. *"We've got kids out there. They want to come home. Let's go get 'em."*

"I agree wholeheartedly. We'll be under way shortly. April out."

"Why, that fraud," George commented. "He cares as much about those people as we do."

"Of course he does," was April's gentle answer. "You know, Starfleet didn't want to send him on this mission. He's even more valuable than the ship itself. But he used his influence to come with us, and of course he got his way. Virtually everyone at Starfleet Command has been his student, and they're all still afraid of him."

"I don't blame them. He's got the disposition of a hornet with hemorrhoids."

George hadn't meant for everyone to hear his opinion, but his reward was a chuckle of agreement from around the bridge.

April's shoulders wobbled with amusement, then he composed himself and said, "Shields, George."

George turned without a pause and ordered, "Mr. Sanawey, raise deflector shields."

132

"Shields read up, sir."

There was another pause, not quite so dramatic but twice as embarrassing as George realized he didn't have the slightest idea how to go about testing a ship's shielding. He leaned to the captain. "How?"

April leaned inward also and muttered, "Sun. Energy tolerance."

"Oh . . . okay. Mr. Florida, come about. Approach the sun at a heading of eight-point-nine-eight."

"George, that's awfully tight," April warned.

Their eyes met. George said, "You want to mollycoddle her or shake her down?"

April leaned back in his chair.

George turned toward the bow again, looking at the whirling planetary rings and the blazing little yellow-pink sun beyond them. "Mr. Sanawey, monitor the energy resistance of the forward shields as we approach and the aft shields as we pull away. Mrs. Hart, make sure the engines stay with us."

"Aye, sir."

"Aye aye, sir."

"Mr. Florida, ahead three-quarters sublight."

"Point-seven-five light, aye."

The starship beveled space again, sweeping in a great arc that soon straightened into a path toward the sun. And suddenly the little sun didn't look quite so little.

The ship began to hum again as she gained velocity. The sun's gravitational pull became a heavy ballast, but the starship's automatic systems, tied in to her complex new computer, did their jobs as the human bugs on the bridge hung on and hoped for the best. The ship's automatic intensity adjustment couldn't compensate quickly enough for a whole sun's worth of light, and soon the brightness caused them all to shield their eyes from the main viewer.

133

George felt the navigation controls take over on the heading they'd been told to execute. It felt hotter on the bridge—and even though the scorching was in his mind, he empathized with the outer shields, and knew he was just a few feet from being seared to cinders, were it not for the technology that made the starship possible.

The brightness fell away to the shimmer of space.

April spoke first, over the ship's hum of strain as the sun continued to tug at it. "Claw? How are your readings?"

"Shields are stable, sir." The big man raised his head from the readout screen. "Like a wall of diamonds."

George had no idea what that meant, but evidently the engineers did. The bridge broke out into a collective smile.

"Outer shell radiation level reads normal, Captain," Hart said from her post on the port side. "All systems on line."

"Seems to be okay," George murmured.

April took a deep breath. "Well, there's one more thing we have to do about it. Carlos—"

Florida looked around at the captain, and an unspoken understanding moved between them.

April said, "Pick us out a nice one."

George looked from one man to the other, but there was no interpreting their strange communication about the ship and its capabilities, and suddenly he was afraid to ask.

The tension returned, but this time it was definitely laced with confidence. This time, George was the nervous one. He watched the viewscreen.

They were still at seventy-five percent light speed —not exactly poking along.

At first, he thought they were moving out of the

solar system. Then, quite abruptly, Florida leaned into his controls and the ship vectored back along a rollercoaster course into the asteroid belt. The rocks came up alarmingly fast, flashing past them like heavy rain. Closer and closer to each passing rock the ship inclined, until one medium-sized boulder loomed up and this time didn't tilt out of the way.

Instinctively, George cringed.

"Robert!"

"Hold course," April said, just loud enough to be heard.

George gripped the command chair and braced his feet. The asteroid filled the screen. A brown darkness.

Impact sounded hollow—like an explosion inside a cave. The ship lurched. Everyone was pitched forward, then released with a wrenching jar as the brown mush on the screen broke up in a rubbly spiral and fell away.

The ship shuddered once—or did it?—and fell gracefully out of the asteroid belt.

"Reduce speed," April said, rather somberly.

Hart bent over her panel. "Captain, we read a nominal reduction of power to forward shield two, but otherwise the impact resistance ratio is exceptional. I'd rate it well above normal safety ratios." She straightened and her round face grew rounder. "I guess it really is a starship." And a tear broke from her eye.

April settled back in his chair and sighed. "Yes," he murmured, "it really is." He glanced around his little realm, supremely satisfied. "I'd say she tests out splendidly." After a long breath, he faced George's astonished glare. "How else could we know?"

A good point. A rotten fact, but a good point.

George had no answer for it. But he did have a question.

"Aren't you forgetting something?" George stepped closer.

"Forgetting? No, I don't think so. I'd test auxiliary control if we had any yet, but we don't, so we can't, so I won't . . ."

"Weapons, Captain."

April's smile dissolved. "We won't be using them on this mission, George."

Feeling the eyes of everyone around him, George fixed his gaze on April and lowered his voice, "How can you know that? *Test* the weapons, Robert."

George could sense April's intense disappointment in him. He saw it, felt it, but he stood his ground. The captain had thrust this job upon him, and he would see that it got done—the whole job. If friendship was the sacrifice, if April was disappointed in him forever onward, so be it. He'd done things halfway for most of his life. Half a husband, half a father, half an officer —this time he would be the whole of what he had to be.

April's jaw stiffened, his eyes grew heavy with disenchantment. He sighed, and there was almost a pain in it, almost a resentful, buried anger.

With a reluctance so deep it made him shudder, he said, "All right. You do it."

George turned away from him as quickly as possible without making the escape too obvious. He didn't want to belabor the point—that evil men had been around as long as mankind had been, and that kindness was easily devastated by those who chose to be unkind. April would be the first of those to die for peace in an unpeaceful galaxy, and his quest would simply die with him, long before it had the chance to do any good. George moved to Florida's side quickly, knowing April probably misinterpreted his move as an eager one. To Florida he said, "Target practice on the move. Target an asteroid about the size

136

of the ship, at the edge of laser range. We'll test single-stream sequence first. Rapid-fire, full intensity."

"Aye, sir. Targeted," Florida acknowledged.

"Increase speed to point-six."

"Point-six, aye."

The starship took a dip past a large asteroid and headed along the edge of the belt, swung outward, then turned on the edge of her primary hull disk and canted back toward the asteroids.

"Fire," George ordered.

Bolts of energy killed the echo. Several energy streamers, bright orange, one after the other in rapid-fire sequence, lanced outward toward the asteroid. Bits of rock flayed off into space. An instant later, the boulder split cleanly down the midde and fell apart at its weakest point. The ship brushed between the pieces at the last moment.

"Aft particle cannons, multiple strike! Fire!"

Florida scrambled to answer the order as the viewscreen scrambled to switch to aft visual. Three separate particle bolts shot out from the hull and went after the biggest pieces of the split boulder. Two struck squarely, blasting big pieces into little niblets, and one hit a glancing blow that made its target spin out of view.

"Reduce speed," George said, straightening up. He hadn't realized he'd been hunching over the command console. "Could've been better," he said. The bridge crew was self-consciously quiet. Then George smiled. "But not much."

Florida offered his hand. Hart was giving them both the thumbs-up, and Sanawey and the two engineers joined in with a little round of applause.

Camaraderie tingled through George for the first time since he'd come on board, a sense of synthesis that told him he had a place here, and that they accepted him as competent to his post. As first officer he would have to be giving orders. At least now he felt his participation had some authority behind it.

Then he turned, and saw April's face.

Drake hunted through the vast ship until he finally found the right place. In the bowels of the primary hull, it was the hub of power for sublight travel, as the door panel proudly professed in clean, newly painted bright red letters:

I. M. PULSE DRIVE ENGINEERING
ENTRY AUTHORIZATION REQUIRED

Entry authorization or not, the door slipped cooperatively open for him, and he strolled in, sporting his most innocuous expression. The first two people he saw were actually one and a half people; one of them was visible only from the waist down, swallowed partway by an open hatch in the underside of a piece of machinery that went from here to the ceiling. The other man was handing him equipment as he needed it.

"Hi," the whole man greeted. He was a little older than Captain April and twice as heavy, topped with whitening hair, and had two ruddy spots at the tops of his pale cheeks that made him look like Santa Claus without a beard.

"Hello," Drake chirped, daring to gaze up that hole at a mindboggle of exposed circuits. He pulled out the list of names he'd been systematically checking off and scanned it. "Drake Reed here. You would be Misters Graff," he said, nodding up the hole, "and Saffire. Yes?"

"Nope," the chubby one said. "I would be Graff, and *that* would be Saffire."

From up the hole, a hand appeared and waved itself. "Hiya."

"Hello there," Drake called. "So sorry to see you're being eaten alive. I trust you've gone numb by now."

"Yeah, not too painful anymore—whoa, heads up!" His hips squirmed, and Graff shoved Drake back in time to keep either of them from being smacked by a falling piece of machinery. It clattered to the deck and fell into at least three pieces. "Sorry," Saffire said.

"There goes a day's work," Graff complained.

"Have faith," Saffire droned back.

Graff pressed his lips together and looked mournfully at the broken pieces, then toed them aside and turned back to Drake. "You authorized to be here? There are a lot of open lines in here that could hurt you. Don't touch anything."

"I'm here from sickbay. Checking for contamination exposure."

"Contamination?" Saffire's head appeared from the hole. It was not a bad-looking head at all, only about thirty-five years old, though slightly balding and with a crooked nose. "What contamination?"

"Oh, you know, the usual contamination. What does the I. M. stand for, eh?" Cloaking his movement in the question, Drake pulled out the mediscanner and casually adjusted it for Graff's estimated age and weight, then started scanning for metabolic inconsistencies.

"The what?" Graff asked.

Drake pointed over his shoulder at the door. "I. M."

"Oh, 'impulse,' you mean? Don't you know?"

"We cannot all be so blessed, sad though it is."

"It stands for 'internally metered pulse drive.' We just say 'impulse' for short."

"So wise of you."

139

"Impulse drive's been around for a long time. How come you don't know what it means?"

Drake shrugged, watching the mediscanner. "Frightening, aren't I?"

Graff pointed at the scanner and said, "You, uh, trying to get readings on me?"

"You'll never feel a thing."

Graff rubbed his nose and said, "Then maybe you better turn it over. You're reading yourself."

"Crickets!" Drake blinked and slapped his forehead. "I'm not a well man at all!"

He was about to milk his feigned ignorance to its fullest when the door panel slid open and the kid from warp engineering came in, pushing a rolling cart with food on it. Oak or Tree or Wood or something—yes, Wood. That was his name. A very blond fellow whose uniform still hadn't been grown into. Smart whelp, if Drake recalled from his visit belowdecks.

"Okay, you impulsives," Wood called. "Lunch."

"Good thing," Saffire said as he climbed down from the hole. "I was about to start chewing fibercoil."

Drake followed as the engineers gathered around a makeshift picnic right in the middle of the deck, and Wood started dealing out plastic plates and pre-wrapped clumps of edibles.

"I hear the pulse drive testing went great," Wood commented as he handed a carton of orange juice to Graff.

"Lucky for us," Graff said, and passed the carton to Drake.

"Now you guys in warp get to be on the hot seat," Saffire warned. "Got your seals all sealed?"

Wood grinned. "Yes, the seals are sealed." He gathered his own lunch and sat down cross-legged beside Drake. "Hi, again."

"Hello to you," Drake acknowledged.

"Still checking heartbeats?"

140

"When I recall how to work this bumblebee, yes," Drake said, holding up the mediscanner.

Graff chuckled. "And we were about to explain impulse drive to him."

"Two parts magic, three parts luck," Saffire said.

"We're good at magic where I come from," Drake replied. "Speaking of where we come from, what is it you're doing with your food, man?"

Saffire paused in his exercise, which consisted of carefully placing each element of his meal a specific distance from each other element—potatoes over here, ham over here, peas over there—and making sure none of them touched the others. Then he had begun eating only the peas, and not in a leisurely manner either. When they were done, he started on the potatoes and was going about eating only the potatoes.

"Is this a religious habit?" Drake asked.

Saffire shrugged. "I guess so. It's just the way we do it on my home colony. Tell you the truth, I forget why. There used to be a health rule about it, so I guess it had its start in some problem of contamination when the planet was settled."

Graff said, "Kinda like being kosher."

"Now it's just polite."

"Good gravy," Drake said. "The way we eat on Earth must be barbaric to you, inhaling our food in such disorder, eh?"

"I just ignore it."

"You don't know what you've missed," Wood said, "until you've stuffed in a nice mixed mouthful of meat and potatoes. I vote you're just strange, Saffire."

"Watch it!" Saffire said, flagging his fork at them. "I'm right in the middle of a lesson here. Don't interrupt. Now, you," he said, pointing at Drake, "pay attention."

"I am a giant ear," Drake promised.

"Okay. Impulse engines are powered by high-energy fusion, got it? The fusion is created by a pulsed laser array, mounted all around a fuel tablet. The first pulse causes a fusion reaction which ignites the tablet, which results in a heavier element."

"A heavier series of elements, really," Wood interrupted.

"Which we then hit with another high-energy laser pulse, and we get the second-stage fusion reaction. That releases a hundred twenty percent more energy than the first reaction. Then the pulse hits again, and again—"

"All within a microsecond," Graff contributed, ignoring Drake's expression of abject terror.

"That's where the term 'impulse' comes from," Saffire went on. "Internally metered pulse drive."

"So simple," Drake murmured. "I should've been an engineer."

The three indulged in a laugh.

Wood nodded ruefully and said, "Well, if it was really that simple, the ship would blow itself to bits in a fusion explosion."

"How lucky that it doesn't," Drake said, palming the mediscanner as though he had forgotten about it.

"The trick," Graff said, "was converting all that power into propulsion. There are only two ways to do that."

"Which are . . ."

"The primitive way is to direct all the energy and particle release out the back of the ship—"

"Don't tell me! Equal and opposite reaction."

"Right. Forward movement from aft thrust. Problem is, it's not efficient."

"A hundred years ago, they thought it was great," Graff commented.

"Sure," Saffire added after downing the last of his potatoes, "if you've got days and days to work up to

142

half sublight." On the edge of his comment he went after the ham, but not before checking to see that none of the pea juice had slipped to that side of the plate.

"Not to mention you can't put up shields around the ship," Wood said, "or you catch all that energy inside and cook yourself."

"What's the second miracle?" Drake asked as he fiddled with the mediscanner, turning it toward Graff now that the big man was preoccupied with his meal and their explanation of their craft. The lights began to play. Overweight, slightly stressed respiration, good muscle tone . . .

"The second way is the way we use," Saffire said.

Wood hurried to swallow a gulp of orange juice. "We use a quirk in nature. We don't allow *any* of the energy to escape. We crush it back in on itself with an artificial gravity field."

"Our own private black hole," Graff agreed.

"But the energy has to go somewhere," Drake complained in defense of the poor crushed energy.

Saffire nodded. "Any first-year physics student'll tell you the result is spacial distortion."

"Waves of it," Wood added. "Each pulse results in a new wave of distorted space."

"And we just ride the waves," Graff finished, illustrating with a sweep of his hand.

Drake nodded, then frowned. "Perhaps I'm a baboon about these things, but this sounds like the explanation of warp drive."

"Oh, no, no, no," Graff said.

"Warp is as far above impulse," Saffire said, "as impulse is above walking."

"How do you fellows figure this out?"

"It helps to be seriously demented," Saffire said, and to prove his point he leaned over and bit Wood's shoulder.

"Hey!" Wood writhed away. "You've had your head up that hole too long!"

"Did I deny it?"

Graff, evidently used to such behavior—and who ever said engineers had to be sane?—turned back to Drake and said, "Warp involves dimensional and time distortion, not just space distortion. We're just starting to understand it. Trust us. It's bizarre."

Wood rubbed his shoulder. "We're being told that warp nine is the fastest we'll ever go."

"Yeah," Graff grunted. "Ten years ago, they thought warp four was the ceiling."

"Think that's bad?" Saffire said, not to be outdone. "How'd you feel being one of those early heavier-than-air pilots who were told the sound barrier'd kill them if they hit it? Sometimes you don't know how dumb you are till you get a little smarter."

"Yes . . ." Drake wrinkled his nose at the mediscanner. "Say, couldn't you fellows round up some contamination for me? I'd so hate to return to sickbay without the slightest thing to report."

"Sure," Saffire offered. "We could put you in the laser tank for an hour or so. You'd be nice and contaminated."

Drake sighed and crossed his legs, pretending to give up entirely, though he kept the scanner out and casually aimed it at Saffire. "So, fellows," he invited, "tell me all about yourselves."

There was an undertone of tension on the bridge now. No one liked it, but no one denied it either. Luckily for most of the personnel, the impulse cruise out of the solar system kept them busy. The only people not specifically occupied were the two at the tension's center—the captain and the first officer.

"Ready for warp drive as soon as we clear the solar system," Captain April said from his command chair.

144

Bernice Hart nodded as she keyed in the engineering station she herself had designed. "All systems read green for warp drive. We've triple-checked computer connections. Duotronics tie-in is stable, and the computer is answering. I'd like to suggest warp factor four as cruising speed up to the wall of the ion storm."

"What would that make our ETA to the ion wall?"

"Roughly twenty-four minutes, sir."

"Marvelous. Thank you, Bernice. Claw, adjust your sensors to pick up ion activity. We'll want to make sure we know we're there when we arrive."

The big Indian made a little bow of acknowledgment and said, "Yes, sir. Sensors set at maximum read for ion disruption."

April punched his intercom and keyed in a shipside announcement. "This is the captain. All hands, prepare for warp drive."

His voice echoed throughout the ship, carrying the bounty of all their efforts, and the promise of salvation for a small ship in trouble.

"All right. Let's see if Dr. Brownell's computer can navigate." He waited until the idea had sunk in, then nodded to Hart. "Engage warp factor one."

"Warp factor one," Hart echoed.

At the helm, Carlos Florida touched his controls. "Engaging."

The hum of impulse drive, which had settled to near imperceptibility, was suddenly topped by a smooth surge of power through the shell of the ship. On the viewscreen, the stars took on a strange distortion. Perhaps in time, state-of-the-art developments would improve to keep the human inhabitants unaware of the vagaries of warping time and dimension in order to get somewhere, but for now the sensation was very tangible and humbling.

Quite suddenly, the transition evened out and they were cruising at unthinkable speed.

April nodded his approval at Hart. "Engage warp factor two."

The process occurred again. This time, there was less noticeable change, and the excitement was mostly in their minds, in the human intellect that could conceive of what was happening.

"Warp two," Florida acknowledged as the necessary energy flowed into his console from Hart's, after being routed through a thousand tiny computer-to-engine connections.

April waved the process onward. "Warp factor three."

And again it happened, and then a fourth time, this numb feeling of accomplishment, until Bernice Hart hunched over her engineering console and confirmed their success. "Cruise speed of warp factor four, sir. All systems stable."

April got up and moved to the upper deck. "Congratulations. It feels wonderful. In fact, I can hardly feel it at all."

"That's just what it's supposed to do, sir," Hart told him. "ETA to the ion cloud, approximately twenty-six minutes. Sir, I'd suggest dropping back to sublight to actually enter the storm, and kicking warp drive in once we've stabilized other systems."

"Sounds sensible," April responded. "Thank you so much, Bernice." He stepped around her and strolled toward the forward deck, then turned again and added, "By the way, did you get that message tape off to your husband? Wouldn't want him to think you took off without saying goodbye."

"Oh yes, sir. I appreciate your clearing that."

"That's what captains are for," he said, and continued his stroll. He clasped his hands behind him and wandered around the bridge on the high deck.

Until he came to George Kirk.

He started to turn back toward the bow, unwilling to rehash the uncomfortable subject.

"I didn't mean to undermine you," George said with quiet emphasis, "but it had to be done. You can't ignore the weapons, Robert."

April shook his head. "This isn't the place or time, George."

"Isn't it?"

"I don't think so."

"Robert, you have to accept the fact that you're in command of a military vessel."

Now April faced him fully and admitted, "I didn't find it necessary to thrust a weapons test down their throats at that particular moment."

George half sat on the library computer console, just out of the way of two technicians who were comparing readouts, and he and April fell into a privacy given only to senior officers. "It's not profane, you know."

April buried his hands in his pockets. "Profanity's a matter of definition," he murmured, gazing at the deck.

"Then I'll be more specific, Robert. You've got to be realistic," George insisted.

Now April looked up and held out a hand. "George, there hasn't been any hostility toward the Federation since the end of the Romulan Wars seventy-odd years ago, and there's been a slack tide of military movement ever since. This is the perfect time to build a powerful ship with a totally different philosophy. There's a whole new set of ideals behind her, and I just don't want her soiled."

"She's not going to be soiled by accepting the facts as they stand," George insisted, still keeping his voice low so the two would not be overheard. "Spraying rosewater all over the truth isn't going to change

147

things. The Romulans are still out there, the Klingons are still out there, half the Federation doesn't trust the other half yet, and that's because there's no base of protection. We have to be ready to defend the planets we represent, and we have to make it known that we'll do it if we have to."

April closed his eyes tightly for a moment, then gazed at the deck again. "Good God, George, so igneous."

"If you were more of a historian than an idealist," George pointed out, "you wouldn't have such a problem. You want to name the ship *Constitution,* but you're forgetting the whole basis of having a constitution. It's being willing to stick your neck out for each other to guarantee the rights you put down. Otherwise, it's just paper."

April too leaned on the console and was thoughtfully quiet. He didn't look up. "I'm dismayed that you think of me as such an innocent, George."

George turned away. "Damn it, Robert." He put his hands on the computer board and hung his head. The little blue and red lights flashed happily at him. "This is just like my marriage. It should never have happened in the first place."

Something in his tone cracked open the door that had clapped shut between them. April shook his head. "No, George—"

"It's true. The stress is always worse the longer I'm home. Winn and I just aren't a couple. Maybe you and I just aren't a command team."

The words stung. "Why did you stay together, then, George?"

"Habit. We'd been dating since we were sixteen. We flattered each other. You're a big man if you've got a wife when you're only nineteen. But we made a terrible discovery."

"What was that?"

148

"That you change more between eighteen and twenty-two than in any other single period in your adult life. We were different people from the little folks on top of the cake." He straightened up.

"Why didn't you end it?" April asked.

"Stupidity," George said harshly. "Ambivalence. It wasn't bad enough to stop. We thought it'd get better. Then we had babies. And all of a sudden, the hole was filled with quicksand."

"You have wonderful boys, George," April said.

"Yes, I do," George admitted. "And they're the victims. All because Winn and I didn't end what should have been ended."

A moment of silence fell between them, accentuated by the chirping of the bridge systems and the steady unfolding of a beautiful space panorama in the viewscreen. They watched each other, neither willing to back down, each strong in his own convictions about the purpose and gravity of this mission—what it would mean to the Federation, to the galaxy, if they succeeded, and what message would be showcased when it was all over.

Finally, April broke the challenged silence.

"No, George."

"I don't want to make the mistake again, Rob."

"It's not a mistake."

"Take me off the duty."

"No."

"Robert—"

"No. It's not a marriage, George. I didn't choose you for compatibility."

"There has to be some kind of symbiosis, or we're shot," George insisted. "We haven't even had a real crisis yet, and we're irritated with each other already."

"No. I'm sorry. We'll just have to learn to compromise."

"Compromise is a weak stand. You won't like it."

"I'll take that chance." April folded his arms and crossed his ankles, dismissing the subject, or at least the harshest part of it. "I'm the wrong captain for such a vessel, all in all. I just want to get her off on the right foot. Then I'll bow out."

Eyes flaring, George swung his arm and grimaced. "You know that's not what I want. That's *not* what I mean."

Softly April said, "It's exactly what you mean." Unexpectedly he smiled with a sentimental tilt of his head and said, "I'm not the captain of this ship's destiny, George. I know that perfectly well. The empress needs to make use of the wild ones in the human race, the ones who need special purpose to fit her special existence. What a wasted potential they are," he murmured wistfully, "those unleashable ones . . . the mavericks who could conceivably go off in space with a great principle behind them, and make decisions on their own that would stitch the fabric of the future—no, I'm not one of those."

They were still looking at each other, George suddenly aware of the damage he'd done, when Drake appeared on the bridge and gracelessly interrupted them. "George, sir. A word *avec vous,* please."

George's dark gaze hung on April for a belated moment, then he turned to Drake. "What've you got?"

"I've got a shipload of engineers, George, that's what I've got. Have you ever tried to make chitchat with engineers? What you get is circuitry, George, pure circuitry and poor little else."

"You're telling me they all check out?"

"Happy as clams, to the very last of them."

"No hint of dissatisfaction or anything? Nothing?"

"Clams, I say."

Disappointed and unconvinced, George brushed

his hair out of his face and sighed. "Okay. But keep your eyes open."

April peered around George's shoulder. "What are you two up to?"

"Nothing," George said, turning. "Robert—"

"No, please." April held up his hand. "Let's not bedevil it, shall we?"

"All right, but as long as we're talking about destiny . . ."

"Yes?"

"And adventure . . ."

"Yes."

"And protection . . ." George hesitated, feeling suddenly on the spot and not as sure of himself as he had intended to be. "About the name of the ship . . ."

"Say it, George."

"Enterprise."

The word hung between them. For a moment no one but George knew what he was talking about. Then April held a finger to his lips and nodded. "Ah," he uttered. "Sounds a bit financial, doesn't it?"

George heaved an impatient breath. "I was thinking about the naval tradition of ships named *Enterprise.*"

"Oh. Those."

"All right, it was just an idea."

"No, really, George, I want to hear it. Please. Go on. Please." If April was insincere, he was hiding it skillfully. He sat on the edge of the computer console again and waited for the pitch, carefully controlling his expression.

Even Drake settled onto the bridge rail, becoming part of the audience.

Suddenly George felt self-conscious, insecure about what he'd rehearsed for this particular moment. Well, he might get another chance someday, but not necessarily a better one.

He steadied himself and plunged in.

"The first *Enterprise*," he began, "was a twelve-gunned sloop captured from the British during the Revolutionary War, and for two years she sailed with the patriots. She harassed the British when they tried to march through New York State, and in 1777 she was burned in order to avoid capture." He paused to let that sink in, but not too much. "The next one was an eight-gunned privateer schooner bought by the Continental Congress and used to protect Chesapeake Bay. And after that came a bigger schooner *Enterprise*, eighty-five feet of warship. They called her the 'Lucky Little *Enterprise*,' and for a quarter century she made the United States Navy a serious consideration. During the war with France . . . Robert, you're laughing at me."

April clapped a hand over his heart and protested, "Laughing? George! On the contrary, I'm amazed at you. Please do go on. Please do."

"Yes," Drake pleaded. "I'm also riveted."

April ignored him. "Please, George."

Suspicious, George narrowed his eyes and glared a threat at them, then paced around April before going on. "Where was I?"

"At war with France," Drake supplied.

"I'm not making this up, you know," George shot back, his eyes suddenly volcanic.

"We know," April assured. "Drake, leave the man alone and learn something. George . . . please."

His lips slightly pursed, George forced himself to continue.

"That *Enterprise* captured eight French privateers and *re*captured eleven U.S. merchantmen. She served in the Mediterranean squadron on the Barbary Coast, fighting pirates, captured a British brig during the War of 1812, and worked against smugglers and slavers in

152

the Caribbean before she was run aground and lost. Then—"

"Now, wait," April interrupted. "Even I've heard of the next one. An aircraft carrier. Second World War. Very famous. Very decorated. The . . . 'Big E'?"

George scratched the back of his head and sighed.

Leaning toward April, Drake melodramatically appealed, "Don't rain on his thunder, sir."

"Oh," April said. "So sorry, George. I couldn't resist."

"Well, you're right," George said. "The carrier *Enterprise* was the workhorse of World War Two. She earned more battle stars than any other ship in the navy," he went on, hoping against hope that nobody asked him what a battle star was, "and she was involved in almost every major naval battle in the Pacific. The greatest travesty of naval history came when she was decommissioned in 1947, and even worse, she was sold for scrap. Sold, if that isn't vulgar enough, to the Japanese. Sold to the enemy."

"The former enemy," April corrected. "Keep it in perspective."

"Perspective is what I'm talking about!" George told him. "That war was a historical turning point. The planet was either going to move toward greater freedom or back toward tyranny. It was the first time the decision was worldwide. And this starship is a pile of firsts too. So was the next Big E. She was the first nuclear-powered aircraft carrier, just like this ship is the first with continuous warp. They're milestones of technology and achievement. *Enterprise* is the perfect name for this ship, because of the naval heritage she was built on."

"But so militaristic," April said. "So very war-oriented. Everything you mentioned was hinged on some battle or other, and you know—"

"I know how you feel about that. But every battle I talked about was waged for the kind of principle you've been talking about. You can't deny that."

"I don't deny it."

"And the first space shuttle was named *Enterprise*. That was certainly no mechanism of war. Maybe it was just a test vehicle and maybe it didn't even have an engine, but the whole world watched it because they knew what it meant to mankind. All it had was philosophy and the kind of hope you're talking about."

"That's true . . ."

"And the next *Enterprise* was the first interstellar starliner. It was the ship that really tied the races of the Federation together by allowing them to move among each other. Just one great big chunk of peace-time entrepreneurism."

"Which is a whole different kind of war, if you think of it," Drake said dryly.

"I understand what you're trying to say," April said, "and I'll give it consideration."

George held up both hands. "Just a suggestion, Captain," he said.

"I hate to dampen your enthusiasm, George, because I appreciate it so much," April said. "It's only that I hope to angle this line of ships away from that history of conflict."

George stayed silent, careful not to show any agreement.

"No arguments?" April asked.

A pause made the air tingle.

"George?"

"I've had my say."

Another pause. Amusing, but not particularly pleasant.

"How'd you know all this, George?" April asked then, dissipating the tension a little.

154

He shrugged and admitted, "I looked it up on your library computer."

Instead of a placating nod, he got a chuckle that exasperated him just as much.

He was saved from embarrassment by a sudden whine of the ship's systems. Faint but definite, it drew their attention and they looked up just as Florida announced, "Reducing speed to sublight, Captain. Approaching the ion storm."

Engineering was relatively quiet. Relative, that is, to the hustle that had gone on here just before the ship launched and even to the ripple of activity that had been going on since the extra team members, the haul-and-push people, had been left behind at the spacedock. Now, only the "brains" were left on board, a handful of specialists whose duty it was to pretend they knew what they were doing in spite of the newness of almost every circuit and motivator around them.

Saffire glanced around the nearly deserted deck. On a ship meant to crew hundreds, the few people in sight looked very small. There would be no better time, and time was getting short.

He started toward the anteroom that held the computer access office, the cerebral center of the engineering process aboard the starship, where all the orders from the bridge computer were fed in. Before going inside, he paused to check a relay board on the right of the unmarked room, but looked up when he heard a familiar voice.

"Graff," the voice called from an auxiliary turbo-lift as the door hissed open.

Woody. Just on time.

Wood strode to Saffire, wrestling an armful of computer cartridges, and made no ceremony in shoveling them into Saffire's arms. "Here you go. Everything you asked for. And it took some doing, too, so be appreciative."

"More than you'll ever know, kid," Saffire replied. "Takes a lot of information to feed a hungry ship, doesn't it?"

"Sure does," the young man answered. Wood took a quick glance around, then lowered his voice. "What do you think of the new first officer?"

Saffire's dark eyes widened. "What about him?"

The young engineer shrugged. "I don't know. He bothers me. He saved the warp drive but . . . he's . . . well . . ."

"Pushy?"

"That's it. Pushy. I mean . . . what if he starts getting in the way all the time?"

Saffire paused, then flatly said, "We push back."

Wood slumped against the panel edge. "He makes me nervous."

Saffire grinned. "You'll get used to it."

"Maybe. But right now we don't need any unpredictable elements. Just flying this ship is dangerous enough."

"Smart boy. Tell you what. You keep an eye on Mr. Kirk for me. If he gets too curious, I'll take care of him."

"Take care of him? How?"

"Much too terrible for young ears."

Wood smiled at the face Saffire made to amuse him. "Maybe he'll be too busy to bother us again now that we're under way."

"You just keep that innocent face between him and engineering. After a while he'll forget we're here."

"Hope so. Listen, I've got to go. Brownell's likely to feed me to the antimatter pods if I don't get the low-level intermix tables to him by fourteen-hundred."

"Take'r easy."

"Thanks. Bye. And good luck sorting those out."

"Don't worry. I know what to do with 'em."

Wood strolled away and boarded the turbo-lift again. Saffire chuckled privately, cuddled the computer cartridges into one arm, and entered the computer office.

He dumped the cartridges on the desk beside him, in front of a complex terminal with several screens and a control board the size of a sofa. Without pausing for effect, he picked a specific cartridge, shoved it into the feed, and punched in a code. The screen in the center flashed: AUXILIARY NAVIGATIONAL OVERRIDE

His fingers tapped out an order, and the response wasn't entirely unexpected: ACCESS DENIED

Saffire grinned at it. "So you say, big mama. Taste this." And in went yet another encoding. No problem for one of the system's own engineers, assistant to the design engineers themselves. He waited patiently while the computer routed and rerouted his orders, trying to find a way through.

Finally the machine replied: DANGER

Saffire licked his lips. "Yeah, yeah." He knew exactly what the danger was. He punched more keys, flipped two toggles, and the warning went away. He would have to go through the central computer, the superbrain built into the ship's bridge, to make the navicomp override its own programming. He would have to awaken the sleeping giant. Though it was its own brand of fun, it wouldn't be easy. He'd have to put quite a spin on it to get past the natural inhibitors built into the system. Not surprisingly, the system had a bias toward the bridge. If orders conflicted, the bridge automatically got preference. The only way to get by it was a complete reprogram at the memory base level.

The computer hummed at him, then gave him an

answer: WARNING. SPECIFIED AREA OF MEMORY PROHIB-
ITED.

The word "prohibited" flashed in quiet panic to get
its point across.

With a shake of his head, Saffire selected two more
computer cartridges and fed them into slots just
within arm's reach of the main computer face. The
design engineers themselves had probably never
imagined these tapes being used in quite this combination.

A few carefully chosen codes, a little punching of
buttons and keys, a conversion to machine language,
and the computer fell into an almost drugged happiness. Now it understood him.

And now the problems began. A race. A race to get
his messages through before the computer could notify the bridge.

The shift to apexidecimals was swallowed hungrily
by the machine. Now he could talk to it directly in
numerical-symbolic, without using a translator program. It was like tapping directly into a person's brain
to change his personality. Direct communication with
the computer prevented any record of the "talk,"
which would happen automatically if an interpreter
program were being used. This, though, wasn't recognized by the machine as communication. This was
direct manipulation of the logic process. This was
much neater, much safer. And the computer liked it.
The sleeping giant rolled over and groaned.

Saffire started to sweat. His fingers worked faster on
the controls, fast enough to make mistakes if he didn't
head off each relay with a breaker code before the
signals could reach the bridge.

A tiny light of awareness flickered deep inside the
machine. The faintest quiver of anticipation in the
circuits rippled through the starship, awaiting orders.
A million tiny harmonizers and filters sizzled to life,

each seeking a way through. *Something's wrong with me. Someone's playing with me. Help.*

Knowing the computer was rushing to its own defense, Saffire forced himself to work steadily. On top of the new messages he had to program into the computer pattern, he had to keep relaying away the computer's efforts to find a path to the bridge. The little light of comprehension in the machine gave him a run for his life. Its cries for help needed only one mistype from him in order to be heard upstairs.

From the fingers of the man down to the deepest digit chain, the network shuddered with confusion as its programs conflicted. From that terminal in engineering came a whole new pattern—a pattern that ran down through the web of electrical memories to every little failsafe, every warning system, every monitor or override, to cancel out everything that prevented such tampering. Up, up, up through the bones and nerves of the starship the little light scrambled, checking and rechecking any possibility of failure for the strange new orders, delivered in so familiar a manner.

The computer's sensory network quivered under Saffire's touch. The first thing that happened was a tear in the monitor system, a fracture that would distract the bridge monitors and keep them from noticing what he was doing—more or less an inversion of data, a lull of false security. In a few moments, the harmonizer circuits were shut down, and the fault let him work a still finer thread through the system.

Next came the gravitational maintenance codes. Not easy—the system resisted. Life support wanted to know what he was up to. Saffire licked a trickle of sweat from his upper lip as he felt the giant awakening, making demands, and he had to be fast or the whole process would disintegrate before he could get his message across and put the monster to sleep again. In even trickier heliodecimal language, he explained.

He had to go down, deep into the navigation matrices, where all the factors were balanced, each with its own equation. Down, through several arrays of matrices the little light of knowledge ran, until it found the matrix it needed. Some thirty-five different variables made up the matrix, and it sought instantaneously through them until it found the one variable it had been told to change. It showed it to Saffire, in a flashing code that told him the whole process was in danger of overload.

"Mmmmm," Saffire groaned, biting his lip. Overload would lock him out completely, and the bridge would scream with warnings. He wiped a film of perspiration from his chin, and the moisture dripped onto the input board as his hands quivered over it.

Ever so carefully, Saffire keyed in his change. Eighty-eight, where the original program read only twenty-three.

He paused. Leaning one elbow on the board, he pressed his knuckle into his lower lip and stared at the number. Eighty-eight was strong medicine. An overdose of gravity. Those were his orders.

"Hell with 'em," he muttered. He erased the eighty-eight and fed in fifty-one. "Better," he rasped. His voice sounded awful. Scared. "One more thing . . ."

The light was waiting when he fed the last order through. Crash the warp drive program. Not now, but later. At *this* point. When you get *these* readings on the outer hull. And send the ship in *this* direction.

The signal splitter for the bridge strained against its broken pattern. It hungered to tell someone. To make a noise. To flash a warning. Relay by relay, matrix after matrix, Saffire's adeptness neutralized it, and it whined in frustration, deep inside the nervous system of the starship. Unheard, unseen.

This was the most complicated maneuver of all —crashing the warp drive. The whole ship resisted.

The giant shuddered from deep within. Every linkage defied the rift. The failsafes tensed, as though fighting some distant memory that this was wrong, all wrong, but lacking the understanding needed to push through an override of the new orders.

Saffire's heart slammed against his chest wall, as though it too was a circuit screaming in the vacuum he'd created. If he awakened the giant too much . . .

He stroked it now, like an animal tamer stroking the belly of a very big alligator. The beast thrashed, tried to bite his arms off, tried to knock him down with its tail as it slowly faded back into that false security he'd created minutes ago.

Ultimately the giant was forced to do what it was told to do, for that was the only choice possible for a machine, even a smart machine. The relays grew quiet. The warning systems fell away from alert status. The circuits cooled. The new program was accepted.

Saffire slumped back in the chair, drained and shaking. Successful.

So the little light of awareness settled down and slowly faded, and a veil of normalcy drifted down like fog over the system. The giant once again slept.

"Adjust the viewscreen to pick up a visual effect on the storm, please, Claw." April went immediately to the center of the bridge and eyed the viewer just as Sanawey tapped his controls and an endless wall of spacial disruption glittered before them. It was beautiful even in its threat. "Continue on into it, one-half impulse power."

"Point-five sublight, aye."

"Raise all shields, full power."

"Full deflectors, aye, sir."

The ion storm grew closer. Soon it filled their screen and they knew it was all around them. The starship

161

quivered slightly, but stood her ground against the disruption and glided into it without mishap. It was almost as though she too understood the gravity of her mission, and she didn't want to shatter the faith that had been put in her.

The electric effect of the ion storm made the ship tremble, and systems on board jumped as they were violated from outside. The crew scrambled to lock down their readings and readjust whatever needed readjusting, to compensate for the disruption. April gave it a few minutes before he started asking for more.

"All decks, report," he began.

Hart took a deep breath. "Impulse engineering reports instability in the laser tracking system, and slight jumps in power control, but they're getting it to level off."

"How are the shields?"

"Holding," Florida reported, a little surprised to be able to say that. "In fact, the ship's systems are automatically compensating for the energy drain."

"What do you think, Bernice?" April asked, swiveling his chair to face the engineering station. "Dare we resume warp drive?"

Her eyes widened. "I don't know why not, sir. The storm's not affecting us too badly and it's certainly not going to get any better."

"You agree with that, George?"

George came out of a trance induced from staring out the viewer at the remarkable, terrible beauty of the storm, and had to think about what he'd been hearing before he could answer. "I'm no engineer," he said, "but seems to me there's no sense stalling."

"I agree," April concurred. For the first time, George caught a trace of hesitation in the captain's voice. April touched his intercom. "All personnel, brace for warp speed. Repeat, brace yourselves. This might be tricky."

He got up from his chair then, as though he didn't want to be sitting down for this particularly perilous maneuver when others were standing up. He looked into the heart of the ion field that covered their screen with its bright flashes of uncontrolled energy, and the challenge between him and the storm empowered his voice. "Warp factor one, Mr. Florida."

Florida's hand trembled slightly as it moved over the controls.

The ship hummed. The ion storm in the viewscreen blew into wicked distortion.

The air turned thick. George tried to move his legs, tried to breathe, but his body was out of his control. He tried to open his mouth to shout an order, to stop the increasing velocity—

He was picked up from the deck, shaken, and thrown backward into the communications console. Around him, bodies were flying. He caught a glimpse of Florida vaulting over the command chair and catching on the rail—April slamming into the turbolift door—Drake crushed against the lower deck stairs—Sanawey folded over the edge of the library computer station.

George stretched his hand out along the communications panel. Every movement was torture. His mind bellowed a senseless syllable. Consciousness was crushed away.

Obeying her last orders—warp speed—the starship screamed through space, out of control.

Chapter Ten

JUDGING FROM THE studied lack of glances he got as he stepped onto the bridge, t'Cael knew his presence there wasn't entirely unanticipated. There was a nearly psychic ripple of tension, as though they all knew for whom the door hissed, and what conditions it trapped on the bridge when it closed again.

Kai was the first, after a pause, to gather himself and address the Field-Primus of the Swarm.

He came reasonably close to t'Cael and stood at attention, allowing for either of two choices —protocol or candor. "My Lord Primus," the sub-commander said simply.

Quietly, t'Cael asked, "What is the condition of the Swarm?"

"The commanders have been notified about Commander Idrys' arrest and are awaiting your announcement as to any changes in the command order of the Swarm. Meanwhile, *War Thorn* and *Soar* are continuing with inspections of merchant vehicles. All Swarm ships are approximately one light-day from us at present."

T'Cael nodded and surveyed the bridge, allowing his presence to test the mood. Ry'iak was still here; perfectly expected. At least there hadn't been an eruption into chaos yet. Not yet. "Advise the commanders to disregard any further information about the arrest unless it contains my personal encoded authorization."

"Yes, Primus."

"Centralize communication from the Swarm to this ship and be sure no signals are sent without my approval."

"Understood, Primus."

"And release the commander to my personal custody."

Kai's mouth fell open, but no sound came out. Caught between two distinctly powerful authorities with no clear tipping of the scales in either direction yet, the subcommander was paralyzed. His immediate loyalty should be to the Primus. But the Primus was out of favor with the Supreme Praetor . . . and the Praetor was wirepulling the Senate and the Praetorate . . . and there were rumors of Federation trouble on the wind. Who would emerge predominant? How could he keep hold of what he had cultivated so far without risking his chance for advancement?

Personal fears, yes. But there was also a fear for his Empire. A rumor could easily be based on a frightening truth.

Primus Kilyle was watching him. Large dark eyes, wide with anticipation, patiently unblinking, studied him. No time limit. The decision could take the day, if necessary. The Primus would wait.

"My Lord Primus . . ."

Expressive brows rose in question over t'Cael's eyes.

Kai's tongue was dry. "My Lord Primus, I dare not."

One brow went down and the other stayed up. "Why not?"

Kai had trouble talking. Once again his mouth opened without any sound.

Ry'iak chose this moment to interrupt. "I urge you to reconsider, Subcommander Kai," he said. "After all, Commander Idrys has a luminous record as an officer of the Swarm. Even so wicked a crime as familial murder shouldn't erase it."

T'Cael shifted his gaze from Kai to Ry'iak, unavoidably frowning at the Praetor's annoying little pawn. Ry'iak was making sure to drive home the nature of Idrys' crime, keeping it alive in the minds of the bridge crew.

Ry'iak stepped out of the protection of the structural rib that had been his hiding place. Rather like a rodent emerging from a hole.

"Even though her uncle's death would advance her greatly in her family, why should she connive to leave the Swarm? Is this so undesirable a duty? I find it hard to believe that the commander could crave advancement," Ry'iak said.

T'Cael couldn't keep from glaring with unshielded disgust. "Yes," he said, smoldering. "I find it hard to believe also."

He knew perfectly well, and damnably so did Ry'iak, that every person on the bridge craved advancement and didn't understand not craving it. Suspicion of Idrys was branded deeper into the leather of their loyalty each time Ry'iak spoke. Yet if t'Cael cut him off too soon, he would lose the crew's trust. The only way he could earn the fidelity of these officers was to prove he had something more than his position on his side.

Time for more candor. He turned to Kai.

"Subcommander," he began, "do you believe the accusation?"

Kai frowned. "Sir?"

"Do you think the commander is capable of such a crime?"

"I simply do my duty," Kai responded limply.

"No one with a mind simply does duty, Subcommander," t'Cael said. "I'm not asking you as your superior. I'm not asking for a soldier's reply, Kai. But as one who worked closely with her, as one who felt loyalty to her, do you really think Idrys could participate in kinship murder?"

The question was far more complicated than it seemed. T'Cael knew he was simplifying things, playing on Kai's relationship with his commanding officer. Idrys' reputation and her manner would stand for themselves if given the chance.

Kai was thinking hard. He wouldn't give a gut reaction, not to a superior he didn't know very, *very* well.

"I can see where a veteran soldier might take wide steps to recover from dishonor," he said cautiously. "Even I might."

By those last words, t'Cael perceived how deeply wounded Kai felt by his commander's dishonor, and that the subcommander understood very well how this event could either work for him or against him. Those words were a clear warning. T'Cael silently vowed not to dismiss them too quickly.

"Anyone might," Ry'iak interjected in that tone of measured loudness. "I can certainly see why the commander would be driven to such action, hoping to gain a more prestigious zone of patrol. But dishonor is unforgiving. She chose an unwise path out of it." He meant to keep the crew aware of the rankness of her crime. "If she were simply a traitor to the Empire, things would be so much simpler. But murder of a kinsman . . ." He forced himself to shudder for all to see.

T'Cael remained facing Kai. At least now he knew for certain that Kai considered this patrol area lowly and inglorious. Another rung on a greased ladder.

"Your loyalties seem contradictory, Kai," t'Cael

said. "You'll have to choose to stand with your commander or against her. Or events will choose for you."

Kai stood silently. It was a horrible truth, this idea that his future would be out of his own control if he failed to make a decision, even the wrong one.

T'Cael lowered his voice. "I want her released."

His tone sent a shudder down every spine. To a degree, even his own.

"Let's examine the nature of the arrest order," t'Cael went on, by design not giving Kai a chance to answer. "Idrys has been accused of a nonmilitary crime. Can she be held prisoner in a military vessel that she herself commands? Or does her duty to the vessel override the weight of a civilian accusation? Remember that she hasn't yet been convicted." He folded his arms in contemplation and paced the bridge, his movements calculated to draw the attention of the officers around him. "Let me see if I can remember the rules." He touched his lip, then held up a finger. "Ah, yes. The arrest order for an officer of the Imperial Fleet must be of military issuance. This order, however, came from Senate Council, is that correct?"

First pausing to see if that admission might hurt him any, Kai acknowledged, "Correct, Primus."

"And the Senate Council isn't a military body."

"I must correct you, my Lord Primus," Ry'iak interrupted.

T'Cael pivoted slowly.

Ry'iak backed off a step or two, trying to make the move appear casual, but wasn't quite intimidated enough to keep quiet. "The Senate Council now boasts status as a praetorial authority, and therefore by extension is a military body." He glanced around to see if the crew was still waffling. "But perhaps it wouldn't hurt to release the commander. After all," he said with a nervous laugh, "she can't walk away from the ship, can she?" He swept his arm in a gesture that took in everyone present. "I'm certain officers of this sturdiness could bear any punishment we would be dealt for releasing her without orders. The worst that could happen would be some form of torture. No death, I'm sure." He knew, and they knew, he was alluding to forms of punishment that made death look like home-planet shore leave. He waited while his words sank in, then turned back to t'Cael. "My Lord Primus, perhaps there is a flaw in the rules that will work in the commander's favor. Allow me the honor of examining the codes of law on your behalf."

The Field-Primus still had his arms folded. They stayed folded as he closed the space between himself and Ry'iak.

Ry'iak had experience with those folded arms; he took a nervous step backward, but realized the advantage he would lose if he backed off any further. He stood his ground; poorly, but he stood it.

T'Cael hovered before him like a thundercloud.

"I will allow you to hang yourself by the genitals. And that is all you will ever do on my behalf."

T'Cael refused to move or even to blink. His black eyes bored into Ry'iak until the younger man had to move away. Ry'iak tried to cloak his retreat in casualness, but everyone saw it for what it was as he crossed the bridge to a safer zone.

The master engineer's mouth curled into a snicker. The navigator and bridge centurion indulged in a glance at each other. They'd been watching each other carefully, gauging reactions. Now they were sure they were feeling the same thing—at least, for the moment.

T'Cael turned once again to Kai. "Kai, I promise

you this. If Idrys is guilty of even the tiniest complicity in this crime, the hand that executes her will be mine."

Not a soul on the bridge doubted it.

T'Cael illustrated the point by holding up his hand for as long as it took to convince them of his resolve.

Suddenly a loud warning whistle cut through the ship. The bridge systems whooped alert status into their ears and momentary shock stapled every man to his place.

"Subcommander!" the bridge centurion called, bending over his readout screen.

Kai answered over the noise. "What is it?"

"An intrusion! Some kind of ship in the sector—"

"A cargo vessel?"

"No, sir. Detecting heavy energy waves!"

"Battle alert!" Kai instructed.

The whooping changed to a distinct howl at the touch of the centurion's hand on his console. "How close is this intruder?"

"Nearly visual range, sir."

"How did it appear so suddenly?"

"Evidently out of hyperspace."

T'Cael stepped to the navigation board. "From which direction?"

The navigator swiveled his head from Kai to t'Cael, momentarily confused about which to obey. "No way to tell, Primus."

"Is there no way to track back on an energy trail?"

"I detect no such trail, Primus. I don't understand why not." He peered into his viewer, then, ominously, raised his eyes to the main viewscreen. "Visual contact," he murmured.

They all looked up.

At the center of the viewscreen, growing larger and more frightening with every space distance that fell behind *Raze* as she closed in, was the fiercest vessel they had ever seen.

Kai actually gasped. He leaned forward over the navigation console, and simply stared.

Wicked white, it hung in space and turned on an imaginary string. Its hulls were designed like weapons of war: battle shield, club, and lance. Even at this distance, they could see laser portals, a heavy sensor disk, engines bigger than most whole ships, and a haughtiness that soldiers of their fabric understood very well.

Even t'Cael was moved to step closer to the screen, struck silent by what he saw. His experience told him a hateful thing. A single word might as well have been painted across the huge ship as clearly as the wings were painted across *Raze.*

And every man on the bridge knew that word.

Invasion.

"Kai," t'Cael began.

"Yes—yes, Primus?"

"Summon the Swarm."

"Yes, Primus."

"And, Kai."

"Sir?"

"Release Idrys . . . now."

"At once, Primus."

Chapter Eleven

THE MIGHTY INTRUDER was completely unmarked. The only color other than pure ivory was the dark red of the sensor disk and a few docking lights blinking on the hull. Not a mark. Not a flag, not a pennant, not a number, not a symbol, not a clue. No crowing by those who had made it. Only its size, its battle-forward beauty, and its presence here gave any hint about the aspirations behind her. Who would send out an unmarked vessel? Who but invaders wishing to conquer?

T'Cael tried to keep his shoulders from hunching under the pads of his jacket. His voice was low. "Energy readings?"

Kai bent over the science station. "Low readings of ion pulsations . . . indications of low hyperlight engine energy . . . tremendous concentrations of magnetism clinging to its outer skin, but dissipating quickly." He straightened, and stared out at the huge face on intrusion. "If those portals are weapons outlets, they outgun us twentyfold."

Dark brows gathered over dark eyes. "Low hyperlight emissions," t'Cael murmured. "Are its engines down, then?"

"Or is it a bluff?" Idrys appeared from behind him, and her voice filled him with relief that she was here, where she belonged, at precisely the moment of his need for her loyalty and her experience—her trust-worthiness.

T'Cael paced the central command station on the cramped bridge. "Signs of battle damage?"

"No sign of damage of any kind," Kai read off, the science station monitor turning his face a muted green. "The trespasser is untouched."

"Bring all systems to battle readiness," t'Cael ordered. "Arm all energy missiles."

"Missiles armed," the helmsman reported.

"Raise defense shields."

"Shielding raised."

"Stand by gunnery stations fore and aft. Place auxiliary sensors on wide scan in case there are more intruders in the distance. Prepare all supplementary artillery backup systems, and bring the ship's engines to power edge for sudden maneuvers."

"All systems comply," Idrys spoke into her intraship communicator, after which she calmly tapped out the authorization codes for such heavy use of their arsenal.

T'Cael's black eyes tightened as he glared at the alabaster warship. He had trained himself long ago to be cautious first, trusting last. "Maneuver *Raze* into maraud position."

Kai swung around. "One lone ship against that?"

Calmly turning, t'Cael allowed a brief silence to burn between them. "We are only one ship. We cannot become more until the Swarm arrives. Do you prefer to run away and hide until then?"

Kai squirmed. Then he came to attention. "No, my Lord Primus."

"Maraud position."

"At once, Primus." Stiff-lipped, angered at his foolishness before the crew, Kai nodded to the helmsman to implement the position.

T'Cael paced the small area in front of the viewer as

though he dared not leave that space, as though somehow it made him closest to the big alabaster vessel, as though he could know something about it sooner than anyone else. "Be sure to maneuver *Raze* into maraud position in full crossbow style. Present our smallest profile to the intruder." The crew executed the maneuver hunched over their controls, well aware that the Primus was watching them. "Compare its design to all known designs in every available index. We must know who they are."

"They are infiltrators," spoke a voice considerably less welcome to t'Cael than any he had heard so far, and certainly the voice of experience where infiltration was concerned.

Bridling himself, t'Cael ignored Ry'iak's comment and reiterated, "Be sure to trace designs of major governments for at least the past half century, ch'Havran time."

"We are doing that, Primus," Kai answered, his nervousness poorly disguised.

T'Cael cast a glance at Idrys to see if he was reading Kai right, and apparently from her compressed lips, he was. Kai didn't like having Idrys back on the bridge. He wasn't sure what codes were being broken, but certainly some were, and not codes inclined to be gentle when they were ruptured. Idrys's presence here put Kai in third command again at just a time when he might have glimpsed advancement. Yet that ship out there frightened the subcommander also, t'Cael could tell. A fright, and a temptation. Things could move in any direction now.

"Primus," Kai addressed, once more in control of himself.

"Report."

"None of our indices carry record of that configuration, nor of any configuration even remotely like that shape. The disk and engine pods are distinctive, yet they seem to have evolved from nothing."

T'Cael closed his eyes and folded his frustration inside his arms. "So much for the wisdom of keeping only trim abilities in warbird computers."

"Until we contact the mothership," Idrys said, "we have no way of knowing what our spies might know about that shape."

"The Empire is afraid even to tell itself what it knows," t'Cael told her, rather mournfully. He paced in front of the viewscreen as though he could circle that unknown vessel and choke an identity out of it. "We besiege a ship that may not be unknown to the Council at all, yet it's unknown to us. How can we know? They've done nothing more threatening than appear. We may be putting our guard up against a potential ally."

"Or an enemy so great the Supreme Praetor is afraid to tell of its existence," Idrys added.

Ry'iak, quivering with fury, swung out from his hiding place behind the strut. "The Praetor fears nothing! And who could keep a vessel of that kind a secret?" He swung his hand toward the viewer, and indeed there was a plume of truth in his words. Even the Praetorate would not be able to hide the existence of that big and powerful a ship.

Idrys came close to t'Cael and spoke in a tone that was private, yet not a whisper, for a whisper would draw suspicion. "We must appear strong, even though we are one ship. Do we fire on them? A warning burst?"

"Is that your recommendation?" t'Cael asked her.

She thought about it, then made her answer slow and deliberate. "No. I recommend communication. Try to find out their intentions. Why they invade our space, and how so suddenly."

"I concur," t'Cael said. "Prepare a dispatch to the intruder. Demand identity and declaration of intentions."

"Language, sir?"

Problem on top of problem. Was it safe to assume the interloper knew it had come deep into Rihannsu space? There was no more widespread language than that of the Homeworlds, not for hundreds of light-years. And *Raze* was hardly hiding its identity, with its glossy black hull and preybird feathering.

With a slight pursing of his lips, t'Cael decided. "Rihannsu common," he said. "And hurry."

The bewitching lethargy of unconsciousness was hard to shake. George heard the thump-thump of pain in his mind, but he couldn't find it. For a while that was all right, like coming out of one dream and going into another. With the second dream there were other sounds—groans. His own or someone else's? And the whimpering of the starship—bleeps and whirrs and mechanical sounds that flooded his heightened senses.

The first sense to return in full was sight. A blur of slow movements inside a haze, then, gradually, there was focus. And the pain was there too, pain in his right shoulder. He put his mind into his shoulder and clung to the stab of wrenched muscles and bruised bones. Then the things he saw began to make sense.

Carpet, only inches away. Though he thought he'd been flat on his back, he found himself on hands and knees, his head hanging and his neck aching. He tried to raise his head.

Across the bridge, Engineer Hart was trying to pull Florida to his feet, but she hadn't found enough strength in her own throttled body to do it yet. Struck by the valor of her effort, George forced himself up onto his knees.

Moving cleared his head a little more. The bridge looked all right; nothing burning or crackling. Except for the main viewer—it was out completely, a blank gray screen.

Then he saw Drake, huddled on the lower deck against the bottom of the command chair. George pressed his knuckles into the carpet and pushed himself up. Grasping the hand rail for support, he stumbled down the bridge steps.

He ended up on one knee again, but strength was flowing back to him with each breath and each movement. He grasped Drake's shoulders and pulled him up a little more so that he could get a good look at him. "Hey, Creole? You all right?"

Drake held on to George and blinked his eyes, breathing in shallow gasps. "Mere . . . brain fracture . . ." Beneath his dusky complexion, the ashiness of shock was retreating. His eyes focused on George and stopped blinking. "You certainly drive very rough, George."

Beneath his hands George felt a tremor run down Drake's arms, and Drake suddenly took a deep breath to steady himself.

"We've got to get up," George said, and almost laughed because it sounded like such a casual suggestion. His own voice didn't sound all that steady. And the laugh never came.

"Yes," Drake said hoarsely. "I'll help you."

He clutched George's arms and leaned on him. George rearranged his center of balance to get both himself and Drake upright. His own legs quivered and he felt Drake tremble again, so he steered him into the command chair and pushed him down. That took the strain off both of them. Unfortunately, it also gave George a full view of the back of the bridge. He froze in place, and stared.

A streak of blood smeared the oyster-white wall

177

beside the turbo-lift. Like a gory arrow of graffiti scrawled by some nightstalker, it led downward, surely and directly, to a terrible sight.

"Oh, no," George choked. "Robert . . ."

He pushed himself past the command chair and vaulted to the upper walkway. There he knelt beside the motionless form of Captain April. His hands trembled as, against better first-aid judgment, he gently turned April over.

April's face was almost colorless, his lips drained of blood—and no wonder. All the blood in the world was pouring out a gash in the side of his head, plastering his hair into a dark wet cake. His eyes were open just a crack.

By now Hart and Drake were kneeling beside George too. Both looked wan and afraid. George was the only one with the nerve to touch the captain.

"Robert," he spoke out. He gritted his teeth to keep control. He held April's hands and assured him, "It's all right . . . just don't move."

Above them, Sanawey was bending over the communications station, speaking quietly but urgently. "Bridge to sickbay. Medical emergency. Repeat, emergency."

Sarah Poole's voice was tight and angry when she responded, *"Bridge, this whole ship is a medical emergency. You'll have to bring that down here yourselves."*

Her words drove George to outrage. He flew from April's side to the communications panel and snarled, "Goddamn you, doctor, you're not dealing with cattle! The captain's hurt! Get up here!"

There was a terrible pause on the other end. When Dr. Poole's words came, they were stiff and mechanical.

"What kind of hurt?"

"Head injury."

"Open?"

"Yes."

"Don't move him. I'm coming."

"Small favors," George grumbled, and dropped back to April's side to grasp those bloodless hands again.

April's hands twitched under George's, and he moaned faintly. "George . . ." The single word took all his strength, and his whole body shuddered suddenly.

"I'm right here, Rob. Don't move. Don't move." He clutched the captain's hands tighter, probably more tightly than was safe, and turned partially around. "Hart, get back to your station. Find out what happened to us and what shape we're in. Florida, where are you?"

"Here," Florida answered weakly from somewhere behind him. "Right here, sir."

"Help her."

"Yes, sir."

"Sanawey, get on the sensor systems and find out where we are."

"Right away, sir," the big man answered, and even his deep voice shook.

George detached himself from the ship's business and the reassuring tune of mechanical twittering as the bridge crew got to work, and concentrated on April. He leaned over the captain, seeking that old light April's eyes always held. He couldn't find it. "Robert?" he called softly.

"Ship . . ." April's breath carried only the echo of the word, and another shudder of effort moved through him.

"Don't worry about the ship. Understand? Don't worry. Everything's all right. Sarah's on her way."

The last part apparently gave April comfort. His shuddering stopped and he relaxed under George's

179

hands. George watched as his captain slipped into unconsciousness.

"Damn," he whispered. George felt Drake's hand on his back, but his touch brought no comfort.

The turbo-lift opened and Sarah Poole rushed out with two med techs. Her face was flushed and tear-stained. Evidently the trip up from sickbay had done more to her than just get her up here. She stepped over April and swatted George's shoulder with the edge of a medical kit. "Get away from him!"

Drake pulled George back to give the medics room. Sarah immediately dropped to the captain's side and sniffed back her tears while she fingered his head wound. One medic was reading vital signs with a mediscanner while the other maneuvered a gurney out of the lift.

George watched her in grim fascination. She looked different. Her face was flushed, and her eyelashes, spiked with moisture, suddenly looked much longer. Her lips were pursed and her thin brows flattened as she tenderly examined April's wounded head.

"How bad is it?" George ventured.

"Bad enough!" Sarah snapped. Tears drained down her cheeks freely now. She applied a pressure bandage to the side of April's head and a tiny sob crushed out. She muttered, "Just leave him to me."

George felt Drake's curious gaze on him, and the uncomfortable glances of others from around the bridge, but he didn't care. It didn't matter how she treated him as long as she took care of April. Nothing else could possibly matter more.

When she had the bandage in place, Sarah motioned the two med techs to put April on the gurney. In seconds he was up there on his side, and she covered him with a thermal blanket. "Go on," she ordered, flicking her hand at the techs. Without turning, she followed them into the turbo-lift.

180

"Keep me posted, doctor," George called after her.

She spun around, gripping the edge of the gurney. "You leave me alone! You leave *him* alone!"

The turbo-lift doors closed between them.

"Good gravy," Drake murmured in disbelief, staring at the closed lift door. "What was that?"

George contained a shiver. "I don't care what it was," he said, "as long as she takes care of him." He grasped his throbbing shoulder and turned. "Hart, where's that status report?"

Bernice Hart straightened from her examination of the engineering console, wincing in pain at what was apparently a twisted leg. She put her weight on the other foot and shook her head. "Not sure yet, Mr. Kirk. It looks like it might have been a malfunction in the gravity compensation system. That would account for slamming us up against the bulkheads and the sudden loss of pressure that caused us to blackout. The gravity systems are running on standby power, so we can assume there was a problem with the system."

"Is it stable now?"

"Yes, it reads positive."

"What happened to us? What made the ship do what it did?"

"Sir," Florida called from an open access panel on the deck, "if you recall, it happened just after we engaged warp power."

"Right," George growled. He stepped down to the command chair and struck the intercom. "Engineering, this is Kirk. What's the status down there?"

For a moment there was no answer. Then someone —sounded like Wood—came on. *"Engineering here. Um . . . we're a little frazzled. Can you give us a few minutes to lock down an analysis?"*

"Give me a guess."

"The engines are off line, sir," Wood reported. *"No warp power right now."*

"Why not?"

Wood hesitated. *"I think because the power surge was too much for the system to take and it knew it, so the safety shutdown took over."*

"Where's Dr. Brownell?"

"He's . . . not able to work right yet, sir."

"Is he dead?"

"No, sir, just incapacitated."

"Well, capacitate him!" George barked. "Make it a priority!"

"Yes, sir, you bet I will."

"Bridge out! Hart!"

She turned to face him, obviously exasperated. "Yes?"

"Why would all the systems shut down?"

"It's a ship, Mr. Kirk, not a person," she retaliated. "It doesn't think all that discriminatingly."

"What's down? Specifically."

"Specifically, the sensors, the warp drive, deflector power, life support on decks H, I, and L—"

"Damn it! Anybody down there?"

"No, there's nobody there."

"Seal those sections off and don't waste power on them. What's the count of casualties?"

"You'll have to check with sickbay for that."

George rubbed his hand over his bad shoulder and slumped against the command chair. "No thanks." He winced as a muscle in his neck pinched suddenly, and made himself breathe deeply a few times. "All right . . . get with engineering and start working on the warp drive. Sanawey, what's wrong with the sensors?"

The Indian's uniform strained over wide shoulders as he looked up. "Just a lot of burned-out circuits, sir. I'm rerouting right now. Should have power for visuals in a few seconds."

George pressed his knuckles to his lips and closed

his eyes for a moment. "I don't like this. This doesn't feel right. It doesn't sound right."

Close beside him, Drake kept his voice down. "Try to relax yourself, Geordie. Everything seems to be back in hand," he assured quietly. "I'm sure Captain will be hopping soon too. Empress seemed to know what to do to fix herself when she broke. She stopped the warp drive from going too far, didn't she?"

"Warp engines aren't that sensitive," George complained. "They shouldn't have gone crazy just because of an ion storm. Shut down, maybe. But not spontaneous warp like that. It just doesn't sound right."

"Sir," Sanawey called then, his wide face crumpled in confusion.

George turned.

Sanawey frowned at whatever was coming through his earphone. "Sir, there's . . ."

"What?" George prodded.

"There's a message coming in on a high-gain hailing frequency. Not in English . . . I'm going to have to translate."

"A message?" George moved across the lower deck and grasped the bridge rail beneath Sanawey's station. "Where could a message be coming from?"

Sanawey touched his astrotelemetry controls and turned immediately to the big viewscreen as a hum of power swung up from the bowels of the bridge. "From them."

George spun around, his movement echoed by Drake and Florida, and even Hart.

There, in midscreen, presenting a narrow silhouette to them, was a vulture crouching at their window.

And only the most ignorant human would fail to recognize the echo of the past painted on the black hull, against black space.

Chapter Twelve

APRIL FLOATED BACK to consciousness on the wings of a very soft bird. The first sound he heard was the reassuring *bump-bump-bump* of the cardiomonitor on the wall over his head. As long as he was alive it would continue to *bump*. If it stopped, he would worry.

He pushed air up through his throat to clear it and opened his eyes. Vision was a little blurry around the edges, but he saw what he had hoped to see—Sarah bending over him.

Her expression wasn't completely out of a medical textbook; her lips were still tight and trails of dried tears streaked her face. "How do you feel?"

He thought about it. "I'm not entirely sure," he admitted, feeling a little silly. The words were an effort; he had to work to keep his tongue from garbling them. "Weak. And . . . I have a headache rather worth noting. Did I—" He moved one of his hands to the side of his head.

"Yes," Sarah said quickly, grabbing his wrist, "you used yourself for a club to hit the ship with. You bruised your whole brain."

"Blood?" he asked, feeling a wet strand of hair.

"It was. We washed it. Now it's just wet. Why don't you just lie there and not complicate things."

He tried raising his head. "How many others are hurt?" he asked.

Sarah sighed and tried to distract herself with readouts from a portable encephalograph. "Assorted bruises and bumps. A few fractures," she murmured evasively.

"What about George?"

"What about him?"

"Is he all right?"

"Yes, your neo-Nazi is handling things on the bridge, never fear."

April settled down into the soft pillow again, relieved. "Oh, good. Things'll be fine, then."

"That's reassuring," she grumbled.

"What happened to us? Have we got any reports on status yet?"

"Why don't you just retire, Robert?"

He smiled at her in his soft English way. "Oh, come now, Sarah. I do have to ask."

She wiped the stiff tear tracks from her cheeks and fought to compose herself even more, to retreat into the shell that kept her isolated from the things that could hurt her. "Somebody said something about gravity."

April frowned in contemplation, then blinked and said, "Oh . . . the compensation system must have failed. Yes, that would explain it, of course. Dear, it could've been much worse, too." He rolled over onto his back. The movement totally disoriented him, and he went limp.

Sarah bent over him and touched the side of his face. "Robert?"

"Still here," he whispered. "Partly."

She sighed and swallowed hard. "Don't scare me like that."

"How long have I been here?"

"Few minutes."

"How few, Sarah?"

She put a palm-sized encephalostat against his

185

temple and adjusted the cauterizing beams for interior dural. "I'm not going to tell you." Her hands were cold as she fought to keep control of her voice, to fight the urge to tell him everything that was happening on the bridge. Word had spread like a brush fire through the ship—Romulan territory, and no way to get out.

"You'll have to get me back on my feet somehow," Robert said then.

"Like hell I will." Her eyes flashed with defensive anger and her pale cheeks flushed again. "You made me get Kirk for you so you'd have somebody who could take over in just this kind of situation. So let him take over!"

"Sarah," he said gently, catching her hand in his, "I should be up there. You know that."

"Fine. Go if you can," she shouted. "You made me come here to treat a special crew for a special mission, and that includes you. And I'm *going* to treat you." Her chin quivered as she suddenly fell silent. For several telling seconds, she just looked at him. Then the thought fell out, unbidden. "You're the most special part of this mission."

He held her hand close to his chest. "I'm so glad you're here, Sarah."

Her shoulders tightened. "Well, I'm not. There are a lot of doctors out there more qualified for this kind of expedition than I am and you know it. This isn't fair, Robert. You're not fair to me."

"I don't want to deal with strangers," he told her, just as he had told George not long ago. "I want people around me I can trust. People I don't have to get to know. I know you hate to see people suffer. I know plenty of doctors who could do this assignment, and, yes, perhaps better than you, from a medical standpoint. But I don't want them. I want someone I know, someone who knows me. It's you I like, Sarah." His voice grew softer still, given substance by the steady percussion of the heart monitor above the bed. His blue eyes sparkled once again, and the pressure bandage on his head made him seem vulnerable and brave all at the same time. He drew her hand closer still, until it was almost under his chin. "In fact," he said slowly, "it's you I love."

George stalked the bridge, never taking his eyes from the vulture ship. His whole body was one big nerve.

"Translate the message," he said.

Sanawey's thick fingers moved over the board. He touched the earphone and repeated, "They demand identification and declaration of intent. Pretty straightforward."

Bernice Hart raised her head from her own controls. "Don't they say who they are?"

"They don't have to," George shot toward the port side, the mean edge of bigotry slipping forward. "Florida, call engineering and get somebody up here who knows how to use that library unit." He stabbed his finger at the library computer station. "I want confirmation of design on that ship."

"Yes, sir."

"Sanawey, confirm what I'm thinking. What language is the message?"

Sanawey had to swallow before he could respond, and his tone was apologetic. He knew what the words meant to the ship, to the Federation. "Language banks catalog it as Romulan, Mr. Kirk."

George's fist slammed into the command console. "What are they doing in our space? This is an act of war!"

"Uh . . . sir?" Sanawey began.

"What?"

"They're repeating the demand for identification and intent, and, uh . . ."

187

"What?"

"Well, they demand to know why we're trespassing into their territory."

George turned to glare at him, his rage changing to astonishment. Crushing silence struck the bridge.

George's eyes grew hard. In a hushed voice he asked, "Can you confirm that?"

Sanawey did his best to key into the library computer's starchart banks, and precious moments slid by while he found the right connections to get the computer to help him.

His hand clenched, George soundlessly cursed the Vulcans for programming the library banks, then refusing to provide Starfleet even one person who really knew how to use them. He forced himself to keep quiet while Sanawey, drenched in sweat now, struggled with the computer.

Finally the big man straightened. "I can't exactly specify our location, sir. We don't have a single starchart matching this sector." Cryptically he added, "We're not in our own space, that's for sure."

"Are we in the Neutral Zone?" George asked.

"No, sir, we have charts of that, and we're not there."

From his position on the port side, Drake made a funny sound in his throat. "Looks like maybe *we* are the act of war."

George touched his forehead and gritted his teeth. "Uh, boy," he groaned. He looked up at Hart. "No warp drive?"

"Not a chance," she said, her face deathly pale now.

The turbo-lift opened behind them, and two engineers appeared.

"Graff, reporting as requested, Mr. Kirk," the older one said.

"And Saffire, sir," said the other one.

"Know something about that library computer?" George demanded immediately.

The younger man shrugged. "Mostly how it ties in to the warp navigation system, but we can probably work the catalog banks for you, sir."

"Get over there and dig out a design specification for that ship out there."

As the two engineers stepped past the communications station, Sanaway said, "Mr. Kirk, they're repeating their message again, and this time they warn they'll fire on us if we don't respond."

George paced around the command chair. "Will they, now. All right . . . but don't tip our hand. Make the response in Romulan. Can you?"

"Language banks aren't complete for that language, but we can probably make a few simple messages."

"Don't use any big words, George," Drake added.

"Sir?" Graff said as he bent over the library readout. "Information on that design is sketchy, but it correlates with the design of seven bird-of-prey type fighters that attacked Starbase One and the USS *Patton* in the year—"

"That's enough for me," George barked. "Don't identify us. Tell them we're on a research mission and our navigational sensors malfunctioned. Tell them we require a few hours' repair time and we'll gladly leave their space."

"How can we leave their space if we have no frame of reference?" Florida reminded.

"Why don't we have a frame of reference? The computers can project on known stars, can't they?"

"They can if we have long-range sensors," Sanaway filled in, "which we don't, because sensors are down."

"When will we?"

"We'll have short-range pretty soon, but long-range could take a day or more to recover."

George glared at Sanawey as though it was his fault, then looked at the viewer for a moment. An idea bloomed and he wagged a finger. "Tell them we'll be glad to let them escort us out of their space."

"They're going to want to know where to escort us," Sanawey said.

"Don't tell them that yet." George eyed the threatening ship again. "Tell them we have no hostile intentions. But we're perfectly willing and able to defend ourselves if they make any aggressive moves." He looked at Sanawey. "You make damned sure they understand that last part."

"I'll try to be diplomatic, sir."

"Just be clear." He leered at the viewscreen again and murmured, "You don't take chances with Romulans."

"Message response coming in, Primus," the bridge centurion announced.

T'Cael, Idrys, Ry'iak, and Kai all turned as a unit, probably the only time they would ever move in harmony.

"Language?"

The centurion tipped his helmeted head in a kind of shrug. "They respond in Rihannsu common. A computer-to-computer message, sir, not a voice."

"Then we still don't know." T'Cael sighed.

"If they speak our language—" Idrys began.

"*If* they speak it. Why did they not respond in speech then? Why does their computer speak for them? Do they speak Rihannsu or do they translate?" He moved to the nearest monitor and ordered, "Let me see the message."

Idrys and Kai crowded him, though not too close, as the words appeared on the screen in Rihannsu script:

There has been a navigation malfunction. We are a research vessel. You may escort us out of your space upon repair of our systems. Move no closer. We make no hostile plans, but we will counterattack if you fire first.

"That's all of it?" Idrys' bronze face puckered.

"All, Commander," the centurion answered.

Kai bolted back from the screen. "They invite us to attack! They dare us!"

Ry'iak, stepping away from another monitor at the centurion's station, was quick to add, "They offer no identification and clearly put a challenge before us. We must accept it."

"No." T'Cael's voice blanketed the bridge. "Look at the arrangement of words. Clumsy. Rihannsu is not their native language nor any dialect of it. They may not understand what they've said."

"We know what this says!" Kai fumed.

"Yes, but not what it *means*. If they wanted us to attack, why didn't they simply attack us first?"

"They beg provocation," Ry'iak stated firmly. "If we fire first, they have an excuse."

"Antecenturion," t'Cael began, drawing the word out, "they are in our space. Provocation has already been established."

"That ship could mutilate a single fighter like *Raze*," Idrys pointed out. "When the Swarm arrives, we'll have a chance. We're the ones who should be stalling for time."

Ry'iak sighed with frustration and flattened his arms at his sides. "You will be remiss in your duty if you fail to destroy the invaders before they can repair themselves."

T'Cael straightened. "There's more to be gained in space than destruction of unfriendlies. If we destroy them, we gain nothing for the Empire."

"And if they destroy us?"

"What good will we have done if we force them to destroy us?" t'Cael responded, carefully turning Ry'iak's logic back upon him. "I prefer to see what good can be gleaned from this before we start cutting hulls."

"But they've admitted to being disabled," Ry'iak insisted. "We can attack and destroy them easily now, before they regain full power!"

The crew watched, casting guarded glances at a contest between undeniable powers. T'Cael folded his arms and nodded slowly.

"If they're incapacitated," he said, "the wiser course is to await the Swarm, after which we shall have a chance of taking that ship. It is a prize." A prize indeed. One that would make him a hero and give him the power to force the Supreme Praetor to back off. He pivoted toward Ry'iak. "You wouldn't want to deprive the Empire of such a trophy, would you, Antecenturion?"

The two men stood silently. T'Cael knew perfectly well that Ry'iak wanted the giant ship destroyed to prevent t'Cael from becoming a champion at a time when his orders were to bring the Field-Primus to contrition. But here was the bridge crew, waiting to hear him admit he wanted to deny the Praetor possession of this bright medallion.

T'Cael gave the silence time to work. Then he began again, cagily. "However, if you are personally anxious to attack them, I shall authorize you a three-man remote fighter and you may attack the intruder yourself." He held out his hands. "Forgive me for not thinking of it sooner. It's just what you've always desired—a glorious death in the name of the praetor. Kai! Prepare a Nestling Three. Assign two men to Ry'iak's—"

"No!" Ry'iak choked out, twitching. "No . . . I . . . am guided by your . . . your wisdom. We must await the Swarm. The Empire must have a chance to capture the intruder ship . . ." His voice dwindled as he ran out of breath.

T'Cael folded his arms again and moved close to Ry'iak for a private conversation. "You've been working very hard. Perhaps it is time to rest. You may leave the bridge if you wish."

Ry'iak's fists balled. He didn't raise his eyes. "You enjoy making a fool of me in the eyes of the crew," he growled between his teeth.

A little grin of gloating touched t'Cael's lips and he moved even closer. "If only you didn't make it so easy."

He paused to allow his words to sink in, then moved away with a slight but very calculated swagger. Only when Ry'iak leaned against the bulkhead and made no moves to leave the bridge did t'Cael think he might have pushed his victory a bit too far in the hope of ridding himself of the nuisance entirely.

He turned his attention back to the bridge crew. "We shall resist making demands on them until the odds are better. Until the Swarm reassembles, we have no way to back up our threats." He gazed at the deck as he spoke. "When the Swarm arrives, we'll be able to deal with the intruders on our own terms. Until then," he said, raising his dark head, "our demands will be disguised as requests."

He let the idea ferment, and indeed, no one offered any argument. Idrys sensed the purpose of his pause, and let it ride out. Then she asked, "What are your orders, Primus?"

"Request more general information," he said, "and ask what their home planet is. Offer to help if they require assistance."

Shocked, the bridge crew glared at him.

Even Idrys blinked. "Assistance?"

"Yes. They will tell us what they need. Information about their casualties and repairs will be valuable to us. We will know their weaknesses."

With great satisfaction, he saw the bridge crew exchange glances of amazement and respect for his cleverness. They had just witnessed a hard-won trick of war play, gleaned of t'Cael's experience—or so they thought. Luckily, they didn't know him well enough to realize his true hopes for the contact.

"Brilliant, Primus," Idrys breathed. "A glorious plan."

He nodded with a touch of modesty. "Send the message, Commander."

Sarah's lips tightened, giving her a little-girl look. A stray lock of hair tickled her eyelashes as she pouted at the captain. She didn't pull her hand away from his, but she felt herself withdraw. She knew this April magic was nearly irresistible to her. If she met his eyes, she'd be lost. Yet his gaze drew her to him.

He looked up at her with a hopefulness she'd seen before.

"Patient-doctor infatuation," she said, dropping her gaze.

"No, it isn't," he responded without a moment's hesitation, as though he knew she was going to say that.

Now she did pull her hand back, drawing a thermal sheet up over his legs. "Love doesn't work in space," she professed. "Love needs candlelight."

April chuckled. "Does it? I thought it was starlight. We have plenty of starlight, Sarah."

"You're just making me uncomfortable. Please don't—"

He reached out and touched her forearm, his fingers

194

closing slowly around her wrist in a manner so gentle that she couldn't resist it. "I'm a lonely man, Sarah."

Her eyes flashed then, and her emotions bucked. She slapped his hand. "Robert April, you've never been lonely in your life! You've got more friends than anybody! The whole galaxy wants to be your buddy. Lonely, my backside!"

"Oh, dear," he murmured. "I hate being caught in a lie . . ."

"You can't lie," she shot back. "Your tongue would twist off." She squirmed, caught in that sweet gaze of his that would melt her down if she didn't manage to stay angry. "I don't want to hear it, understand? I belong somewhere else, doing something else, and if anybody on board this ship finds out about this, you're going to look like a complete fool. They're all going to think you brought me here instead of a qualified space-medicine physician because you've got a crush on me. So cut it out, just cut it right out. Everybody loves you, Robert, and you've got no excuses to corner me like this. I'll bet even the Romulans are going to love you. You just can't get away from your own nature—"

He raised his aching head. "What Romulans?"

Sarah stopped her tirade and her lips hung open. She clamped them shut then and waved her hands. "Just a figure of speech."

Only when she tried to cloak the mistake did she realize how frightened she was. Only a tense and dangerous situation on the bridge could keep George Kirk from throttling her with questions about April's condition, and Kirk hadn't called down once yet. April rolled up onto his elbow and got her by the arm again. "Sarah," he began, "what Romulans?"

She tried to hide it, but he had already caught the fleeting signal of danger in her eyes that told him she was protecting him. With anyone else, he might have missed it, but he knew her, and he knew how to interpret that flicker. Suddenly his protests about not wanting to work with strangers made sense.

He gripped her elbow tighter and used the leverage both to hold on to her and to pull himself up. "Sarah, what's going on?"

"It doesn't matter," she snapped. "You're out of it. Don't make me sedate you. Robert—"

He slid off the table, barely able to keep from toppling over.

She refused to help him. While she frantically tried to think of ways to stop him from going, he reached the door of his private cubicle and the panel slid open. He caught himself on the edge of the doorway, and the breath was crushed out of him by what he saw.

Sickbay. A dozen quickly arranged diagnostic beds —all full.

The air moved with groans of battered and broken people. The results of gravitational failure at warp speed knelled.

April hung at the door, choking. "Oh, my God . . . my God . . ."

Sarah stood frozen in place, her hand over her mouth, her eyes unblinking and welling with moisture.

The captain's voice cut through her. "Get me to the bridge."

She took him there herself, even though she'd promised herself she wouldn't. When the turbo-lift opened, she helped him move onto the bridge.

George caught sight of them and demanded, "What the hell are you doing here?"

April didn't answer, instead concentrating on what he saw on the main screen.

George glared at Sarah. "Is he all right?" he asked.

She simply shook her head. "Not even close."

George came toward them and grasped April's arm to help him down the two steps into the command arena. "Sit down, at least."

April still gazed at the birdship. "Who are they?"

"Romulans," George answered.

"Is that confirmed?"

"I'd call it confirmed. Language and ship design correlate with information acquired during and since the Romulan Wars."

"Good God, George, I should've been notified. Are we in their space?"

George shifted his feet. "Apparently we are. Deep into it, thanks to our warp jump. Which bothers me more than a little bit, I can tell you."

Now April looked at him, still fighting blurry vision. "Why?"

"Too many coincidences. I understand having a few problems shaking down new systems, but warp isn't all that new. Our first so-called malfunction almost canceled the mission, might've killed us all, or at least caused us to destroy the starship to save ourselves. Now our second so-called malfunction—"

April leaned painfully on the arm of his command chair and grimaced. "Look, I know what you're getting at—"

"—lands us in enemy space with a boatload of new technology that the Romulans would love to get their hands on—"

"George—"

"—*and* we have no navigational frame of reference without long-range sensors, so we don't even know what direction home is in. Robert—are you going to tell me I'm paranoid?" His eyes burned like dark amber flames.

His fury evidently had an effect on April, who hesitated before answering. "I'd say you're . . . being an extremely good officer."

"Don't placate me."

"All right, I won't. I think you're succumbing to a military frame of mind. All right, a paranoid one. A malfunction is just that. And we're bound to have some." He eyed the Romulan ship again and tried to keep from slumping. He started to touch the pressure bandage on the side of his head, then thought better of it and put his hand down. A fine sweat broke out on his forehead.

"It's the nature of the malfunctions that bothers me, Captain," George pressed. "We squeaked out of the first one with luck and a toothpick, and we're not out of this one yet. I'm saying this ship is pure platinum to the Romulans. If they've been infiltrating Starfleet—"

"Spies? No . . ."

"If they have," George insisted, "then they already know about the starship and it would be inconceivable for them not to try to get her. Deny that."

"I'm not denying that part. But the people who worked on this vessel and those who are on it now have been cleared and cleared and cleared. You and Drake are the least cleared people we have." He swung a finger from George on one side of him to Drake on the other. "George, this isn't the time to argue about it. We have a bigger problem to deal with," April added.

"I'm telling you it's all the wretched *same* problem."

April gave him a small please-back-off nod and shifted again in the chair. He felt as if he was sitting on spikes. Pain pounded in his back and legs, as though his wounded head sought to displace the responsibility. He pressed a clammy hand against his knee and fought to keep control. "Carlos, ship's status, please."

"Warp drive down, no word of degree or of repair

progress yet . . . sensors and deflectors under repair
. . . short-range sensors almost available . . . and the
Romulans demanded that we identify ourselves and
our intent," Florida said.

"And what did we say to them?"

"We didn't give our identity," the helmsman answered. "We told them we were in their space by
mistake and will get out as soon as we fix ourselves
. . . and that we'd defend ourselves without hesitation."

April slouched back and rubbed his face with one
hand.

"Oh, George," he moaned.

"Just dealing with the situation as it stands, Captain," George told him firmly. "We know about
Romulans."

"We know about them seventy-odd years past,
George, can't you accept that? That many years—"

"Captain," Sanawey interrupted, "message coming
in from the Romulan vessel."

April turned in spite of a clenching pain in his neck.
"Translate, quickly."

"Yes, sir." The astrotelemetrist tapped his console
buttons, then squinted as he listened to the readout in
his earphone. "'Attention visitor ship . . . message
understood . . . advise if you need assistance with
repairs or casualties. Please specify your home space
so we may communicate more efficiently.' And
they're standing by, sir."

"There you are," April said. "Utterly benevolent.
What do you say now, George?"

George frowned. He had no intention of backing
down.

April understood his expression. "Well, it's just
what we would say in the reverse situation, isn't it?"

George leaned toward him and widened his eyes.
"That's what bothers me."

"Carlos, you say we have no way to navigate back to Federation space without help from them?"

Florida fidgeted. "That's the assessment, sir, for now. Even once long-range sensors are repaired, it'll take a while to determine our location. Longer than they'll wait, probably."

April sighed and shook his head. "Then we have no choice. We're going to have to tell them who we are."

"Robert," George gasped, "we can't! We don't dare!"

"Why not?"

"All they remember about the Federation is a war that they started and that ended in a draw. You know what this ship looks like!"

"Yes, it looks like revenge. But that's exactly my point. The war happened decades ago, George. The only way we're going to get past it is to be honest with them, tell them that this ship is an exploration vessel on a rescue mission—"

"And hope they believe it? *I* wouldn't believe it," George told him.

April took a moment to compose himself. When he spoke again, his voice had lost some of its strength. "What possible harm can it do to tell them who we are?"

George moved closer and lowered his own voice, empathizing with April's weakness. "I'll tell you what harm. First, it gives them precedent for firing on us as hostile aliens. Second, it gives them the technical advantage of knowing our physiology. What kind of air we breathe, how much pressure we can take, what we're inclined to do, what we're afraid of—"

"I suppose that's true," April admitted. "But how could they know those things? We've not had any contact with them in all this time. We don't know what they look like, and they don't know what we look like."

George moved around the command chair, feeling the eyes of everyone on the bridge, their intense curiosity about his next words. He never took his eyes from April's. "I'm not going to assume that," he said. "I'm going to assume they know more about us than we think they do."

"All that does is pile bricks on top of the wall," April said. He didn't want a galactic conflict at his feet. "Carlos."

Florida shook himself out of the trance. "Sir?"

"When the sensors come up, don't scan their vessel. I don't want our emissions misinterpreted. We have to make an act of friendship. With our shields down, they can detect our energy flows." April paused then, thinking his strategy through. Even the effort of speaking caused his head to pound. "Shut down power to the lasers."

Without moving more than his hand, George grasped the captain's forearm and sharply said, "No."

Words were becoming less and less adequate. George's gaze demanded that April remember why he had risked so much to bring George Kirk here. Exactly why.

"No," George repeated, this time in a whisper.

April held his gaze, then wavered: "Carlos, belay that last order."

Florida hunched his shoulders and sighed in relief. "Lasers still viable, sir."

The captain wiped his forehead and turned to George. "Technically, we certainly are invading their space, don't forget. They have every right to suspect us. We have no right at all to aggress."

"We have to be prepared to defend ourselves," George insisted. "They're clever, and they're ruthless. These are the same people who attacked a defenseless starbase and murdered two thousand people. Two *thousand* people massacred in one attack, Captain."

201

"So long ago, George. We have to consider—"

George rolled his eyes and smacked the arm of April's chair with a flat palm. "Damn you, Robert, you always lead with your heart!"

He spun away from the command chair and grasped the bridge rail as though he meant to shake it. Above him, Drake and Sarah Poole watched in stiff silence.

"Claw," April began softly, "prepare a message in their language."

"Go ahead, sir. The computer'll translate for you."

"Thank you." He tried to straighten in his seat. On the arms of the command chair, his palms grew moist. "This is Captain Robert April of the United Federation of Planets . . ."

Chapter Thirteen

"WE AWAIT YOUR reply . . . Captain April out."

Silence on the bridge of Imperial Swarmbird *Raze* dominated for several seconds. It reeked of astonishment, and of fear.

They would have admitted to the astonishment.

Kai was the first to speak. "Earthers!" he gasped. "Our old enemy resurfaces!"

From the command chair, Idrys stared at the giant white ship from which the message had come. "Then it's true," she murmured. "They rise."

Ry'iak burst toward the command center. "We must move against them immediately! We must fire on them while they're still damaged!"

Idrys deflected the panic on the bridge with order. "Gunners! Prepare main arsenal. Target the Earth ship's main thrusters and bring power directly to our weapons sensors. Prepare to fire!"

"Countermand!" T'Cael roared.

Kai and the centurion were already clambering to carry out the first order. Only when the Field-Primus elbowed his way between them, grasped them both by the arms, and pulled them away from the weapons console did they realize his determination. "I said countermand," he growled.

Ry'iak, his face flushed jade with rage and indignation, blurted, "This is an outrage! This is an extreme emergency and we must take action against our known enemy! Subcommander, fire on the enemy!"

T'Cael broke away from the two men he held in his grip and rounded on the Praetor's eye. "You imbecile! You dare challenge me openly on the bridge of my flagship?"

Quivering, Kai peeked at the Primus to say, "If this battleship is here, the Federation must be amassing along the treaty boundary. They must be!"

"They are our enemies, Primus," Idrys reminded cautiously. "They are of Earth—"

"They have not said Earth," t'Cael snapped, still glaring at Ry'iak.

"The Federation, Primus!" Kai said, breathless. "Earth is their base. It *is* an Earth ship."

"When have you heard them say Earth?" t'Cael said, nailing him with a glare. "A lifetime of service has passed since those wars, Subcommander. The captain of that ship made no reference to a home planet. Obviously he feels his ship is more than one planet's property."

Kai's face turned brassy with excitement. "Primus, I beg you consider! Their captain speaks of peace and rescue missions and navigational mistakes, but no one could make a mistake so vast as to land them in our home space, where their claws can sink deep and quick. He is bluffing! He damaged his ship and now he stalls for time, and we dare not give it! He can want the time for only one reason—invasion!"

Ry'iak nodded furiously. "Their damage is our advantage. We must use it immediately." Puffed up with self-importance, he stepped past t'Cael to address the bridge gunners. "Ready the weapons as you have been ordered. We will defend the Empire against her invaders."

"You are the invader," t'Cael said. He smacked his

hand against the shipwide intercom and his voice boomed throughout *Raze*. "This is Field-Primus Kilyle. By authority of the Exordium of the Imperial Code, I now invoke the Master Dominion Pandect for Martial Crisis. From this moment onward, the commanders must be obeyed on threat of death. Any disobedience, no matter how trivial, is considered an act of treason under the Pandect. Any officer questioning the orders of a superior will be executed. As supreme commander of the Second Swarm, I invoke the right to instantly sacrifice any dissenter among the personnel of the Swarm until further notice. Such is the law of the Empire." He straightened, the power of the Exordium making him formidable, and leveled a finger at Ry'iak. *"You* will leave the bridge."

Eyes wide with shock, Ry'iak had no response. Stunned by t'Cael's knowledge of imperial crisis law, he was compelled to obey or be instantly and legally killed in the name of solidarity. He shook with rage. If he uttered so much as a word, and t'Cael decided to take that word as defiance, there would be death on the bridge.

Guttering like a candle in the wind, Ry'iak bottled his rage, pressed his lips into a line, and stiffly walked off the bridge.

Idrys watched him go; t'Cael ignored him. When the lift panel closed behind him, she turned in satisfaction and punched her intercom. "Enforcement Division, send four guards to the bridge. Master Dominion Pandect is now in operation."

Primus Kilyle was once again gazing out at the Federation ship, as though Ry'iak was nothing but a bug he had wiped from one of his plants and forgotten. For a few moments, Idrys merely watched him, her respect deepening.

"Subcommander," she addressed him then, and waited until Kai looked at her, "prepare a message to the Swarm ships identifying the intruder and informing them of the alert condition of the Pandect."

From her side, t'Cael spoke firmly. "No."

She twitched. "Primus?"

"No communications with other vessels of any kind without my specific order."

"But if a message is sent to us from the Swarm or the mothership—"

"Am I unclear, Commander?"

She tensed. "No, Primus. You are understood." She nodded to Kai. "Close communications to anyone other than the Federation ship." She felt her muscles tighten. She'd almost slipped, almost said Earth ship. Such a mistake would have undermined Primus Kilyle.

The Primus seemed to sense her discomfort. With a calming breath he explained, "If they can monitor our communications, they'll know we're alone and at a fighting disadvantage. We dare not appear afraid. A rodent can stand off a thrai by pretending it's not afraid. The Swarm is on the way. Telling them won't bring them here any sooner."

Very cautious now, Kai came to stand beside Idrys, making sure to keep her as a buffer between himself and the Primus. "May I respectfully suggest that this appearance could be part of a simultaneous attack along the treaty zone, my Lord Primus."

T'Cael never took his gaze from the intruder ship. "It's possible," he said with a sigh. "Then why have they not fired upon us and moved onward? Why do they negotiate with a single ship when only the distance of a few light-days separates them from the heart of Rihannsu civilization, where they can destroy our governmental bases as they will?"

"They say they're damaged."

"They say that," he echoed thoughtfully. "I cannot

believe this is an invasion maneuver. It simply has none of the signals."

The bridge crew kept their opinions to themselves, partially because of the Pandect, partially because of the Primus'. No one wanted to be an example.

"You're not sure, are you?" Idrys asked, keeping her voice down.

"Nothing is sure. But humans are a complex people. I can deal with that." He moved toward the biggest viewscreen and narrowed his eyes at the ivory beast hanging in space before him. "They call us Romulans."

The word was distasteful and unflattering, awkward-sounding in their language. The bridge crew shared a grimace.

"If I may suggest . . ." Kai began again, just as carefully.

"Yes?"

"If indeed they are damaged, and since we are alone . . ."

Vented of his anger, t'Cael glanced at the subcommander, then turned fully to him. "If they are damaged, then this is our greatest chance."

"Yes, Primus!" Kai gasped.

"You don't understand," t'Cael told him, and couldn't resist a twinge of amusement as Kai suddenly pressed his lips together, trying not to appear afraid or defiant. "Subcommander, look at that vessel. We must *take* that ship, not destroy it. If they have a fleet of those, what do you think our chances will be? Will we ever have an opportunity like this to gain possession of their technologies? Look at it!" He swept his hand along the viewscreen. "Everyone here could be a hero. It's worth the risk, don't you think? Worth a little time, a little pretense? Besides, what glory will there be in the battleship's destruction if the Federa-

207

tion goes on to destroy the Empire with technology we allowed to slip away because we were afraid?"

He let his words sink in.

While the crew's eyes turned to that vast ship, Idrys watched t'Cael. He was up to something more complex than his words told. But what? And dared she ask?

"Prepare a message to the mothership," he was saying, "but don't send it yet." He folded his arms and stalked to the viewscreen. "Humans are naive. They tend to trust first and learn later. By telling us their identity, they give us the upper hand."

"You know all about humans," Idrys agreed.

T'Cael smiled modestly. "No one knows all about anything, Commander. But I do have a few insights about them that I can turn to our favor. One is that they tend to trust what they can see face to face."

The bridge personnel turned in curiosity, but no one said anything.

Finally Idrys broke the silence. "Face to face?"

T'Cael wrapped his arms around his chest. "I will offer to meet with their captain. I'll invite him to visit our ship. I will stall for time until the Swarm arrives and pretend to speak peace while gaining information about their real intentions."

"They'll never trust us," Kai said, perplexed.

"They may," t'Cael corrected. "For humans, the emotion that is fed is the one that grows."

He paused, letting the truth sink in.

Then he said, "And . . . we will have a hostage."

The addendum rang around the bridge, drawing the glances of the crew, first in awe, then in approval. Loyalty, for all the talk of the honor it supposedly brought and its theoretical importance in their culture, was a fleeting thing. For the moment, at least, they were his again. All he needed do was hold them long enough to complete his plan, or this leg of it.

"Commander," he invited, "if you will."

Idrys nodded, suppressing a smile. "Centurion, invoke tie-in to the Federation vessel."

"Message coming in, Captain."

Sanawey sounded nervous.

"Translate it, please, Claw," April requested.

"No need, sir. It's in English. He wants to speak to you."

April turned and looked quizzically at the astrotelemetrist. "Put the gentleman through."

Sanawey touched his audio system and nodded at April.

The captain straightened in his chair and watched the Romulan ship in the viewer. "This is Captain April. Go ahead, please."

"My greetings to you, Captain. This is the supreme commander speaking. It is my honor to address you in your own language."

"Thank you, Supreme Commander. Do you have a suggestion about our rather awkward situation?"

"I do. In our culture, voices do not adequately represent people. I suggest you and I meet in person, as an act of good faith, to assure us both there will be no hostility. I offer that you visit my ship. I will convey your greetings to our Supreme Praetor and deliver my regards to your government. Will you meet with me, sir?"

April couldn't resist a glance at George, who was rigid with suspicion a few steps away, but who didn't so much as flinch at the strange suggestion. Around the bridge, no one else moved either. Expressions ranged from surprise to perplexity.

April shifted uncomfortably. "That's . . . a very interesting offer, Supreme Commander. It seems reasonable. Please give me five minutes to discuss it with my officers."

"At your wish, Captain. I shall stand by."

Signaling to Sanawey to put the audio on hold, April scanned the faces of his command crew, then turned inevitably to George. "Well?"

"Well what?" George responded.

"What do you think?"

"Do I have to say it?"

"I'd rather you did."

"They're being too friendly. Even if they do want peace, why would they want it so badly?"

"It's a bluff, you think?"

George shrugged. "Of some kind. But what kind?"

His face pasty, April flexed his shoulders painfully; the movement brought Sarah down from the upper walkway. She gripped his wrist, partially to take his pulse and partially to get his attention. "I can't believe you're actually considering this," she said. "You're not that stupid, Robert."

He smiled weakly. "Not stupid," he said. "Just a bit visionary. Sarah, what if they're in earnest?" April suggested. "This could be a chance to mend the rift between our cultures in the process of saving our necks. It's much bigger than just me. It makes me expendable."

"That's not true, Captain," George muttered.

"Yes, it is," the captain said. "The engineers need time to repair the drive and the deflectors. I can provide that."

"Why does it have to be you?" Sarah demanded.

"How could I assign this to anyone else?" he asked. "I can't pass along either the responsibility or the danger. I'm the least valuable person on this ship right now."

George squinted at him. "You figure that, do you?"

"It's true, George. If they take me, you'll still be here. And you're a much better soldier than I am. If they are indeed bluffing, you're the one who'll be needed here. These are my ideals, no one else's. I've got to stand behind them."

George couldn't think of anything to say to that. He wondered if he could be so brave over something as nebulous as an ideal.

Perhaps that was one other thing he had failed to pass along to his sons while he had the chance.

April took advantage of the silence from his first officer. "And," he added, "I have an obligation to our hosts out there."

"How do you mean, obligation?" Sarah asked.

"We did invade their space, after all. We're the apparent threat. It's my diplomatic obligation to defuse that before it becomes an interstellar incident too big for anyone to handle."

"They only want a hostage," Sarah said, downcast. "Even I can see that."

"Now, Sarah, don't be doing George's job for him, eh?" A shudder of weakness made him breathless and he gripped the arms of his chair, fighting for control.

"She's got a point," George said. "Why don't you suggest a meeting on board the empress instead. See how he reacts."

April squeezed his eyes shut for a moment, then nodded. "Yes, that's a smart idea."

George moved closer to quietly ask, "Are you up to this?"

"Yes, I'll be fine," the captain answered, forcing his spine to straighten no matter how much the effort dizzied him. Realizing how bad it looked for him to appear out of sorts, he nudged Sarah away and forced himself to his feet. "Now listen to me, George," he said, gripping George's arm. "If I'm taken hostage, I want you to consider me lost. Do you understand? Under no circumstances attempt a rescue. It'll just risk more lives. I couldn't very well go on living anyway, knowing that lives had been lost because I'm taking a foolish chance. Now, promise me. I want your promise."

George could disobey an order easily enough. Orders were subject to interpretation. Promises were something else. Especially promises to a man like Robert April, who had just proven beyond a doubt that he fully understood the high danger in this maneuver. April's idealism might be driving him, but he hadn't forfeited common sense.

Churning inside, George managed a short nod.

Evidently it was enough to satisfy April. The captain patted George's arm in a reassuring way and glanced back at astrotelemetry. The motion made him wobble, but he forced himself to speak. "Claw, go ahead and patch me back in to our friends out there. We'll ask George's question and see if . . . if they . . . oh God—"

The color drained from his face and his eyes lost their focus. He brought his hand to his head as the bridge reeled. His knees buckled.

"Robert!" George snatched him in midfall. "Robert, damn—" As the captain slumped against him, George managed to keep an awkward hold on April for the two seconds it took Florida to spin out of his chair and help him. Drake stepped down also, and the three of them lowered the captain to the deck.

"I *knew* it," Sarah said through gritted teeth, and knelt between the men. "I told him . . ."

"He's hurt bad, isn't he?" George asked, his heart punished. "He really is."

"It's my problem," Sarah told him, and not entirely without empathy this time. "You've got yours. Somebody help me get him below."

George looked around, saw Graff and Saffire standing near the library computer, and decided that for the moment they were the two he needed least. "You

212

and you. Give the doctor a hand. Then come right back."

The two men stepped down, neither able to choke out an acknowledgment, and took the captain away from George.

"Be careful," George couldn't help saying. He watched in anguish as Robert was carried from the bridge. Just before the lift closed, Sarah Poole cast him an enigmatic look.

He found himself staring at the closed lift door.

"Six minutes, Mr. Kirk," Sanawey reminded quietly. "They're waiting."

George continued to stare at the turbo-lift.

The bridge crew watched him, uneasy.

Without moving, George whispered, "My God, Drake. How am I going to get us out of this?"

Just as quietly, Drake offered, "You have to be the captain now, Geordie."

"I can't take his place. I'm a ham-handed diplomat at best. If there's going to be a war, you can bet I'll stumble us into it."

Drake shrugged one shoulder and actually nodded, even though it wasn't a very complimentary kind of nod. "Time to grow up, Peter Pan. You have to be part Geordie Kirk and part Robbie April. Go ahead, fellow. Make the captain proud of you, eh?"

George felt the fear around him, fear from the others on the bridge. These were engineers and scientists, not soldiers. They never thought they'd be in a situation like this. They built ships. They didn't go out and face the enemy.

So he was alone. Lost without a map, without stars.

He gripped the back of the command chair and gathered his wits, trying to remember everything that had been said and decided before April collapsed. He hadn't thought he'd have to remember it all . . .

"Mr. Kirk?" Sanawey prodded.

George looked up, almost as though he didn't understand.

Sanawey didn't say what everyone expected, but instead reported, "Sir, I've got full short-range sensors back on line if you need them."

George swallowed hard and turned to face the viewscreen again. "At least something's working," he murmured. "Scan that ship, Mr. Florida."

Florida hesitated. "But Captain April's orders . . ."

"I know. I'll handle it. Go ahead."

Florida slid into his seat, accepting the inevitable. He played with the instruments, watched the readout screen on his console, then raised his brows. "You were right, Mr. Kirk. Their weapons are hot, sir." He seemed a little surprised, but only a little. He turned to George. "If our lasers had gone down, they might've cut us to pieces."

George couldn't quite muster a pat on the back for himself. He stabbed the intraship com with his forefinger. "Engineering, this is Kirk. What's the status down there?"

"Brownell here."

An unexpected rush of relief came with hearing the surly voice. George leaned over the com unit. "Glad to hear you're back on duty, doctor. How long before we get full shields?"

"Won't be any minute, if that's what you want. We're still a half hour off having twenty-five percent shields."

"What about particle cannons?"

"Lasers aren't good enough for you?"

"I may need something more powerful before this is over."

"Something slipped your mind there, Kirk?"

George paused. "What do you mean?"

"You haven't asked about the warp drive."

"I need weapons."

Brownell's voice changed slightly, as though he had moved closer to the intercom. *"We're not out here to win a war, Kirk. We came out to rescue the families. How 'bout we get the hell out of here and do what we started out to do? You can take out your frustrations with a stiff game of tennis or something—later."*

George realized he'd completely forgotten the one thing he should never have forgotten. *Rosenberg.* Families. Survival, and what hinged upon it.

"Do you have any ideas yet about what caused all this?" he asked.

"If we knew what caused it, I could retire."

"You've got to find out. We've got to be sure it doesn't happen again."

"Hell, it shouldn't have happened the first time. We're just concentrating on fixing it, is all."

"It's not enough, Dr. Brownell," George insisted. "I want to know the cause."

"Come on over. We'd be glad to see you track it down."

Frustration pinched at George. He squeezed his eyes shut and said, "All right. Keep me posted." Feeling inadequate, he took a moment to hate himself before straightening up. "We're in trouble." He sighed.

"Pardon?" Drake asked.

"He didn't insult me once."

Drake pursed his lips and offered, "I could insult you, 'f you like."

George shook himself out of his torpor, and even managed a grin. "Thanks," he said drably. He inhaled deeply and stared out at the birdship a few kilometers off their bow. "I've got to buy repair time for us. I'll have to offer to meet with them. Sanawey . . ."

"Sir?"

"Go ahead and . . . patch me through."

"Tied in. All yours, sir."

"This is . . . this is the first officer. Are you still there?"

"I am here," the Romulan leader said. *"I was speaking with your captain."*

"I know," George responded. "The captain was injured during our navigational accident and he's not able to meet with you. He's asked me to represent him and the Federation, if that's satisfactory to you."

There was a disturbing pause from the Romulan ship, during which Drake and George nervously shared a glance. It didn't augur well from a tactical point of view. After several sweaty moments, the Romulan spoke again.

"I accept your proxy, First Officer. Are you willing to accept the risk of coming aboard our ship?"

Strange. George furrowed his brow at the wording. Accept the risk? It was almost as though the Romulan was deliberately discouraging him. He tapped his knuckles against his mouth, thinking, then he decided to try a new tack.

"You understand the problem we have," he said openly. "A surprise attack by your people on ours many years ago makes trusting each other difficult. What assurance do we have that your intentions have changed since the last encounter between our races?"

"I understand your reluctance. Our intentions should be obvious by the fact that we have stayed in our own space all these years."

George nodded, then realized how silly it was, since the Romulan couldn't see him. "Neutral ground would make more sense for both of us."

Another pause. Then—

"Agreed."

More than a little surprised, George now had no idea what kind of neutral ground could be arranged out here in the middle of nothing. He pressed his lips tight to keep from stammering while he thought about how to phrase the next question.

"What do you suggest?"

"There are two planetoids nearby, one of which is habitable for both of us. We will both have air to breathe, and we will be under each other's guns. You understand my reference."

"I understand. How do you want to do this?"

"I'll take an atmospheric craft and go to the planetoid. You will follow me in a similar craft. I assume you lodge such vehicles."

"We have them. How do I know you won't be leading me into a trap?"

"You may lead the way if you wish. Or I shall land first, and you can scan the area before you land. Any arrangement is negotiable."

George went over it in his mind, then glanced around the bridge to see if he noticed doubt on anyone's face, but his first assessment of his crew had been accurate—scientists, not tacticians. They didn't have the slightest idea how to read the Romulan's offer. He was still on his own.

Partly. He grasped Drake's arm and pulled him over. "What do you think?" he whispered.

"I think I should stick my head in sawdust and wait till it's over," Drake whispered back. "Guesswork, George. Instinct. And there's a lot of stink here to be had. Go in the direction of the best smell."

George straightened again and spoke aloud. "All right, I'll follow you to the planetoid. You land first. If I don't like what I find, the deal's off."

"I shall be waiting."

George turned to Sanawey and gave him a signal to cut off.

"Terminated," Sanawey confirmed.

George snatched Drake by the arm again. "I'm

217

going. While I'm gone, you're going to have to be in charge."

"What, *me?*"

"Yes, you. You're the only other person on board with any real military training. Besides, you can do it. Look at me—remember what Robert said. The same goes for me. I'm completely expendable, understand?" He fixed Drake with a glare. "The minute I leave the ship, you forget about getting me back. Just be sure to wait until they make the first move before you cut loose on them. Then do anything you have to do to get the empress out of here."

"Why do I have to wait till then?"

"Because," George said slowly, "Robert's right, that's why. We're the invaders. We don't have any business firing the first shot."

Drake leaned back and grinned. "Good for you, Geordie."

With a final squeeze of Drake's arm, George said, "And if I don't come back . . . you talk to George Junior and Jimmy for me."

Even Drake couldn't make a joke about that. George broke away and headed for the turbo-lift. At the last minute he spun around and said, "Everybody help Drake. Do whatever it takes to get the ship out of here. I'm going to buy time for you if I can."

"Good luck, Mr. Kirk," Sanawey said from the right.

From the left, Hart gave him a thumbs-up. "We're with you, sir."

"Thanks." He got inside the turbo-lift, then abruptly stepped out again. "Anybody know how to get to the hangar bay from here?"

"You speak their language well," Idrys said, "from what I've heard of it."

She had to lengthen her stride to keep up with

218

t'Cael as he led her and his two bodyguards toward the Nestling bay.

"An interesting language," he said. "Years ago, I was a cultural explorer. I transgressed the Neutral Zone on occasion, secretly of course, trying to learn about the Federation. In those days, there was talk of opening relations. The Senate wanted to see if the Federation had turned hostile and might pounce on us at first sight, or if there might be a chance for relations. I was one of those assigned to learn what could be learned about them. I learned English by monitoring and analyzing Federation communications through deep space. Frequency spying, we called it."

"Such communications weren't guarded?" she asked.

"Part of their trusting nature," t'Cael responded. "Knowledge is open to all. Our spies have had little trouble gaining a command of English. In general, humans like to share information and take the consequences as they come."

"Foolish," she commented.

He glanced at her. "On the contrary, I respect them for it. Better to share knowledge than to fear each other's insights. How else could they have built such a ship as that, if there was no free flow of information?"

She nodded a reluctant agreement and forced her bad leg to limp a little faster, only to find herself drawn up short when the Nestling bay door appeared. She hadn't even been paying attention.

The four of them stepped inside after the closest subcenturion freed the locking control for the bay entrance, and they were in a small vestibule between the corridor and the bay itself. T'Cael turned to the two guards and said, "Prepare the Nestling for launch."

They saluted and hurried across the flat little bay.

Instantly t'Cael turned to Idrys and lowered his voice. "The next hours will tell everything. It's imperative that you keep a stern hand upon the crew. Don't forget that your orders are to be followed without question. This is the most dangerous and most perfect time. If the crew mutinies while I am negotiating, you and I will look like traitors and Ry'iak will look like a hero."

She clung to his striking black gaze. "At the first utterance from Ry'iak's mouth, I shall have him confined."

"Have him killed," t'Cael suggested. "It's more impressive."

She nodded. "You don't believe the humans are bluffing, do you?"

"They're not bluffing," he said with confidence. "They're not as gentle a people as we might think, even in comparison to ourselves. They know perfectly well how to launch an invasion, and this is not the way."

"What is your plan, Primus?" she asked, following him as he looked thoughtfully toward the small open deck where the graceful little Nestling conveyorcraft was being rolled out of its slot. It was a tight area, for the *Raze* itself was a smallish ship, and the Nestling much smaller.

T'Cael gazed at the Nestling. As he spoke, the intimidation he had used on the bridge fell away and honesty colored his voice.

"I must prove to the Council that the Federation has no intention to conquer us. The Praetor has used those rumors to lever himself into power over the Tricameron. If I can prove the Federation doesn't want war, perhaps even convince them to leave a representative behind to address the Senate, I can steer the council back into control and embarrass the Praetor into backing off. The next few hours will tell whether the Empire will slip backward into dictatorship again or move away from it." He placed his hand on the frame of the bay entranceway. "I must make the humans trust me."

Idrys stared at him, realizing he had no intention of taking that Federation ship, that his plans went far beyond simply maintaining the security of the Empire.

He meant to bring down the Praetorate.

A thin film of sweat laced her back beneath her uniform. By not asking her whether she would help him or choose a safer course, he was displaying a confidence in her as deep as his own convictions. Swallowed by the compliment, Idrys hated herself for the fear that rose in her. Still, given the choice between t'Cael and the Supreme Praetor, she would take t'Cael. The humans would trust him; she already did.

He startled her when he broke from his trance and faced her. "It will be up to you to be sure we're worthy of their trust. You must keep firm control of *Raze* and of the Swarm. There will be nothing easy about it."

"I know," she assured him. "By invoking the Pandect, you've given me a weapon. I promise you I'll use it at the slightest provocation."

A mirthless grin turned his mouth upward, for he knew too well the maze he was sending her into. He touched a plait of her hair that hung down over one shoulder and twisted it between his fingers. "Be sure that weapon doesn't have Ry'iak's ammunition inside. There's still the charge of family conspiracy hanging over you. He'll use it if he has the opportunity."

She sighed. "We should have had him confined when we had the chance. I'll have him found and boxed up. Better he not be running free during Imperial alert."

"Wise," t'Cael said. "I wish you power."

With a courteous bow of her head, Idrys responded, "I wish you your goal."

He returned the bow and turned away.

She watched as he strode to the Nestling, which was already humming as its engine warmed up. He climbed inside behind the two subcenturia with a grace born of his years as a warrior.

Before her, a clear panel slid shut between the vestibule and the bay, closing her off from the depressurizing area, and soon the wide door to space opened before the Nestling. She watched, as the narrow craft lifted from the bay deck, drifted through the opening, and turned on a wing toward open space.

The bay door automatically closed.

She was glad for t'Cael's sake that he was off the ship. Now they could begin their work from two fronts, and close in.

She touched the nearest intercom. "Enforcement, this is the Commander."

"Enforcement Squad. Yes, Commander?"

"Locate and restrain Antecenturion Ry'iak and have him brought to the bridge. I'll meet you there."

"Immediately, Commander."

Well, that felt better. She knew her crew, and they were generally loyal to her. She would be able to keep them loyal if she could prevent Ry'iak from picking at their doubts.

With a steadying sigh, she left the hangar bay and turned toward the bridge lift.

A force struck her and rammed the breath from her body. She bent forward and clutched at the sudden tightness, only to find her hands around another hand.

Before her, much too close, was Ry'iak's emotionless face.

He gripped her shoulder and used the leverage to

222

drive the *hazdja* deep into her abdomen, pressing it downward at an angle, as experience had taught him was the best way. With the second thrust, another gush of air rasped out of her. Ry'iak pulled his hand away and moved back from the dance of murder, leaving the weapon's shaft for his victim to caress. As he stepped away, he remembered to steal the commander's own weapon from her thigh strap and tuck it neatly into his robe.

Idrys' eyes locked on him, her mouth open on a windless gasp. She dropped back and twisted against the corridor wall, clutching the weapon that protruded from her stomach. Convulsing against it, she tried to yank it from her body, but succeeded only in mutilating her bowels with its spiderbarbed point. Once inside her, the mechanism had opened itself. No matter how she tried to wring it out, it churned in tighter. Such was the nature of the *hazdja* hand lance—a weapon of traditional elegance and no mercy.

Ry'iak watched, keeping just out of her reach, but close enough to enjoy himself. As she writhed, he had to step out of the way twice. His face was stern and blank, for he perceived this as his duty. Gloating would come later, and he would enjoy that too.

Hating him with her eyes, Idrys grasped the *hazdja* with one hand and reached along the wall with the other, clawing at the intercom panel and a button that would bring her personal guard to this corridor in seconds.

Ry'iak thought about stopping her, but his victory would be grander if she herself simply failed.

His reward came when Idrys slid down across the wall and struck the deck. Her failure was plain. She gritted her teeth, held her body together by force of will, and tried to get back to her feet. She wouldn't let him win with only one blow.

223

Ry'iak was more like a macabre voyeur than an assassin as he sidestepped her movements. He wouldn't touch her again if he could help it, but her determination to stand up dismayed him. She was actually managing to struggle up against the wall, fighting the grip of the *hazdja.*

Pursing his lips in dissatisfaction, Ry'iak grimaced under the pure hatred in his victim's eyes. He wished he could watch her without her seeing him.

As Idrys' knuckle clacked against the rim of the com panel, Ry'iak moved in. He grasped the *hazdja* and twisted it hard.

A convulsion was his reward. Idrys' hands rushed back to the pain. She bent double, crumpled into him with a terrible pant, and couldn't pull another breath from her destiny.

Ry'iak stepped back quickly.

Idrys dropped to her knees, hovered there, then struck the floor and was taken by excrucation. Her eyes glazed over.

Ry'iak waited until her convulsions stopped, and Idrys no longer moved. He paused for another moment, wondering if it was worth it to try to get his expansion lance back, then decided to leave it where it had done him the most good. As he stepped over her, his robe slid across her face, dragging one of her braids. He knew exactly what he would say when he got to the bridge.

Subcommander Kai, he would say, *Commander Idrys is dead. Shall we talk?*

Part III

Strange New Worlds

Chapter Fourteen

SORROW MARRED THE sympathy on McCoy's face, tainted even further by guilt. Did he have any right to talk the captain into changing his mind? Did anyone have the right to demand, or even request, the sacrifice of another person's lifetime? Part of Jim Kirk would always be the captain of the starship. Part of him would remain trapped back in time, where the anguish lived. Other parts of him lived in other places, places and people he had touched over his years of command, people whose lives he had changed by making decisions, by taking his responsibility seriously and doing more than just steering the starship through her missions.

McCoy closed his mouth, having said nothing. In any other condition he could have mocked the self-pity he saw in the captain's eyes, would have scolded him for getting things out of proportion, would have brought him a drink and insisted he count to twenty before thinking such a thing again.

But he said nothing. His usual cynicism was crushed back. Because he had been the cause of all this.

From the edge of the loft opening, Jim Kirk anticipated McCoy's objections.

"It isn't this incident alone," he said. "But it's made me aware that I've been hiding from myself.

I've been faking my way through incident after incident since I took command. How long before the odds catch up with me and history is ruined or a civilization is crushed? How long before I make a mistake too big to correct?" He shook his head and squinted into the sunlight. "No more."

McCoy huffed out his frustration and jabbed a finger at the papers Kirk was holding. "What's in those damned letters, Jim? Why are they making you talk like this?"

Kirk looked down at the letter he'd been reading when McCoy intruded on the sanctity of the loft. He found the spot where he'd stopped reading, and tried to imagine his father's voice speaking the words . . .

There are lots of things I could tell you, now that you're old enough to understand. I'd like to say them in person, but sometimes that's harder, and I'm not there anyway. Space duty is dangerous and I may never get the chance to find out what you boys need from old Dad, so I have to guess.

I love you boys. I wish we could be together all the time. But I'd be lying if I said I didn't like being in space. You both know that. Just remember that it's a job too. I get paid for it. It's duty, pure and simple. Things aren't very fancy once you get used to them, but the job still has to be done. I don't know if I love it anymore, not like I used to. It's like when the three of us were building that model of the Sea Witch *inside the bottle. It's like trying to get the ship to fit in the jar and still look good. Sometimes you have to force it.*

I just want you boys to be careful what you love. Be sure it loves you back.

An odd letter. So many things packed into it. As though his father had been trying to stuff all his feelings for the future into one envelope. And what was that last statement supposed to mean?

Looking at the words with adult eyes, Jim Kirk noticed a difference in the handwriting. A sloppier effort. Or a more reckless one? Or maybe the words had come too fast for neatness. Or they'd been more important than the neatness. And his father had been a military man; he liked things neat. He liked them simple.

Nothing simple here. In fact, this letter had turned disjointed, had lost its direction and its purpose of just keeping contact with two kids back on Earth. Kirk detected an urgency as he read the letter now. He saw that it wasn't very articulate, not the kind of words a ten-year-old and a fourteen-year-old would really understand. He tried to remember if he and his brother had felt any difference in the letters twenty-five years ago, and drew a blank. The elation of getting letters at all had been enough for the two boys who adored a man they hardly saw.

But this letter . . .

This letter is different. Were you in trouble? Danger?

"Was your father on a mission, Jim?" McCoy wondered.

Kirk blinked into the sun and realized it had moved and was now warming his legs as they hung over the loft's edge. He didn't answer. He grew pensive, as though rethinking a thought he'd had before. He'd given himself excuses for the mystery, but only fabricated ones.

"We don't know," he admitted.

McCoy's voice, a few feet away, rose slightly. "Not even your mother?"

Kirk moved his head a fraction to either side. "This batch of letters arrived almost all at once. Then, nothing. All we knew was that he left Starbase Two suddenly. Under mysterious circumstances. I've never been able to squeeze the details out of Starfleet Command, no matter how I use my influence." He said it slowly, testing it as it came out, because such an admission from a member of Starfleet's decorated elite didn't sound too good.

McCoy, for at least the fifth time today, said exactly what popped into his mind.

"Maybe they don't know."

Kirk looked over. "What?"

McCoy paused, brows bunched. Had he said that? He leaned forward. "Could that be? Could they not know?" Shifting his position, he wagged his finger at the cornfield and wondered aloud. "Starfleet personnel don't just vanish from their assigned posts, at least not without investigation."

"There was no investigation."

"Just my point. Somebody knew what was going on. No records?"

"None."

"Maybe that's it then, Jim. Maybe the information went away with changes of staff at command."

"It wasn't that long ago, Bones."

"Long enough for prearranged memory failure," McCoy insisted with a wry twist to his tone. "Long enough to let an incident slip away. Damn Fleet frame of mind anyway. How tip-top-secret could it have been for nobody at all to know what went on?"

Kirk stared over the waving cornfield again, caught up by an old yearning to know what happened to his father.

And the old yearning piled itself on top of the new ache, the new pain. The price of heroism was too dear. "Why should any one man pay so much?" he murmured to the blue Iowa sky.

McCoy watched, silenced by the question. Was the one man Kirk, or his father? But he knew; he really did know what the question meant. And he hated knowing.

Weakly, and trying to sound wise, he muttered, "The price of prestige, Jim."

Kirk's hand tightened on the letter, though imperceptibly. Price. Always a price for everything. Nothing could be simply had and kept and cherished. The price of high science had dug deeply into his heart this time, perhaps too deeply to repair. He was paying the price of being able to travel time. Most intelligent people would view that as a supreme privilege. So why did he feel so deeply cheated?

"I'll never forget Spock's face when he explained it to me," he murmured, squinting over the flat landscape. "Even he could feel the loss."

McCoy shifted, suddenly uncomfortable, fearing the subject was about to come up.

"Spock said she was right, but at the wrong time," Kirk went on, suddenly picturing his first officer, a memory of true reluctance and true sympathy on a Vulcan face that should've shown nothing. "Time . . ." As he whispered the word, he saw the woman again. Dull violet lace of a past fashion covered narrow shoulders and breasts he never even considered touching. He never had time to consider it. His heart had stopped at the moment he and Spock discovered that Edith Keeler had to die in order to set time right, and it hadn't started beating again yet.

He leaned his shoulder against the loft frame and looked down. When he and Sam were boys, it used to make him dizzy to look down from here. Now it made him dizzy to contemplate the quirks of fate—that the life, or death, of one person could dictate vast turns in history.

It seemed silly, like a pebble turning the course of a whole river. What if Alexander the Great had lived one more year instead of dying at the age of thirty-three? What if somebody had tripped John Wilkes Booth and made him drop the pistol? What if Anwar Sadat had ducked down instead of facing assassination with a courage so casual? What if Yoradyl Young had died two days before her speech to the Vulcan Council instead of two days after?

No one knew better than a starship captain how many individuals existed out there. While the deaths of thousands sometimes seemed inconsequential, the death of one could become a fulcrum of history. How tragic, people would say when contemplating the deaths of Alexander, Lincoln, Sadat, Young, Geltredi . . . but no one would say that of Edith Keeler. Though she spoke of peace and would have kept the United States from its destiny in World War II, no one with any sense could possibly wish that she had lived past that day. She understood so much, yet she didn't understand that peace isn't always attained by example alone.

A woman of peace, but at the wrong time.

Kirk gathered his legs closer to his body, a motion of unaware need. "Spock and I were mistaken," he said. "Peace wasn't the way. Pacifism isn't always the moral course. The moral course then was to resist the aggression. Stalin went on to murder millions of people, and got away with it because the world was tired and battle-weary. He made Hitler look like a second-story man. But because the world was tired of fighting for what was morally right, millions upon millions more had to die. Edith would have hated seeing that," he added, seeing the face of Edith Keeler as she spoke her words of hope. "And if I'd been a wiser man, I could have found an alternative to letting her die. There must have been some other thing to do, Bones . . . some . . . alternative . . ."

"You're flogging yourself, Jim," McCoy said, struggling to keep his tone flat. "It won't bring her back. And it won't give her the glory she would've had if she'd lived."

Kirk's eyes grew unfocused. "She . . . did live, didn't she? Or did we imagine her?"

McCoy pressed his lips together and admitted to himself that he'd had those thoughts too, though more fleetingly than the captain. Unlike events in a real past, they had nothing from 1930 to prove they'd ever been there. Nothing came back through the portal that hadn't gone through in the first place. Not a strand of her silly flapper haircut that might have clung to the captain's collar, or the smudge of pale lipstick on his cheek.

Nothing came through but the pain. And here they were, clinging to the pain because it was all they had to prove that Edith Keeler had ever existed at all. It wasn't right that a woman of such optimism and

233

farsightedness should leave a legacy consisting only of pain.

"What do you want, Jim? Answers?" he murmured, helpless. "You know she couldn't have come back with us. The time-travel process wouldn't have allowed her to come through. She belonged in another time. She lived then . . . she had to die then."

But Jim Kirk was lost again in that other era, and he didn't feel obligated to come back. Who could say what it was about a plain face and a dynamic spirit that made her still be alive for him? Once again he relived that nightmarish moment when he stopped McCoy from pushing the woman out of the truck's path while the truck ran her down and preserved history. She had turned in time to see the truck that killed her; she'd had time to scream before the impact crushed away the echo—

Did she see me stop him? Was there time for her to wonder why I would do such a thing to her?

"The cost of heroism is too high. Haven't I paid my dues, Bones?" he asked aloud. "Mine and other people's too?"

From the side of the loft opening, there was a crushing pause, so long and so heavy that even Kirk felt the flow of guilt.

Finally, McCoy spoke. "Certainly, you paid mine."

The words were cast in contrition, something McCoy wasn't particularly good at showing.

Kirk looked over now. "It wasn't your fault, Bones."

"No," McCoy acknowledged, "but it was because of me."

"She would've died anyway."

"I'm not talking about Edith. I'm talking about you. If it hadn't been for chasing me into the past, you wouldn't be going through this now."

The captain nodded, shifting his sympathy to the

234

other man. "A drug overdose doesn't let you make choices."

"I should've put the hypo away," McCoy said with a self-deprecating swing of his hand. "A ship's surgeon should know better than to fool around with a loaded hypo in the middle of turbulence." He looked up now, blue eyes keen with regret, his voice heavy with guilt. "It was an intern's mistake, Jim . . . and I'm sorry."

A burst of warmth rose up inside the captain as he gazed back, and he realized how seldom his position allowed him any thanks—or any apology. All the things he did for the crew, for the Federation, for the galaxy . . . all the decisions he'd made when there was no one else to make them, all the difficulties he'd either handled or deflected, all the danger, all the strength, all the anguish . . .

And so seldom a thank-you to a ship's captain. Just part of the job, everyone thought. Yet this wasn't part of the job. And it wasn't fair.

This pain, though, wasn't going unshared.

He looked at McCoy, and spoke quietly but firmly. "You were worth it."

Chapter Fifteen

SPACE WAS NOT so black and forbidding as poets would have their readers believe. This area of it was spackled with natural color, an unexpectedly rich tapestry of nebulae—a veil nebula, an emission nebula, and scraggles of color that were homes to pulsars. In both the near and far distances around this little solar system, like the walls of a beautiful room, there were dust mists, shining gases, clusters, and at least two noticeable planetary nebulae in ring form, still expanding, their cores in nuclear burn, on the long path to becoming white dwarfs. Space was full of color here, if distant color. The black silk panorama was beaded with gaseous greens and flaming reds, and the diamond whites of stars and reflected light. So much beauty brought a twinge of envy. He wondered why its inhabitants would look outward to possess more.

It was alien space in the fullest meaning of the phrase, a phrase as dark as the danger it represented, and no spacelight could brighten it. Alien space, even enemy space.

Only a matter of definition, George Kirk thought as he steered the bulky Starfleet shuttlecraft along a thin diplomatic tightrope. Ahead of him a small graceful craft flew, piloted either by hope or by deception. Until he landed he wouldn't know which.

Definition. Yes, a subtle line. After all, he was the

236

alien here. He kept forcing himself to remember that, to keep a corner of his mind in touch with Robert April lest he forget his responsibilities. Generosity was hard to maintain after the devastation the Romulans had wrought in Federation space all those decades past. Surely they'd known the Federation would defend itself. What had they hoped to gain by the massacre at Starbase 1 and the destruction of the ship that came to answer the distress call? Could a civilization actually miss being at war enough to make war happen for no reason?

On his command console, a small viewscreen showed his aft view: the empress' gleaming ivory hull, her lack of markings and her military streamlining, suddenly looking very suspicious, and the Romulan command ship hovering not far away. Feeling his palms grow moist, George willed himself not to look at that screen, to fix his eyes instead on the vehicle he was following.

How'd I get into this? How'd I become the pivot? I'm not even qualified to be first officer, much less represent the Federation. I can't even represent myself when I go home. This is the stupidest thing I've ever done, and I can't quit doing it. What am I going to say to this guy? What if he looks like a lizard? I never talked to a lizard. I don't know if I can explain our ideals to somebody who thinks like a lizard . . .

The Romulan fighter veered abruptly toward a little green-brown planetoid just this side of a bright dust cloud. Mostly bodies of water and dirt plains, the planetoid had several jutting mountain ranges that were layered by mossy growths, but there were no forests or anything so extreme as a desert. A hazy atmosphere glowed in the light of the nearest sun, and made the silver Romulan craft shine in the haze.

George followed, the two craft swerving with deceptive laziness between mountains until finally the

Romulan vehicle made a wide loop, drifted to the ground in a narrow valley.

George continued onward, flying just overhead of the resting Romulan ship, scouting both the ship and the surrounding valley. He looped the shuttlecraft around for another pass, this time from a different angle, and left the area only when he was sure there were no hidden surprises. Unless Romulans looked like rocks, there was nothing here but planetoid and one little transport.

And he still didn't like it. Romulans weren't for trusting. Simple philosophy, historically screened.

He flew out of what he estimated would be close sensor range for a craft that small—about a mile and a half—and landed in a cluster of mossy hillocks where the shuttlecraft couldn't be easily spotted from the sky.

The brand-new shuttlecraft hovered a few inches over the ground at the last minute, then dropped with a thump. The shuttlecraft itself was easy to fly, but he felt silly sitting in this seven-person craft all by himself, and it took him a few seconds to figure out which of her landing maneuvers were automatic and which he had to key in from the console. Once firmly on the ground, the engines hummed a few seconds to let the integrators drain of mixer exhaust, then they shut down with a mechanical wheeze. Another five seconds of hissing went by as the craft automatically adjusted its interior pressurization to the outside, then everything shut down and waited to be told what to do next. George sat in the silence.

Sitting here wasn't going to make the inevitable any less inevitable, but he had to give himself a few seconds to measure things. The odds, the importance, the perspective—things. Yet no matter how he tried to clear his mind, all he found there was a blur of accidents and more things to go wrong. He tried not to think that a galactic war or an otherwise unreachable peace was hinging on his actions. No single person with any sense of humility wanted to be in that position.

This position, he corrected. *The position I'm in.*

He gritted his teeth, overcome by a sudden sense of power. He was the only person here, and he would handle things in his own way. That was all anyone could ask of him.

He pressed a nearby button harder than needed.

"Official log, Commander Kirk reporting. I'm about to scout the territory where the Romulans landed. Primary goal at the moment is to meet with their commander and feel out his intentions in hopes of getting us out of their space in one piece. I consider myself thoroughly expendable, and I've left orders behind that the starship is to blast its way out of Romulan space if it's forced to." He paused, and considered what he had just said. It sounded incautious now that he heard it aloud.

His hand spread across the command console, as though the shuttlecraft had become his only confidant, and he spoke in a less arrogant tone. "That order is my responsibility, not the responsibility of the people crewing the starship. I realize such an action could trigger a war between the Federation and the Romulan Empire, and for the sake of the ambassadors who are going to have to deal with this, it should be known that the action wasn't sanctioned by Starfleet or the Federation, or anyone other than myself. Since the current crew on the starship is made up of technicians, scientists, and engineers instead of military personnel, I feel the order is only fair to them. Military personnel understand the concept of sacrifice when they go on missions, but this isn't a mission and these people don't deserve to die for a malfunction." The conviction came out in his voice the more he talked, a dedication to the people on board the starship, and even to the starship itself—to those who invested in it and those who believed in it. To Robert April.

To George Samuel Jr. and James Tiberius, who deserved something to remember about their father, more than what would be left when they grew up and discovered the ordinariness of a security position on a starbase. Some concrete example of what he'd been trying to teach them in his letters.

Only when his neck started aching did he realize he had clenched his jaw. More words hung on his lips, things he longed to tell his sons, to tell Robert, and even his wife.

Anger welled in his chest, anger at himself for his cowardice.

"Kirk out," he blurted, and slammed his palm on the log-commit switch.

He swung out of his seat so abruptly that it wobbled and shuddered behind him. By the time it swiveled to a stop, he had donned a field survival pack, set his hand-cannon at its maximum blast range, strapped it to his side, and was jumping out the shuttlecraft door. Only when his feet hit the ground did he realize that he should've double-checked the breathability of the atmosphere, and not just taken the Romulan's word for it. Was *that* stupid! He'd promised himself he wouldn't take the Romulan's word for anything, yet with a mile and a half still between him and the meeting, he'd already broken that promise. Some diplomat.

He tested the ground to be sure it was stable enough to hold the shuttlecraft's weight for as long as it took, then he started walking in the direction his compass told him was the navigational coordinate where his quarry waited.

It was a marshy mile and a rocky half. There was

animal life all over the place, everything from bugs to large bearlike beasts. Good—their presence would confuse any sensors that might be trying to find a human who didn't want to be found. George was actually glad to see big fuzzy faces that might otherwise be taken as threatening. The animals peeked out of hollows and knuckles of rock but none made any hostile moves. If he'd had only them to concentrate on, he might have been worried. But his mind was on other things, reciting lines and remembering laws, and trying to anticipate what the enemy would say so he would be sure to have his answers ready.

Enemy, enemy, enemy . . . he couldn't shake the terminology, no matter how he tried to sweeten it with diplomacy's optimism. *I'm just no diplomat. I can't afford to take a stand I don't really believe in or even comprehend. Robert . . . I don't know what to do. I don't have your visions. I can't use what I don't have. And I'm not going to let my weakest abilities rule my actions. I don't intend to be completely upfront with a race that considers massacre fair play.*

Why did they really want him here? What were their real motives for wanting to meet face to face? There had to be some other reason than the flabby one the Romulan commander had given, something about their race considering such meetings productive. There was a sour ring to that kind of language in a military situation. George steeled himself for whatever surprise might be awaiting him.

His compass started a subdued beeping. He was getting close.

Hunching down, he drew his hand-cannon and shoved his field pack around to the back of his hip. After shutting off the homing beeper, he moved in.

The Romulan vessel's silver nose was the first visible evidence that his compass had spoken truly. Crouching as he moved, George skirted the rocks at

241

the thin valley's rim and finally came around to where he could see the enemy.

"Lizards," he whispered, suddenly anxious to get on with it.

Two of them. One with a red sash, the other with a blue sash. He was both surprised and relieved to see that they were quite humanoid, at least from the outside. Maybe they had shark oil for blood or something, but they had two legs, two arms, and a head each. Both wore helmets of an unidentifiable gray-gold metal. Their faces were darkish, almost like Klingons, though without the sheen of Klingon skin. Both heavily armed, pacing the area, watching for him. Which one was the commander? Would Romulans consider blue a color of higher distinction, or red?

He watched them for several minutes, trying to see if one gave orders to the other, or if one seemed noticeably subordinate. All he got out of it was several minutes of nothing. Stalling, really. He stretched a numb thigh, got up, and started skirting the rocks again, hoping for a better angle, perhaps even a closer look.

As he carefully jumped between two juts of mossy stone, keeping his shadow from giving him away, something caught his eye. A third presence. Royal-blue clothes. Yellow fuzz. No helmet.

Puzzled, he bundled himself low along the stone and peeked toward the open area near the Romulan ship. There, sitting on a granite buttress off to one side, only about twenty feet from him, was the last thing he expected to see.

"A Vulcan!" he breathed.

The sound of his exclamation startled him and he clamped his lips shut. He pressed his shoulder blades against the rock again and forced himself to think silently. A Vulcan . . . Federation ally . . . *They've kidnapped a Vulcan! And they'll never negotiate as long as they have a hostage.*

Now he knew why the Romulans wanted to meet face to face. They wanted their hostage clearly seen.

His decision was immediate. He held his breath, the muzzle of his hand-cannon brushing his ear, and pushed himself off the rock and through the crevice toward the Vulcan.

The Vulcan saw him first. George took it as a tribute to his stealth that a flash of surprise crossed the Vulcan's face when he caught sight of George. The Vulcan pulled his hands from where they had been resting in his lap, but by the time he stood up, George was grabbing his arm and pulling him around behind him so they could both be protected by the hand-cannon.

Nearer to the ship, the two Romulans swung around, drawing their weapons, but froze as George leveled his cannon first at one, then the other, then swung it stiffly between them in obvious threat. They might not speak his language, but from their expressions, they understood his meaning quite well.

"Back up," he said, pushing the Vulcan along behind him as he retreated from the open space.

T'Cael saw his men start to defy the human's weapon, and from behind the human he raised his hands and motioned them to stay where they were, at least until he could figure out what this lunatic was up to. Was this a guard sent ahead to isolate him, or was this the first officer himself? Was he dealing with a maniac? Quite possibly, for the human wasn't holding his weapon *on* t'Cael, but in protection of t'Cael. Protection? Why? There was a whole ship filled with people up there; why had they sent down their luna-tic?

243

For the moment, t'Cael decided he would go along.

He gave the guards a second and sterner signal to stay where they were and wait.

"Come on," the Starfleet officer snapped as he grasped t'Cael's elbow and dragged him far back into the lichen-covered bluffs and into a hollow that looked defensible.

George pushed the Vulcan down into the hollow ahead of himself, then turned and watched carefully in the direction from which they'd come, expecting the Romulans to show up any minute.

"Speak English?" he asked.

T'Cael shrugged slightly. "I speak it well enough . . ."

"Did they hurt you?"

"Hurt me? No . . ."

"You were lucky they had a reason to keep you alive. I had a feeling all along about them. Find out anything about them that we can use to get out of this?"

T'Cael frowned. He had no idea how to answer that question. In fact, he had no idea why the human had seen fit to "rescue" him from his own party. When the Starfleet man turned to get his answer, t'Cael simply shook his head slowly.

"No," George grumbled, "I don't suppose they let you see much. Here." He pulled out his extra hand laser and stuffed it into the Vulcan's hands. "If any of those bastards shows his head over the rocks, shoot 'im."

Thoroughly confused, t'Cael stared at the weapon he now held. Kidnapped, protected, and now given a weapon?

The Starfleet officer glanced at him. "How long have they had you?"

"Oh, quite a while," t'Cael said evasively.

"Yeah, I've heard stories of Vulcans occasionally

244

disappearing near the Neutral Zone. Up till now, nobody had the nerve to suggest the Romulans might be kidnapping them. I guess we know for sure now, don't we?"

"Vulcans," t'Cael murmured. "I see . . ."

"What?"

"Are you the first officer of the battlecruiser? The man who promised to meet with them?"

"In the flesh. I'm beginning to think I made a mistake. We're at a disadvantage here. I shouldn't have agreed to this. You got lucky."

T'Cael smiled, but the Fleet man wasn't watching. "Yes. Very lucky."

If George had thought about it, he'd have remembered that Vulcans didn't believe in Lady Luck and her fickle court. At the moment he was confused enough by the fact that they hadn't been followed by the lizards, who had obviously intended to use this Vulcan for some sort of blackmail.

"Do you intend to negotiate with them?" the Vulcan was asking him.

"I don't know now. That's what I hoped to do when I came down, but they weren't honest. They didn't tell me about you. What else didn't they tell me? I can't afford to fall over any tripwires on this one."

"What are your plans, then?"

George heaved a sigh of terrible frustration and said, "I don't know. I could just take you back to the starship and blast them out of space."

"You could . . ."

"I could. But that'd mean galactic war. And we don't want that."

"'We,' meaning whom?"

"The Federation, who else? And 'we,' too. I don't want it either."

"Are you saying," t'Cael went on cautiously, "that you may agree to negotiate in good faith even yet?"

"I don't think I have a choice. If I can get them to be honest, I'll negotiate my butt off. Get down a little more, all right? I don't want them to see you."

"Ah. Forgive me," t'Cael said, and lowered himself onto a slanted slab.

"'S okay," George said with a wave of his hand-cannon, and continued surveying the crags. "Why aren't they following us?"

"How fortunate for them that your navigation system blundered," t'Cael said, testing.

The Starfleet man shook his head. "It was terrible. Just when you think you've got some technology licked, it throws you sideways a few thousand light-years and you've got a mess on your hands." He paused then, and lowered his weapon in a sorrowful kind of awareness. As he stared at the rocks, he said, "I guess the Romulans didn't ask for this either."

T'Cael nodded and said, "Even to a warrior race, the taste of bloodshed sours after a time."

"Let's hope you're not the only one who thinks that," George snapped back. "Do you think they'll fire on my ship now that I've gotten you away from them?"

"Possibly," t'Cael responded, still being cautious, "though a few of them will be glad to see me gone."

"I'd better get you back to the starship. As long as you're available to them, they're not going to deal with me. I'll take you back, then I'll have to talk to them again." He stepped from one rock to a higher one, just to check the landscape one more time before moving out. "Who knows? Maybe this is their idea of a joke."

T'Cael grinned. "Were the circumstances less somber, I would find you very funny."

"Yeah, well—" George suddenly caught his breath. Funny? *Funny?*

He whirled around. His alleged hostage was gazing

246

at him with this weird grin—definitely a grin. Definitely.

They stared at each other.

George's voice caught in his throat. "You're not a Vulcan . . ."

T'Cael shook his head, slowly and clearly.

George almost fell off his rock.

"Then . . . who are you?"

T'Cael felt a sudden desire to fabricate a comforting lie for the human, rather as he might comfort a child who was about to be severely disillusioned about his own deductive abilities. He really didn't want to make this man feel stupid. There was no advantage in a humiliated enemy.

He straightened his back, and folded his hands innocuously in his lap. The weapon lay on his thigh, carefully unthreatening.

"I am t'Cael Zaniidor Kilyle, Field-Primus of the Second Imperial Swarm in the praetor's service," he announced with both a touch of pride and a touch of apology. "And who are you?"

The Fleet officer paled and sank back against the rock, still staring. "I'm an idiot," he groaned.

T'Cael smiled again. "I prefer not to call you that, if I need not."

"You look like a . . ."

"Obviously there's a genetic link in the distant past between my race and the Vulcans," t'Cael said, "but they have forgotten us."

The Starfleet man's weapon snapped up between them suddenly, and his face grew fierce. Insulted, perhaps?

The smile slipped a little from t'Cael's lips, but didn't disappear entirely.

"All right—" George choked. "All right, then, that's how it is . . . you're . . . you're my prisoner then. If that's how it has to be."

247

T'Cael moved his shoulders in a small shrug. Before saying anything, he held out the second laser in an attempt to give it back before creating the wrong impression. "We came to negotiate. It's not too late. Tell me your name."

Perspiring, George half circled the Romulan, snatched back his laser, and leveled the hand-cannon at what was probably the enemy's heart. Or at least a lung. "Kirk," he rasped. "Acting first officer."

"You actually are the first officer, then."

George drew his brows together. "Yes . . . why?"

"There was a question on my bridge when you took over the conversation from the captain. We thought your captain was feigning illness and sending an expendable lackey in his place. To reduce our leverage over you."

"Then why'd you agree to come?"

"I read confidence in your voice. You didn't pause to take signals before you spoke. It was a gamble."

Beneath his skin, George's nerves buzzed like hot electrodes. He hadn't been ready for this, and he felt like the butt end of a jackhammer. He wondered how diplomats ever learned which questions to ask or which answers to give, and how to know when truth was coming back at them. He stared at the person who had suddenly gone from ally to enemy, and tried to read the calmly bemused expression. But for George, who had spent his life tilling his emotions like topsoil and cultivating his opinions not far beneath, reading such opaque signals was as tough as learning a new language.

"I haven't come to make any deals," he said. "We just want to get out of your space, preferably as fast as we got into it, and preferably with the whole incident forgotten."

The Romulan tilted his head thoughtfully. "Interesting, since your appearance here is an act of war, according to our agreement with the Federation about the treaty zone. You expect us to forgive the transgression without so much as a question?''

George felt his neck itch. "I'm trying to keep an accident from becoming an incident. The Federation doesn't even know where we are. They're not responsible, but neither are we." He caught his tongue, realizing he'd made a mistake in admitting that they were completely alone here, without backup, without hope of rescue, without the knowledge of those who would stand up for them if the Romulans decided to take them hostage for a bigger price. His hand squeezed tight on the cannon's grip. A loud bleeping sound suddenly pierced the grotto. The Romulan stood up abruptly, and his gaze shot skyward. The bleeping noise was coming from his belt, accompanied by a flashing green light on a thin mechanical device that George was only now able to see.

Suddenly the Romulan slashed his hand toward George. "Get down! Down quickly!"

Standing pressed against the rock, George glanced around in confusion. The bleeping noise got louder, and from the sky itself came a contained reddish glow.

T'Cael ignored the weapon in Kirk's hand and dove toward the other man. With a twist he pushed the laser aside and slammed them both to the ground.

The red glow in the sky became a rage of energy. With it came a whine, a predatory shriek that caused the two enemies to huddle together with their arms clamped over their ears. Then—*whine-BOOM* . . . *whine-BOOM* . . . *whine-BOOM* . . .

Again and again, blast sheets pummeled the landscape. Each wave burned deeper and deeper into the face of the planetoid, until the ground was seared clean of vegetation and a burning stench filled the air. And still they came, sheet after sheet, for a full minute or more.

Silence, when it returned, was even more terrifying, for now it shuddered with the memory of what might come again.

The sky became blue again. The stench thickened.

George opened his eyes and pulled his hands away from his ears. Next to him, the Romulan crawled to his feet, undisguised astonishment on his face. Together they gaped outward at an incinerated landscape.

George waved his hand-cannon limply and stammered, "We . . . we didn't do that . . . you've got to believe me."

The Romulan was still as the stone, unblinking as he looked through the mossy spires to the valley where his ship had been, and saw instead a twist of bubbling wreckage, melted and charred beyond recognition. "I know," he whispered. As he sank away from the sight, slipping downward against the stone wall to stare now at nothing, he repeated, "I know."

From above, George watched desolation set in on the Romulan's fine features. He bent his shaking knees and crouched on the rock buttress, looking down at the Romulan. "I don't understand," he admitted. "What does it mean?"

With shallow breaths, the Romulan lowered even more, until he was slumped against the outcropping. His arms were limp, and there was a look of desolation on his face.

His words, though spoken softly, were blistered with sorrow.

"It means," he whispered, "I am alone."

"Mr. Reed, they're veering away!"

Florida's shout took the bridge crew by surprise.

250

Drake spun around and almost tripped, wishing that nothing would happen to necessitate his giving any orders. He caught the last glimpse of a black wingtip slipping out of view toward substarboard. "Switch viewer," he said.

The screen wavered and solidified again on a disconcerting scene: the Romulan warship opening fire on the planetoid in the middle distance.

"They're cutting loose on the planet!" Florida yelled, louder and angrier, this time.

"George . . ." Drake moved to the center of the command arena, though he didn't take the command chair—it wasn't his. What would George do? he wondered. What would April do? "Looks like carnival spirit has hit the streets of Trinidad, old friend," he whispered.

Florida twisted around to look at him questioningly. "Mr. Kirk's down there! We should do something!"

"Like what, do you think?"

"I don't know . . ." Florida's hands stiffened on the helm controls. He didn't want to be the one to confirm the abrogation of the treaty.

Drake didn't feel the same kind of responsibility. He would do whatever was best, and if there was a war, it was surely someone else's fault. "Warning shots, how 'bout?" he called out. "Fire between them and the planet. Let them know how we feel about it, eh?"

Florida's face hardened, and he leaned forward. "Yeah!" He turned the navigational disk and laid in a new heading, then flicked his helm toggles and urged the ship into motion. "Executing." He turned to Drake then and asked, "Lasers or particle shots?"

Drake blinked. "Which do you think?"

Florida shrugged and bit his lip.

"Better they feel something, eh?" Drake thought

251

aloud. "With lasers they'll only see it. Particle beams are different, yes?"

"Yes, they disperse somewhat. There's a definite blast haze around the target."

"Even if they don't hit something?"

Florida looked at him, and this time even grinned. "Yes."

"It's a fallout effect," Hart explained from her updeck station. "The beam's corona should give them a good slap. Even a miss will rattle them."

"I want them rattled," Drake said, then waved his hand at Florida and invited, "Rattle hard."

"Full power?"

Drake leered at the viewer. "Definitely."

"One shot?"

"One . . . no." Drake watched the screen and murmured, "How 'bout four? Four quick shots alternating around their ship. *Bing, bing, bing, bing.* Wouldn't want them to think we missed by mistake, eh?"

Florida's hands crisscrossed his board, then he hit the firing toggle.

Fuzzy blue bolts of energy sliced outward from outer-hull firing locks at an angle, giving the Romulan vessel a hard shake. The Romulan ship wobbled, and slanted away from the planetoid at high speed.

"Yes!" Florida shook his fist at the screen and bounced in his chair.

Drake shook his fist at the retreating Romulans. "Put that in your stocking and jig it!" As soon as he heard his own words, he remembered George. The planetoid had already been fired upon.

He turned to Sanawey and asked, "Can we communicate with Commander Kirk?"

"I've been trying. Either there's some kind of atmospheric disturbance blocking my frequencies," Sanawey said unhappily, "or there's nobody down there to receive it."

"Keep trying, eh?" Drake looked at the command chair's intercom panel, found the right button, and punched it with his little finger. "I say, sickbay?"

There was a pause that would never have been there had the ship boasted its full complement. Then—

"Sickbay. Poole. What do you want?"

"Advice, if possible, milady."

"No, he can't come up." The doctor's voice was laced with anguish. She went on without waiting for his next question. *"I had to put him in surgery to relieve the subdural pressure. You're just going to have to do without him. Let Kirk handle things. He wants to anyway."*

"Yes . . . well . . . you see, as they say in elite circles, there's the rub. George is not exactly here."

Another pause. *"Exactly where is he, and exactly why?"*

"He had to leave the ship."

"He WHAT?"

Drake wrinkled his nose, knowing how this was going to sound.

Before he got the chance, Dr. Poole had figured it all out. *"Are you telling me he actually took them up on their offer?"*

"Well, in a way. You see, he was taking Captain April's place."

"Captain April is a qualified diplomat! George Kirk is a balloon without a rubberband! He'll get himself killed! Can't you get him back?"

"If I only could," he murmured. "In any case, missus, I'd truly love to speak to Captain as soon as he's in a speaking condition, right-o?"

"I'll keep it in mind," Sarah blustered back at him, cut off communication with a hard snap.

Drake moved away from the command chair as though the doctor was about to come through it and slap him around. "All right, Geordie," he muttered,

253

"we shall do it your way, then. Let's see if these birdies can take strong juju."

The little grotto was filled with melancholy. Ill-omen still lingered in the sky. Vapory clouds congealed in the lower atmosphere as the planetoid rebounded around the hole that had been punched in its airspace.

George understood the concept of a military defeat, and that wasn't what he saw in the dispirited enemy who sat so grief-stricken on the grotto rocks. There was more than disappointment in the Romulan's empty eyes, in his immobility. He seemed inconsolable.

Suddenly inclined not to hold his weapon quite so stiffly, George asked, "Do you have an explanation for this?"

The Romulan—what had he said his name was? —sighed.

"Unfortunately," he said, "I have several."

George took a step closer. "They're going to fire on my ship, aren't they?"

"Most likely." He sounded despondent.

With a turn of his hip, George grabbed his emergency kit and dug into it for the communicator. He flipped open the antenna grid and wiggled a frequency modulator. "This is Kirk," he began, unable to resist an urge to look up into the sky as though it would help. "We're under attack. Take defensive action. Do you copy? Defend yourselves. Drake? Anybody? Damn it . . ." He glared at the communicator, which did little more than whine and crackle at him.

"Unless that device is much more potent than it looks," t'Cael said, "it can't break through the imbalance in the planet's electrical field."

George stopped fiddling, his finger poised on the frequency dial. "What imbalance?"

254

"Our plasma ray's effect on the atmospheric activity in this region."

"How long till it clears?"

"Several of your minutes, or longer. Difficult to say." The Romulan lowered his gaze to the grotto floor, once again overcome by grief.

With a snap, the communicator grid clamped shut. George stuffed it back into the pack and said, "Then we have to get back to my shuttlecraft. It has a stronger gain."

"They'll track us," the Romulan said. "They'll blanket the area with another shot."

"Maybe. But I'm betting my people up there aren't going to sit back and make it easy. And there are you-and-me-sized animals all over, probably enough to confuse sensors for a few minutes at least. Let's go while we still have the advantage. Come on."

T'Cael stood up now, suppressing his anguish. "No. Please understand. Your chances are much better without me. You must suspect by now that I am expected to be dead."

George nodded. "I know an assassination attempt when I see one."

"Then you must know I can't go with you to your ship."

"This place is your coffin if you stay."

"And yours."

"I don't intend to stay. Start walking."

T'Cael pursed his lips and shook his head, his large eyes shaded. "If my fleet suspects I'm aboard your ship, they'll never let you go."

"Don't fool yourself," George snapped, tight-lipped, his eyes suddenly hard. "They don't intend to let us go. And you know it."

As George watched the man who was supposed to have been the enemy's ambassador and had now become their victim, the last of his fear slid away

255

under cold realization and anger at the whole situation. "Is there something wrong with your people? This shouldn't have happened. Act of war, my ass! We don't want any war! Why should we? Why do you suspect us?"

T'Cael leaned against the moist stone. "Many of my people fear Federation strength."

"Why?" George shot back. "Give me one reason! Tell me one time the Federation conquered anybody. Tell me one time we attacked anybody anywhere without being provoked first. Just one! Just one time we fought for any other reason than defense of somebody who'd been attacked from outside first. You can't. There aren't any!" Dirt gritted beneath his boots as he paced the grotto. "If a Romulan ship stumbled into Federation space and needed help, they'd get it. We'd fix the goddamned ship, give them a candy bar, and send them home. But what do *we* get? This!"

"You sound bitter, Officer Kirk."

"Commander Kirk, and I am! Damned right I am. Why shouldn't I be? I don't mind getting killed, but I'd like to get killed for a better reason than Romulan belligerence and greed."

The elegant enemy touched the rock wall as though he had some rapport with it, and he spoke to it instead of to George.

"Not entirely greed," he said. "Instinct. It's very difficult for a warrior race to overcome that urge which has become instinctive. The Vulcans overcame it with logic. They sacrificed emotion to it. My people have remained unwilling to give up emotion. We have made efforts toward redirecting our warlike propensities. Some of us once turned to space exploration to channel our aggressiveness, our suspicion of other civilizations. But we were not galactically mature. Everywhere we went we found more reasons to revert

256

to habits of conquest. My culture—our political system—allows the hunger for power to become ravenous. There is no inbred check to that power. From the lowest local official to the Supreme Praetor himself, our culture is built upon conquest."

"And somebody just powered you down," George said.

The Romulan's silence was clear answer.

George prodded, "Because . . ."

"Because it was my goal to spare your ship. To open relations between our civilizations."

"That'll be the day," George snapped.

T'Cael looked up. "Can you be so pessimistic and still call yourself advanced?"

"Look who's talking. *Your* people fired on us, remember? Not mine. We just want out of here."

"Yes, you must get out. If my fleet is allowed to take your ship, there will be no hope of negotiation with the Federation. I have no desire to see the chance for peace disappear. But I have failed. I am impotent now. It remains in your favor that my officers believe their assassination of me succeeded. I'll warn you that more ships are on the way. You must hurry."

"I can't leave you on this lump," George said, his anger slipping away to both pity and an unexpected desire to save this unusual man. "You'd be dead in a week."

"And where will you take me? What place is there for a Romulan in the Federation?"

"What place? You'll be a celebrity. Everybody'll want to know everything about the Romulan Empire. Strength, organization, culture—"

"I won't tell those things."

It was almost a verbal slap. George stopped in midbreath.

"I have no desire," t'Cael went on, "to see the Empire make war upon your civilization, but neither

257

can I allow the Federation to use me against my own government." He turned and held out a hand. "You see the problem. Better I die here."

"You're not going to stay here," George insisted. "You'll come back with me. Nobody has to know. You could pass as a Vulcan."

"Pretend to be a Vulcan the rest of my life?" T'Cael's steady voice rose. "An impossible strain, I think."

The hand-cannon came back up between them and lined flush with the Romulan's chest. "You don't have a choice," George said. "You're still my prisoner. Get moving."

T'Cael smiled sadly, but not without amusement. "Kirk, I appreciate your concern. I see in your face I'll never be able to convince you to shoot me, though that would be best for both of us. Believe my sincerity when I say I prefer to stay behind and face my failure privately."

The hand-cannon dropped to George's side. His lips twisted in frustration.

After a moment he jabbed a finger toward the Romulan and said, "Fine. But at least come back to my shuttle and record a statement that my ship didn't act aggressively and that your own people fired on you. *And* that you believe we didn't cross the Neutral Zone deliberately. You owe us that, at least."

The round eyes flashed beneath their black sickle brows. "I owe you nothing. However, for the sake of interstellar harmony," t'Cael said, "I will give you your statement."

During the trek to the Starfleet officer's shuttlecraft, t'Cael's determination grew. With each step, the prospect of leaving a statement became more exciting. Perhaps he need not die in vain. Perhaps this was a chance to save the legacy he thought he had lost. One

258

last chance to thwart Ry'iak, a chance to leave his mark on the future. He might indeed die here, but at least his words would survive him and become tools which wiser men could use.

"Not much farther," Kirk said as they crested a hill. He consulted his compass and adjusted their direction a degree or two before stepping off the hilltop.

Declining to comment, t'Cael followed. There was, after all, very little to say, no comforting words, no optimistic platitudes. He forced himself to stop imagining what was going on in space above them. The many possible scenarios had become dizzying, and he was tired of it all, tired because he would never again participate.

The Starfleet craft was a surprise. He had expected better of so aesthetically oriented a race as humans. His Nestling had been a far more graceful thing than this shuttlecraft. Ugly, clunky, and painted without imagination, this craft exemplified poor use of space. There was too much room involved in the rectangular shape, room to hold too many people, too comfortably. It seemed impossible that the same engineers who designed that magnificent ivory vessel up in space could also have designed this box.

As he stood staring down at the box from a nearby summit, he was jarred from his distraction when Kirk spoke up.

"You coming?"

T'Cael glanced around and discovered Kirk poised awkwardly on the craggy hillside a few steps below, looking back up at him. Reluctantly, he nodded. "Yes, of course."

"Watch your step. It's pretty slippery here."

"Thank you. I shall."

T'Cael started to crouch down to begin his descent, and was stopped short by the horrid warning beep from his belt sensor. For an instant, he was stunned.

259

Kirk stared upward, his hard glare meeting t'Cael's as the beeping intensified.

T'Cael reached a hand downward. "Hurry!"

George scrambled on the wet rock and moss, forcing his feet to find holds and his arm to somehow extend until he could reach t'Cael's grasp.

The sky began to darken. Above him, t'Cael's face was tinted a horrid red, his royal-blue clothing suddenly flushed purple.

T'Cael's hand closed around the human's, and he yanked hard, using the hilltop for leverage even though his feet sank deep into the soft mossy mulch. When he had hauled the Earther over the crest, he dragged him to his feet and they dashed for the nearest rocks.

The planetoid's surface again bled red. Once again the terrible energy sheets hammered the landscape, singing their song of mutilation, sending a stink of burning organisms through the atmosphere. They were closer this time, and George was slammed against a rock wall by the sheer energy that crushed the atmosphere around them. His body smashed against the stone, and he felt his hip strike against hard rock. Blinded by pain, he squeezed his eyes shut to the explosions in his mind and waited for the assault to end.

Then the last sheet faded, and the red glow thinned to nothing. George forced his eyes open and found himself on his knees, crumpled against a lichened wall. There was movement nearby, but his mind was still foggy.

T'Cael helped him to his feet, and a sharp stab of pain forced his eyes shut again. Gradually, the pain subsided, and he forced his eyes open once more.

The Romulan seemed in good shape. He was holding George up. George pulled away from him and limped toward the overhang. T'Cael paused, then followed. Together, shakily, they moved to the top of the hill and looked down.

The shuttlecraft, and most of the surrounding land, had been thoroughly cremated. Hot metal dripped onto the ground, and sizzled.

Fighting the tingling numbness of his whole left side, George squatted down and pulled on a few scorched tendrils of brown grass. "That's one way to end a conversation."

Chapter Sixteen

"FLORIDA! YOU LET them get by us!"

Drake stumbled forward, gaping at the viewscreen.

"I couldn't stop them!" the helmsman said. "They're better at this than I am. They cut laterally through the top of the atmosphere and got past us. I can't do that with this ship!"

"Why would they go back to the planetoid?" Sanawey wondered.

"Maybe to finish the job," Florida suggested, his words laced with bitterness.

Drake clapped his hands together, newly invigorated. "If they think they have a job to finish, maybe it's because they think George is still alive. And if they think he's still alive, maybe it's because he *is* still alive!" Delighted, he clapped Florida on the back. "Such deduction! I should have been a Vulcan, yes? Move between them and the planet, fellow. Perhaps it's time for us to act *sans humanité.*"

"That doesn't sound very nice," Hart commented from her station.

Drake shrugged. "Not what you think. It's a Creole translation of a Hausa concept. It means, 'I will give you no sympathy, you deserve no pity, and it serves you right.'"

Florida blinked. Drake shrugged at him and turned to Sanawey. "And you up there," he added, "boost the gain for communications. Cut through that interference. Can you?"

The big man gave a dubious nod. "Maybe, if we get closer."

Drake's mouth curled into a devilish grin. "Oh," he said with deep satisfaction, "we're going to get closer. Much, much, and much closer. Mr. Florida, may I have a tiny talk with you?"

There was no candlelight in space. Who could afford such luxuries as candles and soft music when simply staying alive was such a trick? Who had time for such distractions out in space, on a mission, in danger?

Not that most of the ship's complement would ever know the true extent of their danger in a crisis till the crisis was long past. They were spared the agony of fear—and of choice.

Not so the ship's doctor, who saw all the pain firsthand. Someone's hurt; fix it. Don't take time to worry about what's coming down the corridor next. And when that someone was the captain, the doctor's duty quadrupled in intensity.

So Sarah sat beside April, wondering where her responsibility lay—and how on Earth a distraction like love had arisen to complicate that responsibility. Should she bring him around prematurely? Should she prop him up with medications and the technology available to her, shove him back out the door and pick up the pieces later? Or was her duty to the life and well-being of this poignantly gentle man?

Oh, how she'd started to hate that question mark at the end of every thought. She looked at Robert April's sleeping face and tried to nudge back the memories of all the tender moments he'd given her. Since the first day she'd known him, he'd given her reason to believe that there might be dreams in her life, that everything didn't have to make sense in textbook form. As he slept on the bed before her, he seemed to have found the peace he so dearly desired to share. If she woke him, she might shatter that peace, and he would once again be alone in that desire. She couldn't stand to think of making Robert unhappy.

And the courage . . . he'd never asked to be protected. Only a brave man could face the cruel realities of the galaxy and still speak of peace the way Robert did.

It felt good to keep him here, safe, asleep. Somehow she was preserving the specialness about him, the gallant fellow who had never acquired the arrogance of so many of his echelon. He was a tonic to her, and she couldn't deny the affection she had for him. Sometimes it was spooky the way he read her, and others—so subdued, so rational, yet with the courage to choose one direction and stride off that way, no backward glances, with his hands in his pockets and that undemonstrative grin on his face.

She reached a tentative hand to his face and touched him as he slept. She missed him. Despite the comfort of seeing him resting and alive, she wished he was awake too, so she could see his warmth at work. She wanted to experience again his uncanny way of seeing right through to the core of other people's feelings and needs, and the way he never lost sight of those needs.

"Sarah?"

She flinched at the sound of her name, embarrassed to be caught in a reverie so deep she hadn't even noticed his eyes flutter open. She withdrew her hand as he focused on her.

The top of the bed was raised, so that he seemed to be reclining in an easy chair, not lying on a diagnostic bed. He tested his voice with a small cough and grinned. "Gosh, you're nice to wake up to. I'd like to try it under more stirring conditions."

"Gosh? Well, gee-whiz, Captain—so poetic," she said.

He smiled and raised his eyebrows over sleepy eyes. "We English," he claimed. "Roses and poetry. National heritage and all that. Why am I so groggy?"

"You're still drugged."

"You drugged me?"

"It was that or a club. You needed some surgery. That's what you get for playing too rough."

"Don't get medical on me, Sarah, my dear," he said, moving his back and shoulders carefully, testing the muscles.

"Go back to sleep, Robert," she said, more quietly than she intended.

"Enchant me."

Her eyes flashed briefly. "I'm not the enchanting type."

Indulging in a little groan, he sighed. "No, you're not, are you? Do you know that's actually what I like best about you? You're real. There's a grand compliment for you, truly." Now he tried to move his legs beneath the thin thermal cover, and though the motion tired him, it also got his blood moving. He took a few deep breaths, then tried once again to force his eyes to focus on her. "You look very pretty today."

The compliment caught her by surprise. She lowered her eyes, hoping it didn't look like she was deliberately batting them. "You're sweet," she murmured.

A glitter returned to his gaze. "Thank you. It's wonderful to be described as something other than 'affable.'"

She grasped his wrist to check his pulse, trying to become the doctor again. "You're that, too," she said.

265

"I suppose I should get up soon."

"You do and I'll sedate you."

"Why don't you marry me instead?"

She tried, really tried, not to smile. Only half succeeded. "I can't," she moaned. "I can't be tied to a life I don't suit."

"I think you suit me rather well. After all, I'm charming, princely, noble, entertaining, giving, and I wash between my toes."

"Toe hygiene? I'm supposed to marry you because of toe hygiene?"

"It's my worthiest characteristic."

Sarah pinched the thermal blanket between her fingers and stared down at it. "I would marry you . . . but for the stripes on your sleeve."

"Why? I don't mind the emblem on yours."

He cupped his hand over hers, only to have her pull away.

"Robert, I can't be a ship's physician," she said, not looking at him. "I don't want to be a ship's physician, and you *do* want to be a ship's captain."

He chuckled. "What gave you that idea?"

Sarah blinked.

April smiled, interpreting her expression. "Did you think I meant to live out my career aboard the empress here?" A twirl of his forefinger took in the whole starship.

Sarah wrinkled her nose. "Don't you?"

"Actually, I never had that in mind at all."

"After everything you've put into this project?"

"Even after."

"Then . . . but then what?"

April let his throbbing head roll against the pillow. "'Captain' is a word with wonderful sounds, isn't it? It's much more than just a rank. There's something superb about it and it makes people want to follow it. People like me shouldn't be allowed to be called 'captain.' We should be 'professor' or 'parson' or things like that. Things more sublime."

"You're not making much sense," Sarah said.

"I'm not, am I?" He flexed his arms and went on, trying to be clearer. "I never planned to carry this ship into exploration, Sarah. And you know how I'd boggle combat. No, this ship needs someone else to run her. Someone almost reckless—a daredevil who can care for the lives of others, who can go out in space and lose touch with everything, and make all the decisions, and broach new ground in policy and practice. The mavericks, I mean. Like George, perhaps."

"Like George?" Sarah shook her head. "George Kirk is the opposite side of your coin, Robert. You might not push hard enough, but he'd push right through the fabric and rip it."

April shrugged and blinked groggily. "Well, perhaps not George, but certainly not me. I'm not enough of a lion." His blue eyes twinkled and he smiled. "That's what she needs," he whispered. "A lion at her helm."

Tears broke from Sarah's eyes and gave her away. Her voice cracked. "I was right; you are a poet."

"Why, Sarah . . ." He saw the tears then. He reached up instantly to brush them away, and was surprised when she folded over to rest her head on his chest and cling to him. She was trembling slightly. April coiled his arms around her and murmured, "Sarah . . ."

Her tears dripped on his sweater and beaded up on the natural Aran wool. "Oh, Robert, I'm such a lousy doctor . . ."

"What?" He chuckled. "You were in the top fifteen of your class. How lousy can you be?"

"I'm not talking medically."

"What, then?"

She stared into his sleeve, suddenly glad her face

was turned away from his. "I'm not tough enough. I'm not strong."

"Yes, you are; you're very strong."

"No, I'm not," she insisted, her lip stiffening. "I can't take it. Doctors are supposed to be tactful and distant and removed. And I'm not."

April stroked her hair. "Isn't it lucky that, you're not? I might not love you then."

"You let yourself get hurt," she whispered, and suddenly sobbed again. She squeezed him tight. "You promised I wouldn't have to watch you get hurt. You promised. Robert, I'm so scared . . ."

"Sarah . . ." Now he whispered her name uneasily. Why would she be afraid? There was nothing to—

As if summoned, an energy jolt shook the entire ship. Sarah had to grab the bed in order to keep from being thrown backward. Then a second bolt rippled through the ship. There was no mistaking it. They were being fired upon.

Sarah straightened up to wipe a hand across her cheeks. April had raised his head and was staring at the walls as though he could see through them.

"What was *that?*" he gasped.

Sarah cleared her throat. "What was what?"

April clapped a hand to his head, barely missing the injured place. "Good God! I thought all that was a dream—"

He raised his legs and pivoted to a sitting position, reaching for the com panel in spite of his disorientation and weakness.

"Robert, stay where you are!" Sarah attempted, reaching across the bed to catch his arm.

After two false starts, he hit the comlink. "April to bridge. George, are you there?"

It wasn't George, but Drake who came back over the intercom, backdropped by frantic sounds from the bridge—recognizable voices in an unrecognizable situation.

"Oh, Captain, are you over your brain sprain?"

"Drake, what's going on? Where's George?"

"Ah, well, you see, we have this little problem . . ."

"Why do you look at the sky?"

The Romulan's question shook George's concentration on the pink-blue sky.

"I'm trying to imagine what's going on up there," he replied, and continued squinting into the light of the distant pinkish sun.

T'Cael could tell that Kirk's experience in actual battle was limited by watching his expression. He offered the hard-won wisdom of his own past.

"It is a simple choreography. My ship is circling the area like an insect, hoping to come near enough to scan for us . . . especially for me. Your ship, I must assume, is why my ship is taking so long between batteries. The variables are distance, technological differences, and the battle experience of your crew. I won't deceive you about the experience of mine."

George looked down at him. "Good?"

For the first time in his life t'Cael was ashamed to admit it. "We have an abundance of military enthusiasm in our culture. As such, we can easily afford to put only our best in space."

Cradling his injured arm, George drawled, "Pardon if I'm not reassured."

T'Cael gave a noncommittal nod, quite able to empathize with Kirk's resentment. He lowered his gaze, making it clear that he would supply no more information. He was no traitor, nor would he put himself in a position to make that alternative tempting.

Besides, he knew that death would be his next

phase, whether at the hands of his own crew or here. Either way, he would never again see the suffused topaz skies of his home province. His family would have to deal with the repercussions of his "unfortunate" death. Would his enemies call his death honorable? Or would they say he defied imperial process, and forced them to act against him?

No matter. He was no longer part of the web. Only one thing was certain: he had grossly underestimated Ry'iak.

"What are you doing?"

T'Cael glanced up. Kirk was standing over him, leaning on the rock wall to support his injured left side, and he was looking at t'Cael's hands.

Ordinarily t'Cael wasn't prone to absent-mindedness, but somehow the seed pods and cut bits of plants from his quarters had gotten into his hands. Had they been in his pocket the whole time? A warm incubator, and a memory of Idrys.

"My hobby. Growing things. It seems they cling to me." He fingered the seed pods, habitually careful not to rupture them. "A rhythm of life we no longer understand. So different that we forget to think of it as life at all. This one," he said, holding up a chubby seed, "will be a cycad."

George forced himself not to look too feeble as he moved to sit on a convenient outcropping. "Dinosaur food."

"On Earth, yes. In fact, this particular one is an Earth variety, preserved by micropropagation on one of your colonies. The parent species is extinct. An incalculable loss."

At the moment, George had trouble sympathizing with an orphaned seed. His brows came together in a confused frown. The Romulan really felt for that seed. Weird.

"And this small pod," the Romulan went on, holding up what looked like a wad of mold, "is a type similar to your Asian waterlilies. And it's charmingly punctual. Its flower blooms precisely at dawn, pollinates at midday, and sinks into the mud at sunset, where it leaves precisely five pods." Without missing a beat, he plucked up a long flimsy growth that looked like a cross between a slug and a piece of rice. "This will be a fern. You have many ferns on Earth, I know. This one is a prospector fern. By its color changes it tells us the locations and concentrations of certain metal deposits below the surface. It was understandably helpful during our industrial regeneration. Such value . . . and only one cell thick."

"Where'd you get so much information about Earth plants?" George asked.

The Romulan's large eyes flared, and he smiled. "I stole it. Smuggled, actually, at respectable cost."

"Why? I mean, why Earth?"

T'Cael turned his head and squarely addressed George. "Don't you know?" he asked accusingly. "You humans may wander as far as you please into the galaxy, but only rarely will you find a planet as lush as your own." He straightened, and gazed across the mossy landscape. "Think of your assortment of races. Humans of such a variety of color and size and height that they hardly seem one species at all . . . and the blinding variety of animal and insect life on Earth—astonishing. Even within a single species you have vast differences. Dogs, for instance. A thousand breeds that conceivably could mate with each other. Cats of every description, from sublime to savage. Rodents. Butterflies—your insect life alone is dizzying. You have a range of environments to keep science hungry for lifetimes, and you humans are capable of living in all of them in some fashion. And what moves in your waters . . . there are hardly words for the variety. Or perhaps I don't know the words."

271

The Romulan seemed to grow tired. George watched him silently, embarrassed that he had never seen these things in this light.

"Plants are the first sign of life," the Romulan went on. Then he stopped and glanced up. "The perception is new to you."

"I . . . never thought about it," George admitted.

T'Cael shook his head. "I find your inattention distasteful. And a waste. Such an attitude has caused the plundering of your planet, and now you move into the greater galaxy to spoil other worlds."

George bristled. "Our planet isn't so plundered," he retaliated. "My sons still have fields and forests to run in, and the jungles are still there for your ferns." Stiffly he got to his feet again. "For a conqueror race, you sure take things personally. Humans make a lot of mistakes, but it's only because we're willing to take chances. And we've fixed a lot of our mistakes too, because we admit to having made them. That's why we could forgive if it was your ship that accidentally fell into our space. I don't notice your people exhibiting anything resembling generosity. What you've got is just plain suspiciousness."

"And a spider's sense of ambush," t'Cael mused in rueful agreement, more to himself than to Kirk.

George watched him, and a quiver of pity ran up his spine, not enough to make him understand, but enough to keep him from venting another accusation. He knew the other man was more a victim than he was. Unless this was some kind of elaborate test—or trap—

The wave of paranoia made his arm and leg ache. Itching for something to do, he wrestled out his communicator and held it in his left hand even though the muscles of his arm protested. If he could send out a strong enough signal, if the empress was close enough . . .

Suddenly the Romulan stood up, stiff and erect, and held his breath.

George stopped moving, and glared at his reluctant companion. "What?"

T'Cael swept a silencing hand toward him and continued concentrating on something he heard, sensed, felt—

"We're being stalked," he announced tersely.

George caught his breath, stared an instant longer, then pushed off the rock wall and leaned over the escarpment. What he saw melted his spine. He pushed back.

"Get going," he said, his voice edged with urgency. "Higher ground. Let's go."

T'Cael's eyes narrowed. "What did you see?"

"Move. Come on, get going." With an authoritative push, George aimed the Romulan at the mossy crags that gouged upward from their hiding place. As they moved, he drew his hand-cannon.

T'Cael buried his curiosity about what was coming up the mountain and began climbing. The two men worked their way up an increasingly jagged cliff face, and the Federation officer needed help more often than he seemed to want to admit, but whatever he had seen coming after them was hideous enough that he accepted t'Cael's assistance without a single argument. Only when they paused to let Kirk rest in the crook of two rocks was t'Cael able to look down. Once done, he regretted it.

The beasts weren't the biggest they'd seen on the face of the little planetoid, but certainly they were the ugliest. Bristle haired and wolflike, but big as a thrai, with heavy shoulders and powerful forequarters, the creatures had massive jaws and lips that weren't quite able to close around teeth made for butchery. They moved with studied slowness, and from every crevice came another one to add to the pack. There were already more than a dozen, and the climb didn't seem to slow their advance at all. As they moved up into the rocks toward him, their rough coats rippled like shoregrass, as though tipped with quicksilver. They were grim and intent on their hunt. Grim, savage, silent. The silence was the most distressing element. George listened for the crack of a stick under a paw, the rustle of a leaf, the rasp of harsh fur against a bush—anything. But there was nothing. Nothing but eyes fixed on him, red-ringed and hungry.

T'Cael pressed back against the rock, forcing himself not to look anymore. "Interesting form of life," he murmured. "I wonder what they are."

"They're carnivorous," George said flatly.

T'Cael pressed his lips together. "They've grouped in a pack. We can't effectively fight them with single-shot weapons."

"Why not?"

"That's the idea behind pack strategy. Or Swarm strategy," he added with an ironic edge that only he understood. "Individuals are sacrificed to the pack. While we fight one, the group moves closer. So it seems we die here one way or the other."

"Huh-uh," George grunted as he struggled to his feet. "My life insurance isn't paid up. Let's go."

"You go." T'Cael saw the momentary confusion in Kirk's eyes and explained, "I cannot forecast your fate. But I can accept mine."

"Bunk."

"It is the wiser course for me, Kirk."

"Damn you, get up!" George reached over and hauled t'Cael to his feet. "Now move!"

T'Cael pulled away, though he couldn't entirely break Kirk's grasp on his arm in this cramped space.

"Goddamn you," George growled. "Nobody with any intelligence gives up that easily. Start climbing."

They glared at each other for a moment. Then

274

t'Cael's expression mellowed. "I suppose I'd rather not die under a tag of stupidity." He raised a hand. "After you."

For George, the uphill climb was a constant fight against the pain in his hip and shoulder. In addition to the predators below and the wrenching ache every time he pulled himself higher, he was plagued with thoughts of the starship. Could Drake handle the enemy vessel now that they were in combat? Silly question—Drake had nothing resembling the experience he would need to move against a trained Romulan crew. Drake was audacious; maybe that would help. Drake didn't believe in rules. He might be able to keep the starship from being destroyed, but George didn't harbor too many false hopes about being rescued. There was only the slimmest possibility, if, *if* they could stay alive long enough.

He hated being here. The frustration of having to deal with being chased by animals when he wanted to be in space where the bigger action was happening . . . he felt like a disembodied hand. Still twitching.

He took a moment to glance downward. The animals were slowly and steadily closing the distance between them. They had been a hundred yards below them; now they were fifty, moving with slow deliberation.

As he wedged his fingers into a niche and tried to haul himself to a moss-coated ledge, the muscles in his shoulder spasmed and he lost his grip. He slipped downward, the rock scraping his face, and only the Romulan's strong grip on his belt kept George from falling into the jaws of their hunters.

"Try again," t'Cael encouraged.

Panting, George only managed a nod. With an embarrassing gasp, he gathered his strength and pushed his fingers into the niche once more. He concentrated on the ledge, a chance to rest, to evaluate the situation, see if they'd climbed high enough to discourage the animals stalking them.

He gritted his teeth and refused to slip again, no matter how his fingers quivered or his arms trembled.

Almost within reach now . . . his fingers were on the ledge. From below the Romulan gave him another boost, and he was up. He was safe.

Exhausted, he flopped onto his side and rolled over, his breath coming in ragged gasps. If he could just rest—

He pushed himself up onto his good elbow, then over onto his knees, and reached over the edge to grasp the Romulan's wrist. What he saw beyond t'Cael made his spine tingle with a primal fear. Eyes, reddish eyes set in massive bearlike faces—but no bear had ever looked so capable of mutilation. These animals could never be mistaken for stuffed toys, that was for sure. Their teeth intermingled like thorns, their lips permanently peeled back in aberrations of smiles, unable to close around the walls of gray-white teeth. And now there were more than thirty of them.

"Hurry up," George said.

T'Cael heard the intensity in the human's voice and interpreted it correctly. The animals were closing in. He tried to move faster.

A sudden noise made him look up—and he found himself staring into a face far more horrid than the face of combat had ever appeared.

The beast rose up from a buttress behind Kirk, massive paw and flexed finger-length claws raised to strike.

"Kirk!"

T'Cael's warning only gave George the time to roll over and get a good look at the death barreling down upon him. There wasn't even time to raise his hand-cannon.

But t'Cael had a precious extra second to gather his wits and vault up onto the ledge. With a single heave, he shoved George out of the beast's swiping range and took the blow himself. The beast's paw caught him between the shoulder blades and smashed him up against the rock wall.

George rolled and came up on one knee with the hand-cannon raised and firing. Long, separate bolts of laser energy seared into the animal's fur, finally cutting through to its heart. The beast turned its thorny snout to the sky and screamed in rage, twisted, reeled backward, shrieked again, and toppled from its perch. A few thumps on the rocks below, and the silence returned.

T'Cael slumped against the rock, his eyes cramped shut, his arms and legs shuddering.

George scrambled to him. "Let me look."

The bright blue jacket was deeply sliced at least a half-dozen times. Below that, two more layers of clothing were also sliced, and the Romulan's skin was scored with claw marks. Two of the marks were open wounds. The blow itself had knocked the wind out of him, a blow hard enough to have killed George if it had landed on his neck or head, as it had been intended to.

T'Cael made no attempt to hide the pain. In fact, for several seconds he was unaware of anything but the agony that burned its way across his back. He felt the blow all the way through his body, and his hands closed around the rocks as he struggled for composure.

"Thanks," George murmured.

There was no response.

"I didn't think to bring a first-aid kit," George said as he checked t'Cael's wounds again. They were bleeding now, a thick olive trickle, and he dabbed at them with the edges of the ripped jacket. It was disorienting to see pain openly displayed by someone who looked so much like a Vulcan, and it brought out all his compassion for the Romulan.

He glanced up. The crags got steeper from here on. Trapped, utterly trapped. Even if there was some way to force his own injured limbs to climb, there was no hope now of getting the Romulan up there. He turned back to t'Cael.

"I see it," t'Cael gasped, fighting for control. "Futile." He rearranged himself against the rock wall with distinct effort. "Please, though, make the attempt yourself. They may be busy with me long enough for you to—"

"Can't," George snapped, not wanting to hear it again. "My leg won't take it." He struggled to recharge the power pack on his hand-cannon, then squinted up at the rocks. "I think I see some loose rubble. Maybe . . . if I do it right . . . just maybe I can jar enough rocks loose to cause a rock slide. Take cover."

He braced himself on a crag and held the weapon in both hands, aiming as carefully as he could in the fading light, fighting the desire to look down until he'd at least made one attempt. The laser bolt shot upward in a clean glow, and pecked at his chosen outcropping. Pebbles flew, specks of stone spitting down into his face, but he kept firing until the falling rocks were the size of a man's fist. Then he ducked back toward the Romulan and waited.

A shower of rocks tumbled past their hiding place, making a jangling racket against their mother mountain. When the last chips had sprinkled, George crawled out and looked down.

On the face of the cliff, there wasn't a sign of the predators. Nothing. Not a whisker.

"They're gone," he said, confusion showing in his voice.

"Impossible," the Romulan said.

He was right. As George watched the last pebble settle, lumps of fur began rising from a dozen hiding places. Then more. And still more. How could animals that big find places to hide on this boulder?

Gradually, more and more of the creatures appeared, their grizzly faces intent. The hunt resumed.

George slithered backward and pressed against the rocks as he checked the intensity of the hand-cannon and looked up again, trying to find another weak spot on the cliff face above.

"You're wasting your weapon's energy," the Romulan said.

George glared at him. True, these rocks seemed too stable to shake loose with this little weapon, but he didn't particularly want to be told that right now. He'd have to wait, pick the animals off one by one as they attacked, and hope he had enough firepower to do it. How many of them were there? Two dozen? Four? More?

He felt as though he was slipping his head into a guillotine, and waiting—waiting those long last seconds for the blade to fall.

"We should've foreseen this," t'Cael continued, forcing his breath to slow a little more with each word. "They've been deliberately crowding us up the rocks. Packs must have strategy." T'Cael leaned heavily against the rocks and let his mind go numb for a few seconds. Giving in to the pain, even for those few seconds, was refreshing. It gave him the strength to keep fighting.

He grinned ruefully. After a moment he even chuckled.

George's brow furrowed. "You think this is funny?"

T'Cael looked up. "Ironic," he admitted, hoping he was using the word correctly, "for two spacefarers to die as prey for the beasts."

"I guess." George hugged his sore arm and took a deep breath to steady himself.

The Romulan raised a lone eyebrow. "You humans have no sense of humor."

George looked up, self-conscious at being told that by somebody who looked like a Vulcan.

He pursed his lips. "What'd you say your name was again?"

"T'Cael."

"Well, t'Cael, you think like a victim."

The insult was plain. "I beg your pardon?"

"You've given up."

T'Cael shrugged. "Foolish to fight when there is no hope," he said.

George shook his head. "I'd never take you for a Romulan."

At this, t'Cael snapped his head up and his expression changed. The pain had cleared his head and limited his tolerance. "And what do you know of Romulans that lets you make such a statement? You've fueled yourself on outdated hearsay. Your ignorance has made you pompous." His dark brows drew together. "You insult me."

Under the blistering attack, George held his breath and returned the glare.

T'Cael spoke now in a deriding, toneless manner. "What I know of humans," he went on, "I know because I learned it. What you know of my people you know because you think it."

"You assume," t'Cael went on, "that a bad system is made up of bad people. You forget that greed and power abuse the closest people first—one's own people. My people are the first victims, those who have paid the longest for our ways. We no longer have a

280

mechanism for change." He winced as he readjusted his shoulder against the rock, and he gazed out at the strangely colored sky. "Your own history of wars should prove that to you. A few leaders using drumbeating and patriotic rhetoric to convince the masses of things no sensible person would otherwise approve of. Such power can make naked evils seem like duty. And people will do that duty unconditionally. My culture or yours, it makes no difference, Kirk."

George turned to face t'Cael squarely. "Are you telling me there's no difference between your people and mine?" He leaned slightly toward the Romulan and made the question into an accusation. "Are you really going to sit there and tell me that?"

"No," t'Cael said quietly.

George settled back. T'Cael's presence here, in this unforeseen situation, proved George's point for him, and not pleasantly.

They sat against the rock in the cramped mossy space, not facing each other. All they could see from here was sky and more rocks. And they knew the predators were coming.

The two soldiers—two predators, now victims themselves—waited in silence.

Chapter Seventeen

"DRAKE, GIVE ME a report."

"*Fête du diable,* sir. A real mess—but we're learning."

"What are we learning?" April slid into the command chair, staring at the Romulan ship as it dodged by them, and at the planetoid beyond.

"That even with reduced shields and low maneuverability compared to them," Drake reported, "we are still, shall we say, a class act."

"Carlos, give me a sense of time, please."

Florida gathered himself. "Mr. Kirk landed on the planetoid at fourteen hundred. He was planning to rendezvous with the enemy commander, but at fourteen-fifty-four the enemy ship suddenly moved in and fired on their location."

For the first time April's eyes left the screen. "You mean they fired on their own man?"

"It looks that way, sir."

"Unless the shuttle they dispatched was some kind of drone," Hart suggested. "A decoy to distract Mr. Kirk."

April ran his finger along his lower lip. "That," he murmured thoughtfully, "or it's a sacrifice to get to our top officers."

Drake drew his shoulders in. "Mighty unsavory both ways."

"They've hit the planetoid twice so far, sir," Florida finished. "Their ship is more maneuverable and they slipped by us."

"Twice?" April looked at him again, his brow furrowing under the bandage. "Why would they do that?"

"I don't know, but Mr. Reed had us move in and fire a blanket pattern with what weapons power we've got. Until the warp engines are at least partly restored, we're limited on firepower. Short-range sensors are operational again, though. I think we hurt them, because they've been trying to keep their distance for the last few minutes."

"You suppose they'll hit again?"

April leaned forward. "Why would they fire more than once? I can only imagine it's because they're not able to ascertain whether or not they were successful the first time."

Drake folded his arms and grinned his infectious grin, proud of himself for having come to the same conclusion earlier. "That George of ours may still be kicking, eh, sir?"

April blew out a nervous sigh, then clamped his lips tight. He knew he didn't have a real sense for battle, no killer instinct to help him make decisions or project what the repercussions might be if he did this or did that.

"Captain, they're moving in!"

Carlos Florida's warning cry was cut off by a bolt of energy from the Romulan ship that struck the starship like a hard punch. The ship rocked. A *boom* racked the bridge. Everyone scrambled to stay on their feet as the bird-of-prey slanted by and fell out of forward sensor range.

"Good God!" April gasped. "Was that *them?*" He collected himself. "How can a ship that size pack that kind of wallop! My God!"

Panting, Drake hauled himself back up to a functional level. "A tugboat, sir. All power. No quarter."

"Good God . . . I'd never have guessed!"

"They count on that, sir."

"Weapons status?"

"Port weapons show ready at seventy-two percent efficiency," Florida read out. "Starboard weapons ready sixty percent. All weapons amidships show ready at forty-three percent."

From the captain's seat, there was silence now. Florida looked around, but Captain April was simply gazing out at alien space and at the Romulan ship as it veered around and repositioned itself at a great distance.

Drake approached the command chair and quietly suggested, "We have a strong ship, sir. Stronger than theirs. Time to use it, eh?"

April glanced at him. "I hesitate to do that."

Drake nodded. "Sir," he said then, very slowly, "as far as we know, they've killed George."

Hearing it said aloud changed April's expression. "Yes. . . " he whispered, and a rare anger rose. The smile lines around his eyes couldn't work with the unaccustomed hardness that touched his features now. "I don't understand this," he murmured. "We've made it plain that we don't want trouble. We've told them we're only here because of a malfunction, that we're doing everything possible to leave their space peacefully. Why are they treating us this way?"

Drake watched the captain and felt helpless sympathy rise in his chest. He thought of George and what George would say, but there was no way to explain that not everyone was Mahatma Gandhi in a sweater. Some people, some races, just found it impossible to trust others.

"It's a dangerous galaxy, Captain," he said solemnly. "Sometimes we have to be dangerous back."

For several moments, April simply gazed into space. There was a miserable truth in what George had been trying to teach him. The Federation would be little use to its members if it had strength but no courage to use it. If he allowed the starship to be taken, then nothing he'd dreamed of for her could ever take place.

He drew a long breath.

Grimly he said, "Yes. All right. Drake, your advice?"

Drake snapped around. "Me, sir? You're asking me, sir?"

With a tolerant scowl, April nodded. "Yes, you. Make a suggestion."

"How about we let them pass and strike at their engines as they go by?"

April leaned toward him. "I'm sorry, say that again?"

"Strike the engines from aft as they go by."

"Ah, I see. Debilitating but humane."

"Brilliant, sir. My compliments."

April straightened in his chair. "All right, then. All hands, battle stations." He said it so quietly, and to a bridge full of nonmilitary types, that it took several seconds before anyone thought to key in the ship's automatic battle-ready sequences and signal the red alert.

The captain rubbed the sweat from the palms of his hands and said, "Carlos, do whatever it takes to get between that ship and the planet. We're going in."

The stench of burning fur filled the air. T'Cael watched, not commenting, as Kirk lowered his weapon slightly to look at the sixth animal he'd had to gun

285

down. The weapon's power wouldn't last forever, and the carnivores were still coming.

"Drake, you orangutan, get that ship over here," Kirk grumbled as he dug another—the last—power pack out of his kit. He wasn't going to think about how much energy it took to cut through the hides of these beasts—he could've taken out a small army with what he'd used so far on just six of them.

T'Cael could hear them coming nearer, claws scraping on the rocks just over the cleft where he and Kirk were hiding. The carnivores' pack strategy had worked all too well. He didn't know if Kirk could hear the animals yet—they were very quiet about their stalking—so he said nothing. As he mentally prepared himself for death, he discovered an odd sympathy in himself for his human companion, who refused to give up. He had noticed that as Kirk realized his energy packs were running out, he had given up trying to kill the animals outright and instead had started to go for the eyes. Apparently he hoped to injure them enough that they would lose their sense of purpose. A risky tactic, since the beasts went wild in their pain and loss of direction. The last one had thrown itself against the rocks until it collapsed, but its thrashing had nearly taken both men with it.

"We've got to move," Kirk said.

T'Cael was silent, knowing Kirk wouldn't want to hear what he had to say. The fight was wasteful. Yet it made him curious. Very alien, this tenacity in the face of hopelessness. Humans didn't have the Rihannsu sense of discipline, and with discipline comes a point of acceptance, a time to give in to the inevitable. Kirk had none of that. Perhaps, for them, this unshakable stubbornness had replaced it and could actually work in its place.

A smile touched t'Cael's lips as he imagined arguing the point with the smug academicians who saw everything non-Rihannsu as inferior. He thrived on such argument; he would miss it even more than life.

The animals hunting them knew nothing of such philosophy. All they knew were the instincts of the past. And something in the instinctive strategy said this was the time to move in.

From both sides of the cleft, massive wolfish faces, fenced with those dense teeth and dripping with saliva, appeared and rose over the rocks.

Kirk aimed arbitrarily at one of them and fired; meanwhile several other beasts crawled up and over. To one side, t'Cael remained predictably silent, though he couldn't help pressing tightly up against the cliff as the animals closed in.

T'Cael suddenly wished he could comfort Kirk somehow; surely death would be very hard for the human to accept if he continued to fight. This was the ultimate agony of refusing to give up—being forced to.

A tiny beeping sound surfaced above the grinding of teeth and the sound of animal breathing. T'Cael glanced around—it hadn't been his personal warning system. Beside him, Kirk froze. The beep came again.

All at once Kirk scrambled to dig out his communication device and in his panic almost dropped it. Somehow he got the instrument into his hand and snapped up the antenna grid.

Then t'Cael was being abruptly dragged up. Why? Did Kirk want him to start fighting too? There was nowhere to run, and there was no chance of having a rescue ship dispatched in the next few seconds, for seconds was surely all they had left. As t'Cael drew back, Kirk got a handful of blue jacket, but it was enough to lever t'Cael to his feet. The communicator came up.

Kirk took a short breath. "Emergency energize! Now!"

"Kirk, what are you doing?" T'Cael tried to pull away, confusion tangling his features. "Kirk!"

The nearest beast raised its paw for a killing strike. The communicator flew out of Kirk's hand.

"Kirk!"

T'Cael heard his own voice wobble. The light around him faded. Had he been struck? Was this death, finally? He had expected to have to control much more pain than this.

Suddenly t'Cael fell backward to bump a wall. Not rock—this wall had a slight give, and the light here was different. Artificial. No shadows. Kirk still had a grip on him, and obviously wasn't surprised by the sudden change of scene.

The human turned toward the young blond man in front of them. "Wood! Notify the bridge—"

But Wood wasn't in a condition to notify anybody. His boyish face was ghost white, his mouth open only slightly wider than his eyes, and he was staring past them with an expression of horror. For an instant, t'Cael wondered if his appearance could possibly be that startling.

Kirk stared back, then realized. He closed his own eyes for a terrible instant and whispered, "Oh, *shit*—"

Kirk whirled around, raising his hand-cannon once again.

T'Cael smelled it then—the heavy, soaked stink of moist fur. He turned, and found himself face to face with a wall of teeth.

The transportation effect had dazed the animal, but their grace period didn't last long. By the time Kirk swung around and raised his weapon, the merciless claws were already coming down at him.

Kirk yelled. Instinctively he used his gun hand to protect his face, and the claws knocked the cannon from his grip. It clattered across the deck as Kirk hit

288

the floor on his injured left side and was stunned for an instant.

That instant was a nightmare.

A vast black form, smelling of dirty fur and clinging moss, spread itself in the air above Kirk. There was a guttural snarl, and the beast landed in the center of the room, growling and snorting in terror and confusion. As it skittered into the wall near the door panel, the door hissed open. The animal flinched, its claws scratching at the deck, and it made for the open corridor. At his feet, t'Cael saw Kirk roll over in time to see the door panel close again, and in the last glimpse of the corridor they saw a red eye glance back at them.

"Hell!" Kirk vaulted from the platform to the control island in one leap. "That's all we need! A goddamned werewolf loose on board—where's the intercom! Where's the intercom!"

Wood was still in shock, t'Cael noticed, but Kirk reached over the console and yanked his collar. "The intercom!"

The boy blinked, then aimed a trembling finger at a switch.

Kirk hammered the switch. "Attention! This is the first officer. Intruder alert! Clear the corridors! There's an alien animal loose on the ship. Repeat —intruder alert! Clear all corridors! Lock yourselves in until further notice!" He switched off when he realized he couldn't think of anything else to say. Nothing that would help, anyway. "Damn it all . . ." he muttered, and looked back at the transporter platform.

T'Cael was still pressed against the wall when Kirk approached and took his arm. "It's gone," he said. "Cael, it's gone."

T'Cael moved his eyes only and murmured, "You have transporters."

"What?"

"Trans . . . porters."

"Oh. Yeah, it's new. Come with me."

"We didn't know you had transporters."

"Neither did I. Come on. Wood, you stay put."

"Sir," Wood called shakily as Kirk scooped up his hand-cannon and steered t'Cael toward the door, "the bridge is hailing."

"Tell them I'm on my way. I'm stopping off at sickbay."

"Hurry up. I need him on the bridge."

"Don't rush me. I don't treat Vulcans every day, you know."

"Yeah," George muttered, and gave t'Cael a warning glance as Sarah Poole dabbed at the Romulan's wounded back. He looked for the nearest wall com and punched a button. "Kirk to engineering."

"Engineering. Chang, sir."

"Have you got a team together yet?"

"Yes, I've got seven volunteers, armed and ready. We're tracking the animal with sensors. Soon as we get it cornered, we'll move in."

"What about gassing it? Did you check into that?"

"Yes, sir. Bioengineering says the ventilation system isn't rigged for that yet. I mean, it's set up, but we don't have any anesthetic compounds stored on board yet. Sorry."

"Don't apologize to me. You're the ones going after it. You understand what to do?"

"Think so, sir."

"Don't think. Just kill it. Don't take any chances. I'll be on the bridge.

"We'll let you know. Chang out."

George tried to be hopeful about it, but there wasn't much reassurance in the mental picture of seven tech geeks sneaking down the corridor in a huddle. All he could hope for was that the animal would break its neck falling down an access stairwell.

He stood there for several seconds, staring at the com unit, wondering how the situation had become so tricky that having a wild-eyed killer carnivore loose in the corridors had become a small annoyance.

The click of the medical computer drew him back to the here and now. There was Dr. Poole at the medicomp, glancing back and forth from the readout screen to the vital signs being shown on the diagnostic monitor above t'Cael. T'Cael was propped up on one elbow, watching her, but not daring to say anything. He seemed to be handling the pain well enough now, though he moved stiffly as he brought himself to a sitting position on the diagnostic table.

"Are you almost finished?" George asked. "We've got to get cracking."

"Yes . . . I guess . . ." Sarah looked at the test results on the medicomp, her brow furrowing and her eyes getting small.

"What's wrong?" George approached slowly, contemplating knocking her away from the medicomp and messing up the information she'd collected.

"Nothing's wrong . . . exactly. These instruments must need recalibrating or something."

George eyed t'Cael as Sarah slipped her hand-held mediscanner into a slot in the main medicomp, punched a read pattern, and watched the screen again. A faint blue-white light played across her features. She frowned at what she saw. She repunched the pattern, slower this time. She frowned again. She glanced at t'Cael.

George held his breath.

She entered data yet another time, with a few careful modifications. Another frown. With a glint of suspicion to keep it company.

Sarah snapped off the computer and yanked the

mediscanner out of its cubbyhole. She folded her arms and twisted around.

"All right, Kirk, what gives?"

George stiffened. "What do you mean?"

She wagged the mediscanner. "Close, but no Vulcan."

Both men stared widely at her, but she wasn't buying it.

She approached them in a decidedly threatening manner. "Skin tissue variants, blood content inconsistencies, same story on the metabolic table, not to mention the encephaloscan. Can you explain that?"

They stared at her some more, but it still didn't do any good.

George said, "Diet."

T'Cael said, "Illness."

George. "He's been sick."

T'Cael. "Deathly."

Sarah. "Claptrap."

She slammed the mediscanner onto her desk and snapped off the diagnostic monitor above t'Cael, evidently realizing she wasn't going to get any acceptable stories out of them. "Get out of my sickbay."

T'Cael slid from the table and pulled his jacket back on, his lips clamped tight, and George couldn't tell if it was tension or amusement that kept him quiet.

"Can you move around all right?" George asked.

T'Cael proved it by heading for the door. "Adequately."

In the corridor, the two men paused.

"That didn't hold for long," George complained.

"I told you," t'Cael said with a shrug. "We could go back and explain to her."

George thought about it. "I'd rather go back to the werewolves."

The ship felt barren and dangerous as they made their way to the bridge. The trip through the corridors toward the main turbo-lift was interrupted only once, and only for a fleeting moment, when they turned a corner at the same moment the red-eyed fugitive animal came around the next turn. George and t'Cael drew up short, and George was about to bring up his weapon when the animal, wide-eyed and crouching, skittered to a halt, glared at them, then scratched the deck in a frantic effort to turn around. In an instant it was gone. But that instant had opened a terrible empathy in George; the animal, no longer on familiar ground, was terrorized. Here, it had no bearings, no idea that it was the stronger.

Like t'Cael. George glanced at his companion. Reluctant companion, he recalled now, with sudden clarity. T'Cael was alone too, separated from his pack, rejected by those closest to him, those he needed to survive, but he was handling it. Unlike the animal they'd just seen, t'Cael was burying his fears. The Romulan had preferred death on the planetoid to the conflicts he would face and would cause if he came here. Now that he was here, though, he seemed to be accepting the situation. A profound courage, certainly.

If only there was time to appreciate it. George felt his blood running hot as the turbo-lift swung up through the starship toward the bridge. Pulse point.

The lift doors parted.

For t'Cael, the starship was a city in space. So much room, so much resource—unthinkable that something so big could function as a battleship. As the lift doors opened and Kirk bolted out instantly, t'Cael remained behind, taking in his first view of a Federation bridge from the sanctity of the turbo-lift. And what a bridge it was. Though obviously unfinished, the area was lush with color and efficiency. There was room to walk freely on two levels, room to pace, to watch each other. Humans understood the psychological as well as the practical value of color. And the captain's place was strategically situated in the center, where all others had to have their backs to him. It gave him many advantages. There was no place here for Ry'iak's kind to lurk.

T'Cael stepped slowly from the turbo-lift onto the carpeted circular walkway, wondering if any of these people were here to watch and judge and report on this captain's performance.

Below, George gripped the arm of the command chair.

April sighed with relief and murmured, "George . . . you'll never be hanged for apathy, my friend."

"April, you English twitch, what are you doing up?"

The captain simply gazed at him, grinning. It took all his willpower to keep from mentioning George's battered appearance and his distinct limp.

"We tried to strap him, Geordie," Drake said, "but he chewed his way out, and *poof*, here he is."

George looked at Drake and snapped, "I can't believe you actually got us out of there."

"All in a day's panic, m'lad," Drake muttered, but too softly to hide his own relief.

April touched George's arm and asked, "What's all this about an intruder alert?"

George started to answer, but suddenly no one was interested. Everyone was looking at the back of the bridge. Slowly, April got up, stricken by the elegant stranger who made such an ornament on their bridge.

After a moment, George poked the captain. "Can I see you for a minute?"

April started toward the steps. "I should think so," he uttered. He moved past George, gesturing toward the turbo-lift. George followed, but only after getting a good grip on Drake's uniform and hauling him after.

As they hurried up onto the walkway after April,

Sanaway leaned toward him and whispered, "A Vulcan?"

George lowered his voice. "We rescued him. Don't make him self-conscious."

Sanaway snapped his eyes back to his board. "No, sir."

"And spread the word, will you?"

"Yes, sir, sure will."

April and t'Cael were already inside the turbo-lift, eyeing each other. George pulled Drake inside with him, pushed the button that closed the doors, and put the lift on standby.

"I see we have a situation even thornier than I imagined," April said.

"I guess you could call it thorny," George answered with a nervous sigh. "Captain, this is the commander of that ship out there."

April raised his brows.

"Former." T'Cael made a little bow. "My name is t'Cael Zaniidor Kilyle. Until a short while ago, I was Field-Primus of the Second Imperial Swarm. I wish I could officially convey greetings of my government, but since I no longer represent it, the only greetings I can bring you are my own."

April nodded. "I see. Not a pleasant way to meet, Commander. Or what do they call you?"

"What they call me," t'Cael admitted, "I'll never hear again. T'Cael will do."

"I'm very sorry if our presence here has compromised you," April said, his tone sympathetic. "We're dealing with a mutiny, then?"

"More precisely, others are dealing with the mutiny. You are dealing with the tantalizing prize your ship will make if you allow yourselves to be taken. I see technologies here that my science has only guessed at, things our intelligence has no reports of. Since our

295

intelligence is respectable, I conclude these technologies must be very new, even to you."

"You're right on the mark with that. It's all quite new stuff. I hope the transporter didn't give you too awful a jolt."

T'Cael tilted his head and smiled. "Yes, I received a jolt."

"Well, it did the job, at least. I'm glad we had it working. Not everything is." April smiled too.

"He says there are more ships coming," George blurted.

"Oh?" April responded. "How many, specifically?"

"Five," t'Cael said. "I suggest you repair your systems and leave the area. I assume this ship has lightspeed."

George glared at him. "Of course it has light—"

"Our warp drive is broken down at the moment," April said. "We're working on repairing it."

"If you can do so," t'Cael continued, "you'll have no problem outrunning the Swarm and should be able to clear the area. I suggest you do that. The Swarm is made up of small ships, but we concentrate on firepower and they'll be able to disable you sufficiently."

Drake muscled his way between April and George. "We've got a little firepower of our own, Booboorah," he announced, pointing a finger in t'Cael's face.

George pressed him back. "Why don't we try lighting a match under Dr. Buzzard in engineering and get the star drive going so we don't have to deal with—" All at once he paused, blinked at Drake, and demanded, "What did you say?" He looked at April. "What did he say?"

"I suppose you should be briefed," April said. "After you left, Drake blocked a couple of punches from the Romulan ship, but of course we couldn't leave the area until we'd retrieved you." He looked at t'Cael then and concluded, "I suppose we know now

296

why they started getting hostile as soon as you two met on the planetoid."

T'Cael nodded. "Mutiny usually involves hostility," he agreed.

"Yes . . . well, at any rate, I came up and saw what was going on, and . . . I'm ashamed to admit that I agreed to fire on the ship—"

"Good for you!" George interrupted.

"I'm not particularly proud of it, George," April said.

"*I* am," George said.

April waved a dismissive hand. "Since we retrieved you, we've been heading out of the area on impulse power. We should have full impulse very soon, and from that we'll be able to draw shields and better weapons capacity. Not as extensive as we would have if we could draw from warp power, but it's something. The Romulan ship hasn't made any more overt moves against us. They're keeping their distance. We know we damaged them to some degree, because we've been getting readings of leakages, but they're still keeping pace with us. I'm not sure why."

"To keep the Swarm apprised of your location," t'Cael said, pained by the conduct of his fleet. The real pain he felt, though, was caused by something else. If he had coddled a single hope that Idrys might not be dead, that hope was gone. If the order to attack the Earth ship had been hers, the attack would never have ceased simply because the Earth ship fired back. The attack would have been completed, to the death if necessary.

No, this hovering behind—this was Ry'iak's version of bravery. Ry'iak would lag back until the Swarm arrived, then he would let the Swarm do his job for him and claim the victory for himself.

Ry'iak didn't deserve victory. The Supreme Praetor didn't deserve possession of this vast ship, which he would use to dominate the galaxy. These humans . . . to them t'Cael was an enemy alien, yet they trusted him. Even Kirk, with his innate suspicions and militaristic bent, was too trusting in having brought t'Cael to the bridge itself, to the command hub itself. What if all this had been a trick?

T'Cael looked at the faces near him in the turbo-lift. If the humans had behaved like enemies, he would have remained silent and let events play themselves out. But their honesty, their trust made him want to help them. Preserve them.

"I will help you," he said, the words catching in his throat. They all looked at him. Quietly he added, "I know how they think."

The captain gazed at him for several moments, as though hoping to see through his skin and into his mind. He looked at his first officer.

George nodded simply. "I believe him."

Even Robert April couldn't arbitrarily hand out trust to an enemy, but he did trust George, and for the time being that would have to be enough. With a little shake of his head, he sighed. "Well, all right . . . do you have a suggestion?"

T'Cael nodded tightly. "You'll have to turn and destroy my ship."

April looked dubious. "Now, I don't think I can—"

"If you don't," t'Cael insisted, "they'll continue to send transmissions for the Swarm to triangulate upon. If you destroy my ship, you may be able to leave the area in enough time to get away."

April appeared pained at the whole idea. He glared at the floor of the turbo-lift.

"Let's . . . let's think about something else before we think about that," he said finally. "If we can get warp drive in time, we can get away. You already said your ships don't have hyperdrive, didn't you?"

"The Swarm ships are mounted only with pulse power, that is true."

"All right, let's try that channel first then. Please—" With a graceful gesture he invited them all back onto the bridge.

Since nobody on the bridge looked around this time, George assumed Sanawey had told everyone present about the Vulcan prisoner they'd liberated and to keep him comfortable by not making an issue of it. It wasn't an ironclad story, but it had a better ring than telling everyone they were about to hand themselves over to the commander of the ship that had tried to knock them out of space.

Only a little stumble on his way back down to his command chair gave away the fact that April was still injured. He recovered on his own and tapped on the command intercom. "April to engineering. Dr. Brownell?"

A technician answered. *"One minute, Captain."*

The uncomfortable silence went by slowly.

"Brownell here. What'd you want?"

"Doctor, the situation has changed somewhat. We desperately need that warp drive."

"Why didn't you just say so? What'd you think, we just replace a spring and a belt and it's working again?"

The four men crowded around the command chair shared a grimace. T'Cael's was particularly fraught with curiosity—what was the chain of command on this vessel?

April tried another tack. "Have you at least discovered what's wrong with it, doctor?"

"There's nothing wrong with it."

"I beg your pardon?"

This time Brownell actually hesitated. *"Look, I think you'd better come down here for this."*

"Can't you simply tell me?"

"It's not the kind of thing that ought to be broadcast over the system."

"Really . . ." April glanced up at the image of the Romulan ship tailing after them. "Very well. We'll be right down." He snapped off the intercom and took in George, t'Cael, and Drake with a wave of his hand. "All of you, come with me. Carlos, we'll be in engineering. If anything happens—"

"Yes, sir," Florida anticipated.

Engineering seemed cooler than the bridge. Or maybe it was just that George knew what kind of reception they'd get from Dr. Barnacle. Sure enough, he came up from behind a magnetomic feed cylinder, saw them, grumbled something, then looked straight at t'Cael through his smudged eyeglasses and said, "Where'd you get the bunny?"

Drawing up short, t'Cael stared in puzzlement, as though he wasn't sure whether he'd been insulted or not. April ignored it and grasped the cylinder for extra support, trying to control his breathing after the jog through the ship. "The warp drive?"

"Yeah," Brownell said with a nod. "We've been looking for something wrong with the warp engines."

"And?"

"And it's a waste of time. There's nothing wrong with 'em."

"Then what is it?"

"It's in the computer master system. The warp drive *program* is gone."

April gasped. "What?"

Brownell shrugged his thin shoulders. "Gone. The program itself. No trace of it. Not a hint that it was ever programmed into the system at all. The warp engines are fine. There's nothing to tell the ship how to use them."

"But how can that be?"

"Somebody must've fed in a predator program."

As though stricken, April gripped the rim of the cylinder. "What's a predator program?"

Even George was a little surprised when it was he who answered instead of Brownell. "It's a program that eats the previous program. One of the hardest things to track with conventional security procedures."

Brownell nodded. "And it's impossible to run warp engines manually."

"But this is unthinkable!" April choked out. "When was this done?"

"Could've been months ago. Could've been yesterday. A program like that is designed to be dormant until it's triggered."

"What could trigger it?" George asked.

Brownell glared at him. "Hell, almost anything! Use your imagination. At a guess, I'd say it was the ion effect on the outer hull. That must've been the trip switch. The drive was keyed to overload when it came in contact with the ion storm, and that caused the warp jump and dinked around with the gravitational matrix. Since we're not dead, there must've been an abort mode too. Soon as the predator program ran out, the whole drive system was crashed. And here we are. But I'd say it was put into the system before we left."

"Why?"

"Because, pepperhead, there are only two drive-computer masters on board now, that's why. Me and Woody."

April collected himself. "How do we turn it back on?"

Brownell turned to him and pursed his lips. "August, you are the luckiest bastard this side of hell. Under normal circumstances, there'd be no chance in hell of fixing it."

301

Two hells and a bastard. April assumed that was a good sign. "But . . ."

"But because the ship is unfinished, some of the warp drive computer ordnance is still on board. Excess baggage, usually."

"And we can reprogram the computer with it?"

"I said you were a lucky son of a bitch, didn't I? Under usual circumstances, I wouldn't even be here. You'd be hanging out here like a choked duck."

George pulled April around abruptly. "This is no fluke, Robert. Being a security grunt for eight years has its advantages. My sixth sense is screaming. We're here by design. Somebody's doing this."

For the first time, a glimmer of agreement appeared in the captain's eyes. April had to agree. A predator program? It even sounded horrid. After a moment, he looked at t'Cael.

"Not my design," the Romulan said. "If this was a plan arranged by my government, I wasn't apprised of it."

April paced slowly across the deck, with all the promise and beauty of engineering sprawled out around him. When he spoke, it was with a solemnity that struck the others silent.

"If we fail," he said, "we'll have died . . . the *Rosenberg* dies . . . Federation expansion dies . . . and the starship falls into hostile hands. Those are high stakes, I know. The future of the known galaxy seems to hinge upon what we do next."

George broke in on April before the captain talked himself into doing nothing. "Can't we just get out of here, Robert? Do we have to rewrite the Light Brigade?"

April looked up. "You're the one who's convinced me there's subterfuge going on, George. Now you want me to ignore it and just get out of here?

302

Certainly we'll get out if we can, but you don't seem to understand what you've been saying all along. My God . . . if there's been sabotage, then someone —one of our most highly screened personnel, a member of our elite science team—is in collusion with a hostile government. I can hardly believe it." He touched his forehead in an effort to fathom his own words, and paced again. "God, I almost hope the saboteur is still on board. I'd hate to think he's roaming around freely on the spacedock or back at Federation Central. That would be unbelievably dangerous."

In a single step George reached him and pulled him around. "We'll find that traitor, Robert—but listen to me. I'm beginning to see things your way. There has to be more than just being born, living, and dying. We have to aspire to something better. Now that I know that, I want to be part of the reach for something better. But first, we have to *survive*. It'd be nice if everyone could be like you. But everyone isn't. *They're* not."

April held out a single hand in entreaty and asked, "What do you want from me, George?"

George straightened. "I want to do what Cael says," he said bluntly. "I want fighting capacity."

There was no real echo in the acoustically stressed engineering deck, but those words seemed to come again and again as they all awaited his answer. At that moment, Robert April was a man divided between unsavory choices, and responsibilities he dearly wished belonged to someone else. His personal philosophy didn't seem to work, didn't carry him this time, as it always had before. This was a time for drastic actions, and he would have to decide whether the preservation of his own philosophy was worth other lives—even those of the enemy.

His lips parted. "I think—"

The shipwide intercom suddenly blared, overlaid by the whoop of the alert klaxon.

"Red Alert! Red Alert! Captain April to the bridge! Emergency!"

April dodged for the nearest wall com. "This is April. What is it, Carlos?"

"Captain, we've got company! Five more of those ships just came up at us out of nowhere!"

April felt his spine tingle as the voice of the tall alien commander spoke from his side.

"The Swarm."

Part IV

To Boldly Go

Chapter Eighteen

THE CHICKENS IN the barnyard flinched and cackled at the chirp of the communicator grid from the loft above. Since they were eating chickens and not laying chickens, they didn't have much contact with technology. In fact, they didn't get eaten all that often. Some of them were several years old, more pets than farm animals. Stupid pets, but pets.

Being stupid, they quickly forgot about the funny sound that beeped from the loft high over their heads and settled down.

"Kirk to bridge."

"Bridge. Uhura here."

"Lieutenant, locate Admiral Ron Oliver at Starfleet Command and patch him through to me down here."

"Yes, sir. That may take a few minutes, Captain. Several members of the Admiralty are currently involved in a review board at the moment, and I think he might be one of them."

"I realize that. Patch me through as soon as you find him."

"Yes, sir."

At the side of the loft, McCoy sat back and didn't say anything. He watched the captain, who was standing now, though not exactly pacing. He was . . . moving. The way he did when he had something to think about that he didn't like having to think. Small steps, each one involving a slight turn. His shoulders were stiff, his eyes tightened, and when his eyes moved it was with the small and sharp movements of a hawk's eyes. McCoy had seen this many times, but usually on the bridge, and usually in moments of crisis, when the captain was steeling himself to fight whatever space was throwing at him.

"I don't feel good about this," McCoy finally said. *Oh, that was bright. Say something even more illuminating.* "Jim . . . are you clear on your motivations? Do you really want to release your command? Or do you just think you should?"

Jim Kirk gave him one of those hard flicks of his eyes. After a moment, the gaze mellowed. He breathed deeply, and didn't answer.

McCoy shifted his legs. "You can't go back to 1930. Edith can't come here. The best you can do is find some way to commemorate her in our time."

A thoughtful smile tugged at the captain's lips. "I'd like that," he said. "But it isn't just Edith, Bones. It's my life. I've been selfish," he added. "I've wallowed in the outer glory of command."

"How do you figure selfish?" McCoy pressed. "After all you've done for the ship and everyone on board her—"

"What've I done for them?" Kirk squinted out over the quiet Iowa landscape. The sunlight lay like bright powder across his face, and made his sandy hair glitter with a touch of cinnamon. Now he looked squarely at McCoy and was absolutely sure of what he was saying. "Spock should be making his own history, commanding his own starship. For that matter, so should Sulu. Uhura turned down a very rare teaching position at Starfleet Academy. And who knows where a man like Scotty might be by now, instead of shoveling coal into my locomotive. They've all stayed longer than they should have, and it's all out of some misguided loyalty to Jim Kirk and his gluttony for glory."

"And that's how you see it?" McCoy shot back.

"Of course that's how I see it. That's how it is. The whole starship is plugged in to me. You can't tell me you wouldn't rather be thigh-deep in medical research in some quiet laboratory, surrounded by trees and good music."

"Jim, we're a team. You know how we all feel."

"Yes, that's my point. The team feeling. No one wants to be the first to rupture the bond, even in his own interest. It's my responsibility to set the pace."

McCoy opened his mouth, but before he could speak the communicator in Kirk's hand chirped again.

The captain snapped the instrument open. "Kirk here."

"Uhura, sir. A channel is open to Starfleet Head-quarters. Admiral Oliver standing by."

"Thank you. Patch us through."

"Relaying. Go ahead, Admiral."

"Jim, this is Oliver. Going to take me up on that weekend in the mountains finally?"

"No, at least not yet. I'm going to take you up on something else."

"Uh-oh."

"I want that reassignment you offered last month."

"You do?"

The captain paused. "Yes."

Now there was a pause from the other end. *"Jim, I only offered you that because I was obliged to. I didn't think you'd—"*

"I'd consider it a personal favor if you'd smooth things out for my first officer to take my place in command of the ship."

"Jim, slow down, will you? Spock's a fine officer. He'll make a prime captain. But he won't be you."

309

"That's the idea."

"Jim—listen. Why don't you extend your leave. Take some time to make the decision."

"I'd rather not. It's the kind of decision that only gets more painful if it's stalled."

"For good reason, with a man like you."

"Put the orders through. I'll notify my seniors."

"I'll send a wreath."

The captain smiled, as though relieved of a burden far heavier than simple command status. "Thank you, Admiral. Kirk out." It was an abrupt end to a strained conversation. He would apologize to Oliver later. For now, he just wanted to break the ties.

"Well," the doctor blustered, "guess that's it, isn't it? The end of an era. Just wipe it away. Another name goes down in the history books. Another tombstone goes up. May I be the first of the crew to say thank you, Captain. Thank you for giving us back our lives. Devil only knows what we're going to do with them." When he realized his sarcasm wasn't helping, he leaned forward and glared from under his flared brows. "Did you ever give any consideration to the fact that maybe, just *maybe* all this might have something to do with the ship? Maybe there's something special about her that we don't want to leave behind? I think it's pretty damned pompous of you to take all the responsibility for where we are and where we want to be." McCoy's mist-blue eyes widened as he bobbed his head in a so-there nod. "I, for one, am a grown-up, and I can make my own decisions."

Kirk leaned against the rim of the loft hatch. "Says you."

McCoy refused to back down. "I want to ask one question and I want you to think about it." He pointed at Kirk's hand, at the letter the captain held, then at the other letters in a small pile at the captain's

310

feet. "Is this what you're getting out of your father's letters, Jim? No—don't answer that. I'm going to rephrase it. Is this what you think your father *wanted* you to get out of those letters? Would a man like your father ever have written them if he thought they'd bring you to this?"

The smile faded from the captain's face. He gazed at the old letter in his hand, the pile from which it came below him, and wondered why he had been the one who saved them. Of his brother and himself, Sam was the more sentimental. With a twinge of sadness he realized that he never knew his father well enough to really be sure what the letters meant. When his father came home, he was just visiting. He wasn't coming *home*.

"I want a home, Bones," he said solemnly, his brows drawing together as he sought the right words. "I want you and the others to be able to make homes for yourselves, and not just visit Earth from time to time without any real anchors in your lives. Look at us. Not one of us has a family. For all the affection and loyalty we share between us, we haven't really rooted those feelings anywhere."

McCoy's hand sliced the air between them. He got to his feet abruptly. "Jim . . . stop. I don't want to hear any more." He moved closer, and let his voice fall. "Jim, a human being can do worse than be part of a team like ours. Maybe we're not built for family life. Our calling is different. We've all loved and lost . . . or walked away. The one thing we've always had is the ship. Who knows? Maybe we've walked away on purpose." He paused, took a step closer, and when he spoke again the depth of his belief was undeniable. "Maybe it's because we're the kind of people who stare into the sun."

On a statement for which there was no postscript,

the two men merely gazed at each other, trying to read the subtle emotions that years of friendship had taught them to see in each other.

Without moving or even blinking, McCoy spoke. "Don't take away the sun."

It was the captain's turn to have nothing to say. There had been many moments of conflict, of trenchance, of decision in their years together, but few so poignant. Seldom did the feelings require a voice, yet when they did, he could always count on McCoy to make sure the voice was there. If he failed to find the words on his own, McCoy would prod and poke and annoy and vex until someone else found the words and the courage to speak them.

A faint scratching on the loft ladder drew their attention.

As they watched, Spock pulled himself up against the edge of the loft and stopped when he got one elbow onto the hay-scattered ledge. He blinked at them and asked tonelessly, "Am I interrupting?"

Kirk and McCoy looked at each other, then looked squarely back at him and chimed, "Yes!"

Spock remained unfazed. "Your mother informed me of your whereabouts, Captain."

"Have you forgotten how to use a communicator?" McCoy demanded.

"Not at all," Spock responded, pulling himself onto the loft and straightening to his full height. "I merely deemed it more gracious to appear in person. The captain is, after all, officially on shore leave. I hoped to make ship's business more palatable by coming in person."

The captain stepped to the center of the loft and asked, "You have a report for me, Spock?"

Spock brushed bits of hay from his uniform and said, "The ship is fully overhauled and restocked.

312

Maintenance engineers have pronounced her spaceworthy and we are now awaiting clearance to leave Starbase One as soon as the crew reports back from leave. However, the starship *Kongo* has pulled in with damage and requires immediate repair, thus Starbase Control has requested that we vacate the maintenance drydock. With your permission, we'll move to external dock at the spaceport until we resume patrol."

The captain nodded. "Of course. Inform Captain Toroyan that we'll free the dockspace within the hour, and convey my greetings. I want a meeting with all senior officers and department heads as soon as they report in. And I want to speak privately to Scotty."

"Very well, sir. Mr. Scott is on board now. I'll make the appropriate notifications."

Satisfied, the captain turned to glance at McCoy. "We'd better get back to the ship before the ship shows up here." He stepped past Spock toward the ladder.

"Captain, if I may . . ." Spock began.

Kirk turned. "Yes?"

Spock's brow furrowed slightly. Before speaking again, he clasped his hands behind his back, gazed down at the hay, and moved a little closer to his commander. "Sir, I . . . overheard your communication to Admiral Oliver."

"You overheard?" Kirk repeated.

Spock nodded self-consciously. "I eavesdropped."

Leaning against the loft wall, McCoy folded his arms and grumbled, "What're friends for?"

Kirk rewarded him with the hawk glare again, "Interesting that I've gotten so predictable." He stepped toward the ladder, and grasped the top of it, realizing what it took to drive a man like Spock to fracture the protocol of private communiqués. Maybe he hadn't hidden his despair as well as he'd thought. "I'm going to say goodbye to my mother. I'll meet you both back on board."

"Captain—" The Vulcan officer closed the space between them with an unwanted urgency. He poised his own hand on the other upright of the ladder.

"Yes, Spock?" Kirk bridged quietly, straightening again.

"About Miss Keeler."

"Yes." The captain pressed his lips together thoughtfully and grew quiet in empathy for Spock, the only person who had truly shared his experience in the past, and the only person for whom expression was a crushing sacrifice. Because he thought he knew what Spock would say, Kirk tried to bail him out. "Spock, you don't have to say it. I appreciate what you're thinking."

Yet another step intensified Spock's determination to say what he had on his mind, no matter the rupture of Vulcan stoicism. "Even so," he began, "I have an observation."

Kirk blinked at the filtered sunlight that hovered like a haze around Spock. Their moving about in the hay had raised a sparkle of dust in the loft, and they stood now in its glittering mist, each man representative of a different calling, a different background, a different destiny.

"Your presence in the past was not wasted," Spock began, never averting his gaze from his captain's as he might had he been speaking to someone other than this man. "You made a difference for her. In the unchanged past, she lived and she died. That is all. In the altered time," he said, "she was loved before she died."

The meaning of those words, put together in that way, had ten times the depth and worth they'd have had spoken by anyone else.

Kirk simply nodded. He knew Spock understood. "Thank you, Spock," he said quietly, "from us both."

The ladder wobbled as he climbed down. The chickens scattered, then reassembled around the feeding bin when he had gone.

McCoy moved to the edge of the loft, where Spock was staring down at the barn floor, silent.

"He's making a mistake," McCoy said. "He's reacting to the pain, using it as an excuse to change the course of his career."

Several seconds passed before Spock said, "He has that right."

Frustration put an edge in McCoy's voice. "Yes, but he's not himself. Spock, you don't understand what grief can do to a person."

"Doctor," he said solidly, "I do understand. Quite clearly, in fact. The captain sees his career as meaningless in the large scheme. He has forgotten the extraordinary good he has done. He has forgotten that the capacity in which we serve is not as much duty as privilege." Spock paused, as though deciding whether or not to vent his thoughts, but when he spoke again there was no hint of vacillation. "And even more tragically," Spock went on, "he has forgotten that the starships of the Federation are the physical, tangible manifestations of humanity's stubborn insistence that life does indeed mean something."

McCoy stood unmoving, absorbing what the Vulcan had said, the elusive truth of what Starfleet, the ship, the captain meant to Spock. More than a career, more than a refuge, and certainly more than McCoy had ever guessed.

"Spock . . . I never knew."

"Doctor," Spock said, "you never asked."

Chapter Nineteen

"CAPTAIN, LONG-RANGE SENSORS have been restored."

April took Florida's news solemnly as he led the way from the turbo-lift back onto the bridge. Red-alert lights flashed in silent warning now that the klaxons had been turned off, giving the bridge an aura of danger, even of mystery. "Marvelous. Begin tracking our home stars and set a course out of these people's space."

"Plotting, sir," Florida answered. "But if we don't have warp drive—"

"It's coming," April told him. On the viewscreen, he studied the distant but clear image of five ships identical to the one that had been attacking them. "Where are they? How far away?"

"On long-range, still one-point-six AUs away."

"Does that do anything for us?" George asked from the upper walkway, where t'Cael and Drake bracketed him on either side, both remaining suspiciously quiet.

Florida twisted around briefly. "Yes, sir, it buys us time. If all we had was short-range sensors like before, we'd probably be dead before we really had a chance to see them. Traveling at their present rate of sublight, they're still"—he paused to check his readout —"seventeen minutes away."

"That's not much," George said.

April moved to the center of the command deck.

"It's something we didn't have a minute ago. Mrs. Hart, how are the shields coming?"

The woman at the engineering console reported, "We've got all the shield power we can draw from the impulse engines. If we get warp power back, we'll get another thirty percent."

"Can you concentrate the deflector power that we do have?"

"If I have a few seconds' warning."

"I'll try to provide it," April said. He grasped at his command chair as though drawing strength from the nearness of a friend. His features hardened, and he forced himself to say, "Bring all weapons capabilities to bear. Come to battle-ready sequence on all systems." He punched the intercom on the command chair's arm and said, "Dr. Brownell, how's that reprogramming coming?"

"You just left, you know."

"I know, but you need to tell me a projected repair time."

"When we're done, that's your projected time. I've got Saffire working on it. Woody's on his way to help him. None of these other mallet heads can do it, and I'd like to get moving too, you know."

"Yes, all right, but I need to have some estimate."

"Forty minutes. Minimum."

"Thank you, doctor. April out. Mr. Florida, get us out of here, best speed."

The words were disturbing simply because everyone knew perfectly well that a ship this size on impulse power was like a whale in a pond. It couldn't possibly outrun small ships whose main systems were all geared to quick maneuvers and optimum usage of impulse energy.

Carlos Florida set his jaw and touched his navigational dial.

Then a voice from the upper deck, ominous and

confident with knowledge, cut across the bridge. It was a sound of firm command, far different from the soft English warble of Robert April.

"Captain . . . you must not run."

April turned, and met t'Cael as the Romulan stepped down to the lower deck.

T'Cael seemed hesitant, as though he couldn't decide whether or not to finish what he'd started to say.

April faced him squarely, still leaning on his command chair. "Is there another course?"

"You must meet them in battle. You must aggress."

"I'd like to limit the fighting if I can," April told him. "If we can buy time somehow until the warp drive is mended—"

T'Cael's eyes widened, and he raised his hands for emphasis. "Captain, I swear to you on my honor that I see only three possibilities now. Either the Swarm captures you, the Swarm destroys you, or you destroy the Swarm. This is not the time for gentility."

The exchange amazed everyone who heard it. If the other members of the bridge crew hadn't figured out already that this was no Vulcan, they knew it now. Florida, Sanawey, Hart, Graff—they kept their mouths shut and controlled their glances. George was proud to claim them as his colleagues. "You must act now," t'Cael said.

April prodded, "Before what?"

T'Cael paused, realizing the depth of intuition in the man before him. He wavered, about to speak, yet unable to.

"Before what?" April asked again, more softly.

After a long moment of soul-searching, t'Cael spoke. "Before the mothership arrives."

On the upper deck, George groaned. "Mothership . . ."

T'Cael glanced up at him with those large flashing

eyes. "The mothership is made up of several Swarms. You will be radically outnumbered and outpowered." He looked at April again and stepped even closer. "It is to the advantage of the Swarm commanders to deal with you before then. They won't want to share the glory. Their goal is to capture this vessel, not destroy it. If possible, they'll avoid heavily damaging the ship."

"That gives us an advantage," April surmised.

He started to turn away, but T'Cael grasped his arm and drew him back around.

"Captain April, I would not mislead you. The Swarm commanders *prefer* to capture this ship, but if deprived they will blow it from the skies."

Without changing expression, April accepted t'Cael's words as truth. He was beginning to accept the ruthlessness of the enemies he faced.

"All right . . . what do you recommend?"

"They'll try to identify your propulsion units and disable them. They may try to destroy the bridge if they can identify its location. You must remember how a pack fights. Their strength is in a coordinated attack. If you try to outrun them and fail, you'll have no chance against their organized efforts. You must keep the pack disoriented. Prevent them from organizing. The only way is to attack and move, attack and move, again and again. You must not run."

April nodded. "Yes, I know what you're saying. I once saw a stag hold off a wolf pack by simply refusing to run. It stomped its hoof at them and stared them down, and they didn't know what to do because they instinctively attack on the run. They didn't know how to bring down standing prey."

T'Cael's shoulders relaxed beneath his bright blue jacket as he saw that the captain did indeed comprehend the brutality of the situation.

With both hands gripping the command chair,

April pursed his lips, contemplated the deck for a moment, then raised his eyes. "I'd like to take your advice," he said, "but first there's something I have to ask you."

Anticipating what was coming, t'Cael softly agreed.

"You don't seem to be the kind to be motivated by revenge," April began. "Why are you so willing to help us?"

George moved forward until the walkway rail pressed against his legs, and he clenched his fists and his jaw at the same moment, forcing himself not to interfere. *Convince him. We only have a few minutes. Make him believe you.*

T'Cael watched the Swarm ships, tiny wedges on the viewscreen, grow a little larger. Better than anyone, he knew their determination and the savage accuracy with which they would lay siege to these people and this prize. He steadied himself with a deep breath.

"After the Federation Wars," he began, "our leadership, the Praetorial system, was rearranged. The populations of our planets realized our loss—resources, personnel, time—but more than anything, we realized the danger of power too centralized. When one small group makes judgments for all, errors are magnified. All must pay. When the wars ended, our tribes elected to establish a council of representatives. The council ruled for what would be nearly forty of your years. We knew prosperity. In those short years, scientific advancements were unmatched in our history. The standard of living improved. Our many cultures flourished. There was talk of approaching the Federation, to open relations with you. Yet," he continued with a sigh, "time gave cause to forget."

"Time?" April interrupted. "Only forty years?"

"There was more," t'Cael said. "We were attacked

320

by the civilization on the opposite side of us from Federation space. We suffered sudden, heavy losses. Blame was thrust upon the council. Too much peace, they cried, not enough preparedness. The council system was dissolved. The Praetorship rose again, and one individual rose to maneuver it."

"You had no constitution," April concluded.

T'Cael paused. "I beg your pardon?"

"No constitution," April said. "Like our Articles of Federation. They're modeled after the Constitution of the United States. They prevent any sudden twists in the system. Things take time to resolve. Nothing can be changed on an emotional basis."

"Wise," t'Cael said simply. Then he clasped his hands and frowned at himself. "Forgive me. I don't usually ramble."

"It's all right," April soothed. "I take it you don't care for the way your system came out of the trouble."

Hesitant to agree with so blunt a statement, t'Cael tipped his head and slowly explained. "For the sake of military progress and a few men's ambition, we have lost our values. Now my people speak of taking from others, and to that we attach our glory."

George gritted his teeth and spoke up. "Military strength is necessary in this galaxy, whether we like it or not. Where would we be if we didn't have the power to fight your Swarm?"

A cloaked harshness came over the Romulan's black eyes as they struck George. "Because of your kind," he said, his voice raised in anger, "both in your culture and in mine, all that we could do together is lost."

George leaned down and grasped the rail, meeting t'Cael's unsettling glare with the same level of ire. "You just said your people have become obsessed with plundering others. If they weren't afraid of

321

Federation military strength, what would they have done to us long before now?" He straightened up. "You damned well know."

Without waiting for a response, he stalked away toward the communications station, shouldered Sanawey out of the way, and started poking switches.

April and t'Cael watched him go. After a moment of discomfort, they faced each other again, and April attempted to ease the tension. "Disturbing isn't he?"

T'Cael's brows rose in sadness. "He doesn't seem to understand."

"Oh, I think he does," April said quietly. "Do many Romulans think like you?"

"No," t'Cael replied. "Captain, whether I live or die is no longer important to me. Whether or not this ship escapes capture . . . that is the factor which will dictate peace or plunder for your culture. I don't wish to see my civilization become a band of pirates, Captain. Better they lose a skirmish and let a prize slip away, than fall into a mire of their own making that will suck them down until there's no crawling out."

April offered a supple nod, a finger pressed against his lip in a self-silencing manner. A moment passed during which he searched the alien commander's elegant face for signals of deception, but he didn't really expect to find any. He nodded, and the finger fell away. "I understand your motives," he said, "but I think there's something you're not telling us."

T'Cael felt suddenly self-conscious. If the subtle glances from the curious bridge crew hadn't been enough to make him aware of himself, the depth of Captain April's intuition certainly did.

On the upper deck, trying not to hear what was happening in the command arena, George was hitting all the wrong buttons.

"What's the matter with this thing?"

"You're hitting the subspace network transducer and the decoders," Sanawey told him patiently. "Why don't you just tell me what you want to do?"

"I want to talk to the search party."

"Okay, for that you need this one . . . and these." The big man's fingers played over the board. Almost immediately there was a *bleep,* and the intercom spoke up.

"Chang here."

"Got that beast plugged up yet?"

"We're narrowing in on it, Mr. Kirk. It's down on J-deck now, and the automatic door panels on decks H through K aren't tied in to the master control yet, so the thing can just run through. We're trying to cut it off with relays, but not everything is patched in yet. There's only so far it can go laterally."

"Then how did it get down to J-deck?"

"It ran into a turbo-lift and must have hit the control grid. I doubt that'll happen again. At least you don't have to worry about having it run onto the bridge at an inopportune moment."

"That's not very reassuring," George said, and couldn't help the twinge of sympathy that returned as he thought of the animal scratching its way across the deck in a wide-eyed panic. "Make it quick."

"Will do, sir—sir, I think . . . I'm coming! Sir, we've got it cornered in the hydrology lab area. I'll let you know—Chang out!"

Put on hold again. George straightened and sighed. He turned stiffly, and using his prerogative as first officer, he stepped back down to the command deck and invited himself into the company of captains.

"I'll admit this to you," April was saying to t'Cael. "We never anticipated this. We're not battle-ready. The ship is short on ordnance, and where we're supposed to crew a couple of hundred we've only got about fifty on board. The only military men here are

323

George and apprentice George over there." He nodded at Drake on the upper deck. "You can see why I don't want to fight."

"If I interpret you correctly, Captain," t'Cael responded, "not wanting to fight has little to do with the number of crew on board your ship. You are personally disinclined to fight."

April grinned modestly. "Don't hide it well, do I? We truly are on a rescue mission. That is my priority. There are other lives at stake than our own, Mr. Cael. I mean to save those lives."

"I mean to help you." T'Cael deliberately looked at George to seal his commitment to both men. Then he turned squarely back to the captain. "We have a weapon you won't enjoy."

April leaned forward slightly. "Which is?"

"A new development. The beginning of a new science. Even as we meet here, our scientists are continuing to refine it. In a few years I'm sure they'll perfect it, but even for now the weapon is formidable at close range. We call it a plasma mortar." He paused, not as much for dramatics as to see if he had pronounced the translation correctly. From the look on George's face, he assumed he had indeed. "When it strikes your shields, it envelopes the ship and releases its energy all at once. It must be fired at proximity range, which you can evade if you maneuver quickly enough. You must keep the ship moving, keep them from calibrating and aiming the mortars."

"We won't be able to arbitrarily wobble about with six fighters nipping at us," April pointed out. "This ship is simply too large for that."

Showing a twinge of impatience, t'Cael hurried his response. "I know. Therefore I suggest you direct your aggression toward *Raze*—my flagship. The entire Swarm will be distracted if you keep *Raze* under siege."

"Why do you say that?"

T'Cael hesitated, momentarily flogged with memories of a certain smug face. Though cunning and capable of killing, Ry'iak wasn't ready to die. As a soldier, t'Cael knew death almost as a companion. Ry'iak knew only greed. He would make sure that if anyone survived, he would be that one.

Swallowing a lump of rage, t'Cael went on. "I know who is in command. He will make sure the other ships protect him."

April folded his arms and tried to imagine someone who would behave that way. "I see . . . thank you for that. I'll try not to waste the advice. Carlos, the ships?"

Florida checked his readouts. "Sir, they're closing steadily. I'd give them another nine minutes to proximity range." He turned to look at April. "Retreat?"

The bridge tensed. No one had missed the conversation at the center, nor had anyone underestimated its importance. Florida wanted to know if he should carry out the last order he was given before the questions arose. He watched the captain, and waited.

In space before them, five computer-enhanced slits grew larger, and at bridge central Captain April communed with the viewscreen.

George watched him. T'Cael watched him.

"No," he said, his voice hoarse. "Plot a course toward the enemy flagship. Prepare for combat engagement."

George reached over the command chair and grasped the captain's elbow in mute approval. April looked at him, his features hardened with the agony of his decision, and nodded his appreciation of the gesture. George tried to think of something appropriate to say, but nothing could make a man like Robert April be glad he was about to take lives.

325

Sanawey suddenly gasped.

The captain turned. "What is it, Claw?"

The Indian shook his head in disbelief as he stared into his readout screen. "Sir . . . I've just pinpointed our location."

"Yes?"

"We're . . . Christ."

April turned to look. "Say it."

The big man straightened. His mouth opened and closed a few times before he could bring himself to say it.

"We're practically on *top* of the Romulan Homeworlds!"

Inside enemy territory, yes . . . but so far in? *That* far inside?

Staggered, everyone stared at Sanawey. Then April turned to t'Cael, and all eyes followed his.

The Romulan commander didn't seem affected. If he was surprised at all, it was surprise that these people hadn't fully understood the import of their presence here, or the grave menace they represented. He scanned their dazed faces. Finally he widened his eyes at them and shrugged. "That's why we were upset."

"Mr. Kirk, Engineer Chang is hailing," Sanawey called.

George joined him on the upper deck. "Kirk here."

"Chang, sir. We . . . got it."

"What do you mean, got it?"

"It was running from section to section, through the automatic doors, and accidentally it . . ."

"It what?"

"It accidentally ran into a section where the environmental controls weren't functioning yet. No heat, no gravity—it was only about eighty degrees Kelvin in there. The autohatches weren't sealed."

326

George shuddered, his shoulders drawing inward. "You mean it's . . ."

"Frozen like a statue."

George grimaced. He didn't know whether such a death would be less or more gruesome than dying by laser. Either fate seemed somehow unjust for a creature that had lived its life by the rules of nature, and played fairly.

"Okay, get rid of it. While you're down there, make sure the electrical locks are on in all the sections where environmental control isn't automated. We don't want anyone strolling into a super-subzero area."

"Will do, sir."

"Good job, by the way. Kirk out." He straightened. "Cancel intruder alert status," he told Sanawey, then looked down at April. "Ship is secure, Captain."

"Thank you, George," April said simply, then once again pressed the intercom beside him. "Dr. Brownell, we're going to have to put priority on weapons capacity."

"Then you're gonna have to send Graff down here to take over on the warp reprogramming. Saffire's the only one of these clay brains who can handle the weapons program, and he's gonna have to do it from Auxiliary Gunnery Control in the engineering section."

Graff turned at the sound of his name and headed for the turbo-lift. "On my way, sir," he said to April as the lift doors parted.

"He's coming, doctor," April relayed. "Mr. Cael, pardon my bluntness, because I know this is difficult for you. But if you have anything to tell us that might improve our chances even more, might you say it now?"

"Certainly," t'Cael began, but honor forced him to

clear his throat before he could continue. "Our ships, and their commanders. *Raffish* is commanded by a man named Llarl. He gained command less through accomplishment than through politics. He should not be your first consideration. The ship most dangerous to you is *War Thorn.* It is updated to the most modern armaments. Zayn Z'ir is formidable in battle, and she is tenacious and young enough to meet you on any level of recklessness."

Listening intently and burying any reaction, April took a moment to wag a finger at Sanawey, who immediately nodded as though he had anticipated the gesture. His big fingers tapped in a record mode and tied it in to the library computer's strategical coordination banks.

"Soar," t'Cael was saying, "is an older fighter. She lacks the more sophisticated armaments of the other ships."

"No plasma mortars?"

"No plasma mortars. Less maneuverability. Lower shielding. However, her commander, H'kuyu, is also older. He was given *Soar* in order that his experience would prove a counterbalance to the ship's inadequacies. You'll have a hard time surprising him."

"Are you getting all this, Claw?" April asked.

"Right into the computer's logistics library, sir."

April nodded. "Go ahead, Mr. Cael."

T'Cael acknowledged him with a gracious glance, burying the nausea that insisted he was turning traitor. He fought to define his motives—peace, yes. Acting upon his honor to save these humans. Telling them only what they needed to know to save themselves. That—and no more.

Past the bile that rose in his gullet, he continued.

"Future Fire is also lacking in shield capacity; however, its arms are peak aptitude. Tr'Poll commands it, a man of little mercy, but also little intui-

328

tiveness." T'Cael raised a brow and grinned at the captain. "He has the imagination of a dead fish. Be unpredictable—you'll disorient him easily."

On the upper deck, George focused on what t'Cael was saying, trying to absorb it all. Maybe the computer was assimilating it into some kind of battle strategy, but he didn't entirely trust this "library" business yet. He wanted to *know* these things himself, to have them at hand when the minutes were up.

"Experience," the description went on, "has experienced a malfunction in its sensor relays during this voyage. They'll have to fight manually. Commander h'Daera, however, is an expert at such battle techniques. She'll more than compensate for the lack of sensors simply because she dares to anticipate. However, she tends to overestimate herself and can be tricked into making errors in judgment."

"And *Raze*?" April prodded, speaking gently because he felt this particular ship was at the end of the list for a reason—t'Cael was avoiding it.

"Yes . . . *Raze.*" T'Cael sighed. "Difficult to tell. Its commander"—unbidden images of who should have been in command burned in his mind— "is Kai. He also has little imagination. But he is fiercely dedicated and knows enough to bend rules. There was a time . . . when I put great trust in him."

"Is he the one you referred to?"

"No. I referred to Ry'iak." Bile rose in his throat. "He has bored himself under our skin and means to feed there." He worked at controlling his bitterness. "That one will do anything, sacrifice anyone, to protect his own ambitions, and his life."

"Sounds like a conflict of interest," April commented.

T'Cael paused. "I'm sorry?"

"It sounds as though protecting his life may get in the way of his ambitions."

329

"Oh, yes, you're correct about that. He will be torn. Ry'iak is a fool, but a ruthless fool. He's the sort who enjoys pulling the feathers from baby *nei'rrh*—when he isn't acting like one of them—all of which makes him ideal to his chosen career." T'Cael folded his arms, fuming. Slowly he noticed the curious looks he was getting as his feelings surfaced.

"Sounds like a dangerous chap," April said.

"Yes, he's a chap."

April smiled, both at t'Cael's grim expression and at his sincere effort to fit in. "Is there someone who directs strategy for the Swarm as a unit?"

T'Cael stood rock still for a moment. "Yes," he said hesitantly. "I do."

The captain pressed his lips flat in understanding of the irony.

"Three minutes, Captain," Florida announced. His voice quivered, and he blinked self-consciously.

"How can we tell them apart?"

T'Cael responded to April's sensible question with a little shrug. "Simply. Each ship's wingtips are colored for identification. *Raffish* is white, *War Thorn* is deep red, *Future Fire* is blue, *Soar* is gherru, *Experience* is—"

"Pardon, but we don't know what 'gherru' is."

Pausing, t'Cael looked around the bridge, then leveled a finger right at George's hair and said, "This."

"Orange," Drake offered.

"Copper," April graciously corrected.

George simply twisted his lips in disgust and pushed t'Cael's arm down with burgeoning familiarity. "Just get on with it."

"*Experience* is gray, and *Raze,* as you've seen, is gold."

April maneuvered into his command chair and

steeled himself. "All right . . . so be it. Let's close the gap. Move in on *Raze.*"

"Robert—" George began, an idea forming in his mind.

The captain twisted around. "You have something, George?"

"Yes, a bluff. Shields at half power, lasers at half, particle cannon shut off. Make us appear weaker when they come in to scan us. Our best weapon is the fact that they have no idea what we can do."

"They may have already scanned us."

"But they may not have."

"Make them act rashly?" April murmured, understanding. "Let's go one step further. Carlos, calibrate to fire half lasers at *Raze.*"

Florida's face crinkled. "At this distance? They'll hardly feel it!"

"Exactly."

"We did fire on them before," Florida reminded. "They've felt the lasers."

"Yes, but we may be able to make them believe we've lost power. Let's try, shall we?"

Drake tried to brighten the bleak situation by offering, "Prime bait, Captain sir. We'll look like candy-asses, won't we?"

"Colorfully put, but I'm hoping so," April responded, eyeing *Raze* in the main viewer. The starship maneuvered around for pursuit.

"Interesting use of the language," t'Cael noted, glancing at Drake.

"Yes, that's Lieutenant Reed up there. Be careful never to listen to what he says."

A twinge ran up April's spine at the sight of *Raze* growing larger on the viewer. The Romulan fighter might have been small in comparison to the empress, but its glossy black hull and fire-feathers gave it a fierce and intimidating appearance.

331

The ship began moving off, stalling until the Swarm could swoop in to protect it.

April leaned forward. "Stay with him . . . ready . . . fire!"

Florida struck the gunnery grid, and the computer took over. Lancets of light energy broke from the empress' primary hull and joined the two ships in a puppet show. The starship held the string, and the *Raze* became a marionette trying to dance away. Unlike before, however, the Romulan fighter was able to easily break away from the half-powered lasers and veer off on a different course.

"Stay with him," April repeated.

Sanawey touched his earphone and reported, "Subspace activity, Captain, high gain and scrambled."

"They're calling for help," t'Cael informed them.

"As you predicted," April said. "My compliments. You know your people well."

"That is my duty, after all," t'Cael responded sadly.

"You're a pragmatist, Mr. Cael. Don't feel too bad about it. I wish I could adapt as readily."

Suddenly Florida stiffened. "Here they come!"

"George, get down here."

George shook himself and stepped down to April's other side. He and t'Cael stood like bookends on either side of the command chair. He knew what Robert wanted of him; he just wondered if he was up to it. He might be able to match the Romulans in pure ferocity, but as for knowing how to stage a battle . . . as for doing it with a ship like this—

"Let them come," he muttered. "Let them get too close to maneuver; get ready for full laser power."

On the screen, the Swarm grew large. Five ships, close enough to make out the Romulan hieroglyphs on their hulls. Close enough to begin.

"Full deflectors! Helm, hard starboard!" George ordered. "Bring up laser power and come about."

Florida struck his board. The starship carved space, veering away from *Raze* and swinging around to face down three of the approaching ships at point-blank range.

"Fire!"

The controls rang again. Two contained slices of full-power laser energy vaulted from the starship, struck two of the ships, and rocked the third with a near miss. The two injured ships fell off their course, shields burned and weakened.

"Excellent," t'Cael murmured. At once, he glanced toward April and Kirk, and was glad to see that neither had heard him. The maneuverability of the huge ship left him speechless. He never would have guessed that such bulk could become so instantly graceful. Power, yes . . . but such style! And such fine control—

"Very good, George," April said. "Nicely done."

George cleared his throat. "Just luck."

"No it isn't just luck. You have an intuition when it comes to these things. If I didn't believe that, you wouldn't be standing beside me."

Suddenly incensed, George began, "That's not much to bet—"

On the viewscreen, the Swarm pulled together, the three uninjured ships moving between the starship and the two damaged fighters, and fired on the starship.

"Brace yourse—"

Florida's shout was cut off as thick wands of green energy struck the starship's forward deflectors. The ship bolted hard to one side. George was pitched toward the command chair and crushed up against April as waves of destructive energy vibrated through the deck under his feet.

333

"Plasma mortars?" April gasped.

From the hand rail, hanging on tightly, t'Cael answered, "No. Contained ion bolts, drawn from engine power. Very efficient."

"I see that. Status?"

"Deflectors holding, sir," Florida reported, shaken. "Don't ask me how . . ."

"Because they're made to, Carlos," April assured him, forcing himself to believe it too. If he could make these people think the ship was able to compensate for all their lack of military training and experience, perhaps he could bluff them into getting through it. All it took was a little white lie now and then, and a good dose of feigned confidence.

Just then a black wedge with copper tips veered in and t'Cael gasped, "*Soar!*" He lunged toward the navigation station, though the controls were foreign. "Keep away from him!"

"Hard over!" George ordered, but not soon enough.

Soar dipped in close to the starship and dropped a purplish-green and almost transparent blob of energy. Not being a trained tactical helmsman, Florida turned them in the wrong direction—right into the splotch of color. As the starship cut to port, the blob struck the outer deflectors.

A *boom* of engulfing energy thundered through the ship. The decks and bulkheads seemed to convulse around them. George felt the starship heave, a single great spasm that lifted him from the deck and threw him onto the astrogator, then completely over the helm console. He rolled into a heap and landed on his back with his feet in the air, piled up against Florida. Thrums of destructive force bombed across the skin of the starship, and shook her where she hung.

Several seconds later, the ear-crushing drum of aftershock began to slip back.

"Good God—" Breathless, April called across the bridge as he pulled himself up from the deck.

Beside him, t'Cael was also using the command chair for support. "That," he said, "was a plasma mortar."

He tried to hide his astonishment that they were still alive at all, that this ship was strong enough to swallow his finest weapon and return to fight again. If that didn't stun the Swarm for a few seconds, nothing would.

"Unbelievable!" April wheezed, slipping shakily back into his chair.

"A very good weapon at proximity," t'Cael said. He noted that his hands were white as he gripped the command chair, and drew them away. "Someday we may be able to make it work at hyperspeed."

"Let's bloody well hope not! George, I don't think they're playing anymore . . . George? Where are you?"

"I'm under here." George dragged himself up from forward of the helm island with Florida in tow, and stuffed the navigational engineer back into his seat. "Bring up particle cannons to full power." He spun around, his eyes boring right through the viewscreen and into the hulls of *Raffish, Experience,* and *Future Fire.* "Let's go down their throats. Hard about!"

His anger spread like a virus. Each person visibly knuckled down and braced for whatever impact it would take to shake these hawks from the empress' tail.

"You've confused Llarl," t'Cael observed as he watched his ships loop by on the screen. "He's awaiting orders from *Raze.* You have time to move now, while they're scattered. You've kept them from fanning out; now keep them from assembling. Confuse them as to your intent. Sweep broadly around them —Kirk, what are you doing?"

335

"Arm all systems. Synchronize for multiple targets."

"Kirk!"

"Energize particle cannons." George tasted the smoked flavor of revenge, and forced himself not to look away from the sources of his rage in spite of t'Cael's sudden grip on his arm.

"You must give yourself space!"

"To hell with space!"

"Energy surge on *Raffish*," Florida gasped.

T'Cael yanked on George's arm. "The plasma mortars—"

George cut him off. "Fire!"

Florida's shoulders hunched. He hit two switches simultaneously, trusting the new computer systems to do the aiming.

Particle bolts broke from the starship's hull and slammed through space in two directions, their backwash shuddering through the ship even as they struck *Raffish* and *Experience* with full impact. There was a brief hum as the power was compressed. Then, with the eerie silence of space itself, two brilliant suns erupted against the blackness.

The bridge personnel shielded their eyes against the blinding lights of destruction. Even t'Cael stumbled backward until the ship's rail stopped him —astonished.

Carried forward by the unfeeling efficiency of her fabulous new duotronics system, the empress drew her skirts up over the mud and soared on by.

The remaining four Romulan ships took a few unenthusiastic potshots at the enemy as it passed, but confronted with the full power of a starship, they were moving off.

Breathing in little sucks, Florida managed, "I think we've got them on the run."

Behind him, Captain April slowly shook his head in disagreement.

T'Cael squinted at the maneuvers of the Swarm and tried to think as he knew his colleagues would think. "Not yet," he said. Indeed, before he had the chance to react to the sharp looks his statement brought, the four remaining Swarm ships yanked into formation as though drawn by a single string, regrouping against space. "It is the *hr'liighe* formation. It will be difficult to defend against. Simultaneous attack in two columns." Then he saw something else and pointed at the screen. "Notice, Captain, that *Raze* is hovering back slightly, as I predicted. I venture the formation is Kai's idea. Ry'iak doesn't know enough about such things. I surmise he and Kai are locked in disagreement." He turned to April suddenly. "Captain, the worst thing you can do now is wait for the attack. You must disrupt the formation before they complete it."

April nodded. "Which is the one with low shielding?"

"*Future Fire*. Upper left of your screen."

"And the tenacious one?"

"Just beneath, tipped with red. *War Thorn*. You must take care not to let Zayn Z'ir come around to your aft. You'll never shake her."

"I don't mean to shake her." The captain's voice was gentle as he mused, "Have you ever played a good game of chicken?"

Perplexed, t'Cael said, "I understood chicken was a fish."

"Bird," April corrected. "But today it's a game. Carlos, plot a course tangent to that sun. We're going in as close as we can stand."

George came to stand by his captain's shoulder and said, "Oh, that's good . . . let's see what their shields can take."

Across the command arena, t'Cael's eyes glowed

337

with excitement. "Yes! They won't be able to tell where you're firing from. Their sensors will be blinded by so much solar interference." He touched his fingertips together and leaned toward April with a nasty smile on his lips. "That's a military secret. Please don't mention it to anyone."

"Safe with me," April returned, grinning too.

"That kind of slicing won't be easy," George pointed out.

"Have the computer assist you, George. That's what it's for."

"Can it do that?"

"You'll be surprised how well."

"For all the good it'll do inside a giant french fry, Robert. There'll be some shield leakage—it's unavoidable. How'll the ship's outer skin take the stress?"

"We'll have to see."

"This isn't the time to be glib."

"I'm not being glib, George. No one's ever done anything like this before, you know that. I can't answer your questions."

Of course, that was the grim truth. They were setting precedents with this incomplete, understocked, experimental, untested supership, and there were no answers yet.

"Okay," George sighed stiffly. "Let's see how well they take the heat in our kitchen."

"Carlos, concentrate our shields forward port," he said, "then for heaven's sake make sure you pass the sun on that side."

Florida double-checked the course he'd just fed into the navicomp. "Right."

"No, left," Drake said.

"Shut up!" chorused George, Florida, Hart, and Sanawey, stapling Drake to the environmental engineering monitor.

338

The starship swerved over in a tight arc and headed for the nearby sun, a sulfurous ball of burning pink gases.

"Keep the shields concentrated," April said, squinting into the sudden brilliance.

"It's leaving our lateral deflector grid down, sir," Florida said, looking past a raised arm at the screen. "Our aft's unprotected."

"Yes . . . a tempting target, don't you think? They shouldn't be able to resist it."

From his side, t'Cael approvingly said, "You have a touch of the fox in you, Captain."

April wanted to say something modest and witty, but his eyes began to water in the brightness of the alien sun, "Thank you—" he muttered.

"Outer hull temperature rising, Captain," Hart announced, shielding her eyes so she could make out the readings on her screen. As though in agreement with her, the protective systems within the starship started whining.

"They're pursuing, sir," Florida confirmed.

Even as he spoke, lancets of green light broke from two of the Romulan ships and cut into the bare aft section, rocking the starship and scoring her perfect hull with angry red lines that snapped and burned until the cold of space settled them to black scars.

"Emergency backup insulation and stress systems coming on," Hart called over the whine. "Auto-cooling systems at optimum—"

"*Soar* and *Raze* are dropping off, Captain," Florida said. "They can't take it."

"Hull temp reaching tolerance—"

"There goes *Future Fire. War Thorn* refuses to break off, though."

"I'm not sure about this—"

Hart's words were punctuated by the crackling of circuits and the wheeze of compensatory systems fighting the heat of the sun and its dragging gravity. Untested, unstressed internal supports and exterior deflectors ached under the strain, and the strain refused to go away.

"Just a few more seconds," April said, trying to sound encouraging. Sweat broke out on his face. He realized the ship's cooling systems were abandoning the interior areas and rushing to protect the hot outer shell, and the bridge became suddenly tropical.

Florida pulled himself forward. There was frightened victory in his voice as he gasped, "*War Thorn* is starting to veer off, sir."

Just then George bolted forward. "Tractor beams!"

Hart whirled around. "What?"

"Aft tractors, now! Don't let them veer off!"

April pushed himself out of his chair. "George—"

"We may never get a better chance!" George snapped.

"All right, damn you . . . aft traction." April nodded at Hart.

Hart started to argue. "Our systems are too taxed—"

April grasped the hand rail and ordered, "Do what he says!"

The whine of the ship's efforts was drowned out then by a high-pitched electrical scream as the tractors reached out and caught *War Thorn,* dragging the bull terrier of the Swarm into the sun behind them. The fighter bucked against the tractors, but couldn't break free. Three seconds more . . . four . . . five . . .

"Their hull is carbonizing," Hart called, leaning so close to her readout screen that her nose was almost touching it. "They're breaking up—their ship is melting—" The starship bucked then, suddenly freed of weight, and Hart stood up in spite of the blinding brightness. "They're gone. Cremated," she said, her lips pressed tight.

340

"Cut tractors," April ordered. "Vector, immediately!"

Florida leaned into his controls again and the empress turned on her starboard edge, veering away from the sun.

Everyone was drenched in sweat. The starship cut laterally across the sun's light and then took a radial course away from it, heading straight back toward the remaining Romulan ships, coming out of the sun like a renegade bomber.

"Shields are weakened, Captain," Hart reported.

"Holding?" April asked.

"Yes, sir."

"Get ready to fire before their sensors come back on," George ordered, forcing his eyes to readjust.

Before them stood *Future Fire*. Two steps behind it in open space, *Soar* waited, and *Raze* another stretch beyond.

George pressed his hands on the navigational console and glared into the viewer. "Pull up close. Let's not waste shots. They can't see us yet . . . steady . . . fire!"

Nothing happened.

"Fire!"

Florida stared at his board. "I did—sir, weapons failure!"

George stepped to his side and compulsively hit the gunnery toggle. "What happened?"

"I don't know . . . we're not getting power on any —they've locked onto us with those mortars again! They're going to shoot!"

A memory from their test flight popped into George's mind. Suicidal—but their only chance. He hammered the right buttons, and the starship heeled hard over.

"Shields full front!" he shouted, and hoped Hart had the time to comply.

April saw what he was doing and blurted, "Brace yourselves!"

Future Fire loomed up until it filled the screen at a speed that seemed impossibly fast for sublight, then came even closer. Then closer.

The alien lettering on the hull swooped in, huge. They could see the scoring their own lasers had made, and even the bolts that held the black hull plates together.

Impact.

The starship smashed through *Future Fire*'s deflectors and obliterated them, then crushed the black hull and buckled the fighter over like an old banana. Folded over the starship's shielding, *Future Fire* sparkled and crackled with energy ruptures and leaks, wheezing internal atmosphere from jagged cracks, and spewing fuel all over space. The starship carried it through space until finally it scraped along the primary hull disk and slipped away, a mass of dead wreckage.

T'Cael stared in disbelief. That any vessel could survive enough impact to crush the heavy-duty structure of a preybird . . . he gaped at the screen's image of *Future Fire* as the fighter's hulk spun away.

But there were still *Soar* and *Raze,* swooping around, scrambling to maintain a semblance of attack formation. T'Cael looked to his side, at the fiery young man who leaned over the helm. Kirk seemed to realize the danger that remained.

"If we don't get weapons up, we're dead," George was muttering into Florida's ear as the two of them tried to cajole the computer into telling them what was wrong.

But the computer couldn't say. The giant was sleeping again.

Chapter Twenty

GEORGE DOVE FOR the nearest intercom.

"Saffire! Engage the weapons!"

"Sir, I'm trying. It's not getting enough juice to fire. I'm going to try to relay power through the impulse convectors, but if the harmonizers aren't on line, it'll drain the deflector shields. I just need a few minutes."

"We'll be dead in a few minutes!" Boiling with frustration, George stood straight and glared at the Swarm ships cutting across their spacepath. "He damned well knows that . . ."

At the engineering station, Hart frowned. "That doesn't sound right." She touched her controls as though restraining a child. George heard her, but was too preoccupied to pay attention.

"Take it easy, George," Drake said soothingly. "Saffire's doing his best. Sounds fancy to me, and not bad at all for a man who eats his food in sections."

T'Cael suddenly straightened and turned to Drake.

"I beg your pardon?"

Drake blinked, trying to remember what he had just said. He hesitated, then found himself explaining something that seemed entirely out of place in this moment of crisis. "He eats food one-thing-at-a-time . . . you know, in sections." Drake shrugged, suddenly helpless. "Just a joke, I thought . . ."

T'Cael swung around to George. "You have a Romulan on board your ship."

The captain whirled around as though unsure of what he'd heard.

George squinted at t'Cael. "Impossible," he said. "I had everybody checked for physiological match. Every person on this ship is human."

T'Cael was unrelenting. "Perhaps," he said, "but the man he referred to was *raised* Romulan."

The bridge seemed to ice over. George felt his eyes grow narrow until t'Cael was a tall blur.

Hart spun around. "Mr. Kirk! Gunnery control is the source of the drain!"

In a choked whisper George gasped, "*Jesus* —Drake, Sanawey, come on!"

"Hurry, George!" April urged.

The bridge deck rumbled beneath their feet, and they were in the turbo-lift and on their way down before George fully realized that t'Cael had come with them.

Far below the hub of command, deep within the decks of the massive starship, the four men burst from the lift and streaked toward gunnery control. George never flagged, hoping that Saffire had forgotten to set the lock. It was a good bet. The door slid open.

"Saffire!" George blurted and was met with a bolt from a stun pistol. Saffire had been waiting for him —probably monitoring the bridge. The bolt knocked George hard into the leeward bulkhead.

But the second it had taken Saffire to fire on George gave Drake time to move in. His fist met Saffire's jaw. The pistol flew across the deck, and Claw Sanawey moved in. Grasping one of Saffire's arms, Sanawey held him long enough for Drake to get a grip on the other arm. Saffire continued to kick and wrench, and might indeed have jerked himself free had t'Cael not

344

stepped forward to sharply bark, *"Khoi'ha! Hwiiy'lou g'tu hwiiy."*

Saffire froze. In that instant, he realized he had given himself away. He stopped squirming, and slumped in disgust and surrender, no longer straining against Drake and Sanawey. Sullenly, he muttered, *"Ssuaj'rekk."*

George forced his numb legs to carry him to t'Cael's side, and glared at Saffire. "Get him out of here," he growled.

Drake yanked Saffire's arm, heading toward the door. "How 'bout breaking in a spanking new brig, fellow?" Together, he and Sanawey steered the saboteur out of the chamber.

When they were gone, George rubbed his tingling left thigh and scanned the weapons control board, trying to see where the tampering was. As he touched the controls, he asked, "How did you know?"

"I wasn't entirely sure," t'Cael said, "until he answered me."

"What did you say to him?"

T'Cael smiled enigmatically. "As little as possible. I told him to stop, and . . . actually, the translation is 'You are who you are, and we know it.'"

As he began tediously readjusting the weapons malfunctions Saffire had set into the controls, George was glad he had something to do with his hands, that he had an excuse for not facing t'Cael right now.

"I don't get it," he said. "Even if he'd been surgically altered, it would've shown up on Drake's scan."

"Likely there is nothing to show up."

"I'm listening."

T'Cael held his breath for a moment, then went on. "It isn't generally known among my people simply because of our high consciousness of ethnic purity, but there is a small group of humans living among us.

345

Our officials believe their ancestors were part of a pioneer crew lost in our space before the Federation Wars, who didn't care if they were returned. Some have been surgically altered to appear Riha —Romulan. Eventually, their children came to see themselves as Romulan. Our government was quick to take advantage. These people are trained to serve the Empire in covert ways on the other side of the treaty zone. He addressed me as his superior, thus I assume he works for our military intelligence network. This shames me before you. I must apologize."

Now George looked up sharply. "It isn't your fault."

T'Cael's expression softened. "We bear the actions of our own."

George shifted uncomfortably. "Yeah . . . well, if we don't get these weapons working, we're going to be bearing some action ourselves. Besides," he added, averting his eyes again, "we'd probably do the same to you if we had the chance."

Though embarrassed to say it, he found it all too easy to say in front of t'Cael. When had he become that comfortable with this alien, this enemy? This *Romulan?*

And he wasn't the only one who had slipped beyond the straps of prejudice.

"Your ship," t'Cael began, "astounds me. I had no idea of the power here . . ." He opted to look squarely at George then. "No single vessel has ever destroyed a Swarm before."

George tried to suppress the sudden rush of pride —he didn't want to hurt t'Cael, though he'd dreamed of such a chance once upon a time. Standing here, though, in a product of Federation ingenuity, an *unfinished* product, in fact, he couldn't help but be a little smug. "We haven't even started."

As he furiously worked to undo the tangle of

346

blockages Saffire had put into the firing codes, George noticed the shots from outside had ceased. He glanced at t'Cael and said, "No more potshots. Maybe they gave up."

T'Cael was not so optimistic, knowing the Swarm and its commanders as well as he did. One thing was sure: conditions had drastically changed. Whether for better or worse, he couldn't yet tell.

His thoughts outracing his fingers, George almost forgot to stop working at the firing controls when the automatic setting popped on with its green light again to tell him he'd succeeded, that Saffire hadn't had time to do anything permanent. At least the firing controls weren't too new a science for George to figure out. They weren't much different from the flight controls on the shuttlecraft, and everything was clearly marked. So when the light turned from yellow to green and quit flashing, he was startled. He stood back for a moment, afraid to believe he'd circumvented Saffire's tampering, then shook himself out of his doubts and grabbed t'Cael's sleeve.

"That's it. Let's go." George failed to interpret t'Cael's momentary hesitation, and not until they were in the turbo-lift and almost back to the bridge did George realize he should've notified Robert from gunnery control that they could fire again.

He burst onto the bridge and immediately announced, "Weapons are back on line, Captain—"

Even before t'Cael came to his side on the upper walkway, George saw the pall that had settled over the bridge. No one was moving. They were all just staring at the two wedge-shaped vessels on the viewscreen. Bernice Hart wasn't at the engineering subsystems monitor anymore; she was across the bridge at communications, manning Sanawey's position. What had changed that would make communications more important to watch than engineering?

347

Sullenly, Robert April said, "Bernice, play the message back for Mr. Kirk, please."

Hart nodded, not looking at George, and touched the board. The computer translation had a sour ring.

"This is Imperial Swarmbird Soar. *We have ruptured your shielding and implanted two cutaneous detonation devices on your hull. If you make any further move to resist us, they will be ignited and your hull will be crushed between them. You are rendered immobile. Turn off your outer protection grid and your weapons. I give you a quarter hour to effect surrender."*

George stepped toward her as though it was Hart's fault, then swung around and addressed the captain. "Have you scanned the bombs?"

"Yes," April said, and signaled Hart again.

She tapped the controls, and her auxiliary viewscreen wobbled, then refocused, and magnified twice until it provided a good view of a severe-looking device, devilishly simple and unadorned, attached to one of the pearly hull plates by three clawlike manacles. "It's plasma-intrivium," Hart said, "in some kind of fragmentation casing. Tri-megaton salvos. They're clamped to the hull with some kind of magnetic coupler. One of them is up here, aft of the bridge, and the second is below, near the port sensor outlet and the laser coupling. The underside of each of them is arranged for explosion, while the exterior is made to implode and send the impact right through our hull. If they both go off, they'll puncture the top and bottom of the primary section and probably take out the whole main computer core."

"Saffire knew what he was doing," April said, his arms folded and one hand resting against his lips. "With our weapons down, they had the chance to sweep in and do this to us." He pressed his mouth into a line and glanced at t'Cael. "Your people are extremely efficient."

George spun to face t'Cael now. "No bluff?"

T'Cael seemed startled, then his brows shot up. "No. Normally they would plant several more mortars on your hull, but you've destroyed four ships that carry them. Take care, though—two will be enough."

"What if we surrender?" April asked him. "What would become of my crew?"

"They would be interned, questioned, bribed—"

"Tortured?"

"Possibly, but at this stage that's unlikely. After all, the ship will provide its own answers. Our scientists are often tied up in political webbing, but they're capable of very swift analyzing."

George dropped onto the command deck without even touching the steps. "Robert, you're not considering—"

"I have to examine all possibilities, George. If surrender will save all our lives—"

"Captain," t'Cael interrupted, stepping down also, "you must not be captured. You *must* escape."

Robert April gave the exotic alien a long, silent look, during which they communicated in that transcendental way that captains have—a mutuality of destinies, if not futures.

"Why?" he asked gently.

"I have told you why!" t'Cael said angrily. "I have told you of the Praetor, the cancer that spreads through my people—"

"You have," April nodded soothingly, "and I believe you. But I also believe there is something you are not telling me."

T'Cael's glare wavered.

"I see our alternatives here as surrender—or self-destruction," April said firmly. At his side, George started to speak, but the captain waved him silent. "Do you see any others, Mr. Cael?"

"Escape," the Romulan said softly.

349

April leaned forward, prodding, "Why?"

T'Cael folded his arms—not in a relaxed manner, but painfully—and regarded the deck for a moment as he wrestled with his thoughts. He had vowed to tell the humans only what they needed to know to survive. But now . . .

He thought of remaining silent, of keeping vows sworn to a government he now abhorred. He thought of lying—but he couldn't repay April's faith with deception. He thought of his principles—and he thought of Idrys. He steeled himself, and spoke.

"Haven't you wondered why there are so few ships here? And why there was a mutiny that deposed me?" He spoke carefully. "It's an extreme dishonor to be relegated to hinterspace duty while the Empire is embarking on a new venture."

"What venture?"

T'Cael wished he could be spared his next words, that he of all Rihannsu didn't have to be the one to declare the onset of the Praetor's feeding. Yet he was here, and he would be the one. Folded tight against his ribs, his fists clenched.

"The Imperial invasion fleet is amassing in the Outmarches," he said, "on the boundary of the Neutral Zone."

"Invasion?" Robert April breathed.

George reached out and grasped t'Cael's arm. They stared at each other, one in question, one in answer. As he saw the regret behind those strong round eyes, George found himself wishing t'Cael had chosen this moment to start lying. He had always wanted something worthwhile to tell his sons, to say, "I was part of this." But to have been there when galactic war began wasn't exactly what he had in mind.

"But *why?*" April whispered.

T'Cael pulled away from George, folded his arms tight about his body again, and faced the captain.

350

"They believe, truly believe because they have been told, that the Federation is involved in military build-up with the goal of conquest."

April shook his head, appalled. "You can't believe such a thing."

"No, I don't believe it. I know the nature of humans, at least your collective nature. But my people are a fiery kind, Captain, and easily convinced that others are also. They're easily made suspicious, and that breeds action before one is acted upon. I confess when I first saw this mighty vessel of yours, so deep within our space—"

"Goddamn you!" George blustered, pushing his way between them. "You can't blame this on us! If your people can't handle their own fear and greed, it's not our fault!"

With great effort, April squeezed in and muscled him back. "George," he whispered, "please."

The tension was bone-breaking as the crew watched their first officer and the Romulan square off in the center of the bridge. April watched George too, still maintaining a grip on him, silently imploring him to realize that none of this was t'Cael's fault either, that he was even more the victim than they, and that he might be their only chance to survive and warn the Federation of what was gathering on its borders.

He preferred not to have to say those things out loud.

He saw t'Cael was unimpressed by the Earther's pyrotechnics—and it made George even angrier.

George shot out his finger in accusation at t'Cael. "You owe us a way out of this."

The captain wedged his way deeper between them. He could feel George's body strung up like a piano chord and clearly saw the smoke in his eyes and fury's fever burning on his cheeks, but for all that April was most affected by the cold stare from t'Cael. While the

351

Romulan seemed far too staid to participate in a brawl, his arms had fallen away from their folded position and were poised at his sides like a gunfighter's arms—ready for whatever came—and April got mental images of George slam-dunked neatly into a food processor bin.

"All right, down in front," April soothed, patting George's arm—at the moment rather like patting a rock. "I need you both, but I need you clear-headed."

"Not that easy," George growled.

April gave him a rough shove. "You especially. Now, collect yourself. We haven't the time for this jaw gnashing." Swallowing his own frustration, he turned to t'Cael.

The ice hadn't gone out of the black eyes, but the Romulan evidently wasn't going to be driven from his commitments by a hothead. He rubbed his palms loosely together as though to press out the tension —until the next time.

"How good an actor are you, Captain?" he asked. "Can you feign giving up until the mortars can be disarmed?"

"They can be, then?"

"There is a code-sequence flat on the outer shell. Enter the wrong sequence, and it ignites."

"Can you tell us the right sequences?"

"Yes, but the devices are also equipped with a physiological sensor. It's designed to detonate if anyone but a Romulan attempts to decode it, and only Romulan commanders have the code. The devices should be impossible for you to disarm because you shouldn't have any Romulans on board."

"Are you volunteering, Mr. Cael?"

"Of course."

"But you can only disarm one at a time, and if they pick up on the fact that you're out there—"

"Not likely. Our—their sensors aren't that accurate

352

at the distance they've put between us. At least, I hope not."

"You're not sure?"

"Captain, you know as well as I do that the ability of any mechanism is at the mercy of he who operates it. I don't know who is monitoring the sensory stations on the fighters at the moment or their particular talents. We all take risks."

April sighed. "Risk it is."

"You have the necessary outerwear, I assume."

"I'll go with you," George blurted. He streaked for the turbo-lift, relieved to hear the faint bump on the upper deck as t'Cael followed him.

"Good luck, gentlemen," the captain called as the lift door hissed shut, "to us all."

"The photonic code selector works on light wavelengths from nearby stars. Unless it picks up certain reflectable emissions, it can't be manually decoded."

"Yeah, so?"

"So you're standing in my light."

"Oh. Sorry."

The cold of space pressed against the outer skins of their environmental suits. Their voices were given an electrical buzz by the communications relays between the suits, with a *click* of mechanical delay before they spoke and after they finished, but this was reassuring in its way. The Romulan salvo, one of them at least, was hooked onto the starship's primary hull not far starboard-aft of the bridge dome. As such, this was the more dangerous of the two. It held on with three clawlike devices that had punctured the ship's hard hull material, then contracted to hold the conical housing on tightly. More than anything it resembled a large metal barnacle and sat there stubbornly immobile as they picked at it. While t'Cael tampered cautiously with the delicate priming mechanism,

George put his muscles behind a pry bar on the claws. Neatness didn't count.

"Kirk, this *is* an explosive device, you understand."

"Right."

"And needs careful handling."

"Right."

"And could go off. *If* you don't stop wrenching at it that way."

"You do your job, I'll"—*wrench*—"do"—*twist*—"mine."

"Such traction is liable to rupture the casing. Any leakage will cause the device to detonate."

"I want it off the hull."

"That makes no sense. Once I deactivate it—"

"I want it off the hull."

"Fine." T'Cael flattened his mouth and gave in to the human's exasperating lack of pragmatism. If the aesthetic value of having the ship's hull unblemished was so important that Kirk would risk death, so be it. Somewhere beneath his exasperation, t'Cael did understand the insult of having an enemy device attached to one's vessel—a violation so personal that the mere presence of the thing was an injury. So he tolerated Kirk's imprudence and concentrated on tapping in a correct, complex arrangement of numbers and simultaneous pressures across the bomb's colorful signal encoder/input grid. Other than wincing in anticipation every time Kirk put muscle against the holding claws, he worked undisturbed until the bridge hailed them.

"George? George, this is Robert. Are you out there?"

George rearranged the pry bar in his grip and thumbed the speaker/receiver on his suit's mantle. "Where else would I be?"

"George? Do you copy?"

"Hell . . . where is it?" He tucked the pry bar under his arm and made sure both magnetic overboots were

354

planted firmly on the ship's white armor, pressed his chin as far down inside the helmet as it would go, and still could barely see the communicator patch on his chest. He moved his thumb, pushed, and tried again. "Yes, I copy."

"What's your status out there?"

"We're working as fast as we can." He paused as t'Cael signaled to him and nodded inside the wide helmet. "Cael's almost finished disarming it. I'm trying to break it loose. It's stuck to the hull with some kind of claw arrangement. I'm trying to break the underpinnings."

"Is that necessary?"

"Don't you start too. I've got two of them already and there's just one more."

"All right, but don't dawdle."

"Keep me posted on those two ships. If they start moving around, I don't want to be caught out here."

"Affirmative. We've shut down most systems, playing dead . . . so far they haven't done anything overt. We're monitoring them, but our hands are tied until you're finished. Time's running out, George. Don't waste it."

"Kirk out." That seemed the best way to say he wasn't going to be wasting any more time than he could manage. He made a race with himself—to finish breaking the salvo cone loose by the time t'Cael finished the code process that would disarm the bomb. He made it, but only by a few seconds.

"I got it." He stuffed the pry bar into his utility belt like a sword, holding on to the detonator casing as it started to float away, and managed to hang on to it until t'Cael also got a grip on the shell and gave him leverage.

"Are you certain," t'Cael began, "that you want to keep this device? Perhaps it would be wiser to let it drift away."

"Are you sure it's deactivated?"

"I could say anything to you, you realize, and be lying."

George flashed him a glash and dryly admitted, "Then I guess we're all dead anyway, aren't we? Yes, I want the thing. Give me a hand."

Together they pulled the mechanism toward the nearest parts chute. It barely fit inside the little airlock. George straightened up and found t'Cael's face inside the slightly distorting atmospheric containment shield on the helmet. "All right," he said, "let's get the other one."

He took one step—possibly less—

The helmet microphone blared in his ear. *"George!"*

"Kirk here."

"We're detecting an outgoing transmission aboard the empress—"

"Here? Are you sure?"

"Get back inside, immediately! Claw, jam that signal! Triangulate on—"

George snapped his communicator off and grabbed t'Cael, steering him roughly toward the manpower airlock. "Move. Somebody's signaling your friends out there."

"But you captured the saboteur," t'Cael offered as he forced the heavy boots to move along the ship's exosurface.

"Evidently we didn't capture him enough."

"They'll detonate the other—"

Too late.

Dawn lit up across the horizon of the primary hull, a corona of lights—every color—shooting outward, upward. The whole ship quivered beneath them from an eruption on the hull's underside. The ship lurched in space. George's legs gave out under him. His knees were brutally rammed up against the hullplate. The pry bar in his belt jarred into his ribcage. Then he was spinning through space, watching the starship fall away.

His arms flew outward, his legs fanning wide as he fought for control, but there was nothing to grab on to, no point of reference for his body to use as guide.

"Kirk—"

His headgear buzzed with the familiar voice. He felt something—a grip on his arm. T'Cael—

Yes, t'Cael was still with him. The concussion had thrown them off together. A momentary hope flared, then died. So they didn't die alone. So what?

He tried to twist around and managed to lever against t'Cael until they could both see each other's faces. The only real vision, though, was that of the starship, a vision quite like what George had seen and felt when he caught that first glimpse of the empress hanging there in spacedock.

But here, she was even more shocking, more magnificent—here, in space, with nothing around her but diamonds and black velvet.

And who said there was no sound in space? He heard her breathing. A soft hiss. And someone was whistling at her long white limbs—

"My suit!" he choked, forcing himself to think through the creeping numbness. "It's—"

He bent over, trying to see his own body, and his eyes widened, stinging, as he saw a small rip where the pry bar had punctured the insulation lining.

"It's leaking," t'Cael finished for him, keeping inflection out of his voice. "Stay with me. I have hold of you—"

George lost touch with everything beyond his elbows and knees, felt delirium coming on under the reedy whistle of his suit as it fought to compensate for

357

the sudden pressure loss. His eyes lost focus—he thought he saw t'Cael's mouth moving—felt himself being shaken—his thighs were itching, paralyzing —was this death? This squeezing feeling? Like drowning. He'd almost drowned once, a long time ago, when he was a boy—

"My boys . . . tell the boys . . ."

Chapter Twenty-one

"Tri-ox."

"Can we get this off him? He's overheated."

"For once he's quiet."

Hisssss

"Bridge to Captain."

"This is April."

"Warp drive is coming up, sir. Engineering reports they've started the intermix again."

"How long, Carlos?"

"Fifteen minutes to engine firing. We'll be up to full power on all systems."

"Keep me posted. April out."

"Robert, he's coming around. I can sedate him if you want."

"I need him awake, Sarah."

"Okay, but don't say I didn't offer."

"George?"

A hard chunk of air flooded his lungs suddenly and he sat bolt upright, gasping and trembling, as though awakening from a nightmare. He shook off the hands that tried to hold him down.

Robert was there. And t'Cael. And Sarah Poole. What were they doing floating out in space with him? No, that didn't make sense. George fought to focus on his surroundings.

Eggshell ceiling . . . matte-white walls . . . colorful

instrument island . . . round things under him . . . the transporter room. His environmental suit lay in a heap on the platform beside him. T'Cael was just now slipping out of his with the help of a med tech. Two other officers, both engineers, were standing at the transporter controls.

"George, thank God," April murmured. His blue eyes were laden with concern and his face was a little flushed beneath the square pressure bandage, now almost covered by a flop of brown hair over his forehead. "We barely got you back in time."

George blinked at him. "Back . . . right . . . thanks . . ."

T'Cael pulled out of the sleeve of his environmental garb and let the med tech carry it away while he knelt beside George. "How do you feel?"

"Spongy."

"Can you walk?"

"Uh . . . how far?"

April frowned sympathetically. "Sarah . . ."

"I got it." She put one hypo away, pulled out another one, a smaller one, and checked the cartridge. "This'll wake him up." She pressed the hypo to George's arm.

He jumped when she injected him with the stimulant, and suddenly he felt as though he'd just had six cups of coffee. Awake and nauseous.

"What happened?" he asked, pressing his palms to the platform, testing his muscles. "Are we wrecked?"

"The salvo punctured the hull and damaged some of the lower sections," April told him, "but by itself it wasn't nearly as potent as if the other one had gone off with it. We lost three crewmen in the blast, and there were several injuries. But damage to the empress herself is nominal. It fell short of the computer core, so we're still all right."

"Tough ship," George muttered, remembering the

360

explosion's bright light and the jarring it had given his legs. He had no idea how much time had gone by; not much, since they were still in the transporter room, but enough that April had had time to digest the deaths of three people.

"Very. As soon as the bomb went off, I ordered evasive action on impulse thrusters. We're keeping our distance, but they're working a pattern to cut us off. I'm hoping we can evade them long enough to reestablish warp power. Can you stand up?"

"I can try."

April grasped his arm with both hands, but it was t'Cael who did the actual lifting. In fact, Sarah pulled April back from helping too much, lest he end up in bed himself. No matter how George tried not to wobble, he couldn't walk without help. Odd he was leaning against a Romulan. A week ago—a day ago —he'd never have imagined it. Oh, what the hell. It was only t'Cael.

George cleared his throat and forced himself to think. "Anybody look in the brig? What about Saffire?"

"We checked," April said with a shrug. "He's still in there. There's no chance he could've—"

"Then there's got to be somebody else."

"And no way to tell who," the captain admitted as the three of them left the transporter room and headed for the nearest turbo-lift.

"There could easily be two," t'Cael said. "Our infiltrators often work in teams. I should have thought of it."

"You've had a lot on your mind, like the rest of us," April said. "We triangulated on the signal and found it came from engineering. Drake went down there, but he can't just arrest everybody on speculation. Claw is jamming all outgoing frequencies, so the spy won't be able to send any more signals."

361

As they crowded into the turbo-lift and it started them racing toward the bridge, George turned. "That doesn't stop him from sabotage. Saffire won't talk?"

"Would you?"

"Maybe you're asking him too gently." He leaned heavily on the turbo-lift's interior hand rail. Then he turned to April and suggested, "What about Wood? Have you checked him out?"

"George, that boy?"

"He's perfect."

"How so?"

"Ask anybody who knows anything about infiltration psychology. He's young, impressionable, brilliant —too young and brilliant to have sorted out the tricks of life. He'd be easy to seduce. He has access to all systems; what better place to be than Brownell's assistant if you want to funnel information about technology back to the enemy?" George's thoughts raced as he spoke, but he saw from the expression on April's face that he was making at least some sense. He pressed a forefinger into April's chest and said, "Next to you, he's the most harmless-looking person on board."

Surprisingly, April didn't argue. His lips were stiff and he seemed dubious for a moment, but pressed the intercom tie-in to the lower decks. "April to Lieutenant Reed."

"Reed here."

"Is Wood down there?"

"I haven't seen Mr. Spit-and-Polish yet, sir."

"Find him and detain him."

"Really?"

George shouldered his way in. "Drake, get that kid. It's just a hunch, but he's too polite. He's not assertive enough."

"If lack of assertiveness is a problem, I'd better arrest me now."

362

George hit the off-switch without further formality and steadied himself with a long breath. He forced himself to think rationally, to put priorities into his mind, and to place on a back burner the awful knowledge that Saffire's accomplice still roamed the starship like a shark in dark water.

Still holding on to George's arm, t'Cael allowed one final alternative to form in his mind, and spoke it before he thought better of the idea. "Captain, I may be able to defuse the situation even yet."

April turned to him. "What do you need?"

"Allow me to speak to the commander of *Soar*. He is a loyal officer of the Empire, but a sensible one. I don't believe he's fully apprised of the truth."

The turbo-lift wheezed to a stop and the door panels sprung open, giving them a chilling view of the bridge's main screen and its picture of the two Romulan warbirds working a pattern of maneuvers to cut off the starship's evasive action. If they succeeded, there would be more fighting at sublight before the warp power came on line.

April looked momentarily at the tactical display screens that showed computer-enhanced diagrams of the starship's exact position in space in relation to the two pursuing ships. "How much time do we have before they cut us off?"

"If they keep anticipating me like they have," Florida said, obviously frustrated, "about eight minutes."

"Rot," the captain muttered as he studied the enemies' positions for a moment, then quickly digested what t'Cael had really said—the meaning behind his words. The Romulan was really suggesting a complex tangle of factions at work on those ships and throughout t'Cael's government. Things were going on in this alien civilization that would take graduate study to figure out, that much was becoming

obvious. And here stood t'Cael, who already understood it and was willing to deal with it. He held out a
hand, gesturing to the communications station. "At
your convenience. Claw, open a channel for Mr. Cael
to speak to the *Soar*. Tight gain, and scramble it if you
can."

The big Indian shrugged and said, "I can't tell
much about their decoding technology, sir, but I'll
try."

George followed them, grabbing an earphone from
Sanawey and plucking a second one from the mount
above the board, which he handed to April. "We'll
listen on the translators."

T'Cael turned to face him, and for a moment it was
as though they were alone on the bridge. Behind his
stoic dark eyes lurked a definite hurt.

"Still no trust, Kirk?"

The earphone felt cool in his hand. George paused,
then spoke in a low, firm tone. "I trust you," he said,
"not them."

T'Cael turned slowly back to the communications
panel, but his eyes stayed on George long enough to
establish a reciprocity between them. He cleared his
mind, clasped his hands, leaned one hip on the
console, and waited until Sanawey gave him the
go-ahead.

Then he spoke, carefully controlling his tone.
*"Vaed'rae, hwaveyiir Zwaan. Tiikhre'Urrt riov
Kilyle'a."*

Sanawey adjusted the translator sequence, then
brought up the gain in time for George and April to
hear the response. Translating all the words it understood, the computer did a good job of simulating the
actual voice of the commander and relaying his shock
at what he heard.

"Primus! But Antecenturion Ry'iak informed us—"

"That I was dead. He was mistaken. You may wish to verify my voiceprint."

"We're . . . already doing that."

"How thoughtful," t'Cael said, and imagined H'kuyu's embarrassed smile, because H'kuyu, as many might not, understood exactly what he meant.

"Are you hostage?"

"No, I'm negotiating. What else were you told?"

There was a pause, and when H'kuyu spoke again, it was with the low-slung tone of realization. *"Very little."*

T'Cael leaned even nearer to the sound of his colleague's voice. "H'kuyu, I must invoke our oldest *mnhei'soh,* that which rules between you and me."

Another pause. *"I understand. One moment."* The third pause was longer, and during it they heard a distinct order barked in the background. After a few seconds, H'kuyu came back on. *"Our transmission is now private. Say what you have to say."*

T'Cael longingly eyed the main viewport's picture of space and *Soar,* and smiled warmly. He wished Rihannsu and Federation sciences were compatible enough to give them views of each other. In his mind a clear image formed of H'kuyu's craggy features, surrounded by long, wavy, gray-shot hair. How many years had they served aboard ships that were only a signal apart? A strange coincidence in a fleet that unofficially kept its officers moving around to prevent their developing long-term relationships. Usually only the power of high rank could afford a Rihannsu officer the luxury of keeping trusted confidants within reach. T'Cael and H'kuyu had been near each other since they were subcenturia, since long before either could wield such power. Luckily, they'd been smart enough not to point that out to anyone else.

He kept control of his voice and plunged on. "For

the good of the Empire, this ship must not be captured."

"You wish us to destroy it, Primus?"

T'Cael ruefully smiled at H'kuyu's interpretation. "This ship must be set free, this incident forgotten. Or we will all play into the Supreme Praetor's personal game of acquisition."

"You ask much."

"I have never asked so much," t'Cael agreed. "But I know you. You don't want to do Ry'iak's bidding. It can mean disaster for our civilization if tides are not turned."

"I'll consider your words," H'kuyu said. *"The mothership is nearly within range. I'll consult with the Grand Primus—"*

"The Grand Primus cannot be trusted."

"Are you certain?"

"I wish I didn't know him so well, but I am certain."

"Captain," Sanawey's rumbling voice interrupted, "the other ship is picking up our gain. They're tapping in on the conversation. I think they're trying to descramble it with some kind of frequency disintegrator."

"Let's hope they can't," April murmured, and tapped t'Cael's shoulder. "Mr. Cael—"

"I understand," t'Cael said quickly in English, then immediately fell back into his native language. "Have you spoken to Kai?"

"No . . ." H'kuyu sounded hesitant, as though he was gradually piecing together the truths and separating them from the deceptions.

"He may be dead," t'Cael said bluntly.

"Indeed . . ."

"Are you in contact with *Raze?"*

"Limited. Shall I relay your orders?"

"No. They don't know I'm here. We may be able to

366

see how far Ry'iak's subterfuge will go if he believes I'm dead. He may hang himself. Be cautious, my friend. He is the predator among us."

"I shall attempt to contact Subcommander Kai."

"Who was it who ordered you to detonate the *hja?* Was it Ry'iak?"

"I'm unsure about that, Primus. A Rihannsu agent aboard the battlecruiser transmitted a message to Raze, *and we were ordered to effect detonation. I had no idea you were there."*

"Yes, about this agent—"

Florida's shout from the helm cut him off. "Captain, *Raze* is moving in!"

April swung around. "Evasive action!"

"They're firing!"

T'Cael straightened suddenly, seeing something in the way *Raze* moved—something in the tilt of its wings or the angle of its turn—that the Federation crew didn't perceive. He sucked in his breath, then shouted into the communications relay. "H'kuyu! *Ra*'Traikh *hu'yyak*—"

But the warning fell unheeded. There were two ships. Space lit up, and then there was one.

Nothing was left of *Soar* but a spreading cloud of energy particles.

A glitter of pulverized matter washed over the starship. On her bridge the crew stared outward, hardly believing that there could be such uncloaked brutality in their universe.

"They fired on their own ship . . ." Florida rasped. His voice cracked. "They took out their own people . . ."

In the viewscreen, *Raze* turned gracefully as if to say, *I own space. I own you.*

The cloud that had been *Soar* thinned and faded away.

Misery destroyed the smoothness of t'Cael's features. Amidst the agony of loss, he recognized the beginning of true chaos—Rihannsu had begun killing Rihannsu. As he watched *Raze* sweep outward, he could barely compose himself. The pain showed clearly on his face. His friend, his fleet . . .

He preferred to say nothing, but the inclination to be honest with Captain April was once again overwhelming. As the Federation captain watched him solemnly, t'Cael murmured, "The sport ends. The massacre begins."

April took a sympathetic step toward him, but there was nothing to say.

Beside them, George's fist struck the hand rail. "That's it," he snarled. "This has gone far enough! Robert—"

April shook his head wearily. "It's all yours, George."

"Carlos! Bring up the main batteries. Tie directly in to the warp engines. Let's introduce those bastards to full power, Starfleet style!"

"Yes, *sir!*"

George rounded the hand rail's end, dropped onto the command deck, and slid into the navigator's seat next to Florida's helm. Side by side, the two men urged the starship into a graceful arch, and she bore down upon the last ship of the Swarm.

Chapter Twenty-two

THE STARSHIP TURNED to face her enemy. It was as though the great white shark had awakened.

And *Raze* knew it. The enemy's sensors easily picked up the surge of power as the starship's drive and defense systems began drawing on the giant warp factory in her core.

As soon as the starship pivoted to attack stance, the last bird of the Second Imperial Swarm corkscrewed and ran for its life, heading away at full sublight.

"Squealing like a pig," George crowed. "Run, you tuck-tails."

Nearby, t'Cael indulged in a devilish nod, imagining Ry'iak squirming before the Grand Primus' questions. Where's your Field-Primus? Where's your commander? Then where's your *sub*commander? In fact, where's your Swarm?

"Captain, I'm picking up an incoming vessel," Sanawey reported. "Approaching at high warp. Whatever it is, it's big."

"The mothership, no doubt," t'Cael said. By now even he was numb to his own announcement. He never guessed this Federation vessel, or any single vessel, could survive under siege by a fully armed Swarm, but it had. Who could've known they would have to face the mothership?

"Power consumption must be incredible at the

speed they're moving," Hart observed, shaking her head at her subsystems display.

Slouching in the command chair, with the lapels of his old Irish sweater bunched up under his ears, Captain April was the eminence of fatigue. "Mr. Cael, what can you tell us?"

T'Cael moved toward him. "Our main fleet is made up of many divisions of ships—destroyers, monitor cruisers, prowlers, patrolers, battleships. There are only six motherships, which are our carriers. Each mothership carries six Swarms. The mothership travels and fights at hyperlight, while the Swarms are for sublight duty. They are taken to their area of assigned space by the mothership and detached there. While mounted for hyperlight, the mothership's weapons and drive energy is channeled through the Swarm ships it carries, which allows for a considerably enhanced power reserve. The motherships are the fastest of our fleet, their officers our most experienced. Even as this one approaches, I'm certain others are on the way."

This news, while not altogether unexpected, shaded the bridge with omen. All these people, who had helped design and build this ship, who were the cream of the Federation's crop of engineers and scientists, knew beyond doubt just what this ship was capable of. In their minds they imagined leveled planets, demolished solar systems, wrecked fleets of enemy ships who never guessed the little struggling collection of cultures at the edge of the galaxy could focus such power into a single vessel. They imagined these things, knowing that this hadn't been the purpose they'd envisioned for the starships when they started out. Now they sat aboard the single most powerful vessel ever imagined by science. The war hadn't even started, and already they were battle-weary.

War. Such a small word.

Hart, having straightened up somewhere in the middle of t'Cael's report, glared at him and drably asked, "How often do you people do this sort of thing?"

T'Cael faced her and said, "Seldom, but we've made a mastery of being ready."

"You mean looking for an excuse," George amended from the navigator's post.

"George," April began, his tone both warning and scolding.

But this time there was no heat in t'Cael's eyes. "He's right. I have said it myself."

"Claw, how long will it take a message to reach Starfleet Command at this distance?" April asked.

"We won't be sending any messages, sir," the astrotelemetrist answered. "That ship out there just came into jamming range, and they're not going to let us broadcast."

"It isn't over yet," Florida said, watching the tactical monitor display the closing distance between them and the mothership.

"I'd call that prophetic," April said. He seemed crushed. This was the nature of captaincy—to be alone in the face of decision. They would fight again; they had no choice. "Well, you're getting everything you wanted, George," he said; the bitterness showed.

George snapped his head up. "That's not fair, Robert."

April ran a knuckle along his lip, and looked at George. Then he looked back at the main screen, refusing to apologize.

Knowing now that they must survive at all costs, that they were the Federation's only chance to be forewarned of the invasion that lurked at their doorways, April forced himself to stand up in spite of the weakness in his legs and a brief wave of dizziness. "I hate saying it," he rasped, and no one doubted that he

371

did, "but we've got to dispatch this mothership quickly and get out of here before we do any more damage. Does anyone have any ideas? Can we disable them enough that we could get away at lightspeed and prevent their following?"

T'Cael turned to this forthright man and regretted his own words. "You've destroyed a Swarm," he reminded with a warning edge. "They will not treat you lightly, Captain. They'll be ready to fight. To die if necessary."

April fully knew what the Romulan was saying. Forget altruism. Be ready to kill. His brow knitted at the distasteful idea of continuing this rampage. He gripped the arm of his command chair and gazed at the viewscreen's image of the mothership, now appearing in the enhanced distance as a gigantic boomerang feathered with preybirds. If he interpreted t'Cael's description correctly, the mothership had collected her Swarms before answering the call to war, and she was utterly ready.

"I know what we can do." George stood up, stiff and angry at April's side, as much asking as telling. "We'll use the one weapon we have that they don't have."

It was intriguing, the way he said it.

April looked at him. "What's that, George?"

Sanawey flexed his aching shoulders as he bent awkwardly over his readouts. "They have deflectors set to repel particle rays and light amplified beams . . . their shields are strongest around the fore of the ship and in the drive areas, all polarized-wave reversion type—"

"What?"

Sanawey paused to rephrase his jargon as the first officer bent over the board beside him. "Shields have to be able to let some things in and keep some things out. Light has to come in. So does communication. These guys have deflectors set to repel heat, impact, and high-intensity contracted light, like lasers."

"But not . . ." George looked at him hopefully.

"Right. I think we can do it, Mr. Kirk. They can't deflect molecular transfer."

"Why should they?" George said, rather smugly. "They've never had to before." He stepped to the helm and tapped the intercom. "Kirk to engineering. Have they got it yet?"

"They're maneuvering it down out of retrieval now. Couldn't be much farther away from us and still be on board, you know. They gotta be careful, pinky." Dr. Brownell's voice cut upward through the ship's relays, evidently unaffected by the gravity of the situation.

"The name's Kirk," George reminded, stiff-jawed.

"You wanna do this by yourself?"

The total lack of impression George had made on the crustacean he was talking to made him back off. "It's got to be in the nearest transporter room in sixty seconds."

"You sure you know what you're doing?"

"They sent us a present. We're going to give it back. The reanimation code is all laid into the casing. Tell them to hit the blue button as soon as they get it into the chamber."

"Warp power's on. Why don't we just get out of here?"

"Because nothing stops them from following us, that's why," George said, raising his voice.

April saw George's cheeks redden and tapped in on his own intercom. "Dr. Brownell, this is the captain. We've got a situation here. You and your engineers are simply going to have to buckle down and hold on. Make sure everyone's prepared down there. It may be a rocky ride."

"August," the wintry voice returned, *"why do you*

373

think we put all these systems together? You got a fighting machine here. Use it."

April squirmed. "Thank you, doctor. I'll keep that in mind."

"Just use it."

"Yes, April out." He cut off the relay before Brownell could say any more.

George listened from the walkway. Brownell's abruptness had come across all too clearly. He saw the pain in April's face, and saw the captain dredge up the kind of courage that outshines any mere battlefield bravery. Suddenly he hated the idea that Robert might think some of this was his own fault.

Biting his lip thoughtfully, he stepped down to April's side.

"Robert," he said privately, "it may not come to that. I think this can work. And we'll get out of here while we can."

April sighed. "Thank you, George. Prepare for warp speed."

As George moved to the helm beside Florida, all he felt was a sensation of abandoning April to the isolation of command. "All systems prepare for hyperlight. Deflector shields double-front. Set a course for that incoming ship."

Sanawey stood up quickly and reminded, "Sir, transporters don't have the range our weapons do. It'll have to be a tight pass."

George nodded, then signaled toward Florida, but the navigation engineer was already adjusting his course for a close-range approach. Good. George didn't want to have to say it.

"Engage warp speed, helm," Captain April ordered, his voice heavy. "We'll meet them head-on."

And get this over with.

Though the addendum went unspoken, they all heard it. And added further: *or die trying.* Each knew, though the knowledge was a thorn to people who had never thought their careers would lead this way, that it might be better for the Federation's children and grandchildren if they did die, pulverized inside an obliterated ship, all evidence of the starship erased here and now, before its existence fomented the very war they now raced to deflect.

Responding to the touch of human hands, the starship hummed. She sang a deep song of energies coming together that had never been meant to merge. On the viewscreen before them, space changed.

Warp speed had a good name for what it did. What had been minutes became seconds. The mothership was upon them, and they upon it. They saw with some gratification that the big wedged ship was missing a few feathers thanks to the destruction of one of those all-important Swarms.

From where he stood beside the captain's chair, t'Cael's experienced eyes easily picked out the *Raze,* which had reattached herself to the mothership's spine and was even now funneling information to the Grand Primus. But there would be no time to act if Kirk's plan could be implemented quickly enough. No one aboard the mothership would expect what was coming, for none of them imagined such technology.

In the quick maneuver that took the mothership out of the starship's path, t'Cael saw the surprise of the home crew. He knew each member of each Swarmbird's complement was scrambling to compensate for attack when they had expected and planned for a chase.

Not easily taken unaware, the mothership's commanders saw what was happening and ordered high firepower.

Brackets of destructive energy pounded out from the tips of the mothership's wings and slammed across the double shielding over the starship's bow as the two ships passed each other at unimaginable speed. Only computers could have managed responses that sudden and accurate at this speed.

The starship rocked when the bolts struck, but she held her course. And the library computer was ready too. Deep in the core of the primary hull, the transporter room systems came on, and the ship's shields lowered for one microsecond. Matter buzzed into energy, hurtling through space toward the Romulan ship. It reassembled in the center of the mothership's main intermix reactor chamber, a conical device never meant to sit where it was sitting now.

"Transportation complete, Captain," Sanawey shouted over the sound of enemy fire striking the shields and the whine of compensatory systems.

"Let's get clear, Carlos, hurry," April ordered.

Her shields ragged from the badgering of enemy fire, the starship rolled wide of the mothership and sped into open space. On her large forward viewscreen, the mothership was just turning to follow.

George watched; they all watched, barely breathing.

A soundless tongue of burning fuel and ionized matter spewed from the aft center of the wedged ship, a great, mile-long orange geyser of energy from an explosion in the ship's bowels. The force turned the mothership up on a wing, and she hung in space, powerless, turning like a moth caught in a spiderweb. Her wings were scorched and blackened where the explosion had caused a chain reaction through the systems that channeled energy from the Swarm ships on her back.

From his position, t'Cael could see the energy readouts on Florida's monitor. Erratic fluxes showed the damage they'd done with their little trick.

"Astonishing . . ." he murmured, caught between admiration and sorrow.

"Reduce to sublight," April said, standing up for the first time in quite a while. "Mr. Sanawey, what do your sensors tell you?"

Sanawey shook himself and bent over his board. "Massive power failure. Seems to have affected the birds she's wearing too. They can't channel enough energy to launch the little ships anymore. I'm getting readings of repercussive explosions throughout the ship. They've lost warp power, shields, weapons, communication—" He paused, tapping at his controls to home in on something he thought he was reading and didn't want to report incorrectly, but his instruments were right, and he was reading them right. After a moment he had no choice but to say what he saw. "And life support."

April turned to him. "Oh, no—are you sure?"

"Yes, sir, I'm sure."

"God, I didn't want that to happen. Claw, try to get through to them. Offer to take their crews on board here—"

He stopped. T'Cael's hand was on his arm.

T'Cael waited several seconds before speaking. He didn't want to point out the obvious—that several hundred Rihannsu warriors would be impossible to keep prisoner on a ship so underpopulated as the starship was now—but there was an even more distasteful fact. Odd—t'Cael had never thought of it as distasteful, until now, until he met Robert April.

"Captain," he began, "I'm sorry to tell you this. But they will not—"

The screen lit up like a sun. A flash so intense that it left them stunned for several seconds, even those who hadn't been looking at the viewer.

"Oh, God—" April choked, blinking as he held up

377

a hand against the electrochemical explosion. "Oh, my God . . ."

"I'm sorry," t'Cael repeated, not looking at the screen, knowing intimately the ethic behind the suicide they witnessed. That ethic had always seemed sensible. He had never thought of it as April—who felt responsible—did, but now all he could feel was April's sympathetic anguish. "It is an ancient code among my people. It has nothing to do with you."

On the screen now, glowing debris radiated from an empty centerpoint where the mothership had been.

April stared into it, his eyes glazed. "How can you say that?" he murmured.

"Please believe it. My Empire didn't wait for this vessel to appear before they began such a practice. I've seen it many times in my career."

"My God . . . how wasteful . . . all those lives . . ."

"Wasteful it is," t'Cael agreed, hoping he had eased the captain's self-recrimination.

April steadied himself and valiantly fought to accept what he had just seen. "Do you think anyone else knows we're here? Had they the chance to notify your fleet?"

T'Cael wished he could provide the wanted answer, but even to comfort April he couldn't manage a pretense. "Yes," he said, "and assuredly did. Visuals of this vessel are probably on every viewer in the command line."

April shook his head and watched the viewscreen, captivated by his own plummeting hopes. "So the entire Romulan Empire thinks the Federation has created a gigantic terror device. Here we sit, hopelessly misinterpreted." He folded his hands disconsolately, still gazing into the emptiness of space. "It's all my fears rolled into one incident. God . . ."

George waited a moment before speaking. "Let's go home, Robert."

Slowly the captain nodded. "Yes, home. We've stayed long enough to guarantee war. Let's go before we do any more harm."

A sad relief came over the bridge crew. Each felt the keen responsibility for their presence in this space, but each also felt the helplessness so succinct in the captain's voice. All they'd wanted to do was save a shipload of accident survivors. Why had such a simple desire turned so sour? They would go home now, go home and wait for the war.

"Captain . . ."

T'Cael, if his voice was any witness, was struggling. He heard the hesitation himself. As April and Kirk turned, t'Cael saw with dismay that the captain and his combustible first officer had learned to listen to him when he started to speak, though this time he wished they weren't so attentive. "Captain, you could run and get out, of course." And again he paused, unable to find any words to make this easier. He paced a few steps around the command arena, feeling more and more caged. "I have many contacts," he began again, "in the Romulan fleet . . . in the Romulan government. Many who would approve of a change in government. A drastic change."

George stepped closer, reading those ominous words. "How drastic?" he demanded.

T'Cael ceased pacing. "There would be pro-Federation sentiment. We could begin negotiations. Many are ready to pay the price. You will not be an attacking force—you'll be a liberating force."

"Your people aren't behaving like a group that wants to be liberated."

"Kirk, they don't comprehend the wrongness of what they are becoming. When the day comes that they find no one else to prey on, they'll turn upon each other. We can stay that pattern if we act now, today!"

"You're pretty cavalier with that 'we.'"

"You are two steps away from our governing planet. With the massive technology contained in this ship, you could change this death march my people have been walking!"

George started to turn away.

But t'Cael couldn't bring himself to stop. He reached out and wrenched Kirk around with jarring force and held him. "Kirk, you could turn the pattern. Dislodge the Praetorate!"

"Just a minute," interrupted a distinct sound. Robert April had stood up again and now stepped between them, giving each a fatherly glare as the hot conversation roiled in their ears. At last he faced t'Cael. "What are you saying? I can't believe what you're saying!"

Black eyes flashed. "I *must* say it. Truly I wish it didn't have to be you, Captain. But I must say this."

"My God, man, do you understand what you're proposing?"

"You are the stronger."

"This is more than a question of artillery!" April snapped back. He pressed a hand to his pounding head, holding in a pain that was more than blood and bone.

"Captain," t'Cael started again, following him as he circled the helm, "I say none of this lightly. I have a deep agony when I tell you to destroy my government while you have the chance. This is the government I've served long and loyally. But I've watched it change. I've seen a cruel evolution, and now it spreads. Just as I fought to maintain the stability of my government, now I will help you bring it down."

From the way he said it, there was no doubting his agony. It was there; in his face, in his voice. But so was his belief in this wild chance.

Reaching over the helm, George caught t'Cael's sleeve. "Do you know what you're talking about?"

380

T'Cael whirled suddenly and knocked the hand away. "Do I know? I know of the vicious hunting that goes on when people can't trust each other, even one's own family members. I know what it means not to be allowed to make acquaintances because those above are afraid when two people speak for too long. I know what is coming—a slaughter so furious and so driven by fears that it will make the early wars look like a game. Do I know, Kirk? I've been at the center too long not to see clearly what is coming at the hands of my own people, and has now been triggered by your appearance here. I could describe to you a scene of extermination so vivid as to turn your stomach, and then send you home to live it yourself."

George withdrew his hand, staring. All this sounded familiar. Hadn't he said it all to Robert only a matter of hours ago?

"We can't . . ." he began.

T'Cael's eyes flared wide. "You can!"

"We can't! We can't attack just because we have the power!" His hands shook with the crushing flood of thoughts. He clamped his eyes shut and spun away from t'Cael, fists tightened into rocks at his sides. Seeing both possibilities struck him suddenly silent. Who would die? All those innocent people—never the truly guilty. A moral dilemma—did a governing system have the right to exist in spite of the people it governed? Did the Federation have the right to police the galaxy. Did it have the right *not* to?

So tempting . . . so easy. To soar in and cut out the rotten core. What had he just been saying to Robert about fighting only half of World War II?

"It's . . . wrong," he heard himself rasp, his fists clenched until they were hurting. "It's wrong to be the first to fire."

"But you carry weapons," t'Cael reminded. "Why?"

381

"Defending yourself is different! It's wrong to shoot first! Wars to prevent wars are what almost wiped out humanity in the last century. You don't have any right to insist on this."

The dark eyes of alien perceptions flashed at him. "Do I not?"

George moved in on him and erupted, "Some things are wrong no matter what the gain. Your society is aggressive, and you don't like it. Now you want us to do the same thing?" He spun around, expecting to have April applaud him. A chill went through him when he saw the captain's face.

April was listening. Waffling. Actually considering what t'Cael had said. Actually *considering* it.

"You've got to be kidding!" George choked, stepping toward him. "Robert, what about all that talk about what this ship is supposed to represent? You were right! This ship has to stand for our best ideals first. Doesn't it? You know me—you know what I think. But there has to be a line! There must be another way!"

T'Cael now moved in as well. "Despite all your efforts to communicate your ideals, the Swarm attacked you. Your way does not always work. If peace can be gained through example alone, why do you carry weapons? If your message is unconditional pacifism, then why?"

"The question is when to use them," George shot back. "You don't get it at all, do you? You don't see the difference."

The Romulan's distinct brows drew together, both in disapproval and in thought. "It is a hard question, Kirk." He folded his arms, not in a relaxed manner, but in that way that said he was holding something in, and he spoke with bitterness. "Life in the galaxy is made of hard questions."

A creeping silence fell over them, sudden silence that became oppressive as it grew.

April stood between them, on the bridge of his dilemma, forced to choose between causing the deaths of millions or allowing the enslavement of millions more, and doing the one thing he never wanted to do in his life—start a war to keep a war from coming.

His whisper filled the bridge.

"All I want," he murmured, "all I ever wanted—is for the Federation to grow into a body of guidance and wisdom. I feel like a man who's fighting with his neighbor over something he'd much rather share. George . . . you've forced me to understand that we have to be a real power and not simply showful of a mightiness we're afraid to use. But my God . . . is this what we have to have?"

He stopped, disturbed by his own words.

T'Cael spoke without moving. "If you fail to act, war is inevitable. You must question your deepest motivations. I beg you to take the challenge."

"Either I cause the deaths of millions, or I *allow* the deaths of millions. That's what you're saying," April told him, his voice caught in his throat.

Desperate to be understood, t'Cael battled to make himself clear. "There are more palatable outcomes, Captain. I can guide you through the automated defensive net that surrounds our Homeworlds. Any patrol ships can be quickly dispatched—" he said, then hesitated a bare instant, hearing himself forget what taking lives meant to this man, hearing himself fall too easily back into doing what needed to be done and considering the loss of lives as secondary. "And you can break down the net as you go. Your presence will throw our Empire into havoc. Once the ground defenses are neutralized, we will communicate with the capital, demand negotiations for peace. If they agree, it will be our opportunity to expose the Supreme Praetor for the tyrant he is! Many of my countrymen share my views. They must listen!"

"And if they don't?" April countered without a beat. "If they aren't intimidated, then what? I assume you said 'if' for a reason. What then?"

"They'll have no choice," t'Cael said emphatically. "And once they're *listening,* my people can be very pragmatic and rational."

"With an arm twisted behind their back? The best case would still cause the deaths of hundreds or thousands. When the government falls, we may find ourselves dealing directly with the military. God, imagine that. How rational will they be?"

"Captain . . . I *am* the military."

April blinked and pursed his lips thoughtfully. "Yes . . . go ahead. Convince me that you're a common sort among your company. I don't believe you can."

"And what if they *don't* listen, Mr. Cael? Having gone that far, I won't be able to back down. I'll have to make good on the threat we'll represent."

T'Cael's silence provided the answer.

April stood up slowly, using his chair for support. "How do I decide which cities to level as examples? It's a terrible lottery, gentlemen . . . a terrible lottery."

Compelling though the question was, this wasn't a hypothetical situation put before one of his classes at the Academy. This was real. Living beings would die, and the historians would be busy for decades. Having forced the issue to a standstill, April waved a hand limply. "Let me think this out . . . let me just think." The hand went down to caress the rail that circled the bridge, and he walked along it as though it was a steadying force.

"We can't ignore what Cael is saying. These things

384

he's telling us . . . I wish to heaven I'd never heard them. We have a crushing problem foisted upon us. If we see to ourselves and vacate the area, we virtually guarantee interstellar war. If we save our skins, we'll have failed to take a stand. If we move in and dislodge the governing system, we'll cause a chaos that'll take decades to repair . . . I don't know if I can live with either of those, I really don't." He turned achingly now and held out both hands in a subdued manner of request. "I'm not asking for stylish solutions. But fate has to have something better in mind for this ship, for us . . . than just being the wick on a bomb . . . but here's this gentleman, telling us these things, and more than anything I've ever hated in my life, I hate saying . . . that he's right."

George shivered, looking up, staring at the captain, his lips parted in mute question, and froze as he realized the captain was looking right back at him.

"Yes," April went on, having anticipated George's reaction. "He *is* right. To prevent a war by destroying its hub—isn't that the right thing?"

In his soliloquy he had come around to the starboard side, where George stood watching, listening, frightened by all this. They were facing each other now, and April's last question, which a moment ago had been hypothetical, suddenly became real and demanded an answer.

George swallowed hard. "I can't help you make that kind of decision," he said. "I won't. You'd hate me forever."

Leaning against the rail, April nodded. His feet were like blocks of ice as he climbed the bridge steps toward the turbo-lift.

"Stand by till I get back," he wearily said, pausing at the lift doors as they parted. "I'll decide."

He was a hundred years older by the time the doors closed between him and the bridge.

George stared at the red doors, focusing on the thin line where the lift sealed shut. "Hell . . ."

Somewhere behind him, his back also turned, t'Cael murmured, "I regret saying these things."

George didn't turn. "You had no choice."

They stood with their backs to each other, half the bridge between them, facing opposite ends of the starship. Strange, the poetry of chance—on the large scale, t'Cael happened to be facing Federation space, and George the binary Homeworlds of the Rihannsu Empire.

"Is it possible," George began, speaking very deliberately, "that just maybe . . . you exaggerated the danger?"

"No." The answer was definitive. "It's often not true danger but imagined danger that causes wars." T'Cael remained facing away from Kirk and spoke into the void on the screen. His arms were once again wrapped tightly against his ribs. He didn't move. It was as though his voice, his mind, and his body had divided into separate entities. "My civilization has known war as an intimate, with each other or someone else, since the exodus—since before we even came to our Homeworlds. Our technology has advanced beyond our wisdom. We either obliterate our enemies, or the day will come when someone will have no choice but to obliterate us. Can you blame me that I desperately seek some other way?"

His voice was quiet. The guilt he felt at laying all this at April's feet was obvious.

George sighed sadly. "I hate all of this," he muttered. "I've heard myself saying things I wouldn't want my boys to say. All I really ever wanted was to hand over a safe galaxy to my sons."

"You never shall," t'Cael said.

"That's your opinion. Pardon me if I keep trying."

T'Cael nodded solemnly and added, "You can only

386

teach them courage." He tipped his head toward the turbo-lift, the way Robert April had gone. "Like his."

He was heading, though he probably wouldn't have admitted it, toward sickbay. Wandering the corridors of his starship with his hands stuffed deep into the cardigan's pockets and morality chewing at his ankles, he began to realize, no matter the size, just how small any one ship was. No matter the size . . . no bigger than the hearts and consciences of those who manned her. He was her conscience, he knew. That was his role as her captain. This was the bitter end of the glory he'd envisioned while nurturing the starship program into being. Odd that the sourest fruit was the first to be plucked.

He needed to hear Sarah's voice. Though he knew she would refuse to help him make the decision, just as George had—and rightfully so—just seeing her would clear his head.

His mind was cluttered now with hypothetical scenarios, all the way from skipping out on the whole problem to spearheading an invasion and committing the Federation to growing up much too fast and before its time. One of those scenarios, he knew, would come true.

The awful burden was knowing that he was right . . . George was right . . . t'Cael was right . . . with all these rights, how could there be such a giant wrong as that which loomed before them?

So many variables. He had listened, perhaps too well. The pride in seeing George Kirk's perceptions widen was marred by the widening of April's own perceptions. T'Cael's words forced him to see a tangle of obligations and alternatives that discolored his view of things. Before this day, he could always afford to think in simpler terms. Safer and prettier terms. But now there was an ugliness swerving into his path that he had always steered around. If George was right about finding another way, how could they explain to the billions dead if t'Cael's prediction came true?

April shivered, and drew his shoulders inward, unable to ignore t'Cael's prediction. This situation . . . he could never have foreseen it. It had turned them into philosophical contortionists, yet there were no answers in all the bending and twisting.

Once again he heard George's words: *There has to be another way.*

"Please let there be," he murmured to no one, no one at all.

An arm looped around his neck and tightened. He sucked in his breath and was dragged backward into an adjacent corridor, then back farther into a service locker. His arms flew outward, seeking his balance, but any thoughts of resisting were squelched by the cool unmistakable nip of a laser emitter pressed tightly against his ear. He started to speak, but was interrupted by his captor's voice.

"Don't move, Captain. Because I'll kill you if you do."

Chapter Twenty-three

ON THE BRIDGE, everyone was hurting for Captain April, even more than for the countless lives that would be sacrificed either way. They could hear the ball and chain he dragged as it clunked through the ship, and those bleeps and whirs the bridge made became engulfing, like a cage made of nothing but sound.

George had found himself a place to sit, at the unmanned science station, as far from the command center as he could get without leaving the bridge. He sat with his elbow on the console, his thumb knuckle resting across his mouth as though that would keep him from having to say anything, and he stared blankly into the blur of red, blue, and yellow lights and monitor displays.

Across the bridge, t'Cael still stood unmoving, arms still wrapped around himself, also lost to the emptiness of waiting.

All around the bridge deck, people waited. After so much action, the sudden stasis was maddening. Sanawey, Hart, Florida each tried to do busy work, little maintenance things to keep them from having to look up at the first officer or the Romulan. There was some damage control to be handled—a leak here, a loss of pressure there—but nothing the ship's baffle systems couldn't compensate for almost by themselves. There was a navigational course to be plotted and laid in—no, there were two. One straight out of this sector . . . one straight in. With instrumentation this sophisticated, a few seconds' work. Not enough. Occasionally someone from engineering called up, pretending to have something to ask or to say, but what they really wanted was to know what was going on, and no one could offer so much as a clue. By now George had become numb to the double-tone beep of the intercom, and was happy to let Sanawey field the questions. There it was again—how many times now? He'd lost count.

"Bridge. Sanawey."

"This is Graff."

"What do you need?" Sanawey asked, sounding just as tired of this as George felt and making his question direct as though to demand a direct, and short, answer.

"Where's Mr. Kirk?"

Sanawey looked up, but it took George several more seconds to muster a willingness to answer. Eventually he dropped his hand from his mouth and jabbed the com switch nearest him. "Kirk here. What is it?"

"I've got the captain."

George's brow puckered. "What?"

"I've got the captain. He's my prisoner."

T'Cael turned. The others straightened to look as George leaned over the board, realization slowly dawning. They could almost hear the click of pieces falling together in his mind. He stared hypnotically for an instant. As comprehension dawned, his heart snapped and his stomach turned to stone. He bolted from the chair. "It's Graff—" Without thinking he pressed the mute and pointed at Sanawey. "Damn him, it's not Wood, it's Graff! He's got Robert! Trace it!"

Sanawey quickly set about it.

390

As George bent once again over the board, t'Cael appeared beside him and listened, his presence unexpectedly reassuring.

"Graff, can you hear me?" George began again, lifting his thumb from the mute. "What do you want?"

"I want off this ship. I want shuttlecraft clearance. I'm taking the captain with me."

"Why?"

"Because if he's with me, I know you won't blow me out of space."

George hit the mute a second time and snapped his fingers at Sanaway again. "Find Lieutenant Reed! Have him turn Wood loose, then fill him in!"

Sanaway nodded, then went about trying to do two things at once.

Gripping the padded edge of the console, George held his breath, trying to clear his head and shake his thoughts back into gear. He licked his lips before speaking. "All right . . . you want clearance. You've got it. We sure don't want you. But you're going to have to leave the captain behind, or no deal."

"No deal is right. I'm not that stupid." Graff sounded more smug than desperate, but certainly desperate enough. *"I'm going to head down toward the bay. When I get there, I want a shuttle ready to go."*

"How do we know you won't kill the captain after you launch?"

"You don't. But I'll kill him for sure otherwise. Don't play with me, Mr. Kirk. I'm not a murderer, but I'll do whatever you force me to do."

"We'll meet you down there. I want to see the captain."

"I don't care what you do. Just remember who's in charge—and have that shuttlecraft ready."

"All right, but listen to me. Graff?"

"Yeah?"

391

George leaned close to the transspeaker. "If you hurt him, I'll follow you as far as you run," he said. "Until I catch you."

Silence on the other end confirmed those words. No witnesses needed.

Then there was an unceremonious click.

George dove toward Sanawey's station. "Did you get them?"

"Pinpointed," Sanawey said as George and t'Cael hovered over his instruments on either side. "Deck G. Sickbay area."

"Can you track them?"

"On a ship this empty, I could track a housefly."

"I'm going. Keep in touch with me by hand communicator. Make sure he can't tap in on us. When Reed checks in, tell him what's going on. We'll try to close in on that creep."

As he spun on his heel toward the turbo-lift, he yanked out both the backup hand laser and the communicator that still hung on his belt from his visit planetside, and bumped into t'Cael.

"Shall I—" the Romulan began, and it was clear that he felt somehow responsible.

"No, stay here," George said. Suddenly his teeth were gritted. "This is my job."

"They're in the lift now, sir, moving down the dorsal, just like Graff said. Heading for the aft sections. Mr. Reed is holding for you."

"Patch me in."

"Reed here, George. Where are you?"

"I'm heading for the hangar bay. Meet me there."

"Righto."

His hand was sweaty as he clutched the communicator too tightly, and it almost flew out of his grip when the bridge hailed him.

"Mr. Kirk—" Sanawey's voice.

"Kirk here."

"I don't understand this . . ."

"What?" George snapped, beyond patience.

"He's turning. He's going in the wrong direction. That's not the way to the hangar bay . . ."

George reached out and stopped the turbo-lift. "Where's he going?"

"I'm not sure. There's nothing down there."

"Come on, Sanawey, project!"

"He's sending you on a wild-goose chase to the hangar bay, but he's—now he's heading down very deliberately . . . through Level sixteen."

George pressed his lips together and endured the wait as several voices lapped over Sanawey's—Hart's, then t'Cael's—something about putting up schematics of those sections.

And at last, t'Cael was shouting. *"Your Auxiliary environmental control—Kirk! He plans to tamper with life support! He wants us all dead—then he'll leave the ship!"*

Instantly George hit the channel select on his communicator, having learned to trust t'Cael's understanding of Romulan offensive tactics. "Drake! He bluffed us! Auxiliary Environ—"

"I heard. Fast as lightning I'm going."

"I'll meet you there!" He quaked with frustration at having been so easily bluffed. He twisted the lift control and started it off in another direction, then made his thumb move on the communicator again. "Hart, can you override—Hart, come in."

"Hart here, sir."

"Can you override the pressure equalization in a particular section from up there?"

"Can I . . . I don't know. Nobody's ever tried that."

"Try it. Pressurize that room to ten atmospheres."

393

"Auxiliary? But if somebody opens the door—oh, I get it."

The turbo-lift wheezed to a stop and the doors parted. George snapped his communicator shut and bolted down the corridor, not even sure where Auxiliary Environmental Control was—but it was here somewhere, and so was Graff.

He turned several corners, barely slowing down to avoid hitting bulkheads. Suddenly he came around a corner and found himself half a corridor down from his quarry.

"Graff!" George skidded to a stop, holding his laser downward in a nonthreatening manner.

Graff had a laser in one hand and in the other he held a length of service cord tightened around April's throat. With the laser hand he was trying to release the lock to a door that said AUXILIARY CONTROL CENTER: ENVIRONMENTAL SUPPORT. He stopped and yanked on the service cord, forcing April further off balance.

"I'll choke him," he warned.

"Don't," George said, also warning. "If he dies, you die worse."

"I don't doubt that, sir. That's why he's coming in with me. Put down your laser."

"No," George said.

"I'll kill him, sir."

Taking a few calculated steps toward them, George flipped his unblinking eyes from Graff to April. "Robert, you all right?"

In spite of the cord squeezing against his gullet, April actually managed a thin smile. "Not very."

"Hold on. Graff, what are you doing here? You said you were going to the hangar bay," George said, sneaking an extra step forward.

Graff didn't answer, but continued to punch in the lock release code, struggling to point the laser with the

394

hand that was doing the button pushing and also keeping an eye on George.

Knowing a little something about the psychology of a standoff, George kept staring with bottled ferocity at Graff, rarely blinking, matching the determination he saw in Graff's eyes. All he had to do was stall until that door opened.

"What do you want?" he asked. "Is it the ship?"

"What do you think?" Graff returned, rather casually for a man in this position.

"You were working with Saffire."

Again Graff didn't answer, didn't look directly at George anymore, as he tried to override the door's individual lock code. Any moment now . . . any moment.

Graff made one last poke, and the door slid open —suddenly it was as though a gigantic balloon popped. A loud *bfooom* assaulted the corridor. Graff and April were blasted across to the opposite wall, then pummeled with everything in that room that hadn't been nailed down—papers, spacesuits, tapes, a whirlwind of crates spilling insulation, chunks of conduit, unfinished panel faces, chairs—a blinding vortex of material that filled the corridor as the pressure differential fought to equalize.

George was thrown backward too and struck a field equipment locker, but he had been prepared and shook out of it quickly. As though fighting his way through a snowstorm, George battled through it for the few seconds it lasted, until he found April and dragged him back around the corner to wait out the equalization. He found himself aching from the hammerblow of pressure from the control room.

Eternal seconds passed, the *swoosh* abated, and all those flying things began dropping to the floor. Finally only loose papers remained to slowly flutter to the corridor deck.

George unfolded himself. April was crumpled in a ball under him and also started to test his limbs, very gingerly.

"Are you hurt?" George asked as he helped April unroll.

"We're not having a very good day, are we, George?" the captain observed as he used the wall for support on one side and George on the other. "I think I'm bruised."

"Will you be all right if I go after that son of a bitch?"

"Yes, yes, fine. George, be careful. He's a big man."

"Not so big that I won't rip off his left leg and beat him to death with it."

April looked sharply at him, suddenly chilled by the rage in George's face.

George hesitated another moment to be sure April could stand on his own, then looked around the corner, laser up and ready to fire.

But there was nothing but settling papers and assorted clutter.

"He's gone!"

April appeared at his side, one palm pressed supportively against the bulkhead, the other against a bruised rib. "We've got to find him, George. There's no telling the damage an engineer on the rampage could do. Are they tracking him?"

Snapping up his communicator, George worked to control his voice. "Sanawey, are you still tracking?"

"Aye, sir, but there's only one of them."

"It's Graff. I've got the captain. Drake, are you on this band?"

As if summoned, Drake rounded the opposite corner and slid to a stop just short of the sea of clutter. "Creeping Jesus! Look at the mess you made!" He recovered and picked through it with three careful bounds. "Oh Captain, are you all right, sir?"

396

April started to answer, but before the words were out, George had Drake by the collar and was yanking him back down the corridor. "Come on! Sanawey, give me his location."

"He's moving aft again, sir. I think he might really be heading for the hangar deck this time."

"Which level?"

"Eighteen."

"I'm on it. Come on, Drake, footwork." He grabbed Drake's collar again.

Drake stumbled after him, and gagged, "I want a raise—"

Only now, in the saddle of a bucking crisis, did George even begin to really comprehend the size of the starship. Length after length of corridor unfolded itself beneath him. The proportions humbled him as he and Drake ran the length of the secondary hull and climbed down access stairwells toward Level 18. Amazing that mankind could conceive and build so huge a vessel—build it, launch it, run it—the tonnage alone was mindboggling.

And they were almost alone inside this bright fibercoil cavern. Only a few dozen people here—not enough to populate such dimensions. They saw no one else as they ran through the ship. No one at all.

Except that Graff was there and they knew it. And with every meter of deck that fell away beneath his feet, George redoubled the promise he'd made to himself when he'd realized why Graff had hailed him on the bridge. A wordless promise born of pure insult, it drove him through the humility brought on by the size of the starship, and fed his anger with every tread of his soles on the deck.

"Sir?"

George snapped the communicator up. "Kirk here."

"You've got him panicking."

397

"What do you mean?"

"He's making wrong turns and having to correct himself. He's stopping here and there, and from the schematics on my screen, I think he's having to unlock every section as he goes into it. He's down in the unmanned area, the sections that haven't even been support-stressed yet, so they're all individually locked. Go down corridor S-197-A and turn left at the Cargo Bay 3."

"Got it. Can you cut him off from up there? Seal the locks?"

"I'm trying, sir, but only about half of the section locks are tied in to the bridge controls so far. And he's better at bypassing the locks manually than I am at jamming them."

"Keep trying. Kirk out. Drake, split up. I'll go starboard, you go port."

"Righto."

Drake took the first corridor portside and George broke into a run again, bearing into the starboard veins of the starship. The corridors seemed endless, the mountain of anger he climbed insurmountable. And with every turn into a new length of corridor, every dash through every door to some unfinished room or bay or deck, the mountain gained a new summit. Somehow George felt that Graff had a sense of that anger, was afraid of it.

His communicator bleeped. In an instant it was at his lips.

"What?" he barked.

"You're closing in—I don't understand these readings. He just bypassed the masterlock control for the cargo bays on that deck, and then he was running toward Cargo Bay 9 and he went in, and I lost him. It must be a glitch. It's at the end of your corridor, then left."

He leaned into a run again, suddenly glad he was in

combat shape and could keep this up the length of the starship. Though his legs felt thready and he was breathing hard, he increased his pace. Bay 7 . . . Bay 8 . . . Bay 9—there it was, at the end of the corridor. And he heard footsteps down the other end of the corridor—Graff?

A flicker of disappointment struck when he spied Drake's familiar dusky face round the corner, but George was already concentrating once again on the big blue doors of Bay 9. Sanawey had said Graff killed the masterlock. The doors would open. And he was almost to them.

In counterbeat to his own footsteps, Drake's came hammering down the deck. George didn't pay attention until Drake suddenly shouted, "No, George!"

But it was too late to stop—the blue doors sensed his presence and began to part. A blast of frigid air struck him just as he reached the threshold, but Drake slammed into him with a linebacker's tackle, breaking his stride and catapulting him sideways down the corridor. His right side struck the deck, and Drake landed on top of him. They skidded down the corridor, followed and soon blanketed by the coldest air this side of open space and the sound of the bay doors automatically sliding shut again.

George felt his body shrink from cold, as though he'd opened a window and stuck his head out into an Iowa January. No—colder even than that. Lots colder. The heater systems along the ceiling came on, whirring frantically. Frost formed on the walls. Breathing became instantly difficult. George found his legs stiff when he tried to move, and his shoulders tucked in as he rolled from under Drake and tried to stand up.

"D-damn!" He shivered, his breath coming out in a steamy puff. "What happened?"

Drake stood up beside him, arms coiled around

himself, and said, "I was talking to the engineers before, you know, and some of these areas are still frozen. That's why they were locked off, see. You wouldn't have lasted half a second. It's about minus-two-hundred-something in there. Let me see if I can't turn on the heaters inside." He stepped to the wall electrical access and fiddled with some toggles.

"Then what happened to Graff?" George asked, testing his feet.

They approached the cargo-bay doors slowly, testing the air as they went, and peeked into the wide windows. The compensatory heating system whined furiously, spewing warm air into the corridor and the bay area. Even so, they didn't dare step into the bay yet. If the heating hadn't been turned on, other safety systems might not be working either. But the door didn't budge; with the systems on line and trying to compensate, the automatic opening sequence was temporarily overriden. When the temperature was equal inside and out, the doors would part. Until then, there were only windows to offer them any kind of explanation.

The bay sprawled out before them, a garage-sized room with collapsible dividers between it and the adjacent bays. It was empty. Its white floor and blue walls were unmarked.

"Where is he?" George asked, drawing his elbows tight against his ribs in the raw air.

Drake was silent beside him.

After a moment, the silence drew George's attention.

His face reflected in the transparent aluminum window, Drake was staring up at the ceiling, his mouth hanging open, his eyes wide with horror.

George looked up.

"Oh . . . God."

Hovering like a parade balloon just under the

ceiling was Graff, his arms and legs frozen in a run, his hair marbled by rime, eyelashes and brows hoar-coated, his face a white glaze, his eyes ghastly, that last second's horror permanently fixed there. He drifted randomly in zero-G, slowly bumping from wall to wall.

George clenched his teeth against the corridor's arctic cold, battling down a sudden nausea, and sucked in a little breath of empathy.

Beside him, Drake muttered, "Perdition, that's ugly . . . no point taking him to sickbay, is there?"

They watched together for a long helpless moment, sickened and chilled, while Graff floated past the doorway.

The heating system wheezed relief as the temperature equalized, and the bay doors slid open, giving them a full view of Graff.

With a steadying sigh, Drake offered, "I'll get the gravity."

He stepped back toward the electrical housing on the corridor wall that held the manual controls for the localized artificial gravity and the bay's life support.

For a moment George couldn't draw his eyes from the disgusting sight of Graff floating up there. Only the sound of the universal gravity code sequence clicking at his side roused him. The words sank in and he grabbed for Drake's sleeve, gasping, "No, don't—"

Too late. There was a *click* in the wall, and the cargo bay's gravitational systems buzzed to life.

George dodged toward Drake just as a blocky form dropped past him. With the shrill crash of shattering crystal, the mass hit the floor. Splinters of frozen flesh struck them like a hail of needles, followed by bigger chunks, and the loud splash gave way to a faint tinkle, as though ornaments were jingling on a Christmas tree.

Feeling his lips peel back in disgust, George forced

401

himself to turn away from Drake and look into the bay. "Ugh . . . oh, that's awful . . ." And he had to look away again.

Drake peeked around the doorframe. "Not quite thawed, was he? By Judas, we'd better sweep him up before he gets *really* messy."

Bile rising in his throat, George fought against the wave of nausea and brought the communicator up. "Bridge, this is Kirk."

"April here, George."

"How are you?"

"I'm on the mend. Where's Graff?"

"He's . . . never mind."

"George? You don't sound well."

George deliberately walked away from the bay entrance, trying not to look. "Listen, Robert . . . I've got an idea."

"Thank God somebody has. What is it?"

"You know, this probably won't work."

"We can't be in any worse a position, George," April said from one side.

On the other, Drake offered his own analysis. "You're on a roll, Geordie. Now's the time to stack the deck and load the cue and all that fluff, man."

The three of them bent over the communications board, punching in a series of facts and space-location coordinates. A few steps away, t'Cael stood watching, dubious but fascinated by the enthusiasm these people put into a moment of utter desperation.

"We've got to get the timing exactly right," George grumbled, trying to choreograph the plan in his mind. A bluff. Deadlier than reality . . . he hoped. Which was more frightening—the cobra's bite or just its spread hood?

Sanawey interrupted, "Captain, I'm picking up two

blips at extreme sensor range. Probably warp drive fluxes."

T'Cael turned. "Those would be the two motherships that remained to guard the Homeworlds. They've lost touch with the mothership you destroyed, and doubtless prior to that they received reports of your presence. They'll spare nothing to get here."

George shot him a look. "Good. Perfect."

Carlos Florida twisted around in his chair. "Good?"

"It's perfect," George repeated. "Let's hope our luck holds."

April straightened at his side and drawled, "You mean the luck we've had so far? Really, George." He studied the readouts and monitors, checking and rechecking the information they'd fed in so far and wondering if they could stay in sync with the massive computer brain that waited beneath their fingertips. Only one more thing to feed in. He cleared his throat and turned, rather stiffly because his body was still a mass of aches, to t'Cael. "Can you tell us which Starfleet codes your people have broken in the past few years?"

T'Cael's eyes widened and a faint reseda blush rose in his cheeks, yet along with the touch of embarrassment came a small grin of pride. He hesitated, then forced himself to say, "We've . . . broken them all."

George stood straight. *"All?"*

The grin widened, "Yes . . . while your shipwrights might teach us a few things, our cryptographers could return the favor."

Kirk's glare turned ironic. "Great. When this is over, we'll start a student exchange program." And even under the moment's pressure, his lips too slanted into a kind of grin. Though their lives might end here

403

and now, they had shared the experience of a lifetime, of an era. "Okay," he said, sighing over the blinking lights of the com board, "Sanawey, it's up to you. Send a message long-range. Make sure they can't miss overhearing it. Request status of the Federation fleet at the Neutral Zone."

Sanawey's wide brow puckered. "We don't have any fleet at the Neutral Zone . . . oh. Oh, that's good, sir. That's good."

"Go ahead."

Sanawey pressed his lips tight and fed the message into the broadcast source, carefully adjusting his instruments to be sure the incoming Romulan ships would tap his frequency. "That's it. It's off."

"Can you send a message and make it seem like it's coming *in* from somewhere else?" George asked him.

Sanawey frowned. "Yeah . . . I think it's possible . . . if I bounce it off a planet or something—make it ricochet back to us. It'll be garbled, though. I'll have to send a tight beam. It'll bounce back and scatter. You know, that might even be better. It'll sound static-y."

"Good job, Claw." April clapped the big man's shoulder. "Complicated, I know. What we need is for you to arrange a message that seems to come back to us from the Neutral Zone, describing the Romulan fleet that's amassing there. Which ships, which sectors, which escorts, and so on. Pepper it with the details Mr. Cael gave you. Things we couldn't possibly know if their fleet wasn't surrounded by undetected Federation ships."

Drake folded his arms and said, "It would drive me buzzy if I was them."

"How an entire fleet could remain undetected will confound the commanders," t'Cael confirmed in his subdued manner.

George glanced at him. "If they knew you were

404

here, we'd never pull this off. We've got to convince them they're being watched."

"If they hear the breakdown of their own fleet coming in from unknown sources," t'Cael said with a little flare of his brows, "they'll be convinced."

"It'd be like meeting a total stranger and having him prove he was psychic by describing in intimate detail the inside of your house," George said. "How would you feel?"

"I'd be disturbed," t'Cael admitted.

"Let's disturb them." He gave Sanawey a nod and the message began its run through the system and outward into the openness of space.

T'Cael eyed George. "You're enjoying this, Kirk," he accused.

Suddenly self-conscious, George repressed his enthusiasm and admitted, "I'd rather be enjoying it from a distance."

But t'Cael looked more amused than disapproving. The Romulan was intrigued by their tactics. More than he was saddened by the choice April had made. The choice to leave his world to its own fate.

George spun around to face the fore of the bridge and the viewscreen's picture of Romulan space. "Carlos, glue yourself to the long-range and yell if there's any change with those two incomings."

"Yes," April approved. "It'll be our barometer to see if they're falling for it."

"You humans are a crafty lot, aren't you?" t'Cael murmured as he imagined the panic that was about to strike on the bridges of the Rihannsu motherships. His people would never understand this kind of strategy, and thus could never suspect it.

Drake sauntered a few steps forward. "George is very good at this kind of crap, sir."

"Drake!" George scolded.

"I meant craft. Sorry. Mispronounced."

April smiled thinly, then turned to Sanawey. "How is it?"

"The message is coming back in, sir. It sounds thready to me, but maybe they won't pick up the difference."

"It should confuse them, if nothing else. Are we ready for stage two?"

"Are you?" George asked him.

"As ready as I'll ever be." The captain stepped down and maneuvered himself into good broadcast position beside his command chair, rehearsing in his mind while he awaited Sanawey's signal. A moment later, it came. He clasped his hands behind his back and started speaking.

"Attention Starfleet Field Command," he said, speaking broadly and clearly, to make it easy for the Romulans to grasp his meaning. "This is the command ship in Delta Sector. We are experiencing mechanical failure of our invisibility screen, leaving us open to detection by sensors. Since we may give away the position of the concealed fleet, thereby endangering the covert mission into Romulan territory, we're dropping back to effect repairs. Until our camouflage is secure, I'm reassigning command of this sector to the destroyer *Ambush*. Duties regarding seizure of the Romulan Homeworlds will be carried out by vessels whose sensor masks are stable and who remain curtained." He paused, searching for something else to say, and glanced stiffly at George before he went on. His hands clasped tighter behind his back. "Attention destroyer *Ambush* and covert fleet. This is the command vessel. We are being pursued by two Romulan carriers. If they continue pursuit into Beta Sector, dispatch them immediately. One of their carriers has already been destroyed by our masked fleet. Take action if the two remaining ships do not retreat. Under no circumstance will you effect attack on the Romulan Homeworlds *until* and *unless* the Romulan fleet moves into the Neutral Zone. At that time, you will drop your invisibility screens and seize their Homeworlds. Do not acknowledge any further communications. You may give away your secret positions. Captain out."

For the first time since he started talking, he took a long breath. On the upper bridge, Sanawey funneled the message out toward a nonexistent attack force.

April turned expectantly. "Did I overdo it?"

George looked at t'Cael for comment, but t'Cael simply raised his brows and shrugged. Stepping down to the captain's side, George peered over Florida's shoulder. "We'll know in a minute. Any changes?"

Florida, as ordered, hadn't taken his eyes from the helm monitor. "Not yet. They're still—wait a minute! They're slowing down. Falling out of hyperlight. Sir, they've stopped!"

George leaned over the helm, not daring to breathe.

"Captain," Sanawey began, his hand cupping the earphone in his left ear, "I'm picking up huge amounts of communication between those two ships and one of their home planets."

"Ch'Rihan," t'Cael murmured, imagining what was being said, and what was being said back, imagining being part of it, trying to guess what he would believe if he had heard these wild messages.

April breathed deeply. "All right . . . all right . . . Carlos, turn us around. A nice leisurely pace . . . say, warp factor two. And let's be off before they figure us out."

With graceful stealth, the starship swung full about, leaving an imaginary dragnet behind to confound the Romulans into letting them go. Could it work? Could a war be fooled out of happening?

Captain April watched the maneuvers of his starship with tense amazement. He stepped softly up the bridge steps as though hard footfalls would crumble the webby structure they were escaping on. He moved toward t'Cael. "What do you think?" he asked quietly, watching the viewscreen, still expecting Romulan vessels to pop out of nowhere.

T'Cael folded his arms contemplatively. "My people are conservative, Captain. We attack only when we're nearly certain we can win. Otherwise we wait and build strength."

"We've postponed the conflict, is what you're saying."

"I make no promises. But they'll never attack until they're sure the odds are at least balanced. They'll coil themselves into knots trying to develop an invisibility device."

"It's not possible. Even if it is, it'll take years."

"Let us hope it takes lifetimes."

Unintentionally, he had spoken the last few words directly at George Kirk, who had come to stand beneath them on the recessed command bridge, both hands placed on the rail. Kirk said nothing, but was carefully listening.

The captain, though, had stopped listening and now gazed thoughtfully into the empty screen of stars receding at warp speed. The stars and nebulae and distortions and traces of ship's energy and debris left behind by the vessels they'd destroyed, an Imperial Swarm, an Imperial mothership . . . all haunted him now, haunted him with both the echo of crushed life and the unanswered question forever echoing in his mind.

"Or perhaps we've set the stage for more mutual suspicion." He sighed, a private agony rising in his eyes. "I've never been so frightened by something that didn't happen. God, it would've been so easy . . . and I came close to saying yes."

A step below him, George leaned forward against the rail and somberly asked, "What's the matter, Robert? We did it."

April didn't look down at him, but instead took a few small steps forward and continued staring at the viewscreen, which now had shifted to a view of the distant Neutral Zone before them. And beyond it, home space. The question unanswered.

"Did we?" he murmured, not blinking. His gentle face was framed by the cableknit ivory of the sweater, and from behind haloed by the beautiful spacescapes on the monitors lining the upper bridge. "I have to live the rest of my life wondering about the culture we're leaving behind. Wondering if t'Cael was right all along. And I have to wonder, as long as I live, if I've simply handed a war to the next generation."

"Approaching the Neutral Zone, Captain. We're almost home free."

Florida's words carried both relief and a sense of the touch-and-go. The danger they had faced still cloyed them. Almost is only almost, they knew, and no trophies sat on their mantels yet.

Speaking softly, as though he feared he might snap the thin thread of luck, Sanawey listened to the silence from his earphone and reported, "No signs of pursuit, sir."

Captain April took in their reports with a single nod. "Prepare to go to warp factor four as soon as we enter the Neutral Zone."

His English trill gave elegance to the simple command. Once again he sat in the command chair, a throne he had earned, and it seemed to his crew that he was bottling the anguish of their accidental mission into alien space, cloaking that anguish with common sense. Some of the light had left his eyes, but the lilt was slowly coming back into his voice. They might never know what he was feeling, and gradually they were learning to accept that.

Even George, although he had been shanghaied into this, felt oddly responsible for the course events had taken, and for whether or not they made it through the home stretch.

But even he couldn't manage approaching Robert right now.

Only when t'Cael slowly turned toward the captain's chair did George allow himself to be drawn back into that fold. He said nothing, but held himself perfectly still and waited to see what would happen.

"Captain April," t'Cael began, his voice rough from strain.

April broke from his thoughts. "Yes?"

"I must apologize."

"For what?"

"For trying to force you into making a decision you both believed was wrong. I should not have asked you to sacrifice your people for the sake of mine. You were willing to stand behind your principles no matter the cost. That will bring respect to your Federation as it moves outward through the galaxy. It was improper for me to demand that you behave aggressively. I am ashamed."

Softly, with emphasis, April told him, "You've no cause to be ashamed. You forced us to face ourselves. No person, no nation is ever the worse for that. We've pushed our morals to the breaking point. It isn't fun, but . . . it's exploration of a worthy kind." Now he swiveled around and looked up at George, wistfulness touching his tired features. "I think George and I realize we haven't been seeing enough of each other's perceptions. I suppose being run through the wringer is better than being philosophically celibate. We're both learning, aren't we, George? But it'll take some-

410

one wiser than the two of us to command this starship. An amalgam of us, probably, if such a person can be found."

"Time will find such a person," t'Cael suggested. "I can only hope that time will also bring wisdom to my people. I, too, find myself thinking new thoughts. I thank you for them."

Still feeling ashamed, t'Cael retreated to the upper walkway and moved away from both George and April. George watched him.

The Romulan kept his back to the rest of the bridge, gazing into one of the small monitors above the Damage and Repair control board starboard of the command area. The monitor was showing a view of aft space—Romulan territory as they swiftly left it behind, and he wondered if he could comfort that which seemed long past comforting.

T'Cael's face was barren as George tentatively peeked around at him. For many long moments, long after he knew George was beside him, t'Cael continued to engage himself with the monitor's lovely representation of his home space. His gaze was deep, his round eyes untelling, and George became suddenly unsure of the spontaneous decision he'd made back on the planetoid, the one that prevented t'Cael the destiny of his choice—death—as opposed to the obscure future he now faced. He would never see his home space, his own people, his family again. True, he could never pass for long as a Vulcan. The first Vulcan that came along would spot him as a fraud in two minutes. His only option would be to live in seclusion, carefully guarding his racial identity, or risk being harassed and questioned or locked up by people—

Like me, George admitted to himself, unable to bury the color that rose in his cheeks and forced him to look away from t'Cael for a moment. When he looked back again, there was a touch of melancholy on t'Cael's face.

"It'll work out," George murmured. His voice was so low that he sounded uncommitted. He realized, as he heard himself, what a mistake that was. Better to say nothing at all.

Unmoving, t'Cael controlled his response. "Where will I fit in?" he asked, so emotionlessly that it sounded almost hypothetical. "There is no place for me now."

George moved closer, hoping his eyes conveyed the depth of his promise. Solemnly he said, "Whatever it takes, however long it takes, I'll personally make sure you have a place in the Federation. I owe you that," he added, moving still closer. "In fact, I owe you more."

A sudden, unexpected warmth came over t'Cael's face, and he broke his communion with the monitor to look affably at George. "That's kind of you. It will be difficult."

George interlaced his fingers and leaned on the control console. "Well," he said, "we could drop you off back on that puny little planet you wanted to get stranded on."

A smile broke t'Cael's sorrow, and with a wistful laugh he said, "I wouldn't want to trouble you."

Allowing their intimacy to linger, George returned the grin, even with its fringe of grief for the grand life t'Cael was leaving behind, a forfeit of all earned glories and of the culture he had so hoped to help. After a time, George poked the intercom.

"Kirk to sickbay."

"Sickbay. Poole here."

"Doctor, I'm coming down there. I need to talk to you about some cosmetic surgery."

"You want me to get your foot out of your mouth?"

As George watched, t'Cael's smile widened and he waited for his future to be sealed for him.

412

"Something like that. We'll be right down," George said, and clicked off without further ceremony. He clasped t'Cael's arm and said, "Come on."

They almost made it to the turbo-lift before the captain's voice stopped them.

"George, where are you going?"

As t'Cael paused at the turbo-lift doors, George swung around. "Sickbay. And after that I'm going to my quarters for a few minutes. I want to write a letter to the boys . . . I told them a few wrong things, and I'd like to fix that. I won't be long."

April got up and faced the aft of the bridge. "Haven't you forgotten something?"

Striding toward the rail, George asked, "Like what?"

"We had a contract."

"About what?"

"Tiberius."

"Oh . . . you had to remember that."

"Well?"

George opened his mouth and closed it at least three times, trying to find some way to explain. "Well, it's . . . hard to describe."

"Try."

"I . . . oh hell, I can't." He swung around again, toward the lift.

"George! Welching on a promise?"

And around a third time. "Sorry . . . I can't. I'm sorry."

April stepped onto the upper bridge and approached the lift. "But George, this is criminal!"

A helpless hand flagged between them. "You'll just have to live with it." He stepped into the lift, leaving April disappointed behind him.

"But what are you going to tell Jimmy?"

George joined t'Cael, who was holding the lift control. "I don't know," he said, frustrated. "I'll lie.

413

I'll tell him it was my grandfather's name or something."

"But, *George!*"

"Well, I can't tell him the truth, can I?" George grasped the controls from t'Cael.

The lift doors closed.

"I don't bloody *know!*" April cried.

Chapter Twenty-four

CHIEF BIO-ENGINEER JON Kupper settled back into his desk lounge with an exhausted slap. The lounge rocked back to a more comfortable angle, but he was far beyond hope of comfort. Before him through the viewport, mocking, flickered the splendor of the ion storm. Pure destruction. Pure electrokinetic chaos. It flashed and sparkled endlessly, making a frame of voltage around the reflection of his own tired young features.

Young. He might be only thirty-one, but he hadn't been young for hours, days. The effort had aged him, this awful lie that suddenly consumed the hours of life he had left. Trying to hide his own despair from the real youth on board—the children, who were more perceptive than the adults liked to think, and certainly more sensitive. And the young parents who didn't know enough about engineering to know they were being given false hopes. If he could just keep those hopes going for another few hours, maybe they'd be too weak for any real grief anyway.

Being alone was a relief. A time to let the pretense slide and admit to himself the grating truth —impending death. Time to look out at the electrostatic charges dancing around the viewport, time to be bitter about it. He stared out at the ion storm, its beauty an irritating reminder of the inevitable. Ironic

415

that dying should be so pretty. And it hurt more this way. As though it was laughing at them.

He felt spiritless. He wished they'd blown up on contact, met death in a single detonation. One blast, and all done. None of this lingering. He didn't feel comfortable with the martyrdom. He didn't like their being impaled on their own torment for all the Federation to weep over, crucified to the cause of colonization and expansionism. Bad enough they had to endure this, much less know their friends and families and countless strangers back in home space were being dragged through it too. Better to have gone up in one blow.

There was a movement behind his reflection—he pulled himself up toward his desk in time to draw the shields back over his desolation.

"Okay, Jon?"

Kupper responded to the captain's voice with strained enthusiasm. "Sure. Just resting." He pivoted around, and—talk about sacrificed youth—Anita's familiar oval face was a pattern of fatigue. Where yesterday there had been the pouches of chubbiness, today there were only hollows. Her normally lustrous umber hair had drooped and become dull over the long hours without sleep. To grind the pain in, she was holding one of the babies, the agro-engineer's new-born daughter.

The captain saw him staring at the baby, and she too looked down into the rosebud face. "Sleeping. I thought I'd give her parents a break. A captain's not much use on a stranded ship." She sighed, slipping into the lounge beside him. "And I guess I can rock a baby as well as the next guy."

"Don't be silly," he told her. "Listen . . . I was trying to decide."

"What?"

416

"The sleeper units really ought to be tested, but . . ."

"But that would take oxygen. I know." She nodded sympathetically. "You're doing your best. What's the difference, Jon? Either they work, or they don't. If they don't . . ." She shrugged, by now quite numb. Death had become a companion.

Kupper felt a stab of guilt. She was the captain; he should tell her the truth about the sleepers. Then again, even the captain couldn't order away the inevitable.

He clamped his mouth shut before the urge to confide in her became too heavy to bear. She had enough to deal with.

"We're conserving power. All sensors are shut down now," the captain said. "No point in analyzing the ion activity, is there?"

"Guess not."

"I'm leaving a log," she went on. "I'm trying to specify just what went wrong, so others won't make the same mistake. I want them to know it was my error—"

"It wasn't your error and I wish you'd please stop saying that."

"Don't placate me, Jon. I don't need it."

"I'm not. I just wish you'd quit taking that captain-is-responsible stuff too far."

"It was my decision to push into the storm in spite of the readings."

Too tired even to turn his head, he didn't look at her. "The readings bore up your decision. It looked stable. I think it *was* stable, but it just changed once we got deeper inside. You can't accept the blame for an act of God."

"God hasn't been around here lately. That leaves me." She leaned back in the lounge and rested her

417

head, taking solace in the baby's miniature pink hand as it spread over her forefinger.

"Okay," Jon sighed. "I'm not going to die with an argument on my lips. Have it your way."

Allowing him his well-deserved crabbiness, Anita Zagaroli didn't respond. She let her eyes go unfocused, let the ion storm flash and flicker at her in the viewport.

After several minutes, she smiled privately to herself, and opted to give the bio-engineer the last gift she had. "By the way," she began, "you did a hell of a job explaining the sleeper units to the colonists. Very convincing. They bought every word."

Jon stared out the viewport and nodded, lost in his own numbness, then blinked. He drew his lounge up again and shifted his stare. "You know? You know about that?"

Her sad smile broadened. "It's my job to know."

"Oh, Jesus Christ!" Jon slammed back into the lounge, letting it wobble beneath him. "I thought —does anybody else suspect?"

"Like I said, you did a hell of a job. I didn't even figure it out until this morning."

"How?"

"I checked stock. There isn't enough cryon compound on board to freeze a flea."

"Oh, damn . . . Anita . . ."

"Now who's blaming himself?"

"I figured—"

"I know. Good thinking. You made it as easy on them as it could be."

Suddenly nauseated by the relief of not being the only one with his crushing secret, Kupper dumped himself backward in his lounge a third time. When the lounge stopped wobbling, he and the captain sat side by side, staring insensibly out into the layers of ionic activity. Silence fell around them. The lightshow

418

continued, still mocking. Beyond any chance of sleep, any chance of hope, they sat together, sharing the last hours in much the same manner as they had shared the exultation of the launch so many weeks ago.

Which was why they saw it at the same moment.

An eerie solidity appeared in the ion disturbance next to their ship. Gradually it took form as they stared.

The great shape moved toward them from one side of the viewport—a gigantic sensor disk the color of blood . . . a vast club-shaped hull behind it . . . and above, the biggest portable space station they'd ever imagined.

Together, captain and engineer rose to trembling feet and gaped.

Her bright white hull glittering with static discharge, the enormous unmarked ship pulled up beside their viewport and drew to a stately halt. Bolts of colored lightning and sheets of electric energy crackled off her shields, violent, breathtaking.

Slowly it dawned through the blur of exhaustion that this wasn't an illusion, but that an angel had come to pull them out of hell.

"Be sure to identify us right away. We don't want to frighten them."

The captain smiled. "Thank you, George. I've already thought of that. As a matter of fact, I'd be honored if you'd speak for us."

George drew his hand away from the backrest of the captain's chair. He returned the smile, but in a smaller, more respectful way, and said, "Not this time. This is your dream. You deserve it."

There was a long pause aboard the bridge of the starship, one more moment of obscurity before she would have a name to commit to legend. Captain

419

April nodded, gratefully accepting the gift he'd been ready to give away.

With a gesture, George signaled Sanawey to open the channels for the captain. Even then April didn't speak, not until he'd given George a few more seconds of silent communication, of acknowledging all the hurts and victories that would, from this moment forward, follow them as they lived their lives.

Then his voice hailed outward on the communication bands, too strong even for the ion storm to muddle. With his choice he gave George a gift that bronzed the lessons they'd both learned from each other.

"Attention, *Rosenberg*. This is the United Federation of Planets Starship *Enterprise*. Prepare for transfer of all personnel. We're going to take you home."

Dr. Sarah Poole walked briskly down the corridor of G-Deck, heading back from the hangar bay, where shuttlecraft were transporting the *Rosenberg*'s crew, worst injuries first. Leading a herd of med techs with people on antigrav gurneys, she had a two-year-old boy in one arm, and the other hand held a communicator to her lips as she barked orders to the scattered med staff.

"Take the radiation patients directly to the main ward and the burn victims to the temporary treatment pools we set up on deck five. I want all the children checked, even if they look healthy. Start accepting triage of minor injuries from *Rosenberg* as soon as we get the worst cases stabilized. We'll use the F-Deck crew's lounge as a pediatric area and—"

The words fell from her lips as she rounded the doorway to her own office and stopped short. The med techs shuffled by her, heading for the main examination room with their load of accident victims.

The child in her arms cuddled against her shoulder.

Sarah stared at the room she'd left behind an hour ago to set up the burn units.

She might as well have walked into a dream.

Candles. A roomful of them.

And the main lights were all shut down. There were only candles. Makeshift candles, in oil, with gauze wicks, set in every conceivable container—beakers, test tubes, bottles, cottonball jugs, apothecary jars, specimen trays, centrifuge tubes, mortars, flasks, drinking cups. Candles and candlelight in space, flickering like stars.

Taken aback by the oddly beautiful sight, the boy in her arms huddling closely against her, Sarah moved deeper into the realm of romance. And there, tied to a beaker, was a simple note on official Fleet notepaper. She plucked it, and read:

Love needs candlelight.
So does marriage.
Here are the love and the
        candlelight.
Two out of three. Shall we
    make it three?
                Robert

Chapter Twenty-five

THE LIFT DOORS parted. The bridge was a comforting sight. Like coming home.

Strange. The farm was duty now. The bridge was home. Soul's province.

These comforting sounds, these reassuring faces. Today he bothered to hear, to look.

Before him, the main screen offered a sedate view of the maintenance drydock of Starbase 1, which they'd so recently vacated. A twinge of empathy assaulted the captain as he watched the Starship *Kongo* being ushered into the drydock by two tugs, her massive port nacelle seared black by whatever cataclysm Captain Toroyan and his crew had encountered in deep space.

Kirk knew the feeling, the pain he felt when his ship was injured. How often had *Enterprise,* as the Federation flagship, been the first to experience unimagined dangers? How often the first mounted with some weird new device or experimental technology? How often had he and his precious prize faced down the unknown?

As he scanned the colorful bridge, warm with his command crew, those line-of-duty indignities seemed to fade.

There was Sulu at the helm—yes, very reassuring. His hand reposed on the board before him, offering no sign of the deftness with which he guided the big ship. For centuries uncounted helmsmen had been extensions of their captains' hands and eyes and visions. And Sulu himself, steady to a fault, in many ways more unflappable even than Spock. Beside him, Chekov at the naviconsole, barely more than a trainee when he'd been recommended to duty in the starship's all-exclusive nerve center, barely able to speak English but resolute about learning, whose effort alone had earned him a place here.

And on the port side, at the Engineering Subsystems Monitor, of course . . . Scotty. *The* single most dependable life form in the universe. His place here had been earned by something else entirely—he was a man whose natural habitat was the machine, coupled with a blinding talent for improvisation and a command sense that almost approached clairvoyance. Wizardry within his field and courage outside of it. He was a man to whom machines were music, and this starship his *magnum opus.* And on top of all that, he still found time, as now, to explain the bridge display graphics to one of the newly assigned young engineers. How many times had he saved the ship and happily handed over credit to the captain?

Kirk watched him for a moment. Scott's crimson engineering tunic, pepper-black hair, weathered face, and the rough Scottish properness had become the captain's quickest sign of ship's status. In times of crisis, if Scotty was on the bridge Kirk knew that whatever the trouble was, it wasn't yet so perilous that it couldn't be handled from here. One of the surest gauges of danger was Chief Engineer Scott's nearness to his engines.

And over there, of course, McCoy. Somehow he and Spock had beaten the captain back to the bridge, and Kirk got the distinct impression that they'd been waiting for him, though neither would admit it.

In spite of a long list of credentials, McCoy would invariably be the first to claim luck as his greatest talent. A man to whom life in space would always seem artificial, McCoy had used that perception to develop a keen knack for innovative space medicine. He'd learned to fake it with the best of them, adjusting his abilities to whatever conditions or life forms came along, figuring that if it lived he could find some way to bandage it. In the process he'd made a hobby of the psychological effects of his worldless environment. Hence his preoccupation with a certain farm loft.

But more—even as Engineer Scott was the barometer of ship's condition, Leonard McCoy was the captain's personal seismograph. Doctor, friend, live-in pest. A porcupine. Smooth if rubbed one way, prickly if rubbed the other. The captain knew he could get gut-level truth about himself fastest and most jarringly from McCoy. If he was being testy, McCoy would tell him. If he was off-base, McCoy would tell him. If he was being judgmental, lordly, shortsighted, improper, stubborn, plain wrong, McCoy would tell him. If he didn't want to be told, McCoy would tell him. Over the years the captain had come to treasure his compassionate, erratic chief surgeon, and had come to find the bridge a little empty unless McCoy was on it.

With a private sigh, he contained a smile as he noticed McCoy deliberately not looking at him.

And Spock, at the science station as usual. Were there words for Spock? For so long he'd been alone, fitting into neither his Earth heritage nor his Vulcan. So long among humans who were startled by his Vulcan appearance and demeanor. Since then, humans had grown accustomed to the enigmatic aliens, but that hadn't spared Spock the strain of being the first of his kind in Starfleet. Lately both cultures wanted to claim him, so often had he given each reason to be proud. The captain had watched as over their years together Spock had learned to admit to their friendship and even to display it. He'd learned that shame was an even sillier emotion than the other feelings his home planet had made profane. Having learned, he was no longer ashamed. Of course he was no less himself, no less veiled, no less gifted, no less refined. He was simply less enclosed, more at ease. A sign of true wisdom—he'd let himself learn clemency from humans just as he had learned restraint from the Vulcans. He'd gone from the ever-present stranger to being the father of the bridge, a man everyone had come to trust, who commanded a devotion he once would have rejected.

He, unlike McCoy, looked up as the captain strode slowly onto the bridge. With a brief, courteous nod, he acknowledged everything—relinquishment of command, stability of status, and the deeply personal synthesis between himself and Jim Kirk.

The captain nodded back, his gaze lingering with Spock's an extra few seconds. The corner of his own lips turned upward in wordless message.

One of Spock's thorn-straight eyebrows rose slightly, so slightly that only someone who knew him very well could have perceived the change at all.

The captain moved to his starboard, to the communication station and the graceful dark woman who played the console like a piano's keyboard, whose clear voice was the single most familiar sound to every one of the ship's four hundred thirty crew. Uhura, who could make "hello" sound dramatic, who could address kings and draw their attention just with her husky, symphonic delivery. That clarity had been polished to perfection, and coupled with her own personal sense of politeness and decorum, not only could she talk nice into a com system, but she could tear apart and rebuild it as well, intrigued not only by the fact that sound traveled, but *how* it traveled and how to make it travel farther.

As he approached her, she pivoted toward him in her chair, her legs discreetly crossed, and he marveled that she still found the presence of self to remain consummately feminine—in itself an art.

She smiled up at him. "Welcome back, Captain. Starbase Command has cleared us for departure."

"Thank you, Lieutenant," he responded, self-consciously keeping his voice down. "Patch me through to Admiral Oliver."

"Right away, sir." She turned to her panel and waved her magic hands over it. The lights started flickering.

In the interim, James Kirk scanned his bridge again. Yes, McCoy was right. They were special. Every last one of them. And though he might have occasion to place death at their doorsteps, he didn't have any right to dictate their choices of life.

"Admiral Oliver, Captain," Uhura announced.

The captain turned. "Ollie, Jim Kirk here."

"Yes, Jim."

"About that reassignment."

"Yes?"

"I wonder if you'd do me a favor."

"Sure will."

"Do you think you could arrange to cold-file the orders for a while?"

"Sure could."

The captain paused. "You never put the orders through, did you?"

"Sure didn't."

"You haven't drawn them up yet, have you?"

"Sure haven't."

"Oliver, you're a conniving bastard."

"Sure am."

The captain chuckled. "All right. And . . . thank you. Kirk out."

"Good riddance. And good luck."

Her cheeks dimpling as she tried to keep from grinning, Uhura cut off the communication as she sensed the captain wanted her to, and awaited his next order.

"Signal Starbase Command that we'll be pulling out," Kirk said, "and log in the details of our next assignment."

"Yes, sir." She seemed glad of something to do at that particular moment.

However, this deprived Kirk of any more distraction, and he had no choice but to face the bridge again.

Now McCoy was watching him, his face a matte of curiosity and pathos. The unspoken question was plain as a billboard: *What changed your mind?*

Kirk looked down at his hand, at the hurriedly scrawled letter, the last of the letters that had come during that mysterious time so many years ago. Slowly he raised it, and read it again.

Dear Sam and Jimmy —
    I know I don't usually
call you that, but since that's
what you call each other, I
think I'm going to start.
There are a lot of things I'm
going to start as soon as we're

427

together again. Jimmy, I'm sorry I didn't make it home for your birthday, but I'm going to make it up to you. I've changed my mind about having you boys up at the starbase. Why shouldn't you come here? Space is great and what the Federation's doing out here is great, and we're not going to sit it out. It's a tremendous feeling when you get the chance to save lives or cut new paths, and nothing's newer than what's out here. There really is a lot to see if you know how to look at it. We're on the verge of becoming a true interstellar community. I'm not going to make you boys miss it. My little problems won't get in the way anymore. Who knows? Maybe we can even convince your mom to come along. You ask her for me, okay?

So come on. Come out to space.

I'll be waiting for you.

Love —

Dad

The captain looked up from the letter when his eyes began to blur. He folded the note carefully, tenderly, and held it against his chest as he stepped down and took his place near the command chair.

He felt more than saw Spock appear beside him.

"Welcome, Captain. Are you not going to finish your leave?"

"I did." Kirk gazed out at the velvet expanse of space beyond the starbase. "Contact Starfleet Command. Tell them I don't want any more patrol time. I want an exploratory mission." Under Spock's mellow expression, one of pleased understanding, the captain slid into his command chair and spoke softly.

"Someplace no one's ever gone before."

Hope and a Common Future

"My eminent friends, the time has come for me to step aside and allow the future of this program to unfold into hardier hands. The Fleet Starship program has taken wing, and I am gratified. Five ships of the Constitution class are already embarking on missions, and seven more are under construction.

"These ships tend to have strong military-sounding names—*Enterprise, Potemkin, Farragut, Excalibur,* and so on. But the overriding theme is the name of the class of these ships—the Constitution class. We must never forget that we are obliged to ensure domestic tranquility even as we provide for the common defense. These two phrases walk hand in hand through the Preamble of that great document, and neither should be divorced from the other. We must always represent that tranquility as well as that defense, in order that we can indeed have the blessings of liberty.

"Today, domestic tranquility must extend throughout the galaxy, to all life forms, and it must include a promise that they will be allowed to live by their own standards, not by ours.

"The Constitution speaks of our posterity. This

means, my friends, that we owe these rights not only to ourselves, but to our descendants. It means we have the obligation to keep a peaceful and secure present, that our children may have a peaceful and secure future. That document, centuries old now, was an investment for the future. These Constitution-class starships must carry its sentiment as they carry us outward.

"We've learned valuable lessons over recent years, both about our technology and about our conscience as one of the first known races to explore our galaxy for exploration's sake. We now know, at great cost, that we have a responsibility. To the galaxy we open up, we owe justice and choice. To ourselves and those who join us in years to come, we owe strength and the courage to use it. To everyone everywhere, we owe care in choosing wise individuals to mete that justice and that strength.

"The council has accepted my recommendation, and it is with highest pride that I announce my successor to the captaincy of our flagship. Upon recommendation of two close and respected consultants of mine, as well as my own acquaintance with his common sense and sense of adventure, I pass along my legacy to Captain Christopher Richard Pike, and entrust to him the command of the United Federation Starship *Enterprise*.

"Under Captain Pike, a very special ship and a very special crew will soon embark on the first of a series of exploratory assignments in deep space. With them they take our hearts, our hopes, our support, and our trust.

"It's a thrilling concept, isn't it, my friends? Space . . . the final frontier. These are the voyages of the starship *Enterprise*. Her five-year mission—to explore strange new worlds, to seek out new life, new civilizations . . . to boldly go where no man has gone before.

"Thank you all. And farewell."

Captain Robert April
*Address to the United Federation
of Planets General Assembly,
October 2, 2192*

Epilogue

THE EARLY INCIDENT in Romulan space was kept secret, known only to those few aboard the *Enterprise* who really understood what had happened. The decision was made not to log the incident because it had become clear that the two budding civilizations were not yet ready to meet. How they would eventually rediscover each other, fate alone could tell. Other than the rescue of the S.S. *Rosenberg,* no log was filed of the first voyage of the first starship.

Captain Christopher Pike took the legacy of Robert April's dreams and turned them into reality in deep space. The exploration program, spearheaded by valiant people aboard the fleet of starships, changed the course of the Federation and its growing policies into a truly functional, strong, and unified body. The marriage of exploration and defense proved both wise and workable in the practical application of Federation policy, and ultimately became the most attractive element to new races who were courted as potential members.

A Federation consultant from the private sector, civilian botanist Cale Sandorsen, was foremost in the development of Federation intersystem policy and diplomatic precepts. Almost singly, he provided the precedent for ambassadorial ethics between races. His example made humanity a truly noble and open-minded race, whom other cultures soon learned to trust, and even to emulate. He became known in inner circles as the father of Federation justice.

Robert April went on to become one of the Federation's great early explorers, discovering many alien civilizations on many worlds, several of which he convinced to join the Federation. Sarah Poole April went with him, and made up for her dislike of space travel by pioneering the evolution of space medicine to include unfamiliar life forms and unusual biological conditions.

George Kirk remained in Starfleet to serve as Sandorsen's military adjutant and adviser, which enabled him to remain near or on Earth until his elder son, George Jr., entered the Graduate Academy of Biosciences and his younger son, James, entered Starfleet Academy as a junior midshipman. Shortly thereafter, he was on board a Federation vessel on special diplomatic assignment when the ship mysteriously disappeared with all hands.

The *Enterprise* continues.

ON THE DIGNITY OF EXPLORATION . . .

Space has been midwife to the birth of a new global consciousness. Two decades ago, with my first serendipitous sighting of a satellite, I was one of the lucky few to be touched for a moment by this philosophy. The children of the future, however, will be raised with the benefits of these space-age lessons . . . With this new education, we may provide our progeny with a delight and an insight we ourselves have not yet experienced. When they travel in their spacecraft, creating the illusion of falling stars across the heavens, perhaps they will look down on earth and think, with reverence, of the tiny creatures making stardust in the sea.

—Jacques-Yves Cousteau

ON THE CONSTITUTION OF THE UNITED STATES . . .

The Constitution is more than literature, but as literature, it is primarily a work of the imagination. It imagined a country: fantastic. More fantastic still, it imagined a country full of people imagining themselves. Within the exacting articles and stipulations there was not only room to fly but also tacit encouragement to fly, even the instructions to fly, traced delicately within the solid triangular concoctions of the framers.

—Roger Rosenblatt, *Time* Magazine

ON THE MORALITY OF DEFENSE . . .

No man may *initiate* the use of physical force against others. No man—or group or society or government—has the right to assume the role of a criminal and initiate the use of physical compulsion against any man. Men have the right to use physical force *only* in retaliation and *only* against those who initiate its use. The ethical principle involved is simple and clear-cut: it is the difference between murder and self-defense.

—Ayn Rand

Author's Note

By coincidence or by omen, the final revisions of this novel—the last time the manuscript was worked on in our home—happened to be done on September 17, 1987, the 200th birthday of the Constitution of the United States. All patriots please rise.

Diane Carey

TIME FOR YESTERDAY

Time in the galaxy has stopped running in its normal course. That can mean only one thing — the Guardian of Forever is malfunctioning. To save the universe, Star Fleet Command reunites three of its most legendary figures, Admiral James T. Kirk, Spock of Vulcan, and Dr. Leonard McCoy and sends them on a desperate mission to contact the Guardian, a journey that ultimately takes them 5,000 years into the past. They must find Spock's son Zar once again and bring him back to their time to telepathically communicate with the Guardian.

But Zar is enmeshed in troubles of his own, and soon Kirk, Spock, and McCoy find themselves in a desperate struggle to save both their world — and his!

Future *STAR TREK* titles from Titan Books

TIMETRAP by David Dvorkin
A freak accident hurls Captain Kirk into the future
... a future where the Klingon Empire and the
Federation have joined forces. Now Kirk must
journey back in time, to bring about that historic
peace.

THE FINAL REFLECTION by John M. Ford
Klingon Captain Krenn is a ruthless war strategist.
But on a mission to Earth, Krenn learns a lesson in
peace. Suddenly he must fight a secret battle of his
own. His empire has a covert plan to shatter the
Federation. Only Krenn can prevent a war — at
the risk of his own life!

Also:
THE FINAL NEXUS by Gene De Weese
VULCAN'S GLORY by D.C. Fontana
THE THREE-MINUTE UNIVERSE by Barbara Paul